VAMPIRE

KNIGHT

The Immortal Knight Chronicles Book 4

Richard of Ashbury
and the Hundred Years War
1346 - 1377

DAN DAVIS

Vampire Knight

Copyright © 2018 by Dan Davis

For information contact :
dandaviswrites@outlook.com

ISBN: 9781723983535
First Edition: September 2018

1

A KING'S COMMAND

THE MESSENGER WOKE ME before dawn. It was Saturday 26th August 1346 and there would be a grand battle that day between the kings of France and England. And, although I did not know it that morning, by nightfall I would discover a new and terrible immortal enemy in the midst of the French army.

"What was that?" I asked the figure standing over me in the dark. He had spoken before I was fully awake.

"His Grace summons you, sir," one of the King's men said, speaking softly but with some urgency.

It was dark inside the church in the small village of Wadicourt.

"Where is the King now?" I asked, rubbing my eyes.

"His Grace is yet in the other village, sir," the messenger said. "In Crecy."

I climbed to my feet and stretched the aches from my muscles. Over the decades, I had become accustomed to sleeping in my armour, when necessary. The mail hauberks from my youth had slowly been replaced by various other forms of armour. Many of my men wore coats riveted or sewn with small plates to provide protection. Those of us who could afford it though wore larger, close-fitted iron pieces. Sleeping in a breastplate and back plate along with armour on the front of my legs and the outsides of my arms, and armoured feet and gauntlets, took some getting used to. After decades of campaigning experience, along with my immortal strength and endurance, I was capable of getting a fair night's sleep in it.

I left my helm with a page and stepped around the sleeping bodies on the floor of the church. It was damp outside and colder than an August morning deserved to be but it would soon warm up once the day got going.

We traipsed across the ridge following the rutted track between the two villages, walking past thousands of English men-at-arms and archers beginning to bestir themselves. Scores of campfires were being lit along the slope. Few of us expected the battle to start any time soon. Still, many men were eager to arm themselves immediately upon waking and the sounds of steel plate and mail clanging filled the air, along with gruff complaints, coughing and the clearing of throats and the odd bark of laughter. Every man in the army wore a steel helm of some kind and although most were darkened with grime or painted, still they glinted in the gloom.

I approached the village of Crecy, walking past a windmill at the top of the ridge, its furled sails stationary in the dawn light as if it was some giant sentinel watching over us. In between the thatched houses and kitchen gardens, soldiers and servants busied themselves by fetching water from the stream running at the back of the village. Beyond the village to the south was a woodland, deep in shadow. Young pages led groups of horses to and from the stream, or brushed them down, or walked them to warm them up. Many were led back behind the ridge to the wagon park where they would be both safe and out of the way, assuming the French came at us from the way we were expecting.

The messenger led me past the King's pavilion tent into the small church. It was stifling inside and dark despite the candles and packed with men in armour. A priest was concluding a mass and I waited by the door for it to finish.

"Is that you, Richard?" the King asked as I approached. His helm, with its ring of gold around it, stood higher than almost all of the priests and lords surrounding him.

King Edward III of England had grown into a very fine man. Already wearing his harness, clad in the finest plate armour and helm, he was ready for the battle and yet appeared relaxed and comfortable. The King's surcoat was quartered with the red field and three golden lions of England and the blue field and gold lilies of France. His visor was even affixed, though he had it hinged up so that his face was exposed.

"Your Grace," I said, bowing.

"Come closer, sir," the King said.

The lords clustered all around him were unwelcoming, begrudging the attention I was receiving. For many of them, it would be a day for them to shine before their enemies and peers, to win renown and solidify their already-glowing reputations as fighting lords of England.

The King brought me a step further away from the crowd and waved away one of his priests who made to follow.

"We will fight in three battles, as planned, with most of the bowmen on the flanks and some in front of the men-at-arms. The first two battles will form a line across the ridge, two thirds of the way up," he said, speaking clearly but softly, so that his words would not carry. When he said battle, he was referring to our formations. A *battaile* was a semi-independent division and our armies were almost always divided into the van, middle and rear guards, or battles. "My battle will hold behind the main line, on the ridge in the centre, forming the reserve. You will keep your own bowmen with you and the rest of your company at the edge of my battle on the centre of the ridge. I would ask that you stay within earshot."

I nodded, and attempted to keep my disappointment from my face at being held in the rear. My men would be frustrated at being so far from the action. Not least because that meant thousands of Englishmen would plunder dead Frenchmen before they could. Assuming, of course, that we won the field.

"You have a specific task for me in mind, Your Grace?" I asked. I had known Edward for many years and even though I kept my true strength and speed hidden from mortals, the King knew me as a consummate knight who could be trusted with any task. It would not be the first time he had given me special instructions for swinging a battle in our favour.

The King lowered his voice further and turned his back on the great lords waiting on him. "The Prince fights in the van on the right, by this village. You will have noted how the slope on that flank is gentler, easier. Our enemies will press him hard. Perhaps, if events necessitate it, you might consider providing him with just a little support?"

"I understand, Your Grace."

He pursed his lips, cleared his throat and punched his fist into my breastplate. "I know, Richard."

When he turned back to the great lords of his kingdom, our conference was over and I had been dismissed. Pushing through the priests and lords who ignored me or scowled at me, I went back to prepare my men.

I was posing as a mortal, as always, and as a somewhat impoverished knight at that. Edward had favoured me ever since I helped him to take control of his crown from the traitor Mortimer sixteen years earlier.

Yet, I was a man with an invented lineage, pretending that I was the latest in a line of minor knights who had fought for Henry III and Edward I. The lords considered my pedigree to be non-existent. And the great men of the realm disliked my closeness with Edward, from the days of his youth through to that morning in France when he was in his prime at the age of thirty-four.

More than their needless petty jealousies, though, I was beginning to run into the problem that I always encountered.

The fact that I had apparently not aged in the sixteen years since I came to prominence was now often commented on, and the young men who had laughed and joked with me over wine when we were twenty years old were now beginning to go grey and bald and fat.

Eva, who had once been my wife, had told me that I unnerved many men just with my presence. She suspected that they sensed there was something different about me, something wrong. Something dangerous. For young men, that is all very well. Exciting, even. But old men grow suspicious and bitter and so it would soon be time for me to move on. To remove myself from England and the English for twenty or thirty years so that most of the men who knew me would die. Then I would return and perhaps once more claim to be the son of the man I had pretended to be.

The other members of the Order of the White Dagger, especially the former monk Stephen Gossett and my friend the former Templar knight Thomas de Vimory, had urged me to leave before it drew any further attention to me that might endanger the Order itself.

"You already arouse great suspicion, sir!" Stephen had said at our last meeting in London. "We agreed to this. You agreed, Richard. You agreed!"

Though he claimed his concern was for the continued secrecy of the Order, I suspected he was more worried that his growing mercantile empire in London would be threatened. He was right that I had sworn to flee when the whispers against me started.

But I could not leave King Edward. Not when he was poised to smash the French and reclaim some or all of the lands that the English crown had held in my youth, over a hundred and fifty years earlier.

Not yet.

It was early morning when my company assembled from the

places around the villages where they had slept. There were eighteen men-at-arms and twenty-nine archers in my company and before I spoke to them all I relayed the essence of our orders to the leading men in my company.

Many in my company were drawn from the few capable men on my estate, along with a few retainers I had picked up over the years. A couple were pardoned criminals and more were already professional soldiers looking for hire when I found them. However they had come into it, they stayed for the money, as well as for the love of it. They were men who made war for their private profit, neither knights nor squires but men of little worth who would not do a thing without their six pence a day and thirty marks a year.

Together, we had fought for years in Brittany, on the far north-western tip of France. A rugged land in places but a fertile one and a good place for small companies of men to commit mischief. We helped to take towns and win small battles, and we raided and lived off the land.

"The King wants us in the rearguard?" Black Walter cried. "Don't he know we can win this battle for him, sir?"

Walter was one of my best men but he was a mortal who had no inkling that I was anything other than a capable knight. He was a commoner and had such a simplistic and shallow view of the world that for many years I had thought him a halfwit. Even then, I had recognised his unusual ability, strength and courage when it came to feats of arms and so I had equipped him with good armour and commanded him to fight as my squire. He even rode superbly, despite never mounting a decent horse until he was a man grown.

His father had been from the Welsh Marches in the far west of England, and his hair and beard were shiny as obsidian and his skin somewhat swarthy. Walter denied that he was a Welshman by blood but most of my men liked to doubt him. I trusted him to watch my back in battle and tried to avoid speaking to him otherwise.

"Hold your tongue, Walt," Thomas said. "The King will ultimately send the rear guard into the fray to turn the tide of the battle and so win the day."

Sir Thomas had been fighting at my side for close to a hundred years and we knew each other like brothers. He so often spoke my own mind that I rarely needed to disagree with him.

"Come on, Walt, you know this," said John, grinning. "It is precisely because we are so well regarded by the King that he wishes to use us in the most critical moment."

"That is right and true, John," Hugh said, eagerly. "Surely, our company shall carry the day."

John and Hugh were the newest and youngest members of the Order of the White Dagger. Formerly a member of the Knights Templar, Thomas and I had freed Sir John and the squire Hugh from gaol in France when the French King had arrested and prosecuted their order. I had been reluctant to offer them the Gift but allowed myself to be persuaded.

John was a tall, fair, handsome and chivalrous man who had always fought and acted honourably, despite being a Frenchman on his mother's side. Thankfully, his father had been one of the Anglo-Normans of Ireland, which meant he was almost a proper

Englishman.

Hugh, a Frenchman by birth, was a squire when we found him thirty years earlier and he remained a dutiful though unimaginative fellow. I found it impossible to think of him as anything other than a young man, even though he was over fifty, because of the wide-eyed earnestness he had somehow retained.

"Aye, sirs, I suppose you be right enough about that," Walt said, cheering at the thought of being able to fight by the end of the day.

"What about my lads, sir?" Rob Hawthorn asked.

Another mortal, like Walter, he commanded my archers. Once, Rob was a wild youth, much taken with brawling and chasing women. By the time my company left Brittany, he had become as steady and trustworthy as a commoner could be. He was not tall but he had an archer's build. John had once cried that Rob was built like the Minotaur. Once the myth was explained to the archers, they found it highly amusing. "Can I take my men to join the flanks of the van? Or the middle?"

"You are all to stay with me throughout the battle and you will hold on to your arrows until we need them," I said. Rob nodded, pressing his lips together. I continued. "Right then, you all know what you are about. Get the men some food, make sure they are well watered. Get the weapons sharpened and armour repaired. Make sure the servants keep our horses ready at the rear."

"Horses, Sir Richard?" Walt said, scratching his face under the edge of his mail aventail. "Ain't we all fighting on foot today?"

"Indeed we are, Walt. And yet one never knows how a battle may turn." I raised my voice so that the rest of the men could hear me. "Make yourselves ready. John, set my banner on the right of the vanguard, at the front, so that we may advance without hindrance when the time comes. I shall see you all there, men. God be with you all today."

"Stick by Sir Richard," John cried, "and we'll get to murder a dozen Frenchmen apiece."

The entire company cheered, bringing bemused glances from the other men gathering on the ridge.

While they busied themselves, I glanced at Thomas and we walked a few paces away down the slope, looking down the hill and out across the valley.

"What is our true task?" Thomas asked when we could not be overheard.

"The king wants us to protect the Prince," I replied.

Thomas narrowed his eyes. "And yet Prince Edward commands the vanguard while we shall be in the rear."

"By honouring the Prince with such responsibility," I said, attempting to gather the strands of my thoughts into what I believed was the truth behind the King's words, "a victory this day will establish the Prince of Wales as a great warrior. He will be famed across Christendom as a mighty king in waiting. His reputation will be made. All will know that England has a bright future."

"Only if we win," Thomas pointed out.

"Well, yes," I said. "And only if the Prince lives through the day, more to the point."

Thomas took a deep breath and then sighed. "He will be hard pressed indeed down there. Gentle slope that side. If I was charging our lines, mounted, with my lance couched and looking for an Englishman to impale, that is where I would do it."

We stood looking along the slope, imagining thousands of knights charging our men.

"Imagine if they took him," I said. "What would England's future be then?"

"So why are we to be held back from him at all?" Thomas asked. "We can protect him from the start."

"His victory must not be tainted with my name. Although Suffolk is my lord, all men know that I am the King's man. The victory must belong to the Prince. If he is in danger, we shall save him for as long as we need to. But we shall not say that is what we have done. We shall deny it. And so shall our men."

"A shame."

"We will know," I said. "God will know."

He bowed his head and turned to look out once more. "Dear Lord, here they come."

2

THE KING'S
CAMPAIGN

THE BATTLE WE WERE SOON TO FIGHT had been a long
time coming. King Edward had needed to obtain an enormous
amount of money, to raise thousands of men along with
purveying the victuals to supply them, and then ship that army
across the channel.

We had been through it before, in 1338 and 1344, when we
had relied on our Flemish, Breton and German allies but their
endless dithering, fickle nature, and endless petty demands had
scuppered our attempts. Now we would invade France properly.

With Englishmen.

To find the funds, Edward had forced loans from the Church
and from towns all across the country. Foreign clergymen, some

of whom were astonishingly wealthy, were fleeced three ways from Sunday, which all true born English folk rejoiced to see.

But all this was still nowhere near enough and so Edward had borrowed money from a syndicate of London merchants led by none other than my immortal friend Stephen Gosset.

It was of course not right for the wealth of the Order of the White Dagger to be employed in funding a mortal's war but finding immortals had proved incredibly difficult and we increasingly expressed doubt that there were any left to be found. Besides, it was the King of England who needed the money, and Edward III had turned out to be rather a good one.

Stephen wanted to provide the funding because he claimed we would, eventually, recoup our investment many times over and also that it would buy favour from the Crown that would enable us to leverage even more influence. That is to say, it appealed to his ambition.

And I wanted to fight. If that meant loaning a king some of our massive wealth, so be it.

The King wanted a vast army of twenty thousand men and so he implemented the innovation that was compulsory military service. Every man in the kingdom was expected to serve based on his level of income. If you made five pounds a year then you would be expected to fight as an archer, with all the necessary equipment and ability that entailed. Men who earned ten pounds a year would fight as a hobelar, those fellows who formed a versatile light cavalry of sorts which we used for scouting and foraging and anything requiring rapid mobility. Those who were assessed as having an income of twenty-five pounds were required to serve as a man-at-arms, with proper weapons and armour and a horse, along with the necessary servants to support him on campaign.

The king required every man to serve not merely in defence of the realm against invasion but also if we were to fight on the Continent. Also, any man who claimed to be too old or ill to fight would have to provide a substitute or pay a fine instead of their service. It was a shrewd move on Edward's part but in other years, before and since, he would have faced opposition to his money-raising schemes. It was only the fact that so many of his lords were looking forward to the fight that he got away with little more than grumbling.

In spite of my considerable secret wealth and immortality, I was playing the part of a minor gentleman who was lucky enough to have been knighted during fighting overseas before returning to England as a young man.

As I had done a number of times already, I left England for twenty years and then posed as the son of the man I had formally been. This time, a few older fellows here and there had given me hard stares before swearing that I was the spitting image of my father. It was a simple enough thing to pull off successfully because who would truly suspect I was the very same man? It was hardly credible.

Very soon after my most recent return, I had moved immediately into supporting the young King Edward just as it appeared he was being usurped by the traitor Roger Mortimer, the new husband of the King's mother.

When he was aged just seventeen, I had urged the powerless king to act before it was too late and together with a group of young lords we seized Mortimer in Nottingham and hanged the traitor a few weeks later. Edward subsequently favoured me considerably and I had fought for him in various ways ever since.

But, as we stood to prepare for battle outside the village of Crecy, that night in Nottingham had been sixteen years before and the time was drawing near for me to flee once more. My apparent youthfulness was remarked upon by men who were beginning to feel the ravages of time in their aching limbs and the tightness of their clothes across the belly. It is merely a matter of eating beef every day and drinking good wine, I would say, but increasingly my words fell on deaf ears. Even the King was beginning to look at me askance, though for now he protected me against the detrimental effects of rumour by his continued favouring of me with tasks of a military nature.

For Edward, I had fought against the old enemy the Scots, in the Low Countries and in Brittany against the French and their allies. During the Battle of Sluys off the coast of Flanders, I had led my men across the bloody decks to take ship after ship, winning considerable glory and fame for myself and my men. In that great victory we slaughtered tens of thousands of Frenchmen but due to the weakness and untrustworthiness of our allies the Flemish, we could not take advantage of it and so the war foundered.

In Brittany, for many years, I took and defended towns and raided for supplies to provide for garrisons. The mortal men who survived that crucible with me became as hard as iron and it was those men who were with me at Crecy. Men-at-arms and archers who had learned to fight as a unit whether we were on our own or fighting with other companies in a more significant battle.

My men believed me to be blessed.

Or cursed.

Some said I was protected by an angel or by God Himself, while others whispered that I had done a deal with the Devil. But all had seen me recover from wounds that they swore would have killed King Arthur or Alexander and, whatever the cause, ultimately, they thought that I was blessed with that most precious of all soldierly traits. Luck. And they all loved to serve me because as every soldier knows, luck is contagious. And the regular plunder also helped.

And so I came back from Brittany to join the King's army in Normandy for the invasion of France, bringing my small force of hardened veterans with me.

Edward had not, in fact, managed to bring an army of the size he had intended. The treacherous Scots were massing in the North and thousands of Englishmen had to be left behind to face them. Similarly, there was thought to be great risk of French attacks by sea on the southern English coast and so the King ensured that the men of the coastal towns stay where they were to resist. What is more, a diversionary force was sent to Flanders to distract the French and to drag them to their north-eastern border.

Our main force landed from 12th July 1346 and spread out into the countryside, only to discover that the villages, towns, manors and monasteries were abandoned; the people fleeing into the woods and marshes at our approach. Immediately after stepping ashore, King Edward, God bless him, proclaimed that, out of compassion for the fate of his people of France, none of us should molest any old man, woman or child, or rob any church or burn any building on pain of immediate death or horrific mutilation.

It was a fine sentiment and he even offered forty shillings to anyone who discovered men breaking the King's orders, which proved that the King perceived the essentially mercenary nature of the common man.

Of course, every village, town, manor and monastery with twenty miles was burned to the ground on the first or second day but at least he tried. The fires were so widespread that on the first night in Normandy we lit up the sky so brightly that the reddish glow filling the horizon all around was enough to play dice by.

And so we continued. We rampaged across Normandy, heading always east with the coast on our left, sometimes so close we could smell it but other times ranging miles inland.

Those poor people. They would have been King Edward's subjects, had their lords but sworn fealty to him as their rightful lord but I suppose they knew he could not protect them from King Philip. England was considered a poor and weak kingdom and France was the mightiest in Christendom. What is more, Normandy bordered the core of the Kingdom of France, whereas Brittany and Gascony were further removed. All the King of France had to do was lean from his palace window and reach out his arm to take Normandy. They were loyal to him and so we burned the duchy from one end to the other.

Before then, though, we had taken the city of Caen. It had to be taken because the garrison inside was big enough to cut our supply line and threaten our rear if we left them in there. What is more, it was immensely rich and somewhat vulnerably located.

Even before we landed, we knew where we were headed and it was within striking distance from the coast. Still, few of us expected the siege to be over quickly.

Caen was a vast city and even the men who had never seen it knew that it was one of the biggest in the whole country, not counting Paris of course.

"It is bigger even than London," I had said to my men.

"It never is, sir," said Black Walter, a man of astonishing ignorance and impudence who I liked to keep at my side because he was so good at killing my enemies, despite him being a mortal man.

"Wait until you see it," I said.

The castle on the north side was formidable and they had high, thick walls around the city itself. Those walls, we saw when we approached, had been draped with colourful banners to display to us that it was defended by powerful and wealthy men. Atop the walls, standing shoulder to shoulder, were those who would defend their homes with crossbows and rocks and, if it came to it, swords and spears and daggers. Inside, Caen was packed with magnificent homes and enormous churches with grand spires jutting up in every quarter and on either side of the city were two abbeys, both huge and fancy and with high walls that joined with the ones ringing the city.

"I stand corrected, sir," Black Walter had said.

"This was William the Conqueror's city, Walt. The bastard robbed Saxon England from top to bottom and spent all our gold enriching this city here."

"Pardon me for asking, sir," Walt said, "but ain't you come from Normans yourself?"

In fact, I was descended by blood from Earl Robert de Ferrers and through him to a lord who had fought for the Normans at Hastings but I never revealed such things to mortals.

"My mother was as English as they come," I said, which was true. "And my father's line, well, that was all a long time ago. I am as English as you are, Walt."

"If you say so, sir," he said.

"But Walt's a Welshman, sir," Rob said, in a false whisper. It made the men laugh and Walt cursed the lot of them.

To the south of the city was a large island in the centre of two broad rivers that flowed around Caen. The island was filled with splendid houses and ornately carved churches and even had plenty of green, open spaces. All of our eyes were drawn towards it because it alone out of everything in sight was unprotected by walls. Of course, the rivers served as a moat of sorts but we knew from our approach how tidal the rivers were and also that such watercourses tended to be slow and shallow at low tide. Still, even if we took and looted that island, the rest of Caen would remain untouched.

I knew how it would play out. As I explained to my men, we would dig in, offer terms which they would refuse and we would fling rocks at the walls for months until it became clear no French army was coming to relieve them and then they would surrender.

I was proved wrong almost immediately.

On the very first day, before our vanguard even established

themselves around the walls, groups of archers drifted closer and closer to the city. Some of them noticed that the inhabitants of the town were fleeing across the stone bridge that linked it to the wealthy island. The cannier ones saw that there was a steady stream of soldiers, too, pushing their way out of the city and into that island. It made no sense at all for the French to contest that island. All it was good for was plunder.

More and more of our archers stopped preparing camp and drifted closer to stare, confused, as the French soldiers barged through the denizens. After a while, our men began jeering and mocking them. And then, without any orders being given by anyone, groups of archers started an assault on the bridges, on the island and on the city that the Normans seemed to be abandoning. Archers waded through the river, and used barges and boats, to approach the island and bridges, and other Englishmen hacked their way into the city and assaulted the bridge to the island from the rear.

"Have you ever seen anything like this before?" I asked Thomas, looking down on the madness from afar.

"An impregnable city being abandoned for no reason?" he replied. "One could argue Baghdad ninety years ago but..."

"Come now, that is hardly the same thing," I said.

"Indeed, it is not," he allowed. "And I can only think that God has driven the Normans mad."

It was hard to argue with that. My immortal knight John and his immortal squire Hugh, both former Templars, charged in amongst the heaviest of the fighting, leading Rob Hawthorn and my archers deeper into the fray. Black Walter begged me to give him leave to join in.

"Old Tommy here can watch your back all right, sir," Walt said, in a pleading tone. "Almost good as I can, sir."

I laughed, because Old Tommy was the affectionate name my company had awarded to Sir Thomas the former high-ranking Templar who was about a hundred and fifty years old and who had fought in more battles and killed more men than anyone alive, other than me.

"Go on then, Walt. But if you get killed, do not come to me complaining of it."

Despite not being a straightforward assault, for the enemy fought hard, it was one of the unlikeliest victories I have ever witnessed, or even heard about. For days after Caen was plundered from basements to belfries, I saw many a man laughing and shaking his head in wonder.

After that, it was all marching and plunder, marching on a broad front and going always east and north and east again. Following the coast.

"We are heading to Paris," some fools would say. "We shall make Paris into England."

"We are heading to a port on the coast," the wiser would answer.

"But where?"

No one knew.

We were practically unchallenged the entire way until we reached the River Seine. We wanted to cross at the city of Rouen but the bridge had been destroyed by the canny French. There was talk of taking the town but Paris and King Philip were so close that it would have been foolhardy to dig in for a siege. What we feared as much as anything was being cut off from the coast. If we could reach the coast, we could reach our ships and then we were as good as back in England, or so we felt.

We headed upstream for another place to cross but after doing nothing for weeks the French finally made some tactical decisions. Every bridge or ford was destroyed or defended. Some we contested but, as Edward feared committing to any one place and being trapped, we were always driven back.

And then we were so close to Paris that those who stood in the right place or climbed trees or spires could see it on the horizon and everyone else could smell it when the wind blew the stench in our direction. So close to Paris that when we burned the hunting lodges and mansions of great nobles everywhere about, the smoke billowed into the sky and announced that we were so close that we could be at the gates if we so wished. No doubt the Parisians panicked, as they are a people prone to hysteria. And yet still King Philip did not attack us.

We knew from reports that he had been raising an army for weeks but where was it?

In the meantime, we brought more havoc to the country as our army, spread out for miles in a number of groups, probed the river until we reached the town of Poissy. The garrison had fled after wrecking their bridge but our men repaired the span and we were across.

Only to find ourselves now trapped by the River Somme.

Again, all bridges were destroyed or guarded and suddenly we felt the noose tightening. The word was that Philip's army had taken so long to assemble because it was so vast. An army created for a single purpose; to crush the English and grind us into dust once and for all.

My men began to feel the ravages of the march. They grew hungry and tired. Bone-tired from never getting enough rest. Their feet were in a bad way. The horses were suffering. We ran out of meat and the men grumbled that the dried peas sat heavy in their guts.

"Be grateful that you have boiled peas," I upbraided them. "You lucky bastards ate onions yesterday. You should be on your knees thanking God for those onions."

My weak jests were always tolerated and perhaps even appreciated but it grew increasingly difficult to keep their spirits raised.

"We will thank God, sir," cried John so that all in our company could hear. "We will thank Him when we scythe through the French knights like they are sheaths of wheat and take their stinking spiced sausages for ourselves."

They cheered that, at least, even though John was almost a Frenchman himself. My men were common as muck but they knew John first as a man who had risked his own life for all of them in battles past. I thumped John on his armoured shoulder as I made off, grateful as ever for his God-given charm.

Still, our army as a whole seemed to contract and shrink and the rambunctiousness of the march became pensiveness and men's eyes drooped and shadowed. Soon, we were cornered by the Somme and I had to lead my men in the crossing of a ford at low tide. Our archers drove the waiting enemy away from the water's edge and when I waded ashore with Thomas and John at my side, we carved our way into the French and held them as more English men-at-arms and archers crossed.

It was hard fought for a while but then the French fled and our entire army, including all our scores of wagons and thousands of horses, made it across in a single tide which may just have been the most remarkable moment of the whole campaign.

For a day or so we stayed on the river because the French army had come up and thousands upon thousands of them stared across at us from the other side. They could have forded the river, for they had the numbers on us, and we waited for them to attack.

In the end, they quietly went away again. My men shouted their thanks for the day of rest across the river at the retreating French, to much laughter. In truth, our army was still exhausted and low on supplies.

We marched on, hoping to drive on through and join with the Flemish.

But it was not to be.

King Philip had finally acted decisively to pin us in place with his numbers and so Edward found an excellent position to defend.

The ridge between the villages of Crecy and Wadicourt, with a slope at our front and to the flanks and woods behind.

"This will do very nicely," I had said to Thomas from atop the hill after the King had made his decision.

He shook his head. "It is unseemly to be so cheerful when so many Christians will likely die in this valley."

"I have known you too long, sir," I replied, "and watched you

25

too often rejoice in the blood you have spilled to believe that your disapproval runs deep."

Thomas spluttered in protest. It was his French blood that made him so melancholic but that was understandable considering we were going to be fighting his countrymen. Having said that, John and Hugh did not appear overly concerned that morning as John went amongst my men to jokingly berate them for their lax standards. I watched from afar how the squire Hugh followed closely at John's side, all the while gazing at him in adoration.

They had both been very young men when Thomas and I had rescued them from a French gaol, saving them from execution. It had been about thirty-five years since that night and yet in many ways they had both retained their youthful manner. Thomas had been old when he had become one of us so perhaps that better explained his grim mood.

The mortals in my company seemed happy enough, although, being commoners, they lacked the depth of character necessary for considering such things and so it was to be expected. They wanted to win, to fight well in the eyes of their friends, the King, and God, in that order, and then to plunder the dead or take a man for ransom. They were not troubled by the whys and wherefores.

And so, after a night of preparation and my brief morning meeting with the King, we stood ready to face the onslaught of the massed ranks of French nobility.

The common archer and man-at-arms knew one thing as well as any knight amongst them.

That if we broke, we would be slaughtered to a man.

3

CRECY

EVERY ENGLISHMAN WAS ORDERED to fight on foot. King Edward himself walked amongst us, speaking to the men-at-arms, the archers and even the occasional Welshman.

What is more, he took the time to personally adjust our dispositions even within the individual battles. Many of the knights and lords who trailed after him also engaged the men in similar fashion and so the bonds of friendship and loyalty and duty were strengthened before the horror of the battle was to begin.

The army's priests went from man to man, blessing them. Our soldiers would be hard pressed by the massing ranks of the French knights and if any of us broke, we would all certainly be lost because it was only when an army fled that a right slaughter could occur. We needed to hold against whatever onslaught we suffered, no matter how long and how terrible it was.

For all of our recent victories against towns and small detachments, none of us was under any illusion about the enemy that day. The Frankish knight, armoured and mounted and delivering a thunderous combined charge with their enormous war horses, was the most devastating force on Earth. They were famed as Christendom's finest troops right across Europe and far beyond. Nothing could stand against the French knight when used properly. Not massed ranks of savage pagan Lithuanians in the north, nor the horse armies of the Turks of the East.

King Edward took his position near the top of the ridge, with the huge windmill behind. His bodyguards, lords, messengers, marshals, secretaries, heralds, and servants surrounded him. Each of the lords had their own men on hand, so that there were scores of men about the King in the centre of the rear battle. My company was many yards down the hill and I would certainly not be within earshot of the King unless I moved back.

"The men will stay here," I said to Thomas and the other key men of the company, "and you shall accompany me further up the hill."

The first of the French standard bearers arranged themselves in the valley a couple of miles away to the south, their colourful fabrics rippling in the wind. Behind them, thousands upon thousands of soldiers emerged from the roads and deployed in formation. Even after midday, they were still deploying.

"By God, sir," Rob Hawthorn, the leader of my archers said to me. "How many of them are there?"

"A good few, Rob, a good few. But we should have an arrow or two for each of them, what say you?"

He frowned. "Aye, that may be, sir."

We had fought smaller battles before, my company and I, while in Brittany, and one or two of them had begun with similar respective positions, writ small. A few hundred English against a thousand or two French. And we had always come away from them rather well.

But however keenly they are fought, a small scrap is a world away from a mass battle. It is often a slower affair on account of the masses of men and horses that must be arranged but the momentousness of the occasion stirs men's hearts, for good and for ill.

On that ridge by Crecy we held an advantageous position and yet it was by no means unassailable. What passes for hills in that part of France would not count as a molehill in Derbyshire.

The men knew it was to be the sort of battle they had heard of all their lives but had never really fought. These men had battled for their lives in Scotland, Wales, or Brittany, climbed town walls as the denizens fought to resist, forded freezing rivers while under attack, faced down charges from mounted men-at-arms. And all of those events were filled with moments that they would boast of when drunk, or weep for when very drunk, or recall in silence before the next action.

And yet that morning outside Crecy, there was a feeling in the air. Every man knew that his king's fate hung in the balance. And so, England's fate hung in the balance.

I wondered if the French felt that also. Indeed, they would

have felt the desecration we had committed against the sanctity of their God-given lands and the people who served them. A knight's duty was to protect his lord, his king, and his people and the French had been held back from us for so long. They must have been desperate to do their duty and run us down.

"Will they come?" Thomas asked, looking at the sky.

John laughed. "Of course they will, brother. How can they not?"

Walt scratched his armpit through the mail there. "Why do you say it so certain, sir?"

John shrugged. "They must, that is all. They simply must."

I knew what he meant. It was what knights had lived for, since the days of Charlemagne. To charge the enemies that despoiled the earth with their presence.

The bannerets of France were rich and prominent knights who had made a career of war and commanded sections of cavalry in battle and flew their banner, which was a rectangular flag bearing their arms as opposed to the triangular pennon of an ordinary knight.

These men too often recruited their own companies and some did so among their dependents and neighbours like we did in England. But that was unusual. Most of the French army was made up of hundreds or thousands of individual noblemen and gentlemen, each one with his own personal retinue of a squire and a page and often no more than that.

When they mustered in France, they would line up wearing their armour ready for inspection by the officers of the Crown. The archers had to show they could use their bows. Horses were valued and branded so they could not be swapped for poor ones later, with the useless horses sent away and the man rebuked or fined. These men were then assigned to one great nobleman or another for the duration of the campaign. This meant that they would be fighting alongside men they did not know.

But despite all these weaknesses in organisation when compared to our superbly professional armies, the ordinary French peasant and the knights and lords, all threw themselves into the army with great heart for they loved the Crown and wished to do their duty.

Although King Philip himself was not loved, the idea of kingship had to be served. Our hearts compelled us to do so. Of course, the hope for financial reward and personal glory was just as important for some men.

Knighthood was yet a glorious thing, especially for the French. The ballads of the day yet celebrated knighthood as an idea, an ideal, more than it did the act of war. Not just knights but the common folk were able to recognise the banners and blazons of the most famous knights of the realm. Membership of the chivalric orders was much coveted by French and English alike.

Before every great battle, young men-at-arms queued up in their scores or even in their hundreds to be knighted on an occasion that would do them great honour if they survived and they sought to cement their newly-won status by challenging enemies to jousts between the lines.

Men wanted to be knights even if they did not want to be a soldier because they knew it would win them respect from their peers. The ideals of knighthood were perhaps rarely reflected in the practice of war itself but it was a knight's greatest duty to fight in a war for his king and fulfilling that duty felt truly glorious. Riding amongst your brother knights with the cacophony of horses' hoofs and armour and the trumpets and kettle drums, the brilliant colours of the pennants and banners snapping in the wind above your head. There was nothing like it for feeling right and true and powerful.

But changes were already on the horizon. Indeed, many were already present and being felt.

Men who were not knights still became great soldiers. Of course, our great armies were always commanded by the King, or a duke, a count, or an earl. But an experienced English squire could find himself leading a company and commanding knights even when he himself had not been dubbed. And, indeed, a mere knight could find himself in command of counts and barons if the King so ordered it. Something unthinkable in my youth. And men like Black Walter, who never wanted nor expected nor deserved to be knighted, could fight alongside them and be as skilled as any of them and just as well equipped.

Again, in my youth, we had a far greater expectation that battles would be decided by knights fighting knights from horseback under agreed and understood codes of behaviour. But the lessons learned over the years, especially from combat against the horse archers of the Steppe and the slippery Saracen cavalry, meant that we came to favour mobility and victory over honour. And so all of the men and even the archers used horses for mobility but all would dismount for combat itself. Most of my men had coursers, light and swift and trained for war. We needed at least two and ideally three horses each. The archers tended to ride rounceys or hobbies which could vary in quality from the sublime to the God awful.

When I was young, swords were worn and used by what would later be known as gentlemen whereas commoners were more likely to be armed with no more than spears and bows. But even archers had swords by the time we were fighting in France, though plenty preferred axes, maces or hammers and could afford to buy or loot whatever they liked.

Armour, too, had changed almost beyond recognition. Once, we had worn mail from head to toe, with a surcoat over the top in our colours. But by Crecy, we knights and lords mostly wore steel breastplates and back-pieces, along with close fitting plate covering our limbs and only the insides and exposed parts protected by pieces of mail. The steel would discolour and rust something terrible and pages and servants had to scrub them every night that they could to keep them in good order.

Our helms had changed from the old style to a lighter, rounded one called a basinet which protected the top and back of the head and was fitted with a gorget to protect the throat. A movable, conical visor hinged at the top or side meant one could open the helm to breathe, speak and see clearly. A basic style of basinet was worn by almost everyone, even the spearmen and garrison troops. Though for the rest of their armour they often wore a habergeon, which was a mail jacket that a man could shrug on by himself. Some men could only afford, or simply preferred, to fight in a layered linen coat which was easily good enough to stop all but the most terrible of cuts.

Their trumpets sounded in the distance, the blasts brought to us on the wind and calling in ever more of them from miles around.

The foremost of them was an enormous mass of crossbowmen, growing ever larger.

"There be the Genoese, sir," Rob said, unnecessarily pointing at them with his unstrung bow.

Black Walt pointed down the hill at the numerous cannons being prepared on the flanks of the archers at the extreme ends of the battlefield. "What do you reckon our smoking monsters will make of them?"

The dozens of small cannons were protected by a line of parked wagons on either flank, the bizarre, squat things pointing out between them. Most were *ribalds*, cannons constructed from clusters of narrow iron barrels attached to a wooden frame that fired out iron rods. Some had four, or eight, or a dozen barrels. There were a handful of *bombards* amongst them, which were single, more substantial, iron barrels that shot out larger iron arrows or clusters of balls.

"The cannon will do nothing," I said, confidently. "A cacophony of thunder, belching foul smoke and nothing to show for it other than to frighten the birds. Same as we saw in Scotland."

Thomas coughed and spoke under his breath. "That was over twenty years ago, Richard."

Most of my men had been babes in arms or barely much older at the time.

"These devices are ever improved by the cunningest Italian

minds, Richard," John said, his smile wide. "One day soon we shall see these ribalds or the bombards wreaking havoc upon an enemy army, mark my words, sir."

"Nonsense, John," I replied. "I have heard those very same words for how many years past? And, let me tell you, the Tartars used trebuchets to launch barrels filled with oil, *naphtha*, black powder, and the like which would explode upon impact with the ground and throw terrible fire directly onto the men nearby. I have urged the King to seek out these proven weapons but, sadly, he has fallen for the deceits of these Italians who have promised devastation for decades and yet who deliver only smoke and belch out ever more vague promises."

My men chuckled at me, for they had heard it all before. What I could never tell the mortals amongst them was that I had witnessed the effects of these Eastern weapons with my own eyes.

Some part of me still enjoyed being well-regarded and respected by other men. It was a terrible weakness of character and one I would soon seek to eradicate altogether, but I even drew satisfaction from the approval of commoners like Rob Hawthorn and Black Walter, men who served me and would be far beneath me in every sense even had I been a mortal knight

Our own trumpeters sounded the call to arms once more, as if there was an Englishman in all France who was not prepared and ready to meet the enemy.

"God Almighty," Rob said, "they don't half love their bleating."

"It is a wonderful sound," I said, loudly. "It rather stirs the blood, does it not?"

"What's the point of stirred blood if we be all the way back here?" I heard Black Walter mumble. I chose not to respond to his grumbling.

"There's too many of them to assemble properly before nightfall," Thomas said, with what was possibly more hope than judgement. "Do you not see, Sir Richard?"

I looked at the height of the Sun and held out my fingers to measure the distance between what was probably the horizon and the Sun itself. "There is a good few hours yet. All depends on how keen they are."

A little while later, it clouded over and a light but steady rain began to fall.

"Surely," Thomas said, "surely, they will not attack this evening."

Men cried out up and down the line as the French trumpets sounded, the kettledrums resounded and the Genoese crossbowmen began marching forward, closing the distance toward our forward battles.

Our archers, on the flanks of the battles, began stringing their bows from their horned nocks and readying their arrows. Their linen arrow bags were coated with wax to keep the arrows dry. Those bags were bulky things, stiffened by a wicker frame so that the fletchings did not crush each other.

They wore their lords livery over their brown, russet, or undyed tunics. The surcoats displayed the yellows, reds, blues, or greens of their lord's colours, scores of different styles from every county and hundred in England. But all were faded and most filthy with mud and food and wine stains.

As the Genoese came within the farthest range of their weapons, in groups they began to shoot their bows. Once they had shot, they would reload and advance further. In this way, they made their way closer and closer while unleashing a steady stream of bolts at us.

Sadly for them, their bolts mostly fell short of our lines.

The English bowmen, however, were in their element. Those men could shoot a dozen arrows a minute, if they had to and if they had enough arrows. They rarely did shoot at such a rate. Doing so would use tens of thousands of arrows in a couple of minutes and although that would cause an orgy of destruction it would also use up wagonloads of ammunition and leave the archers with little to do. What they tended to do instead was loose a mass volley of one or two shots and then they would pick their targets, being mindful of how many arrows they had left and how many enemies were on the field.

Still, they swiftly shot down hundreds of the Genoese. The mercenary crossbowmen stood in formations that were as loose as their vast numbers would allow so that our arrows would be more likely to fall on empty ground rather than on a man. Yet they dropped, killed and wounded, faster then I had expected to see.

"Quite a harvest this year," Hal Brampton, one of my men-at-arms, quipped. "Sizeable crop of crossbowmen we be scything down, is it not?"

"Do my eyes deceive me," Rob Hawthorn said, "or have the Italians gone and forgotten their bloody shields?"

I squinted into the crowd for a moment. "By God, how right you are. Is there a shield amongst the lot of them?"

Rob laughed in disbelief, as did the others. And well they might, for part of the strength of the Genoese was that each man carried an enormous and quite sturdy personal shield which would protect him from return shots while reloading or marching. But these thousands of men had no shields at all.

"Why ain't their bows reaching our lads?" Walt asked Rob. "They be in the range of them now, ain't it so?"

"Their cords are wet," Rob said, nodding once. "That rain fair soaked them through. Ain't so easy to restring a crossbow as is a real bow." He patted his own weapon like it was a faithful old hound. The hemp bow string was coated with wax but that only went so far in keeping the things dry, so archers kept them rolled away in a leather pouch on their belts, along with a spare or two. Some even kept a coil of cord under their steel helms.

"Hate this bit," Walt complained. "When the archers just stand there and shoot at each other for bloody ages while we hang about with nothing to do."

"Patience is a conquering virtue, Walt," I said.

Walt sighed. "Want to get on with the real fighting, is all, sir."

Rob and my other archers were offended on behalf of their profession. One of them, Deryk, cried out at Walt.

"Should you not be down amongst your brother Welshmen, Walter?"

"Shut your damned mouth, Deryk Crookley, or you shall find it filled with my knuckles and your own black teeth."

Our trumpets sounded and orders were shouted and relayed by heralds and sergeants that our bowmen were to increase the pace.

Before any man could respond, a great cacophony split the air along with billowing smoke and fire, as our cannons began firing, one after another and often many at once.

The ribalds and bombards spat their fire and their iron arrows and pellets down at the Genoese. How many of them were killed by the cannon, I could not say, as the arrows began to take them apart at the same time. Italians fell all across the field, and the foremost among them began backing away into their fellows behind.

I shot a hand out to grab Thomas by the armour of his upper arm. "They are going to break."

"Begging your pardon, sir, but not them lads," Rob said. "Genoese don't break, don't they say? Retreat in good order, the Genoese."

For a while, it seemed that he was right, for the Italians steadied themselves despite the astonishing number of them that fell to English arrows. Still, they were on edge and shuffling in that way that men do before they lose heart.

"Quick charge would do for the lot of them," I said to no one in particular. "It would be well if we had a hundred men mounted and ready for just such a moment. See them off once and for—"

The cannons sounded again. Not as many as before, perhaps merely a dozen of the squat little beasts coughed out their fire. It was impossible to tell if any of the projectiles even reached their targets but the fear of the machines was enough to do the job that a hundred charging men and horse would have done.

The Genoese broke.

Some of them at the fronts and edges of their formations

backed further and further into the men behind, forcing those men to edge back themselves until some men turned and walked toward the rear, pushing past men still loading and shooting. More and more followed until the walking turned into running as fast as they were able with their large bows. Some men tripped and fell and—if they had any—their friends helped them up. All the while, the arrows fell upon them, driving them away.

A cheer went up from all the English battles as our men jeered the fleeing Italians, for it is a sight to stir the heart when your enemy breaks.

"You ain't looking happy, sir," Black Walt said from beside me. "You neither, Tom."

"It was good work," I replied. "Yet now we face the true test. See, there, how they are already making ready. Look at them, the magnificent bastards."

The French mounted men-at-arms moved forward on their great destriers and in their bright colours and shining steel. They were so many, massing together in a curved, broken front that stretched halfway across the vale and many more ranks pushed in from the rear.

"Once the Italians get free, the true battle shall begin," Thomas confirmed.

Instead, the French pushed into the fleeing Genoese and the mounted men's weapons were drawn and they began laying about them. Cutting down the Genoese, who could put up no defence against the onslaught.

"What are they doing?" Rob shouted, outraged at the sight of archers falling to knights, which was a deep-rooted fear for all bowmen. "They slay their own men."

Walt scoffed. "Shouldn't have run, should they. Bloody cowards." We ignored him.

"They are not their own men," I said to Rob. "We are watching Frenchmen murdering Italians."

It was a horror of a sight but we did not have long to ponder it, for the French had their blood up and in no time they barged through the Genoese and came charging in a chaotic mass straight across the field toward our first battle on the right.

"Here they come," Rob said to his archers. "Now let's see our lads do their work."

I had loved English bowmen for over one hundred years but only in the wars against the belligerent Scots and the factions in Brittany had they begun to come into their own. Successive English armies had included more and more bowmen in their ranks to the point where we had twice as many of them as we had men-at-arms. With masses of spearmen supporting them, our archers could shoot their powerful bows into enemy horse and men at will. We had done so before in Brittany but never on such a scale.

And we had likewise never faced an enemy of the scale and quality of the French nobility, the knights and squires of the greatest nation in Christendom and perhaps of anywhere on Earth. It was impossible not to be moved to fear by the sight, even though their initial charge was as ragged as any I had seen.

As they came within range of our foremost bowmen, the orders were given to shoot. Arrows darted up in their hundreds and fell in amongst those riders.

The arrows the bows shot were murderous bloody things. A yard long and thick so that they did not snap when the massive force of the bow thrust them skyward. At their head was the small, dense bodkin point which could penetrate mail armour and force its way through visors or between sheets of plate.

Horses fell, stumbling and throwing their riders as they tumbled or sank to their knees and keeled over. Men were hit and rode on, or else veered away. Others were spilled from their saddles like the hand of God had swatted them. The fallen impeded the charge of those behind.

Our cannon fired. I jumped in fear at the sudden noise, as did many of those around me.

It terrified the charging horses and disrupted them further as they turned to flee from the appalling crashing thunder and evil stench.

And yet through it all, the courageous and the lucky reached our first battle in their dozens and then in the hundreds. All along the front line of the English battle, horses swerved and their riders hacked down on our men in a whirling storm of steel. A terrific clangour filled the air, growing louder even than the roaring cries of the men.

The first battle, on the right, was packed with great lords, their banners held high above where they stood.

In the very centre was the tallest banner.

That of Prince Edward.

Already at sixteen, the young man himself stood a head taller than most of the other men around him and he made for an unmistakeable and irresistible target.

"Going for the Prince, ain't they, sir?" Walt said. "Great bloody pack of the lordly bastards. Perhaps we might have a wander down there and lend a hand now, sir?"

"All is well," I said, though it certainly seemed as though the fighting was heaviest where the Prince was. I chanced a look behind me at the King, who stood watching all impassively.

More French came from the rear, streaming in as if there was no end to them. Our arrows fell in their thousands, coming in an endless stream. Those shooting from further away on the farthest flanks aimed up so their arrows dropped from a height into the massed French and the bowmen but those closest to the men-at-arms shot at the mounted knights before them.

Small groups of riders in the dozens attempted repeated charges against the archers on the wings but the tightly packed spearmen formed a wall of points that horses would die on, while the archers picked off the charging men at will.

The French edged away from the wings and clustered further in the centre where they could engage with our men-at-arms but this only served to give our archers even more of an oblique angle to shoot from, so that even men fifty yards back from the fighting were dropping from the arrow storm while they waited their turn at the English.

Still, they were skilled and brave and they were so many, and they forced their way into the Prince's battle right at its heart.

Right where the Prince stood, fighting for his life, for his people and for the love of glory.

The sky grew darker. Surely, many a man ventured, surely the French would have to break off soon. And yet still, they fought with a mad fury, sensing that all they needed to do was to break through the lines or to kill the Prince and they would have victory.

The Prince's banner fell.

A great intake of breath went up all around us and a rumbling growl began from our men as the horror of it dawned on them.

"He's fallen, by God," Black Walter said. "There, told you so."

"Hold your damned tongue," I snapped. "A banner is not the man."

Sure enough, in a few moments the banner was heaved aloft again and ten thousand Englishmen roared.

I sidled away from my men so that I was within hailing distance from the King as a knight came panting up the hill, covered in the grime of battle.

The messenger dropped to a knee in front of King Edward.

"Get up, sir, and relay your message," said one of the King's men.

When he stood, I saw wild fear in his eyes. "Your Grace, the Earl of Northampton begs you send the reserve to assist the Prince, who is sorely pressed. All about him, men are falling and the Prince can do only so much. Please, Your Grace. We must have more men, or the Prince is in the gravest of danger."

King Edward barely blinked. "Is my son dead or injured? Does he lay upon the earth, felled?"

"No, Your Grace, but he is hard pressed. Hard pressed, indeed."

The King radiated disapproval. "Hard pressed? You return to Northampton and those that sent you and you tell him to beg me for nought while my son yet lives. Tell them also that they are fighting so that my son may win his spurs and so that this victory may be his alone. Do you hear me well, sir? Then go now."

The poor man withered and bowed as deeply as he was able, mumbling his confirmation as he backed away.

Watching carefully, I noted how the King looked out from his helm, searching for someone and I pushed my way forward to appear at his side while more celebrated knights and lords than I protested in outrage.

"Your Grace?"

"Richard," he said, using his private voice, "I wonder if you might take your company forward a little way?"

"At once, Your Grace."

He turned away, dismissing me, but I noted how his eyes locked onto his son's wavering banner down below.

I pushed through the courtiers and called to my men. "We shall push forward now." I grabbed my senior archer. "Rob, keep your men to our rear but ensure they stay with me. You will be close to the enemy but hold your shots for now. I know it will much pain them but they will not shoot near the Prince and yet keep them in place in case the bastards break through our line."

The archers carried a variety of secondary weapons. Most of the younger lads wore cheap swords that were liable to bend or break if they struck a piece of armour at an odd angle. Older men could afford better weapons or had learned to favour a hammer or mace. Every one of them, though, wore a long dagger which was the sweetest thing there was for slipping through a man's armour and right into his offal, or to open his veins. Even the ones who barely knew one end of a sword from the other had grown up with a dagger in his palm and by God did they like to use them.

Rob nodded. "They'll not wander off, sir."

"Walt," I said, "you stay by my side and do not get carried away like last time."

"Don't know to what you be referring to, sir, but you can trust me, sir."

I raised a hand to Thomas, who lifted his hilt in salute. John grinned from ear to ear as he drew his sword and kissed the base of the blade. He and Hugh clapped each other on the shoulders before closing their visors.

Leading them, I pushed down the hill toward the battle while Walt shouted out for men to make way. He had a loud voice when he needed it, uncouth as it was. In no time, we were in amongst the wounded and the exhausted who sat or lay upon the ground while their servants tended to them. Some men guzzled water or wine. Others cried out in pain. We passed a knight who was having a great dent hammered out of his breastplate while he directed his servants and swigged from a cup of wine.

"Good evening, Sir Richard," he grinned, raising his cup to me. "Rare old fight, this one. Have at it, sir. Have at it!"

I nodded and continued on, pushing into the massed ranks of men. The sound grew until hearing a single voice in amongst the shouting and clash of arms grew impossible. Keeping my eyes fixed on the Prince's banner, I shoved and yanked men aside, calling out that I was on the King's business, for all the good it did.

The masses around me surged like a wave and, all of a sudden, there he was.

Prince Edward.

The sixteen-year-old prince fought like a lion fending off dogs. From afar and in his armour and similar red and blue quartered surcoat, the Prince looked exactly like his father. His magnificent harness was covered in muck and his armour much bashed about but the Prince stood tall and thrust at a horseman with a broken lance in one hand and swung a mace in his left at a French knight who rushed him on foot.

At his side, Sir Humphrey Ingham, a strong knight but a sour bastard, held the Prince's great banner aloft with an arm wrapped around the pole while he slashed at the French with a drastically bent sword. Even as I watched, more French horsemen pushed their way into the clear space before him. But the Prince smashed his mace into the helm of the man charging on foot and a moment later stepped forward and thrust the tip of the broken lance into the groin of the mounted man with such force that it threw the man down even as it rent his loins apart. The horse reared in panic but the Prince swatted its thrashing hooves away with his mace and stepped aside to knock a lance away from his chest.

In the space he created for himself, he half turned to those men being pushed back beside him.

"Come, my lords!" The Prince shouted, breathing raggedly. "For England!"

In response, the great cry of our people went up. "Saint George!"

"Prince Edward!" I shouted as my battle cry, for my heart was greatly stirred by the young lord's heroism and his skill. "For the Prince! Prince Edward!"

I hurled myself into the fray beside the heir to the throne and Thomas and John were with me, as was Walter, who put himself in harm's way for me many a time, though he was but a mortal man. Bless his black heart.

Humphrey Ingham, the Prince's friend, fought like a lion even with the hindrance of the great banner, throwing his body before Edward's time and again so that he became much battered.

For a time, I all but lost myself in the battle. The enemy faltered and returned, time and again. And we threw them back, time and again.

Night was almost upon us when the heat went out of the enemy. Prince Edward stepped closer and, exhausted beyond speaking, briefly placed a hand upon my shoulder. I clapped him on his arm, with a little too much enthusiasm, and he staggered away.

John grabbed me, leaned his helm against mine and shouted through the metal into my ear. "Now is the time, is it not? Now we should rush out and finish them?"

I looked to Thomas close behind us, who chopped his hand down in a signal that meant we should not act.

"Still too many," Thomas cried to John. "How many more do they have out there? Ten thousand mounted?"

"Numbers count for nought!" I shouted. "Remember the Mongols, Thomas."

I could tell by the set of his shoulders that he scoffed at me because he thought I was half mad with the urge to kill more men.

"King Philip holds the other side of the field," he said. "We had the best of it today. Perhaps we shall decide this tomorrow, no?"

"They will flee, the damned—" I said, in half a growl and caught myself before I spoke an insult aimed at all Frenchmen. "Come, the Prince is safe for now. Come, all of you, come."

I led them out of the fray, back up of the hill.

Black Walter flipped up his visor, panting next to me. "French still coming, ain't they, sir? Should we not stay with the Prince until he be safe and well?"

"Be quiet, Walt."

Almost to the King, I turned and looked out at the heaving to and fro of the battlefield.

It was clear to me that we had triumphed over the French. No matter how often the mounted French charged, fell back, rallied and charged again, their attacks could not break us.

We stood and watched, all of us wondering when would be the right moment to throw a good portion of our reserves into the fight on the front lines.

I coughed and pushed through the powerful knights until I drew close to the King. "I wonder if we might advance and engage now, Your Grace?"

Edward pondered it for a moment, as if the thought had not occurred to him, and as if every Englishman in France had not been urging him to do so for hours.

He nodded once.

"Let us be about our business," the King said, his voice raised, and the cry went up to advance down the slope and join the slaughter.

For slaughter it seemed to be. We were giving no quarter, no ransoms were taken, and no corpses were stripped of riches. Even the archers restrained themselves, somehow overcoming the natural acquisitiveness of the common man in order to continue killing French knights and nobles.

It was when we were fully engaged and the field was strewn with corpses, that one of the most remarkable things happened.

A charge of knights came full pelt for our centre, right where the King's banner was held aloft. They were in the very finest armour, riding the most magnificent beasts, and in their centre was a great lord in all his finery.

As they drew close, I realised in shock that they were shouting the war cry "Prague!" and those men around me called out in surprise that this was the John, the blind King of Bohemia. Once a formidable warrior, he was about fifty years old and had been blind for years after losing his sight on crusade against the pagan Lithuanians, and so no one had expected to see him fighting.

Yet there he was, charging headlong toward his death. John of Bohemia's bodyguards were slaughtered and the blind old soldier was surrounded by our men, dragged from his horse, and killed. By God, it must have made those poor men sick to their stomachs to kill a king rather than take him for ransom.

Darkness was falling. At the rear and edges of the masses of French cavalry, I watched small groups failing to reform and peel away from the main body.

"We have to finish them," Thomas said to me. "Now, before they escape."

I was surprised to hear him, a Frenchman originally from a place not far to the south, near Paris, urging us to kill his countrymen. But then Thomas had been amongst the English for almost a hundred years and a century was enough time to turn even a Frenchman sensible.

"Yes, yes," John said, "now is the time."

His good-hearted squire Hugh raised his axe above his head. "Let us kill the damned bastards."

That surprised me even more but then the reasons for their passion became clearer. I recalled how they and their brother Templars had been persecuted by a French king. It had been almost forty years since we had rescued John and Hugh from execution at the hands of the fourth King Philip, and it was that king's nephew, Philip VI who we faced across the battlefield that day.

Thomas especially wished we had saved more Templars but John and Hugh were all we could manage. To save their lives, I had granted them the Gift of my blood and we had welcomed both into the Order of the White Dagger.

John had been a very fine addition to the Order. He was a well-made young man, well-spoken and chivalrous. He retained his vows of poverty and chastity, so he claimed at least, and I had never met a man who did not like him. As a man often disliked by my peers, it was a wonder to me.

Hugh was a born follower but there was nothing wrong with that. Almost every man on Earth is the same and he was skilled in war and dutiful in nature.

I pushed my way back toward the King's massive dragon

banner once more and forced my way through the press of men who wished to defend him with their person. A few fellows attempted to stop me but I did not allow them to.

"Your Grace," I called out when nearing him. "Might we not now mount and drive them off?"

William de Bohun, the Earl of Northampton, answered me. "The command to retrieve the horses has been given, Richard. Do you think we are fools or children who need you to hold our hands? Take yourself back to the fighting where you may be useful."

A few men about us chuckled. I ignored them all.

"Your Grace? Is that not the standard of King Philip out there at the rear?"

"Of course it is," Northampton said, irritated. "Are you as blind as the dead King of Bohemia, man?"

More laughter.

"We can kill Philip," I said, using my battlefield voice. "Or take him, if you prefer. Your Grace."

The laughter died and the King turned to me. "You will wait until our main charge begins. If you and your men can find a way through, then you may take my cousin the King of France."

"I will, Your Grace."

He reached out and grasped my arm as I turned. He leaned in close and I heard him over the terrible din. "God be with you."

"And with you, sire."

Northampton spoke up again, aiming his remarks at Edward but speaking loud enough for all about us to hear. "Philip will never surrender himself to a mere knight."

"Then that will be his choice," King Edward said, allowing his irritation to show. "Go, now, Richard."

With a bow of my head and a final glance at the Earl of Northampton, I began to push my way out of the King's circle and back to my men.

Sir John Chandos clapped an armoured arm around my shoulders. "Richard," he shouted in my ear. "The King said to take him, yes? He is worth everything alive. Dead, he brings us nothing."

I liked Chandos. He reminded me of myself. A Derbyshire knight barely above a commoner, he had risen as high as the likes of us could rise. He was about twenty-six or so and yet his tactical ability was evident to those of us who were able to recognise it. I had taken him under my wing when he was younger but now he was reaching the prime of his life and he was growing to consider himself as a greater man than I.

"I will treat Philip as gently as a babe in arms," I said, pushing Chandos away to arm's length. "But babies sometimes get dropped on their heads."

He looked concerned as I turned away but I wanted Chandos to know that his patronising advice was unwelcome.

When I returned to my company, I dragged our wide-eyed pages to me and shouted for them to bring our horses up immediately.

"We join the counter charge?" Thomas asked.

"The King has issued a command to me. This company will follow close behind the counter charge in the centre. When the lines clash, we shall punch our way through and we shall take King

Philip in the name of Edward."

"My God," John said, a grin forming across his face.

"Rob?" I called to the leader of my archers. "You will stay close behind us, save your arrows if you can. When we reach the banner of the King of France, you may kill the horses of the King and his bodyguard. But please, Mister Hawthorn, do not murder a king this evening."

Rob nodded. "We'll give you dead horses, Sir Richard."

I have always appreciated the simplicity of the lower classes.

Darkness was falling and we were running out of time to complete our victory. The haste with which hundreds of horses were brought forward was impressive and was a testament to the fact that the professionalism of our army extended from top to bottom. My company mounted just as the first line of English cavalry formed and charged at the French. They were themselves readying for yet another desperate and foolhardy charge at us, no doubt because they witnessed the relative disorder in our lines as the horses were brought up.

"Stay together. Stay under our banner. And take no man but Philip." I urged my men before closing my visor.

We were going to capture a king.

4

THE BLACK KNIGHT

IT WAS WONDERFUL TO BE MOUNTED again. To rise up above the heads of men on foot and so see that much further. Feeling the power of the animal beneath me and the mass of those beside me as we advanced behind the English men-at-arms. They smashed into the French and the sound of metal clashing echoed through the dusk. Banners waved everywhere and rallying cries filled the air as groups of men were broken apart before desperate attempts to reform.

All the while, I kept my sight fixed upon the banner of Philip; a vivid blue covered in countless emblems of the bright yellow fleur-de-lis.

Beside it was the Oriflamme itself, the ancient and holy battle standard of the French crown. Bright red and unadorned but long and narrow, with two enormous streamers doubling its length and flown from a gilded lance. Flying it over the battlefield meant that no quarter was to be given, echoing the orders of Edward for the English.

I aimed directly at those banners and, after ensuring that Thomas, John, Hugh, Walt, Ralf, and Simon were with me, I forced our way through the press of men and horse until we reached Philip's companions and bodyguard.

Touchingly, there remained some levies of townsfolk on foot about the French king and they were being cut to pieces even as the lords and knights of France turned and fled from everywhere else on the field.

Our advance was halted by a line of beautifully armoured men on enormous horses. They looked like they had been untouched by the fighting and I meant to change that forthwith. As we clashed with them, a few arrows slipped by me to hammer into the flesh of the French horses. The man before me struggled to control his maddened destrier and I shoved him sideways from his saddle, sending him down into the deep shadows between the horses.

I pushed through deeper and found myself surrounded on all sides, though it was increasingly difficult to tell. Men were losing the breath necessary to shout through their visors and the growing darkness was dulling heraldic colours and designs.

But I could see King Philip clearly now.

He looked magnificent and I was thrilled to be so close to him. To be the one to capture him would be a great honour.

We were close, and his men were falling all around him. When a gap opened up, my archers hit his horse with a volley of arrows, some slipping through its protective coverings and it went down, taking the King with him. A cry went up from both sides and we heaved forward against the mass of men protecting him but they pushed back at us with equal ferocity. In mere moments, Philip was up on a fresh horse and his men took up their battle cry with renewed vigour.

"*Montjoie Saint Denis!*"

While the English, including Thomas and John behind me, roared for Saint George.

I hacked and shoved further in, closer and closer to Philip. My armour received terrible punishment and my entire body would be a mass of deep bruises in the morning unless I could sup on a goodly amount of blood after the battle.

And that was when I saw him.

A French knight hacking his way toward me. He wore black over his old-fashioned armour and he was followed by a handful of men-at-arms also in black.

One of the pair of squires bore a banner of plain black with no emblem or image upon it. He threw down the English who stood against him with such ease that I was astonished to see it.

Philip used the opportunity to begin to withdraw and, seeing this, I shouted at my men to bring him down. My command was passed back to my archers who loosed a volley at the group of bodyguards. A roar went up. Philip had an arrow shaft jutting from a gap in his visor and his new horse was also wounded and both man and rider fell.

Good God, I thought, *we have killed the King of France.*

But they pulled him up and cheered as they helped him to

mount a third horse. The mass of loyal men dragged the mounted King away toward safety.

As the French pulled back, space was created and the fighting intensified at once. The knight with the black banner swung his polearm at Thomas and knocked my friend senseless on the back of his horse.

John shouted and jabbed at the attacker with a broken lance. The man-at-arms bearing the black banner whirled his hammer down on Walt's horse's head with such force that the animal was killed. It dropped like a stone, throwing Walt down with it. John's lance was ripped from his grasp and tossed spinning over the heads of the riders swirling behind.

Hugh rushed in with his axe and smashed the breastplate of the black knight, who reeled from the blow before returning one of his own with such speed and power that it crashed against Hugh's helm. He fell to his knees, dazed or dead.

Such strength was inhuman. I could barely believe what I was seeing but there it was.

These men were surely immortals.

Charging my horse at them, I raised my weapon and thrust it at the squire with the black banner. I noted his red shield with three white escutcheons hanging from his shoulder. It seemed familiar but I had no time to think on it as, somehow, he swiped my attack away with the head of his hammer and struck me on the shoulder so quickly I did not see the blow coming.

Instinct caused me to lean away and so the rising backhanded blow merely clipped the top of my conical helm rather than hit me clean on the side of the head. Even so, it knocked me momentarily senseless.

I was falling.

The bastards had struck my horse and he was dropping.

When I looked up, the three men-at-arms beneath the black banner were riding away after the King.

John helped Hugh to his feet but he was unsteady indeed, despite the immortal blood in his veins.

"Get after them!" I shouted at my company.

"King Philip?" Thomas asked, lifting his visor and peering about, clearly still dazed from the blow to his head.

"The knight with the black banner!" I shouted, pointing with my weapon. "And his squires."

My archers were mounted on all kinds of horses but mostly hobbies that would not fare well when fighting through the mad swirling cavalry before us, of both sides. I watched John force his horse forward and raise his sword above his head.

"Saint George!" John cried with primal harshness. He was outraged that they had so wounded Hugh, who was very dear to John. He was an honourable man.

John was the finest horsemen of us all and mounted on the biggest, strongest destrier. He could force his way ahead through the crowd while I brought up the company.

I lifted my visor and raised my voice. "John, hear me. Get after him, John. Slow him down, if you can. Yet be wary."

"Wary?" John cried, with outrage in his voice.

I reached across and grasped John's arm. "You can see that he is one of us, John, do you not see it? In receipt of the Gift. One of William's creations. His squires also."

"Of course they are," John snapped, still angry, before calming himself somewhat. "I will stop him, Richard."

"We are taking the knight of the black banner and his men," I called to my company. "Twenty marks to the man who takes one alive. Ten for each one dead."

They all roared their approval and we chased them through the battlefield. A handful of my archers, the best riders, pulled ahead of us. They wanted the money and they wanted the glory, too.

The sun had set and it was almost full night but there was just enough light to see by, though my vision was severely limited by my visor. I could just make out John and a couple of archers racing ahead of me, taking their own paths through the chaos in pursuit of our quarry.

The black banner was still held aloft by the small group fleeing amongst the rest and yet almost all the banners began to look similarly dark. I forced myself to clamp my eyes upon the one I wanted and trusted my horse and my instinct to avoid whatever came in front of us.

Likewise, I had to trust that enough of my company remained with me. As far as I was concerned, my archers were worth their weight in silver, for they could bring down a knight in armour with a well-placed arrow to the man's horse. I prayed to God that we would catch them before they escaped.

Years, I had searched for William's hidden immortals and now I had three of them almost within my grasp. I could barely contain the passion rising in my throat and I roared a wordless cry. It was echoed by my men behind me, crying for Saint George and some calling my name as their war-cry. It stirred my heart greatly to hear it.

We were charged in the flank by a group of knights from Hainault. Their shouts and the drumming of their horse's hooves filled the air at the same moment they hit my company. I avoided the lance aimed for me but a charging horse's shoulder collided with my destrier's head and neck and we were knocked quite desperately aside. It is a wonder my magnificent animal did not fall and instead we recovered, wheeled about and charged into the affray. I assume they believed we were in pursuit of King Philip for, after only a short engagement to delay us, they fell back and rode away.

It was growing difficult to see anything at all but I hurried on, with ever fewer of my men behind me.

"John!" I called, lifting my visor. "John!" The noise of the battle was growing ever quieter but still I barely made out his answering cry from up ahead.

An isolated farmhouse appeared before us. The structure and the building around it had formed some sort of nexus for the fleeing Frenchmen, perhaps seeking to hide overnight or to use the structures to mount some kind of defence against their pursuers. And the English had swarmed here, the foolish ones perhaps expecting to find food and the more experienced-aware that the place would likely have been commandeered by some lord before or during the battle—looking for wealth they could carry away.

I lifted my visor again and left it up so I could see better in the darkness.

Men shouted and fought all around. A pair of men even struggled high up on the thatched roof, grappling and sliding down the sides. They could have been men of either side, perhaps fighting to the death over a ring or a chicken. There was madness in the air already when I saw a flash of yellow and turned to see a man attempting to fire the barn.

In the light of the growing fire, I saw the black knight.

I saw so much in a single instant.

Far across the yard, the figures like ravens against the flame. On the ground, bodies writhed and died.

The black knight's helm was gone but he was silhouetted against the fire and I could make out no features.

But I knew it was him, for he held a grown man aloft in his hands as if his victim weighed no more than a rag doll.

And it was John that he held in his grasp. John was also without his helm and indeed his armour seemed to hang off him in tatters, with buckles and straps hanging down.

My friend and companion struggled to free himself but he was dripping with blood from injuries elsewhere on his body.

The black knight brought John's neck to his mouth with a savage jerk and began drinking from what must have been a gaping wound. He pulled back, tearing a long strand of skin and flesh and blood with it. As he did so, John let out a terrible, mournful cry.

I rode blindly toward the knight, determined to destroy this monster, to smite him with a single mighty blow. The rage filled me.

Something hit me in the face.

Then I was falling, the flames and silhouetted figures twisting as I tumbled to the ground.

Even as I crashed into the compacted earth and the pain hit me, I had a dreadful realisation of what must have happened.

As if I was some impetuous young fool in his first campaign, I had left my visor up as I attacked.

And a crossbow bolt had hit me in the face.

The shaft jutted from my cheek and hot blood gushed into my throat and I was wracked by coughing. Crawling on all fours, I had to hang my head down to let the blood pour out of my face rather than fill my throat and drown me. My eyes streamed so that it was hard to see and I groaned, unable to speak. Still, I got to my feet and stepped forward into the blurred streaks of shadow and flame.

"Sir Richard!"

Friendly voices surrounded me and hands were on me.

I recognised the voice of Black Walter, the commoner who was not an immortal and who did not know anything about the existence of the Gift, or the Order. But he was strong and did not know hesitation.

"Walt? Pull this bolt from my face!" At least, so I tried to speak but instead it came out as a series of grunts and ended in wet coughing.

Frustrated, I grabbed the slippery bolt in my fist and began to draw it out.

"No, no, no!" Walt and my other men shouted at me and they seized my arms so that I could not pull it from my face.

I was strong but was held by half a dozen English archers who were as strong as mortals could be and they heaved my arm away from my face. I almost screamed in frustration because I knew that once I got the bolt out and I could consume a mortal's blood, I would heal my wound and I could return to the fight.

"Leave him be!" Thomas shouted. "Move back, you fools. Spread out and stand guard. Catch your horses."

He forced me to kneel, bade me hold still and muttered a prayer as he pulled the wooden shaft from my head. It was excruciating and I felt the shattered bones of my cheek crunching and grinding as the iron point of the bolt made its way back out. More blood and chunks fell into the back of my mouth and I shook as I held my breath and braced myself against Thomas, fighting the urge to jerk away from the source of the agony.

With a wet, sucking sound, he pulled it clear and held it up to the firelight. The barn and the farmhouse were both burning with enormously tall, bright flames and their heat washed over me in waves.

Holding a palm over the ruin of my face, I attempted to speak but Thomas hushed me.

"Blood. Yes, Richard, I know. Come."

He guided me into the shadow of a chest-high stone wall, sat me down and dragged a dying French spearman into my lap. He was probably a locally raised levy, called to defend his homeland and his town from the invading English brutes. He had a deep laceration in his skull and his movements were weak and he was clearly dying from his wounds. Thomas said another prayer but mercifully for me did not wait until he was finished before slitting the spearman's throat and holding the wound up to my face.

66

I drank down his blood, swallowing as much of my own as I did his.

And yet I felt it working in my belly before I had finished drinking. The strength of it filled me, lessened my pain. I felt or perhaps merely imagined the bones of my face knitting back together.

"John?" I asked, the moment I was able.

Thomas helped me to my feet and escorted me to him. Our company had already cleaned him up somewhat and bound his wounds even though he was dead.

And dead he was, with no hope of recovery. His head had been severed almost all the way through and his eyes stared lifelessly, reflecting the light from the fires that were already burning themselves out.

Hugh cradled the body of his brother, friend, and closest companion, weeping freely over him. They had been together, knight and squire, friend and brother, for over thirty years. And now Hugh was alone.

"Two of Rob's archers also fell," Thomas said, his voice flat. "Deryk Crookley and Paul Gipping."

It was my fault that John was dead. And two of the best archers. I had sent them on ahead, alone, without considering that even an immortal knight like John might be vastly outmatched by the men he was pursuing.

Even at the last moment, when John was still alive, I could have stopped it if only I had pulled my visor into place.

Decades, I had been searching and waiting for the chance to find and face down one of William's immortals and when it finally happened I was somehow unprepared and useless.

It was an irreparable personal failure.

"I could not stop them," Thomas said, his voice flat with his own sense of failure. "And then when they fled, I lost them in the darkness."

"As God is my witness," I said, "I shall find the knight of the black banner and his men."

"I swear it also," Thomas said.

"And I," Hugh said, wiping his eyes.

"I shall find them," I continued, "and tear their God damned hearts out."

5

DUTY

"BY GOD, SIR!" Black Walt said in the pre-dawn murk the next morning. "Your face, sir. It is a miracle, sir."

"Avert your eyes from my face, Walt," I growled at him, for I was still in pain and had hardly slept as we lay by the smouldering ruins of that farmhouse. "Else it shall be a miracle if you live to see the sunrise this day."

He ducked away in false obsequiousness but I could hear him muttering under his breath as he went.

It was dank but not cold and the sun would burn away the damp when it rose. Smoke drifted through the morning. Normally, blackbirds, warblers and song thrushes would be chorusing at that hour but all I could hear was the cawing of a hundred malicious crows off in the shadows, already feasting on the carcases of the fallen.

I hid my healed face behind my visor, hoping that my soldiers would assume my wound was shamefully hideous, and gathered my company. We had lost men due to my foolishness but those that remained seemed not to blame me. Indeed, they all wanted to take their own revenge for John and Deryk and Paul. Their bodies we wrapped up as best we could and brought them with us for proper burial later.

I knew we had little chance of finding our prey by that point but I also knew that our chances would dwindle to nought if we delayed much longer. We assumed that the French would withdraw but we did not know whether they would contest the field again that very day. Some battles ran over more than one day and I thought that perhaps the French, who undoubtedly outnumbered us, might have another crack of the whip.

"It may be that the black banner knight laid low in the darkness nearby and may yet be within our grasp," I told my men. "We must get after them now, before they can get further away."

My company was ready almost immediately for they had no camp to break and little equipment. We had not gone far and were picking our way through the pre-dawn gloom when a cry went up from Black Walter and Rob the archer.

"What is it?" I asked, approaching to where they had stopped, looking south. There was a slight rise in the land there, and a line of trees across the horizon forming a darker band of black beneath the lightening sky.

"Listen, sir," Rob muttered. "Men marching. Hundreds."

"Marching? Not riding?" I strained to hear anything through

my helm as Black Walter removed his own.

"Sounds like thousands to me."

"Where?" I asked.

They both pondered it, heads tilted to one side, listening. Rob pointed and Walt nodded in agreement.

"Coming up from the south," Rob said, "up the Abbeville road, I reckon."

It seemed as though the French would contest the field once again and they were making an early start of it, hoping to catch us unprepared.

"God damned bastards," I said, as Thomas came up beside me.

"The French have returned?" he asked, his visor open but his features lost in shadow. I detected a hint of pride in his voice, along with the frustration. "We must warn the King."

"If we do, we will lose the black banner," I replied. "Lose our chance to take revenge for John."

"I wish to kill that black knight. I wish it with all my heart," Thomas said. "Yet it is our duty to warn the King."

"Other men will send word," Walter said. "Perhaps word is sent already."

"Or one of us can return," I said, "bringing word of this fresh attack."

Thomas turned to me and though I could not make out his features, I knew him so well that I could imagine precisely how they were set. "None of us would be heeded by the lords. None but you."

"They would listen to you, Thomas. You are a knight."

"I am French. And they know me as a squire in your service."

"Very well," I said, growing frustrated, "I will return to the King and you will continue the pursuit."

"We ain't going to leave you alone, Sir Richard," Walt said, with his infuriating, base sense of honour. I ignored him.

"You know that I am not afraid of an honourable death," Thomas said, "but I do not hope that we can best the men we pursue without you there."

I almost growled at him. "What then would you have me do, sir?"

"It is our duty to return to our lines, raise the alarm, and join the battle."

I grumbled but I knew he was right. My men were frustrated also and they had no wish to fight another battle after the exertion of the day before but they did as I commanded and returned with us.

"Where have you been?" the Earl of Northampton said to me when I reached the village of Crecy as the sun was almost up.

"In pursuit of our enemies."

He scoffed as his men finished dressing him in the final pieces of his armour, most of which he had apparently slept in. "Did you even make an attempt on seizing Philip?"

I recalled how my men had killed Philip's horses, twice, and had even put an arrow in him, driving him and his men from the field and confirming our victory for King Edward. Perhaps de Bohun saw something of the violence I felt bubbling up within me and he addressed me again in a more agreeable tone.

"We are grateful for your bringing us news of the French

attack," he said.

More and more men were coming in from the south, bringing word of the massing French troops.

"My lord!" one lightly-armoured squire on a fast horse cried, riding close and calling out. "They are two thousand strong. And, my lord, they are all levies and all are on foot."

Northampton's face lit up in joy and he turned to the other lords within hailing distance. "Suffolk! Warwick! Did you hear? Two thousand local levies!"

"It is a ruse," Warwick said, confidently. "They are drawing us in for a counter attack."

"Never, my lords," I said. "The French are not sufficient in cunning to bait such a trap."

Sir John Chandos mounted his horse. "Sir Richard is correct, my lords. Shall we slaughter them to a man and then return to break our fast?"

Our cavalry could not have been more thrilled at the opportunity to run down the enemy formations. It was the perfect situation for mounted men-at-arms to bring to bear the heavy cavalry charge and hundreds of us formed up in lines with remarkable ease and as the sun came up we thundered across the battlefield, already churned by yesterday's struggle, and crashed into the front ranks of local levy troops.

They were astonished by our attack and they crumbled almost immediately.

When they turned to run, we forced ourselves in amongst them and cut them to pieces. I broke off quickly and returned to my company but the English pursued the fleeing commoners for miles as they scattered in all directions.

By the time I reached my men, the sun was fully up. The field was strewn with bodies and with men and horses wandering, dazed and wounded, singly and in groups.

It seemed that the dead were all French, or at least practically all of the men-at-arms were. Heralds from both sides picked their way through the field, checking bodies for identifying heraldry as clerks marked down lists of the deceased. There were hundreds of dead English archers and Welsh spearmen being prepared for burial.

"We may continue the pursuit of the knight of the black banner now," I said to Thomas and the rest of my men. "But in which direction should we go?"

"South, sir," Black Walt said. "Let us get back to the edge of Paris."

"And what is your reasoning, Walt?"

"Good plunder, ain't there."

I ignored him. "Thomas? Rob?"

"I heard from some of the other lads that the French knights and lords ran on past Abbeville to Amiens, sir," Rob said. "So they reckon."

"If that is so," Thomas replied, "it would be madness for us to ride that way. There must be ten thousand men-at-arms in that direction."

"And yet if our quarry is there, we will go nonetheless," I insisted. "Assuming the men will follow?" I looked at Rob and Walt.

Walt grinned. "Try and stop them, sir."

Rob was more circumspect. He scratched his nose. "Might do it with a bit of encouragement, sir."

I resolved to promise generous sums of prize money but a royal sergeant rode hard toward me and my heart sank. And it was as I feared.

"King Edward requests that you attend him at his quarters in the village of Crecy, Sir Richard," the sergeant said. "Immediately, if you please."

It seemed that God did not wish me to pursue the knight of the black banner. I cursed Him even though I knew it must have been punishment for some sin or other that I had committed. It was hard to know which it might be, as I committed so many.

Prince Edward was leaving the King's tent on the edge of the village of Crecy as I approached. He was surrounded by a gaggle of young lords and he towered over almost all of them. Clad in his magnificent armour, he looked every bit the picture of the chosen prince, the hope of a new generation. The Prince had fought like a Greek hero. I knew looking at him that morning, serious and alert and paying his sycophantic knights like Sir Humphrey Ingham polite yet distant attention, that he would make a superb King of England, just like his father.

"Sir Richard!" he called, surprising me and startling his lords. "They caused you no trouble this morning, I take it?"

"It was like hunting sheep, Your Grace."

He laughed. "And yet they say you do not enjoy hunting of any sort, sir."

"I enjoy hunting well enough, Your Grace. It is simply that I prefer hunting the King's enemies."

Prince Edward nodded at his followers. "A very fine thing to say, sir. And you are in luck, for the King has need of your preferred kind of hunting. God be with you, Richard."

I bowed. "God be with you, Your Grace."

He moved off as if he had a specific task of his own to complete, and I am sure that he did for he was no paper prince but a useful lord and contributor to the campaign. Already at sixteen years of age he was a better man than most. His competence and rightness made us all feel hopeful and secure about the future of England.

His knights hurried after him like goslings after a goose. One of them, Sir Humphrey, turned to glare at me before he went. He had fought well on the field by the Prince's side, bearing his banner, and yet it had been my company that had come to the rescue. No doubt he felt the glory that should have been all his had been stolen by me.

Ah well, I thought. *Another enemy to add to the list.*

"Richard, good. Tomorrow, we shall move northeast along the coast," King Edward said without preamble as I ducked inside the open-sided tent.

All the lords surrounding the King turned to me also. A few of them scowled. I grinned back because I knew it would annoy them.

"We are heading for Wissant, Your Grace?" I asked, stepping forward. A couple of the lords begrudgingly moved aside. Wissant was a common landing place for those crossing from England. It made sense to me that we would want to take it when we disembarked for home.

"You want to leave France, Richard?" Edward asked, seeming to be cross with me. I suspected that he was feigning displeasure but it is hard to know where kings are concerned. Some of the sanest ones are still quite mad by ordinary standards.

"In fact, Your Grace, I would like to ride further into the country."

"Oh? Do you have some heroic deeds in mind? Or are you simply looking for pillage?"

I considered requesting his leave for the pursuit of the knight of the black banner but I could not think of a reason good enough. Clearly, I could not say that he was a blood-drinking immortal so powerful that he and his men had easily slaughtered John, who was himself a blood-drinking immortal knight.

If I suggested that I wanted revenge for John's death, he would dismiss my needs without a thought, for as far as anyone else would be concerned, I had lost a man on the battlefield. No crime had been committed. He may even explicitly forbid me from pursuing the French knight.

If on the other hand I said nothing, perhaps I could find time for my own purposes.

"As you say, Your Grace," I replied.

He glanced at me but I kept my face expressionless and he continued.

"That is well, as I would have your men advance ahead of the vanguard. You shall start today and we shall start behind you tomorrow. Go no further than Calais. The French have withdrawn into their towns, stiffened the garrisons and are no doubt improving their defences but there may be some attempts to delay us or divert us. If you encounter any force who will not withdraw from you, fix them in position and send a man to Northampton who will come up to you in strength enough to drive them away. And ensure you go no further than twenty miles from the coast. Is that all clear, Richard?"

How in the name of God will I know how many miles I am from the coast, I wondered.

"Perfectly clear, Your Grace," I said, bowing.

In the end, it was a disappointingly routine duty and though we ran off a few local squires, we rode through a quiet and empty country. Anyone with any sense had long since fled far from our advancing army and even the fools hid in the woods and dells and ditches at our approach.

Behind my company, the English army advanced in a broad front stretching from the coast deep inland, and they burned every house, barn, outhouse and field so that the sky was filled with smoke. We ignored every walled town, other than to burn their crops and suburbs to the ground, other than a small place called Etaples which was quickly taken, sacked, and then burned. Every market town and tiny village in our line of advance was turned to charcoal and smoke. When the army reached the settlement of Wissant, where I had expected we would embark for England, we instead destroyed it utterly.

Ten miles further up the coast was the small port town of Calais. It was well-known for two things. The first being that the place was a damned nest of pirates and the second that its people reeked of herring.

And yet it would be hard to imagine a small town that was

better defended than Calais. As it was so close to the border of Flanders, it had become the stoutest fortress in the area. The first element in its favour was the fact it was surrounded by water. On the north side was the harbour and between that and the town was a wall, a moat and a fortified dyke. The other three sides had walls and a wide double moat. Beyond the moat was a marsh that teemed with fowl and wading birds but was sodden, boggy and crossed by rivers and tidal inundations. A dangerous place to cross even for locals and the marshland was vast. The approach to the town was by causeways that were anything but trustworthy.

The town itself was a perfect rectangle of high walls and the massive castle in the north-west corner was separated from the town by even more walls, moats and ditches. What is more, the place was well garrisoned and stocked with vast stores, because it existed in constant readiness for a siege by the Flemings, who wanted more than anything to take the place for themselves but never had the resources or the courage to make the attempt.

And it was Calais, of all bloody places, that King Edward decided to take.

6

THE LADY CECILIA

"IT'S THE FLEMISH, ain't it," Black Walt said, picking gristle out of his teeth. "Everyone knows."

The leading men of my company sat at the table in my newly built home in the English camp outside Calais which had been named Villeneuve-la-Hardie in early summer 1347.

We had been besieging Calais for nine months and, in fact, to call Villeneuve a camp was rather absurd. It had become a town and a fortification as grand as any in England, outside of London. Villeneuve had a population of over ten thousand men, and hundreds or perhaps even thousands of women. In the cold autumn, we had dug our defences all around Calais to defend ourselves from assault by any French forces coming up from Paris to relieve the siege. Within our own lines, we built the temporary town.

We knew we would be there for a long time and so considerable effort was made to ensure we could pass the ravages of winter in some sort of comfort. The King had a quite considerable mansion of two storeys built from massive timbers and the great lords each attempted to outdo the other with their own homes around the royal residence.

Not simply grand homes but we also had market halls, public buildings, bathhouses, stables and thousands of hovels thrown up the soldiers made from whatever brushwood and reeds they could bring in from the land all around. We cut down every tree and bush for miles in every direction.

We had in effect created a new and vast English town that happened to be located in France. But ten thousand men could not survive for long on the countryside thereabouts, bountiful though it was. Supplies came from England by a steady stream of ships bringing fuel, food, ale, and everything else needed by a town and an army. Much of it was landed up the coast at Gravelines and then brought overland from Flanders. My company had been active over the months by patrolling that route and escorting the supplies because the French attempted time and again to cut us off. Whenever we were given leave to do so, we raided deep into the French lands.

Even so, I could find little trace of the knight with the black banner.

Our new town sucked supplies from all across England via the ports of the south in hundreds of ships. It was a town that housed some of the richest and hungriest men of England and the meat markets and the cloth markets of Villeneuve were as well stocked as any in the region. We were maintained in our position only by an enormous effort of support by our people. The English were proud of us and willed us toward the victory that would come from taking Calais for England.

Before the full depths of winter struck, we made an attempt to storm the town. I had urged those lords who would listen to me that we should simply take the place so we could spend the winter within the walls rather than without. And I believed that a victory would free me to take up active search for the blood drinking knight.

"How would you suggest we do it?" Northampton had asked me, scoffing. "The land is waterlogged so we cannot undermine the walls. Breaking them would take months anyway, even with the largest trebuchets."

It amused me to be so condescended by young men who had a fraction of my experience. "We storm them," I had said, shrugging at their concerns. "Our men are well rested now. We make hundreds of long ladders and make a rush on the place from all directions. Our archers would be up them in no time."

"The archers?" Northampton had cried, appalled.

In the end, the King listened to me but he also heeded the warnings of his faithful lords, who convinced him that a complicated plan to take the town from the seaward side would be most likely to succeed. They arranged dozens of small vessels to be packed with me and with huge ladders. The assault failed.

Then they built the trebuchets that Northampton and the others demanded and they even brought over a dozen cannon. For weeks and then months they chipped away at the walls but there was hardly any effect. We received an influx of fresh men before Christmas, when it was getting icy, but the half-hearted attempts to storm the walls all failed. By the time of the deep freeze at the end of February, we had entirely given up and all settled in and waited for the townsfolk to starve.

There were some of us who wondered what all this great effort was for. Was Calais really worth it? We accepted that taking Paris was out of the question but many of the veterans could not understand why we did not withdraw before winter and return in spring to engage in more raiding.

"It's the Flemish," Black Walt repeated. "Got to be."

My house was a sturdy one, with two chambers and a loft above for storage. The small bedchamber at the rear was a private space for me and where I would bleed myself to provide blood for Thomas every few days, away from the prying eyes of our company. The main chamber was a larger space with a fire which I used for company business which meant in essence it was where we drank ale and talked and played dice every night.

"The King would not do all this just for the Flemings," Rob countered. "It must be for England's benefit."

"Aye," said Hal, "but what's good for Flanders be good for England."

Fair Simon lifted his head, confusion on his face. "We ain't going to hand the keys of Calais over to the Flemings, are we, Sir Richard?"

"Of course not," I said. Though I thought that Edward was the kind of king who would do anything if it served his ultimate purposes. Whatever those were.

"You see, Walt!" Simon snapped. "You don't know what you're talking about."

"And you cannot hold your drink, lad. Why don't you have a lie down before you hurt yourself, eh?" Walt cuffed his mouth. "I never said he would hand it over, did I? What I do say is that we were supposed to be taking possession of Normandy, were we not? I know we cannot secure so much land but if we want a city or a port, why not one in Normandy? Well, we know why. The King needs the Flemings. And so we take Calais, no matter the cost, because the Flemings want it. When you bargain with a man, best you hold what he wants so you may get what you want. Right?"

Black Walt was fundamentally ignorant about matters above the interests of his class but he was wily enough to see that the patterns of human relationships were in essence the same even when writ large on a geopolitical scale. Still, I was bored of the endless talk.

"Hold your flapping tongue, Walt," I said. "Do not concern yourself with the intentions of your betters. If you must speak, tell us of the time the Mayor of Spalding caught you in his bed with all three of his daughters."

Merely mentioning the tale brought smiles and laughter from most of the men but Walt shook his head. "How many times have you blasted fools heard me tell it? I grow weary of it and thus you have gone and spoilt what was once nought but a cherished memory. No, no, do not crow at me, you oafish band. I have a greater tale I would have us hear, if Sir Richard would deign to tell it. What say you, Sir Richard? If I was a sinful man, which praise God I am not, I would place a wager that Fair Simon, Ralf, and perhaps even Adam, ain't never had the pleasure of hearing the tale of the storming of Nottingham and the taking of the traitor at the right hand of our great king when he was but a young man in danger of losing his crown to the usurper."

"Dear God Almighty," I groaned. "I am nowhere near drunk enough for your goading to work, Walt, you ignorant sot and to even make the attempt demonstrates no more than your own inebriation."

"But this is a special occasion, sir!" he cried, staring at each of us in turn with an idiot grin on his face. "It's a Tuesday."

"You are embarrassing yourself, Walt. We are riding to Gravelines on the morrow and I will need you sober and well rested, do you hear me?"

My men, impudent commoners that they were, cried as one that they must have my tale or else their hearts should break and other such nonsense. The more I cursed them, the more resolute they became.

I waved them into what passed for silence. "Someone bring me some wine, then," I said and they cheered their victory.

Yet before I could begin, a messenger arrived stating that the King requested my presence, immediately. It was late in the day and so I was confident we must be facing a military crisis of some kind.

Calling Thomas, and Rob to me, I told them to get the men sober and ready them for action. I did not envy their task for it would be all but impossible.

"Walter, brush yourself off and come with me," I said and followed the messenger to the King's grand residence.

In all the time we had been besieging Calais, I had been seeking the knight of the black banner. I did not have leave from the King to venture far from our lines but I did what we always did in the Order and that was to pay for information. Using tactics employed by the Assassins of Alamut and the Mongols, we cultivated relationships with merchants, jounglers, tinkers and other travellers who could come across enemy lines without rousing very much suspicion.

Initially, I had been hopeful. But all our possible roads to the immortal killer of John led, in the end, to a dead end.

Stephen stayed in London for most of the time and used his existing agents and contacts to ask questions and to recruit further men. We spent a fortune in bribes and in hush money.

All for nought, so far.

After winter had passed, I was expecting the trail to magically grow fresh once more and yet every day into summer I knew that I had failed again. My failure in the battle had led to the failure in the search for the knight. My lack of success was no doubt due to my sinfulness. I had sinned by my complacency, my vanity. For decades, I had fought in battles where no man could harm me. Only when outnumbered and cut off had I felt my life at risk and even then, I was rarely concerned.

And so I had grown lazy and vain.

I had become arrogant.

Lost my way.

And I knew that I could redeem myself, in the eyes of God and in the eyes of the men and the woman of my Order, by slaying the knight of the black banner and his men.

But I had to find him first.

When we reached King Edward's mansion, I was called into the hall without a moment's delay.

Edward and his men were at the far end, seated about the long table, outnumbered by attentive servants. The day's ordinary business had been dealt with and I was relieved to see the men of the court were in good cheer, for once. Wine and morsels of food were consumed as the lords conversed loudly amongst themselves. They ignored me as I took the offered seat at the King's side.

"I have a request to make of you, Richard," the King said, gripping a letter in his hand.

"Name it, Your Grace."

"One of the Queen's friends, the Lady Cecilia Comines has been widowed and requires an escort back to England. There is a ship waiting at Gravelines but the lady is at her husband's estate in Hainault."

"I am sorry to hear of her husband's death. Was he at Crecy?"

"No," the King smiled, "he was with the Flemish forces and never made it to us. His death was due to a sudden bloody flux. And the Lady Cecilia cannot stay in Hainault in the current circumstances and she requires an escort to the coast."

"Forgive me, sir, but is her brother not Sir Humphrey Ingham?"

"Humphrey is back in England. You are the steadiest man I know and you shall not allow any harm to come to her, nor shall you allow her to be dishonoured or insulted in any way. You shall travel with the protection of a letter which states you will undertake no action which would alter the war or any treaty or truce. Do you accept?"

I bowed, for how could I deny my king? "I am honoured to accept, Your Grace."

As I left the royal presence, Walter fell in beside me with his eyes popping out of his head and a broad, idiot grin on his face.

"The Lady Cecilia is said to be the most beautiful woman this side of the Rhine, Sir Richard!"

I chose not to ask what great beauty was on the other side of the Rhine and instead sighed at his ignorance. "Every bloody lord with a spare shilling will pay troubadours to spread word of his daughter's beauty far and wide. In this way, he increases her market value. Do you see?"

"Clever bastards," Walt said, nodding. "But that ain't true of Lady Cecilia, Sir Richard, not in the least bit true. You know Garrulous Gilbert what's with Dagworth's company? He seen her with his own eye, so he did. He swore upon God's teeth that she was more beautiful than a dewdrop on a red rose lit by a midsummer dawn."

I knew the man Walt referred to and his epithet was an ironic one. "Gilbert has not had a tongue in his head for over six years, Walt. Not since that Breton knight had it cut out."

"He speaks with his *hands*, sir. Gestures in a most eloquent fashion. And Gilbert says she's got a bosom like the Lady Helen."

"Lady Helen who?"

"The Lady Helen of Troy, sir."

"And Helen had a fine bosom, did she, Walt?"

He shook his head in despair at my ignorance. "Stands to reason, sir. It is wisdom itself. Why else would them Greeks have run after her like that if she ain't got no apples in her barrel?"

"You have not an ounce of wisdom in your soul, you fool."

"Yes, sir. But what is better than wisdom? A woman. And what is better than a good woman? Nothing."

I cursed his idiocy even as I chuckled but damn me if the fool was not entirely right about the Lady Cecilia.

∞ ∞ ∞

"Might this not be a fine opportunity for ranging inland a little?" Thomas suggested as we rode. "By which I mean we can make enquiries regarding the knight of the black banner?"

"I know your meaning, Thomas," I said. "We must do as the King commands."

He said nothing. A silence full of meaning, which I supplied for myself. We had seen kings come and go and while they ruled, they were everything to the kingdom and to each of us that served him. But then the king would be dead, and his courtiers would be dead, and new men would take their places. Why did the likes of us, who outlived them all one after the other, need to follow the wishes of even the greatest of mortals, when we had our own quest that spanned lifetimes?

I had no answer for Thomas back then, nor even one for myself, other than I felt it was my duty. It was the duty of all men to follow the word of their king, even if that king was young and the man was old. Why should it be any different for us when it came down to it? Fulfilling one's duty is all one can hope for in life.

Of course, it is when duty battles with duty that a man's heart is filled with anguish. But I had been asked a favour by a king, and a good one at that, and so I would see it through.

I escorted the Lady and her servants from a small manor house in Hainault back to Calais. It was not a long way but of course tensions were high and there was an air of lawlessness and fear everywhere we went, although that may have been as much to do with my men—veteran brutes that they were—as it did with the state of France. The entire task would have been a simple one and indeed a rather pleasant break from the fetid air of the army had it not been for one thing.

The Lady Cecilia herself.

For it was true that she was a great beauty. Her skin was pale as milk and her hair fair as sunlight, with lips like ripe cherries and eyes as big and bright and blue as a clear sky over Dove Dale. The moment I saw her, I knew I was in trouble. She was a lady and a widow still in mourning for her husband but I had bedded ladies before, married, widowed and maid alike, when they were lusty enough to make pursuit easy. There would be no privacy to be had on the road, however, and so I resolved to restrain myself lest it cause me further problems with the courtiers. Any more scandals and rumours around me and Edward would be forced to cast me aside. It would therefore be best if I attempted no seduction at all, not even a subtle one.

And then I discovered that I need not have concerned myself with such thoughts.

"The King sent you?" she said, somehow managing to look

down her pretty little nose at me while avoiding eye contact of any kind. "The King sent you and you alone?"

"I have a number of armed men who serve me who will also provide your protection on the road, my lady."

"Those appalling villeins?" she said, her sweet lips turning sour at the corners. "But where is the Earl of Northampton?"

"He is with the King, my lady."

"Surely, Warwick has come for me?"

"The Earl of Warwick is with the King in Calais, my lady, and with your permission I shall escort you there forthwith."

"You most certainly do not have my permission. Summon Lancaster. He may escort me."

"I am afraid he is otherwise engaged, my lady."

"How dare you take that tone with me. I shall not stand for it. You must send for Kent, immediately. Even Stafford would do. Come, come, the sooner you set off with my instructions, the sooner a man of the proper rank shall return. I cannot stand to stay in this ghastly place an hour longer than necessary."

I stepped closer to her and she fell silent, looking warily up at me. Her servants drew nearer, ready to pull her away.

"We are leaving now, my lady," I said with a pleasant smile on my face. "Please mount your horse and instruct your servants and ladies to do the same, or else I shall instruct my appalling villeins to truss them up and carry you all to Calais like bolts of Flemish cloth."

She hesitated for a good long moment and I knew I had her.

"The King shall hear about this," she said, in a far softer voice. "And the Queen, also."

"I am certain that your woes will be the very essence of their attention once we reach Calais. Shall we begin, Lady Cecilia?"

She tossed her head up and rolled her eyes, not deigning to reply.

By the time we made off, it was already late in the day but we had to get moving if we were to reach the first stopping point. My men were ranging all around the Lady's company on their coursers or hobbies, other than Walt who lurked as always within striking distance of my back. I urged my horse forward and called out that we were leaving immediately and that anything or anyone not packed up and mounted would be left behind.

"Do not hurry the lady so," a hulking great servant said to me in a dismissive tone as he tightened a strap across a horse's flank. He did not even look up from where he stood. His voice was as gruff as his manner and I resisted the urge to lean down and strike him with the back of my hand.

"I do not hurry the lady," I replied, my tone level. "I hurried her servants. I hurried you, did you hear, little man?"

Prideful men who consider themselves to be large fellows hate nothing more than to be called small. And so it was with this servant, who glared at me with open hostility.

Instead of pushing him further, I laughed and rode away, turning to Walt as he came up with me.

"Watch that man, Walt."

"I clocked the cove before you ever conversed with him," Walt replied. "His name's Eustace. They call him the Steward and so he is but he's built like a fighter and no mistake. Right bruiser, that one, sir."

"Yes, thank you for your assessment."

Now that Walt mentioned it, I noted how this Eustace fellow stayed close to the Lady and watched her always from the corner of one eye. I should have seen it before but he was undoubtedly an experienced soldier, or a bailiff used to bashing skulls in, or perhaps a former ruffian, but it was perfectly ordinary for a noble to have guards and armed servants and arguably it was vital considering the state of the country.

"Well, Sir Richard?" Walt asked, raising an eyebrow and jerking his head back with a sly look on his face.

I knew what the sordid ruffian was getting at but I pretended ignorance. "What is it that you are asking, Walter?"

He grinned. "You doubted what old Gilbert said about the lady, sir, but now you know that he ain't one to tell a lie and, so help me God, neither be I. That dear lady is a ripe one and no mistake. Wheresoever she goes, the men all about her, common folk and lords alike, must be bending God's ear with all the praying for forgiveness they be doing once she passes by."

"Do not speak of your betters in such a manner," I said, repulsed by his vulgarity. "In fact, do not speak of the Lady Cecilia at all from now on, excepting practical matters."

"Right you are, sir," Walt replied, cheerfully. "So, speaking practically, my lord, how about we inveigle the Lady's wagon into a ditch at a likely spot on the way, so as you can take her into the woods and give her the green gown?"

I do not know what disturbed me more. The fact that Walt's depraved mind so closely mimicked my own, or that I was desperately tempted to take him up on the offer of assistance.

But my reservations remained. Even if I could somehow seduce the woman into civility, I could not imagine her softening so far as to allow me to lift her skirts and attempting to do so and failing could have dire social consequences for me. As it was, it appeared that she was resolved to be insulted by my every action and indeed by my presence and even the maintenance of the utmost public courtesy would only go so far to lessen the blow.

Besides, she would never be left alone. Not by her ladies, nor by her servants. And certainly not by her bodyguard.

"He's watching you like a hawk, sir," Walter said when we stopped at a local manor for the night. "Black beady eyes on him, ain't they, sir. Like a rabid badger."

The little manor hall was a dark and smoky place in need of repair but the lord was a loyal Fleming and so was an ally of ours, though he was away with the army. His servants provided dried herring in abundance and plenty of bread, though the wine was two years old and on the turn. The ale was good, though, and that was enough for my men.

"See that the bowmen are on watch all around and come back for some ale, Walter," I said.

When he was gone I smoothed myself down as well as I could and made my way to the table where Lady Cecilia was eating. She did not look pleased to see me.

"My Lady, I hope that everything is to your satisfaction." I continued before she could voice her displeasure. "We shall rise before first light and look to make the rest of the journey before nightfall tomorrow. I pray you sleep well." I bowed and turned to leave.

"Sir," she said, her voice softer than before. I turned back. "I know that your only concern is for my personal safety and I wish to say that I am grateful for your efforts."

Surprised, I was about to make a gracious reply but she continued speaking.

"And that is why I know you shall grant my request that you and your men shall sleep outside the manor house tonight."

"Come again?"

"I think you heard me perfectly well. I could not possibly sleep for a moment all night long, knowing that such men sleep under the same roof."

I rubbed the corner of my eye. "My men will behave themselves, my lady. Some shall be outside through the night to watch all approaches at all hours. Those not on watch shall sleep within the hall. You shall have the master bedchamber on the floor above. Have no fear, for I shall stand guard myself at your door all night long."

Her face flushed and she gaped at me. Behind her, the steward Eustace stomped forward.

"I shall be the man standing guard over the lady," he said, his voice a growl.

Making a show of it, I raised my eyebrows dramatically. "Oh, it is like that, is it? Well, in that case, do not allow me to stop you."

Her ladies gasped and the Lady Cecilia jumped to her feet, slamming her hands upon the table in a most unladylike fashion, causing the cups to wobble mightily. "It is most certainly not like anything, you unchivalrous oaf. Oh, I cannot eat another morsel, you have upset me so. I must retire to my chamber lest I strike you for your impudence."

I bowed. "I would greatly savour any blow to my person that you could strike, my lady."

She screwed up her mouth and I was certain she was about to toss her wine in my face but her ladies bustled her away from the table toward the stairs at the rear.

I bowed again, grinning as I stood up. The stocky steward glared at me with red murder in his black eyes.

"Eustace, is it?" I said, brightly. "I thought you were to stand guard at the lady's door? Well, hop to it, man. Hop to it, I say. We would not wish harm to come to such a delightful creature, would we? Come, come, good steward, be about your business."

Gritting his teeth, he backed away while fixing me with that dark look.

"You will let me know if you need me to stand watch in your stead, will you not? I hear many a man of advanced years struggles to remain wakeful in the darkest hours."

He hesitated, his face growing a vivid purple, but then he turned and strode off up the stairs.

When I turned to head back outside, I caught Thomas' eye. He shook his head in disapproval. After so long, I could read his mind in just that one look.

Making enemies at every turn, Richard, he would have said.

I shrugged, indicating that I cared nothing if some slab-brained steward thought himself an enemy.

Thomas was unimpressed.

Through the night, as I lay on my back on two old mattresses at the top of the hall, I considered climbing the stairs to check on Lady Cecilia. I would have had to bully old Eustace away but I knew he could be overpowered with ease and perhaps even without much fuss. Once he was removed, I would politely ask if there was anything she needed.

I imagined that she might ask one of her ladies to open the door to me, where I might be admitted into the dimly lit room. I pictured a single candle burning beside the bed and the Lady, sitting up with her hair uncovered, to ask if I might not sit upon the bed to converse with her. It seemed to me that if I could get so far then it would be a simple enough matter to be invited to disrobe entirely and to join her in the bed and beneath the sheets. I thought it likely that her servants would vacate the bed but that was not always the case and if the red-haired girl were there with us then I would certainly allow her to remain. The older ladies were welcome to feign sleep upon the truckle bed. The lady herself had no children, so perhaps her marriage had been a loveless one. It might be that I could awaken a desire in her that was hitherto unknown to herself and so I would proceed slowly and lovingly, caressing her. Stroking her blonde hair and the perfect pale skin of her cheeks as they flushed with desire. Her chest, too, would be flushed when she removed her underclothes and bared herself to me.

Black Walter kicked my feet again.

"Begging your pardon, sir, but it's almost sunrise."

"Damn your tongue, Walter," I cursed. "Damn your eyes, too."

"Yes, sir," he said. "Glad you slept well, sir."

It was an overcast day and we set off under a low sky with very few words spoken. Lady Cecilia appeared just in time, wrapped tightly in a heavy cloak with her hood up. Eustace heaved her into the saddle and we were away. I set a smart pace so that we would make it safely back to our territory before dark.

"A rather bad track for rain," Thomas said, looking at the gathering black clouds.

It was much travelled and the surface was deeply pitted and the soil loose. It would certainly turn into a morass if heavy rain were to fall.

"It may hold off yet," I said.

The rainstorm hit us before midday, driving us all to the shelter of a nearby copse. Mud pooled and spattered everywhere in mere moments and there was no chance of making headway through it. Beyond the copse I could make out the reed-thatched roof of a low cottage and I raised a finger to point at it, about to suggest to the Lady Cecilia that she seek shelter within, when a fox burst from a bush beneath the lady's horse. As much as the surprising streak of red at its hooves, the sudden shouts of warning from the men all around caused the horse to bolt away. Lady Cecilia held on while the animal thundered across a field, flinging mud and crops behind it as it went. I was after her right away, my courser gaining on the palfrey and all would have been well but for the idiot bloody fox veering back across the path of the already frightened horse.

It reared and then bucked, throwing the poor girl over its neck, causing her to fall very heavily.

Flinging myself from the saddle, I stooped to the mud and

lifted the woman into my arms. She was dazed and caked in dark mud but she was awake and mumbling something. I wiped the muck from her eyes and started back to the cottage I had seen, crying out orders for water to be heated and for clean cloth to be readied.

"I shall take her," Eustace said, scowling as he lumbered up to us.

"You shall not," I replied. "I will place her within, where her ladies can care for her."

The cottage was cold and dark and clearly had been abandoned. But only recently, for it was clean and had no smell of mould. There were plenty enough such emptied homes in those parts where armies tramped back and forth looking to take everything a man had and those who could live with distant family readily did so.

"Make a bed of your cloaks by the hearth," I commanded. "Build the fire hot, for she is soaked through."

I laid her down and saw with relief that her eyes were open.

"I am well," she said, faintly. Her eyes closed.

"Glad as it makes me to hear that, my lady, you took a bad fall and must rest. Your ladies will see to you now and you and they shall send to me if you need anything it is in my power to provide."

She reached up and placed a hand on my cheek, leaving a wet smear of mud.

Eustace lurked in the background like an old storm-struck tree trunk. "My lady shivers. You must leave."

"As must you," I said and dragged him from the cottage and

pushed him away while I closed the door. "Thomas, Walt, Rob. I believe we will be forced to shelter hereabouts for the night. Even if the rain lets up, I doubt the lady will be ready to travel before day's end."

"Begging your pardon, sir," Rob said, snatching off his hat. "Is the lady much harmed?"

I pondered it, for I had seen how she had landed on her head and neck and such falls had ended the strength of many a man in my sight. "No, no. She will be well by morning, I am sure of it."

All my men sighed with relief and many grinned. "God be praised," Rob said and many of them took up the prayer.

It is my experience, earned through many centuries of observation, that most men would do almost anything for any woman. A beautiful young woman of the nobility may have men of all ages and all classes gladly laying down their lives for her, should she wish it. This is the proper way of things, for women carry our civilisation within their wombs, and each and every one of us knows this to be true.

Eustace glared at me and I turned on him.

"Where were you, Steward Eustace?" I said softly, advancing slowly. "Why was your hand not wrapped about her bridle? You will damned well do your duty the next time or I'll see you punished myself."

He did not retreat but stood his ground and simply glowered in response.

A group of sodden archers hurried over, their arms full of twigs, branches, and broken dead wood. "Firewood, Sir Richard!"

"Well done, lads," I said. "Leave it by the door for the ladies, will you and fetch more. We shall need to strip that little wood clean, as the Lady must be warm through the night."

"Right you are, sir!" the men cried, happy beyond measure.

It was a sodden afternoon, with nothing to do but huddle against a tree or a wall. Some of the men took turns within the empty pigsty, empty wood store and the outbuildings but I resigned myself to being wet through to the bone and staying that way. Just as night fell, the rain began easing off but a steady wind came up with it and chilled us mightily. I kept moving around between the groups of my men to check at least one of them was alert to danger but mostly it was to keep myself warm and my thoughts away from the memory of holding Lady Cecilia in my arms as she stared up at me with those big blue eyes.

"Begging your pardon, Sir Richard." It was Reginald, one of Rob's bowmen, approaching with one of the Lady's servants huddled under a thick cloak. "The lady here has a message for you directly, sir, from her Ladyship herself, sir."

"My Lady would speak with you, Sir Richard," the woman said. "As soon as your duties allow."

"I shall return with you immediately, good woman."

I ducked in through the doorway and stood for a moment as the warmth from the fire and the silence from the cessation of the wind enveloped me. It was like stepping into an altogether different world from the one outside.

Lady Cecilia reclined where I had last seen her, bundled up by the roaring fire. One servant attended her, while the others were nowhere to be seen.

"Where is Eustace, good woman?" I said to the young red-head who was tucking the blankets up higher over the injured woman.

"I sent him away to see to the other servants," Cecilia said, her voice clear. "I could not stand his ceaseless lurking. And besides, I now know that I am perfectly safe in your care." She glanced at her servant who finished fussing and moved away. "Come closer, Sir Richard. Down here, where I can see you."

I did as I was bid and knelt close beside her on one knee. The firelight shone upon her face like gold on marble and her eyes glittered.

Swallowing, I spoke softly. "How may I be of service, my lady?"

She reached out from her bundled coverings and placed a lovely hand upon the back of mine. Those eyes of hers snared mine in their gaze and I could not look away. "I simply wished to thank you for what you did for me and also to beg your pardon for my rude manner."

"No pardon is necessary, my lady, but of course you would have it."

She smiled and gently patted my hand. It stayed there. "An explanation, then? You see, your reputation preceded you and I had been led to believe that you were a most uncouth and unchivalrous knight. It is known that King Edward favours you for your martial abilities but it is said that you entirely lacked even the most rudimentary courtly standards."

Whatever my facial expression was, she laughed lightly at it before continuing.

"But I see that these were slanderous words spread by your enemies and that you are as true a knight as any in Christendom."

I bowed my head, tearing my eyes from hers for but a moment

before fixing on them again. "Your generous words have moved me, my lady."

"Then kiss me," she said.

I was startled but a woman does not need to tell me such a thing twice.

Bending to kiss her upon the cheek, she grasped my head between her hands and pulled my mouth down onto hers. Her lips were soft and warm and delightful beyond measure. I had my hands planted either side of her, lest I fall down upon her with the weight of my body. She kissed me deeply, opening her mouth and putting her tongue into mine and her fingers dug into my hair like she intended to never let go. She moaned with passion into my mouth, bringing forth a groan of my own, the sounds resonating between us, while her hands moved from my hair to my face and my neck, touching and stroking me while her lips worked on mine.

She pushed me away, gasping and eyes shining.

"You must go now," she said, breathlessly, grasping one of my hands to her chest with both of her. "Lest our servants start talking."

I did not know what to say, so I said nothing as I stood, gazing down at her.

The young red-haired woman took my arm and led me away to the door. The girl was looking at me with passion in her eyes while biting her lower lip and I almost asked her to come outside with me before cooling my ardour. At the door, I turned and remembered my manners.

"I shall pray you rest well, Lady Cecilia, and wake fully

recovered for the journey tomorrow."

"Good night, Richard," she said softly.

In the morning, she carefully ignored me and we continued on, our horses splashing through the remnants of the rain and sinking into the mud. The wind helped to rid the street of the water and then the sun came out and the surface firmed up so that by late afternoon we came to Gravelines. Thomas would take over leadership of the company while I returned to England.

"It is my duty to cross with you to England. My men shall remain but I also have business in London."

"You continue to honour me with your protection, sir, and I have so little to offer in return."

"Your company is more than enough, my lady. The crossing should be swift if the wind remains as it is but the journey can be tedious unless one has diversions."

She blushed and looked down, covering her face with a lovely hand. "I should greatly wish to share a ship with you for the crossing, dear Richard," she said, speaking softly. "Yet my good name is the only thing of any value that remains to me."

"I understand, my lady," I said. "I shall ensure that you and your household reach your estates but I shall do so from afar."

"A true knight, indeed," she said, starting to reach for my cheek before pulling her hand back to place it over her heart.

After we embarked, I barely saw her, even from a distance. But I kept my word and made certain that there were no delays in ports. Our ships both travelled around Kent into the Thames and the port of London. The crossing was as easy as any I have undertaken and I have crossed that channel more times than I care to count.

London was teeming with ships, as ever, with large and small cogs with single masts, the fatter hulks and even a handful of huge Genoese carracks with sleek sides, two masts and more than one sail. They brought all manner of goods from Italy and beyond and in return brought English wool across to Flanders or back home, for our wool was rightly prized for its quality. Between the great ships, hundreds of wherries taxied passengers to and from ships, and across and up or down the Thames.

While I waited on the dockside for her to disembark, her brother, Sir Humphrey, rode up with a dozen men on expensive horses, crowding the space. Walt cursed them for their rudeness but I forestalled him.

"Sir Humphrey," I said, walking directly to his horse. The men around him put their hands on their swords but Sir Humphrey waved them back and called out to me in return.

"Richard?" He frowned, looking between me and the ship. "You travelled with the Lady Cecilia?"

"But of course!" I said, purposefully misunderstanding the specifics of his insinuation. "Did not the King himself order me to protect the lady and see her home safe, sir? I am not a man to shirk his duty."

Sir Humphrey curled his lip and furrowed his brow. "Where is she? Where is my sister, man?"

"I assume she is yet to disembark. I just arrived from my own ship." I jerked my thumb down river and he visibly relaxed and even began to smile a little. Then he looked up and the smile spread across his face.

"Cecilia!" he cried, and fairly leapt from his saddle to run to her.

She was a vision as she stepped onto the dock helped by her servants and a swarm of bowing sailors. She and her brother embraced and he directed a dozen questions at her before she could answer the first one. Eventually, she laughed and pushed him away.

"I am well, I am well. All is well." She looked at me, then, for the first time but so directly that it was certain she knew precisely where I was. "Thanks entirely to Sir Richard's chivalrous attentions."

"I am sure," Sir Humphrey said, all but growling. "I shall have to thank you in some way, sir. Are you going to that manor of yours directly?"

It was clear he was prompting me to make my departure and now that I would be robbed of my planned, passionate farewell with his sister, I was liable to get going forthwith. "I have a house in London and shall stay there until my business here is complete. Then I must return to my company in Villeneuve. Lady Cecilia, I am glad to see you well and back in the arms of your family. If there is anything I can do for you, you need but ask it. Good day, my lady. My lord."

He all but growled at my presumption yet she beamed at me in open affection. It stirred my heart but it was tinged with sadness. She seemed to be perfect. A woman grown, strong and forthright but kind and filled with physical passion tempered with the wisdom to control it. If only she could be my wife, I thought, as I rode away on my rented horse. But I knew just as she would that her destiny was to marry some great lord, perhaps even an earl, and bear him many children.

"To Master Stephen's house, sir?" Walter asked as we plodded by the carts teeming with barrels of salt cod and herring.

"It is my house, Walt," I said. "And no, I am beyond filthy and in need of a bath. I shall cross to Southwark and go home later. Go home and tell Stephen to have my chambers prepared and to ready a fine feast. And good wine."

Walt nodded. "My old man used to say, God rest his soul, if you cannot have a woman, son, then you might as well have a drink."

I shook my head. "I see that you come from a long line of wise fools."

Yet it was I who was the fool for sending Walt away from my side.

7

THE ASSASSIN

SOAKING IN STEAMING HOT WATER, I leaned back against
the side of the tub and sighed. I could not recall the last time I
had taken a bath. Certainly not during the campaign and not for
some time before then. It was somewhat indulgent of me but then
I did so hate coming to London at all and anything I could do to
balance the unpleasantness was perfectly acceptable, as far as I was
concerned.

The Southwark stews, on the south side of the Thames across
from the City of London, served as the bathhouses for anyone
who could pay for them. While they were all private
establishments, some were more affordable than others. The one
I utilised was the most expensive of them all and thus I enjoyed
the privacy of my own small room and a woman to serve me as I
bathed. It was a well-made room, lit by small windows high up on

the exterior wall and a decorative, iron-framed lantern on an ornate dressing table. The floor was tiled quite finely in a white and green pattern evoking the sensuality of nature, an effect enhanced by the fresh lavender and other herbs filling the room with delightful scents.

A most welcoming woman scrubbed my shoulders with a sponge and good Spanish soap, kneading my flesh as she washed. Try as I might, I could not cease thinking of Cecilia. She had bewitched me utterly and no matter if I directed my thoughts to the conduct of the war or the possibilities for our search for the immortal Frenchman, I found myself recalling moments that I passed with the lady, and even fantasising about conversations that we might one day enjoy. Absurdly, I even pictured myself married to her and sharing the truly intimate relationship that comes from daily sharing a bed, a home, and a partnership with another. And, as was as natural and inevitable as the changing of the seasons, I sinfully indulged in base, lustful daydreams where I stripped Cecilia of her clothing while she smiled up adoringly at me.

"That feels remarkably restorative, Pernille," I muttered.

"I do apologise, good sir, but as I have previously expressed to you, I don't be doing that sort of thing no more."

Surprised, I noticed that I was idly stroking one of her hands as she worked on my neck. "My apologies, Pernille. Upon my oath, it was not my intention to initiate~" I broke off from my explanation as I saw that my intention was in fact jutting up above the surface of the grey water.

"And besides," Pernille continued, as if I had not spoken, "I am far too ancient to excite a young man such as yourself."

I stopped, because I knew then that she wanted me to talk her into it. Quite suddenly the wantonness of her subtle proposition turned my incidental lust into a fervour and I grasped her hand firmly in mine, pulling her gently but firmly closer to me by an inch or two.

"My dear, I am a hundred and eighty years of age and you are nought but a spring chicken to my eyes. I would be honoured if you would share the pleasures of this bath with me."

She assumed I was joking about my age, of course, and she laughed even though there was no jest to be found in my remark. "I shall call one of the younger girls, my lord. One more suited to your needs. Surely, you cannot wish to waste your coin and your ardour on the likes of me."

"By all means, call one of your girls in to serve us both while we recline in the waters. Come, come. You are perfection itself."

"Oh, you are spouting flattery, sire, as surely you must know that beneath my clothes my body is quite unbecoming."

"I would never pursue a woman who does not desire me in turn, Pernille, so do nothing that would not please you. But you can see in my eyes that I speak truth when I say I want no woman here more than I want you."

At that, she disrobed and we made love very slowly in the waters. If I had to guess, I would have said she was aged between thirty and thirty-five and she was quite lovely in body and in spirit.

"I truly have not lain with a man here for some years," she said later, reclining in my arms as one of the servants let cold water out from the tub and opened the brass tap to allow the hot water to fill up to the brim once more.

"Then I am honoured by your generosity." It was her job to make men feel wanted, and special, and I suspected that she recited the same words a few times a week. Even so, I was ever contented to be deceived by a comely woman.

"There is something unusual about you, my lord," she said, trailing a finger over the back of my hand where it rested on the rim of the tub. "And I do not speak of your talents in the ways of love, which are quite remarkable."

I sighed, as she was rapidly spoiling my relaxed mood with her professional patter. No doubt she wanted me to ask for her the next time I returned but I wanted a few more moments of peace before I went back to doing my duty to the King, and to my Order and my oath. And I wanted her to be quiet so I could think of Cecilia and imagine that one day it might be her reclining in my arms.

There was a cry from somewhere else in the building, rising over the usual hubbub and occasional barks of laughter.

Something about it called for my attention.

It was the sound of a woman protesting in outrage. After laughter and cries of passion, that was the most common noise to hear in that place and yet there was a tone of terror in it.

Pernille was attuned to the sounds of her bordello also and her body tensed at the cry.

"Go see what that's about, Maggie, dear," she said, her demeanour suddenly serious and commanding, to the young woman attending us. Maggie nodded and went to the door.

A shout of warning went up from beyond the room, far closer

than before, and it was accompanied by the sound of a man's feet approaching along the floorboards.

My instincts kicked in and I pushed Pernille away from me and stood in the tub, looking for my clothing. The rules of the establishment were that no weapons were allowed within and so my sword was in the guardroom along with the two burly porters who dealt with trouble using stout clubs when necessary. No doubt, I thought, they would soon put an end to whatever the trouble was but still I felt somewhat vulnerable as I stood there with the water streaming from my naked flesh, knowing that I was entirely unarmed.

My instincts were always good and they had been honed further by the many decades of danger I had lived. And they had not failed me.

The door to the soak room burst open, striking young Maggie and knocking her aside as a huge fellow barged through with an angry expression on his face and a drawn sword in his hand. Pernille, moving with admirable speed, hopped from the tub, her heavy breasts swinging beneath her, and retreated to the corner, dragging Maggie with her.

The attacker was not interested in the women.

Indeed, he did not even take a moment to look at the naked one and instead had eyes only for me as he paused in the doorway.

My first impression was that he was taller than me, and considerably stouter. He wore the clothing of a middling townsman yet was bareheaded and his hair was unkempt and he sported a rather wild beard, which was really quite unusual at the time.

His eyes were filled with the fury of violence and as he looked rather like a wild bear wearing a tunic I did not waste time attempting to forestall him with words.

Instead, I jumped from the water across the room, away from him, trying to reach my clothing and the knife that was on my belt so that I would at least have something sharp and steel that I could stick the bastard with.

My lead foot, wet as it was, slipped from under me as I landed on the tiled floor and I fell hard, banging my elbow and hip and jarring me to the bone. What often saved me in a fight was my instinct to always be moving and even as I fell, I twisted and rolled and sprang back to my feet. And a lucky thing it was, too, as the bear-like fellow was already slashing his blade down at my naked back.

He caught me with a glancing blow, cutting me obliquely across the skin over my shoulder blade. I cried out in surprise more than pain, as I had not for a moment imagined such a beast of a man would move so swiftly and I knew then that he was an immortal. He had to be.

I glanced behind me as I changed direction, bounced off the wall and dived for the neat piles of my clothing upon the dressing table. The man was growling as he thrust his blade into the air, judging very well just where I was heading.

The point punctured my flank, low on my ribcage, penetrating quite deeply before my momentum pulled me from the blade and I crashed into the table, grabbing hold of it and crying out from the terrible pain shooting through me.

There was no hesitation from him and he followed me with a

stride that brought him to striking distance. Before he could finish me off, I grabbed the heavy lantern on the table top and swung it with all my strength at his head. He ducked but still it struck him good and proper right on his crown and the blow shook him down to his toes. Such a blow would have smitten a mortal man and likely would have felled a warhorse but it did little more than slow my would-be murderer. As his sword point waved, I steeled myself, batted it aside with my forearm and charged into him. I lifted him with my shoulder and carried him across the width of the room until his back crashed into the opposite wall. It was such a terrible impact, even through the heft of the sturdy man's flesh, that the force of it knocked the wind from me and I fell back and down to the floor, as did the other man. The women were screaming.

Before I could recover, he was somehow throwing himself on top of me. My wound was deep and blood was pouring down my side and I felt my strength leaking out of me along with it. The great big bastard forced me down beneath him as I tried to squirm away on my back. He brought the edge of his sword to bear and pushed it down toward my throat. I reached up and stopped the blade by grasping it with both hands, taking the weight upon my palms. He heaved down and the edge sliced through my flesh. His face was contorted in rage and his lips pulled back in a sneer, baring his yellow teeth. A stream of blood gushed from the top of his head where I had split his skull with the lamp. I was strong enough to resist his downward force but he began to saw his sword back and forth and the blade sliced down to the bones of my hands and I knew then that he would cut through my hands and drive the blade through my neck.

His head burst apart. Cloven in two from above by a blade. Pink brains and blood showered down on my face and I twisted his body from me.

Above me stood my man, Walter, looking quite concerned.

"Good Christ, sir," he shouted, "you be in a right bad way."

"God love you, man," I said.

He was grinning at the terrified women, feasting his ignoble eyes upon Pernille's flesh even as she cowered in fear and disgust. The dead man twitched and blood gushed from the large gap between both sides of his head.

"Help me into my clothes," I commanded, "quickly, man."

Walt jumped to help me to my feet. "Sir, I must say your wounds are grievous. Sit here and I shall fetch a surgeon to bind you up."

"No surgeon. Help me to the house. I will recover there."

"As you command, Sir Richard. But should we not wait for the bailiffs? This bastard done killed the stew's porters down at the door. I cannot flee from the body or else they shall say I am guilty of murder myself."

He was quite right. But I knew that I needed blood or else I would not be long for the world and I had no wish to be caught up in an inquest. It would be possible to bribe the right men to keep my name from public mention but only if I was not seen with the body by too many people, and already I could hear folk gathering from elsewhere in the stew.

"We shall do what is right and no harm shall come to you, Walt," I said, hurting quite badly, "as long as you help me to dress and get me out of here."

"Right you are, sir," Walt said, then immediately shaking out my shirt.

"Leave my purse for the ladies."

"Ladies?" He looked around, confused. "The whores? How much?"

"Leave the purse," I hissed. They would know what I wanted in return. "And for the love of God, remove your blade from the man's head."

∞ ∞ ∞

"You must have some idea who he was," Stephen said, pacing back and forth across the width of his solar on the second floor of his house.

It was our house, in fact, belonging to the Order of the White Dagger. We had taken turns to reside there over the decades, though I had used it the least because the decadence and stench of London made my skin crawl. But Stephen lived there publicly and had spent most of the previous century living there, on and off, and as such it was imbued with his personal taste. Having said that, Stephen would rather have by his bedside twenty books, bound in black or red, of Aristotle and his philosophy than rich robes or costly fiddles or gay harps. What décor I could see was far too modern for me to feel comfortable at the best of times and I was already feeling unnerved by my recent close brush with death.

I lay back on a day-bed with a cup of tepid blood in my hand, generously donated by three of Stephen's servants. We always employed servants, in the London house, and also in our smaller residence in Bristol where Eva preferred to live, who agreed to be bled every few days so that someone provided blood once every other day. That volume and at that frequency was enough to keep Stephen or Eva in fine fettle. We explained to the servants when we employed them that bloodletting was necessary for maintaining the good health and proper behaviour and always they had accepted it, for it was a common practice.

"I have no idea who he was, Stephen. How many more times would you like me to say so?"

"And you are certain he was one of us?" He strode away across the chamber as he spoke.

"He was one of William's creations, yes."

Stephen turned on his heel. "Could it be that one of William's men created another? One of the revenants, as the Assassins made in Alamut?"

"I suppose it is possible. The revenants were quite raving mad but they were also burned quite rapidly by sunlight, far more even than you and Eva are. Our fellow today wore no hat or hood and his face was quite unburned."

"Not much daylight in the stews, though, I take it?" he said it lightly, not looking at me.

"Do not pretend you are ignorant on the matter, Stephen. But he must have arrived in the stews through the streets in sunlight."

"We do not truly know where he came from, do we. Perhaps he was lying in wait for you."

"I thought you were the master of reason and I was the dullard soldier? If you recall, the porters were slain when he forced his way into the building. He came from outside. Hence, he came through the streets and was not burned by the sun. Therefore, he was not a second-generation revenant but a direct spawn of William."

Stephen inclined his head for a moment. "And where did he come from before he walked the streets of London, I wonder? Was he English?"

"I told you. He did not speak a word."

"Did he *look* like an Englishman?"

"An English hermit, perhaps. The brute was in dire need of a barber's services."

"And yet he had the build and the skill of a man-at-arms."

"I would not necessarily say so. We did not engage in much swordplay. His build would have made him suitable as the bailiff of a hundred in the northern Marches. A brute, as I say, not necessarily a warrior."

Stephen nodded and continued his pacing. "I shall ask the city watchmen which gate he entered through. Perhaps that will give us a clue about where he came from. Assuming one of the oafs recalls our Assassin."

"Unless he came by ship," I muttered.

Stephen stopped and turned to me. "How did he smell?"

"How did he *smell?*" I sighed. "Stephen, I do wonder about you."

"Think, Richard," he said, approaching and speaking earnestly. "Did he smell of the road? When he grasped you, did he smell like horses? Or did he smell like the sea?"

I laughed. "You have not been on a long voyage for so long. You have forgotten that you would step ashore reeking of stale sweat, vomit, and piss."

"And is that how he smelled?"

I scoffed. "I really do not recall, Stephen, but why do you not pay a visit to the coroner and ask if you can smell the corpse."

He grinned. "What a wonderful idea." Tapping his fingers on his chin, he turned and wandered away.

"Oh, Stephen. Our money can only turn so many heads and close so many mouths. If you go around sniffing corpses then you shall arouse more suspicion than we can cope with."

"Is finding the origin of our assassin not of the utmost importance? Surely, he was sent by the very man we are pursuing? If we can track the path of the assassin back to its source, will it not lead us to the knight we seek in France?" He came close again, dropping to a knee next to me. "What if we cannot find our quarry in France or further afield because he somehow got by us and came to England? The black knight could be in London, Richard."

I nodded, galled that I had not come to the same conclusions myself. "Very well. Do whatever you have to. But, for God's sake, go nowhere without protection, Stephen."

He airily wafted my concerns away. "Oh, I shall be fine."

I shot my hand out and grasped his wrist. "I am returning to the siege, Stephen and shall not be here to keep you safe. That brute would have killed me if Walt had not hewed his skull in half at the very last moment. What if the assassin had come for you first? You have been living comfortably for so long that you have forgotten what it is to be afraid. It is time you remembered."

Stephen was nothing if he was not a survivor at heart and so he listened to me and swore he would arm his porters and servants, hire soldiers to guard the house and to guard his person when he went about on business.

I hoped that the black knight was not in England, as Stephen feared. My duty to the King, and to the men of my company, required me to return to the siege of Calais.

My oath to find the immortal spawn of my brother William would have to continue in France.

8

THE SIEGE OF CALAIS

A WARM SUMMER CAME and inside Calais, the townsfolk starved. Like all who suffer in a besieged town, they ate all the horses, then the dogs, the cats and finally the rats and mice. After that, in their desperation they began to boil up and chew on anything leather. I have been that hungry myself many times down the centuries and it is a kind of madness that grips you and convinces you that you may draw sustenance from gnawing on your own shoes.

Then their wells inside the city began to dry up. Disease broke out within the walls.

We knew how bad it was inside because we intercepted a letter from the commander of Calais to King Philip. A brave Genoese rowed out of the harbour one morning in late June but he was caught and his letter brought to King Edward who read it aloud to us right away.

"We can now find no more food in the town unless we eat men's flesh," Edward read from the letter. "None of the officers have forgotten your entreaties to hold out until we may fight no more and that day is almost upon us. Yet we shall not surrender. Every man here has sworn to rush from the gates to fight our way through the English lines until each one us lies dead."

As he read this, I turned to Thomas behind me. "Take some men and keep watch on the gates until you are relieved." When I straightened again, I caught Northampton's eye and he nodded once at me.

"Unless you can find some other solution, this is the last letter that you will receive from me, for your loyal town shall be lost and all of us that are within it," Edward said. He finished reading it but spoke no more of the content. Then he called his servants. "I shall seal this with my personal seal and then we shall forward it to my cousin Philip."

A few of the lords laughed at the thought of the King of France receiving such a dire letter with Edward's seal on it but most of us, I am sure, felt sickened by the plight of our enemies within the town.

In response, Philip organised and launched a great relief convoy of eight armed barges that he hoped could sneak into the harbour without us noticing. I have no idea what the French were thinking because we easily captured the supplies ourselves, which was a boon to us and served to utterly break the will of the leaders within the walls.

The leaders of Calais rounded up all their wives, daughters

and mothers. They gathered their young sons and their aged fathers. They collected their injured and sick brothers.

And they threw them out of the gates.

It was not an unknown tactic, of course, but it was no less sickening to see for all that. For the sort of men who become the leaders of a town, their primary duty is their duty to their lord. To their king. That duty was greater than the one they felt to their own families.

When I saw the huddled, shuffling, gaunt women with their children clinging to their knees creeping out of the gates, I wondered if Englishmen would have acted in the same way. Our people have always been more independently minded than those from other nations. Not as independent as the Welsh, Scots or Irish, thank God, but certainly more so than the French. The English have always had the best possible balance between civic duty, royal loyalty, and individual freedom. The French, on the other hand, were always more collectivist or, as one might say, subservient.

But we were not going to take on responsibility for the families of the men who had defied us for months. King Edward was under no legal or moral duty to accept those useless mouths expelled by the fathers of Calais. What was worse, though, was that he refused to allow them through our lines and inland to where Philip could care for them.

And so those poor women, those weeping children and weak old men, huddled in the ditches between our lines and the town's defences, starved.

"Let them burden King Philip, Your Grace," I pleaded to

Edward one night after I could take their wailing no longer.

"My lords have always whispered in my ear that you are too cruel and unchivalrous to keep at my side," the King said in response. "But they do not know you like I do. You have always had this absurd weakness. A hidden softness. And because of your weakness, you would have me show weakness when Christendom is watching. No, Richard. They had their chance to surrender months ago. Now they must suffer the consequences."

I wanted to argue. Protest that compassion was not weakness but a virtue and it would be a most Christian and decent thing to let the women and children through our lines.

But just as he knew me, I knew him. I had known him since before he was twenty years old. And I knew that when he had that dark look in his eye, nothing could divert him from his royal cruelty.

I rode away with my men to raid the country for as many days as it took for the last of the refugees to perish.

It did not take long.

By this point, we had been outside Calais for ten months and our army had been growing since spring. The town that we had created to contain them all also grew beyond our defensive lines and so we had to extend them further. By July, we had over five thousand men-at-arms with their horses and servants, along with seven thousand infantry made up from levied townsfolk and Welsh spearmen, plus what I was told was twenty thousand archers. In all my years fighting, I had never known an English army the size of it. Indeed, we would not raise such a force and send it to France for another two hundred years or so.

And what were we going to do with all those men?

The French were coming for us again. King Philip had raised a massive force and he meant to drive us into the sea and so wipe away all we had accomplished since that morning near Crecy almost a year before. He marched it right up to our camp at the end of July and we all knew we would have another fine battle to decide the fate of France. Philip was said to have eleven thousand men-at-arms, more than twice as many as we had. We all wondered if our archers would be able to cut them down as they had at Crecy.

"What is he waiting for?" Walt asked me as we looked up at the distant escarpment miles to the south where thousands of Frenchmen stood, silhouetted against the bright blue skies beyond. Their banners and pennants fluttered and whipped in the steady wind.

"Would you attack us?" Thomas asked. "If you were Philip?"

"I wouldn't attack us," Rob said, "if I was Charlemagne himself, sir."

"Philip is no Charlemagne," I said. "But we must do our duty and provoke them into attack."

My company and many others skirmished with groups of Frenchmen who strayed from their lines. We shot a great many arrows but they were fearful of us. And rightly so.

Our defences were simply too strong and the French took less than a day to decide they would not attack us after all. In fact, they sent word to Edward that it was not a battle they wanted, but peace. And so a truce was declared and my company fell back from the French. My archers were disappointed, for their favourite sport was shooting the horses of French cavalry.

The two sides negotiated for days. Thomas and I got close enough to watch the French delegation closely but we saw no one who might be the knight of the black banner.

"Look," Thomas said, nudging me with his elbow. "It is Sir Geoffrey."

"Who?" I asked.

"Geoffrey de Charny," he said, pointing at a well-built lord in a very fine red coat. He was fine-featured, with a square jaw and piercing eyes. "Do you see? Standing between the Duke of Bourbon and the Duke of Athens."

"Hmm," I said. "The man does not seem to be particularly impressive."

Out of the corner of my eye I saw Thomas turn and stare at me.

"Perhaps you should introduce yourself," Thomas said. "If we are considering one day inviting him to join the Order of the White Dagger."

"Look at him, Thomas," I said. "Why would he ever give away his fortunate life in order to take up a future with us? When Dukes wish to consult an expert on chivalry, they send for that man there. He has founded more than one monastery. He keeps company with the great lords of his kingdom."

"So do you, Richard."

I snorted. *Yes*, I thought yet did not speak aloud, *yes but Charny's lords respect him.*

"I think we must aim a little lower than the living embodiment of chivalry, Thomas."

He laughed a little and nodded. "Very well. Let us look elsewhere."

The negotiations dragged on. The French proposed that we march from our camp and fight an open battle. Of course, Edward could never have given up our impregnable position but the ploy was a clever one because it made the King of England appear to contradict his chivalrous reputation as a man of honour. We wondered how our king would handle the matter but in the end he was saved from having to make a decision.

For the commanders of Calais, the men who had thrown their wives and children out to starve to miserable deaths within sight and earshot of their precious town, declared at sundown on the first day of August, that they were surrendering.

In the dark of the night, the French army under Philip set fire to their tents, spoiled their food and water, and marched away before sunrise. The King of France abandoned his most loyal subjects to their fate.

The lords of Calais requested a negotiation of terms but Edward's message to them was quite clear. There will be no terms. Their surrender would be complete, and England would take everything they had and would kill every man they wished to.

"You cannot mean to put all these knights and squires to the sword, Your Grace?" Northampton said to the King that day.

"I would prefer their heads," Edward said. "But I will be content with hanging."

"They simply did their duty to their king," the capable knight Walter Mauny said. "Just as any of your loyal captains would have done in their place."

"Ransom them, Your Grace," Suffolk said. My lord the Earl of Suffolk had once been a prisoner of King Philip a few years before and had ultimately been ransomed.

I said nothing. It was not as though Edward did not know that the chivalrous thing to do would be to ransom them but he was resolute and I knew from the set of his arms and the look in his eyes that nothing his lifelong companions could say would move him.

William Bohun the Earl of Northampton came around the backs of the men surrounding the King and approached me. He reached out and grasped my upper arm, attempting to drag me away from the rest. When he found that he could not budge me so much as an inch, he lowered his head and muttered. "I would speak with you, sir." I followed him a few paces away. "You must add your voice to ours, Richard. Make him see reason."

I shrugged. "Why should I care what happens to those men? They defied us. They must now die."

He peered up at me, squinting. When he spoke, he did so slowly, as one might explain the operation of a watermill to a simpleton. "It is not the men but the convention we must protect, Richard. It is clear that this war will drag on further, perhaps for years. What if you yourself are captured one day? You scoff but you are often deep within enemy territory with no support and it is highly likely you will be taken. Do you wish to be ransomed or murdered outright in revenge for this atrocity which we are about to commit?"

Northampton clearly had a poor consideration for my intellect and my morality.

"Try someone else, Bohun," I said, shaking his gloved fingers from my arm.

"I can help you," he said. He said it in a way that was loaded with meaning of some sort so I turned back. "Yes indeed, I can help you to find the man you are looking for."

"Where is he?" I asked.

"If you help me," he said, "I will help you."

"Fine. I will persuade him. Now, tell me."

The Earl of Northampton smiled and spread his arms. "If you tell me who it is that you seek, I will find out for you."

I laughed. "You promise a thing that you do not possess. You know nothing, my lord."

"I know that you are always asking questions. Seeking the knights who killed your squire. Wherever they have gone I will find them for you."

In the end, I did as Northampton proposed and had a few choice words with King Edward. I did not know if the Earl would truly be able to help me to find the black banner but having a favour owed to you by a great lord of the realm could be worth more than money, if one knew how to use it.

Edward allowed the lords of Calais to live, although he took everything they owned other than their Earthly lives.

When the French were dragged out, the English entered and raised Edward's standard from the walls to the sound of horns and trumpets as our great king rode within. The booty was dragged out and gathered in one place to be properly accounted for. Calais was filled to the brim with the profits from decades of enthusiastic piracy and there was a remarkable amount of money, silver, and other goods and valuables. I received coats, furs, quilts, tablecloths, necklaces, silver goblets and linen. I had it all sent to Eva's house in Bristol.

Edward held on to a few of the richest leaders but all the other survivors were given a hunk of bread, a cup of wine and a kick up the arse as we sent them south into France without a penny to their names. Those emaciated, humiliated men were an announcement to the people of France that their king could not protect them and that they would do well to consider welcoming a king who could.

Calais was thus emptied completely of Frenchmen and immediately repopulated with Englishmen and the city became a true part of England from that day on for over two hundred years.

The war was not over. Indeed, it grew heated again, for I was ordered to begin making deeper raids into France in preparation for our army's next advance. Not just my company, of course. Henry of Lancaster led a huge force to capture a town thirty miles away. Even the Prince of Wales, God love him, rode at the head of a raiding party into Artois. He made a lot of noise and burned plenty but no one wanted him to range too far from safety. He was our golden prince, after all.

And I was free to take up my hunt for the immortal knight once more.

∞ ∞ ∞

The search for the knight of the black banner continued and

yet it foundered as we entered the autumn of 1347. People still travelled in bad weather, of course they did, but with nothing like the frequency of the summer. And the banditry and general lawlessness that gripped France following the loss of the battle continued.

But then at the end of September, a truce was agreed by both sides which was to last until July 1348. Of course, Philip wanted a truce because he had no hope of beating us militarily. But my men could not understand it. They felt as though they had been cheated of their ultimate victory and I could understand why that was their view but I explained that we had reached somewhat of a strategic impasse and the nine-month break would allow a reduction of the appalling cost and logistical effort it took to keep our vast army in the field.

They were just annoyed that they were going to miss out on all that booty.

It meant that my operations in France were suddenly curtailed. We were going home, and a few men were pulling back into Calais but maintaining my company in the field was out of the question. It would threaten the treaty and to defy it would be treasonous.

When we returned to England, I gave the men of my company their final payments and dismissed them. They returned to their homes and their families, if they had them. Some claimed they were now rich enough to find a wife and start a family. Others went into the degenerate filth of London to spend their relatively huge wealth on drink and women and to waste the rest.

For a time, I returned home and set things in order there. It was a terribly wet summer and the rain fell and fell and there was never enough time between downpours for anything to dry out so that everyone and everything was damp all the time, even indoors. My fields turned to mud and the wheat and barley was much battered by the deluge. The common people grew tense because they could sense that a famine may have been coming.

King Edward and the lords of England, on the other hand, spent that wet summer in a series of sumptuous tourneys across the country. In many ways, Edward was on top of the world. And why would he not be? He was thirty-five years old, and a fifteen-month campaign had brought him the glory that he had been seeking for so long. The leaders of England were rather joyful after such a series of victories. Our small nation had bested the mighty France again and again, in battle and in tactical manoeuvres, overall strategy and even in politics. As soon as winter was over, the tournaments began at Reading, Bury St. Edmunds, Lincoln, Eltham and Lichfield. It was an endless cycle of feasting, competition, dancing, drinking and travelling. Round and round the country they went in an orgy of consumption and splendour.

"As much as I respect the King and the young lords he has cultivated," Thomas said to me during a feast at Windsor in July, "I despise witnessing how they squander their wealth and deck out their bodies with the trappings of frippery, buffoonery and lust."

"Keep your voice down," I warned him, aware that he had unusually consumed rather a lot of wine.

"They celebrate themselves, Richard," he continued, heeding me not at all. "Not one of them seem to realise that their victories were a gift from God, who is the true benefactor of the chivalry of England."

I took his cup from him and pressed food into his hand. "Eat some bread, brother."

Although I was sympathetic with his opinion, I could not hold those elaborate displays against Edward, for he was behaving precisely as a king should. He was demonstrating his power and his majesty to the people of his kingdom, from the great to the common folk. A king's magnificence reflects onto those he rules and so every man no matter how lowly rejoiced to see the astonishing pageantry and splendour.

Thomas saw empty glamour and vanity but then he still carried within him the heart of a monk and his personal distaste for rampant consumption blinded him to the necessity of it. A king who acts with frugality is not loved by the common man. The pageantry was kingship, perhaps just as much as victory in battle was. Both ends of the scale enabled and enhanced the other.

But my pride was mostly in how my people were growing in stature on the world stage. The lords of Christendom had witnessed the King repeatedly overcome the first ranked military power west of Constantinople. The English had become the foremost warriors of Europe and suddenly every prince in Christendom cried out for Edward's attention, whether it was to arbitrate disputes between kingdoms or to offer him marriages for his children or beg for military aid.

The King of Castile betrothed his heir to the Princess Joan who was fourteen years old and as pretty as a picture and as charming as any of her lauded ancestors.

While dreading to hear of it as if I was a young girl myself, I kept an ear out for news of any betrothal that Lady Cecilia might have made to some lord or other but there was nothing. She was almost never travelling with the court and never when I was in attendance, although I was sure that was merely bad luck.

Oftentimes a widow could postpone her next marriage by claiming to still be consumed by grief for her last husband but when a lady was as great a prize as Cecilia, that could only get her so far. I had little doubt that her brother Sir Humphrey was doing everything in his power to arrange a match.

Their family was not a great one and their family was small, surviving the generations with just an heir or two but their wealth was considerable and her beauty was famed so it was likely she could find an older man looking to replace a dead wife or a young lordling who would not object to an older widow, considering all her other attributes.

More than once I sat down to pen a letter to her but I always stared at the confused words in my appalling hand and ended up tossing the letter across the chamber in irritation. What was it that I wanted from her? Her love, of course, but I knew that would never be possible for even if in some mad passion she wanted me, I could never condemn her to a marriage with an ageless knight who could never give her children. It could never lead to happiness.

And so, with the war on hold and the search for the black knight finding only shadows, I commanded that the members of the Order of the White Dagger meet at our house in London to discuss what was to be done next.

∞ ∞ ∞

Myself, Thomas, Hugh, Stephen and Eva were in attendance. Without the good humour and energy of John, it seemed to me to be rather quiet and dour in the hall as we ate up our bread and drank off the wine.

I dismissed the servants for a while so that we could speak freely and I commanded Stephen to provide a full account of his search. And Stephen swore blind that he was doing everything he could to locate the knight but there was the fundamental problem that we had so little to go on.

"I did discover the truth about the squire of the black banner knight who held the red shield," Stephen said. "As you stated, the shield was red with three white sub-ordinary escutcheons and this being the blazon of Sir Geoffrey de Charny, one of the most famed knights in Christendom, we believed it may have been painted in order to distract or deceive us or others on the battlefield. However, the shield truly was one of de Charny's. This does not incriminate the great knight himself, of course, because the shield had in fact been stolen."

"*Stolen* from de Charny?" I was suspicious. "Who would steal a shield?"

It was true that Sir Geoffrey de Charny was one of the most famous knights in Christendom. A lord who was honoured for his chivalrous acts in peace and in war. But the story of a stolen shield seemed like something a guilty man would make up to defend himself in court.

"A man in need of one?" Eva said.

"Sir Geoffrey was not at Crecy," I said to Stephen. "So how could his shield have been?"

"I am cognisant," Stephen said, holding his palms up to me. "I had the story from one of de Charny's squires but, even though de Charny's reputation is impeccable, of course I would not take such a thing on face value. On the day before the battle, Sir Geoffrey's second-best shield was found to be lost and the squire gave the servants a sound thrashing for the loss. And de Charny was diverted from the battlefield itself by King Philip and so he was not present. Other witnesses confirm that de Charny had his squires and servants whipped around that time, presumably for the lost shield."

"How far away was he?" I asked.

Stephen nodded. "The heralds state that de Charny was not present and my contacts say he was on his way to Flanders on the day of the battle. A servant in the King's household said Sir Geoffrey was tasked with ensuring the Flemings could not come to our aid. Sir Geoffrey's squire, on the other hand, suggested King Philip was jealous of the fame and glory that his lowly knight would no doubt win against the English and so he sent him away."

"Both can be true," I muttered. "But why would anyone steal it at all? Who would have the opportunity to do so?"

"As for opportunity," Stephen replied, "there were tens of thousands of Frenchmen roaming north of Paris during those few days before the battle. As to why take it all, I do not know. Perhaps it was misdirection, as we thought. Or perhaps it was meant to inspire those who saw it. Whether they thought de Charny was present or not, laying eyes upon a famed standard could stir the hearts of lesser men, could it not?"

I smiled at Stephen's woeful attempts to appear wise in the ways of war.

"Indeed," Thomas said earnestly, for he somehow remained free from cynicism despite decades of experience, "and ever since, the French have said that if Sir Geoffrey de Charny had been present, the battle would have been won."

I scoffed. "Even a perfect knight like de Charny could not have changed the course of that battle."

"Is he?" Stephen asked, jerking his head up to look at me.

"Is who what?"

"Is Sir Geoffrey the perfect knight, as they say? Or were you speaking in jest? It is often rather difficult to tell, Richard."

"In jest, yes, but it is not entirely untrue. He fights as well as anyone, in tourney and in battle and acts with honour, so far as I know."

"He is a man filled with the experience of years, as much as a mortal man can be," Thomas added. "His family blazon of a red field represents Iron, and the god Mars who was the pagan god of war. He is gifted with profound wisdom and the spirit of adventure and by common repute, a knight more skilled in the art of war than any man in France."

"An exaggeration," I muttered. "Most probably."

"Well then," Stephen said, speaking carefully and watching us closely, "would he not be an ideal member of the Order?"

Thomas snapped his head up at that.

"Have you two been speaking about this?" I asked Stephen and Thomas.

"Indeed, we have not, Richard," Stephen said, his face the picture of sincerity. Thomas would not meet my eye.

"As you well know, Stephen, I would not make a man one of us," I said, "without him being on point of death, as Thomas was, or if he begged me for it knowing everything that it would entail, as you did. And I cannot see Geoffrey de Charny giving up all he has to join us, no matter how honourable we know our cause to be."

"But if, in the wars to come, he is cut down when you are near," Stephen said, "perhaps then you might—"

I spoke over him. "It would be an extremely unlikely confluence of chance that I be on hand for the man to draw his last breath, and also be alone with him long enough to administer half a gallon of my own blood to his lips, do you not think, Stephen? A man of his standing would be attended by a dozen servants, and many peers."

Stephen sighed. "I understand. You have it right, of course. But as Thomas and I have been reiterating for many years now, we need more men, Richard. As our difficulties in finding the black banner knight demonstrate rather well. With more men, men who were absolutely trusted with the knowledge of what we truly seek, we could have eyes and ears all across France. And you also have agreed to find us some men, have you not? Men of high quality, as you have said. If such a situation as his death was to occur while you..."

"Yes, yes," I said, irritated with his presumptuousness and also knowing that what he wanted would never come to pass. "But enough of Sir Geoffrey de Charny. What about the trail of the bloody immortal, Stephen?"

He looked down at his wax tablet, as if hoping that answers would appear there. "We expected that the black banner or his men would commit more murders in order to obtain their blood. But every occurrence I have been able to investigate has led nowhere."

"Perhaps he has his own blood slaves," Eva suggested. "We have managed to go entirely undetected for all this time. It is not a difficult thing to procure blood, if you have means and a few private moments."

I slumped, growing disheartened by the extended failure. I had been so close and yet my momentary lapse in forgetting to close my visor had cost me so dearly. "More likely he has fled France for some other land. He could have crossed into Aragon and beyond, gone over the Alps to Italy and from there, to anywhere."

"Would he flee so far?" Hugh said, ever hopeful. "Why was he here, fighting in that battle at all? Where did he come from?"

We had no answers.

"What of the assassin?" I said. "Stephen, what came of the dead man in the Southwark stews? Where did his trail lead?"

Stephen hung his head. "It seems he came to the stews from London, as he was seen crossing the bridge. Also, he had no known lodging in the city. So we can conclude that he came either from ship to London or by land from elsewhere in the country beyond the city."

"And?" I said. "Which was it?"

"None admitted to his coming by ship. But, as you know, it is possible to smuggle ashore many a hidden cargo, including a man, should a shipmaster wish it. But my agents have always been trustworthy before. And so I believe the brute who attacked you was an Englishman from somewhere beyond London."

"From where beyond London?"

"Ah," Stephen said. "Of that, I do not know. There was no sighting of him coming in through any of the gates. And none from any road to here, either."

"Dear God, Stephen."

"Come, Richard," Thomas said. "It is hardly Stephen's fault that the assassin kept to the shadows."

My frustration grew into anger and although I felt the urge to rant and threaten them all, I resisted it.

They had superior strength and speed and health than mortal men, but their minds had not been enhanced along with their bodies and so I could not expect them to have done any more. Although railing at him further would be futile, I knew it was Stephen's fault, if it was any man's. It was he who ran our core network of spies.

But, there was one other resource we had not yet tapped.

"If you are not competent to complete this task, I shall ask Eva to do so."

Stephen's eyes bulged and he babbled out a series of notions as to why it should not be done. "But, Richard, Eva's agents are far fewer than mine. No offence meant, good woman, but it is true. It would take weeks for relevant messages to reach your people and then weeks more before they could act. Besides, the information that your agents provide is of a more general sort, mostly for trading purposes. And also, the fact that you are a woman means you would find it vastly more difficult to operate away from home if you needed to travel to meet them in foreign parts as I have done when necessary."

"I have managed well enough in years gone by," Eva said, fixing him with a steady look. "And have counselled you in many a matter when you have needed it."

Stephen scoffed and threw up his arms. "A woman's counsel? It was a woman's counsel that brought mankind to woe, did it not? A woman's counsel was it that threw Adam out of Paradise, where he had been so merry and at ease. And also—"

"That's quite enough of that, Stephen," I said, cutting him off as he searched in vain for some other objection. "You have failed. What is more, you have told us, in essence, that you do not expect to ever be successful. And so Eva shall find the man and then we shall go to him, take him, and force him to tell all about the others that he knows. Now, we will start again afresh, under Eva's direction."

Eva simply nodded. "I will begin immediately."

I had embarrassed Stephen in front of the others and he grew sullen. It is good to consider the effects your words may have on your followers but you should always ensure they are men of character who can accept your criticisms and continue to do their duty. Stephen was quite brilliant but he was never emotionally robust. Perhaps it was due to his common birth that he lacked the depth of character that a man of good breeding will tend to have.

Or perhaps it was his lack of dutifulness that was his main weakness of character. He never comprehended, not truly, that doing one's duty lifts up one's soul to greater heights than self-interest ever could. Stephen was always keenly aware of his lowborn blood and I believe he resented being beholden to anyone, even~astonishing as it may seem~to a king. It was a flaw that would eventually have disastrous consequences, as he pushed and needled England further away from the proper, natural hierarchies designed by God and toward ungodly, destructive notions of egalitarianism. But that would unravel in the centuries to come and I had only a glint of it at the time.

"I wanted to ask you Stephen," Thomas said, "and you also, Eva. Have you heard about this pestilence growing in the south?"

Stephen nodded. "The merchants are all in a blaze about it. Word has stopped coming out of Italy but many ports were closed, last we heard."

Eva sighed. "It appears this will disrupt our search."

"Nonsense," I said. "When is there not some pestilences striking down armies and ports and cities and towns? This summer is already the wettest I can recall and no doubt has caused foul air to rise in the heat of the south. This new bloody flux or murderous fever or whatever it is will burn itself out without affecting any of us much at all."

But I could not have been more wrong.

The Great Mortality had come.

9

THE BLACK DEATH

I WAS HAPPY, because I had received a letter from Lady Cecilia.

Dearest Richard, I pray my words find you well. I had hoped so to see you at court this past winter and spring yet found you always absent which caused my heart to be full heavy. I shall be staying at the Tower in London in early June as a guest of the Queen. If you could spare the time and effort away from your important duties on your estates to join me there, it would make me the happiest woman on earth.

As ancient as I was, upon reading the words I leapt in the air and whooped with joy, scaring the messenger and bringing Walt running with his dagger drawn.

It was all I could do to contain my excitement in the following days and every time I recalled that there could be no happy marriage for us, I simply pushed the thought away.

And when I saw her, I forgot it entirely.

After arriving absurdly early and sending word of it to the lady, I stood in the entrance to the gardens in the southwestern corner of the walls, beneath the White Tower. It had stopped raining after days and days and though everything was damp, the sun came out and the world sparkled. The ornamental fruit trees shone with vivid green, though the blossom on them had all been blasted off by the rains and there would be no fruit for the royal cooks to use in the fall.

She was more beautiful than ever and her smile at seeing me took my breath away. She was a vision and I for a few moments I was simply, idiotically happy.

"Sir Richard," she said as I bowed. "It gladdens my heart that you came."

I smiled. "My heart is glad also, my lady."

We were not alone, of course, and her servants followed closely and mine drifted along as far away from me as they would go. And the Tower was busy with other lords and ladies within and without and so our meeting was not some secret liaison but an opportunity to converse and become acquainted, as those who might be disposed to a marriage will often do.

We talked of small things, such as the appalling weather, and ignored unsavoury topics such as the necessary leanness of the coming winter for many in the land. It had been a long while since I had spoken of my favourite ballads and favoured foods and I was rusty with it, doing so was a pleasant change from discussing war and siegecraft. In truth, any topic would have been joyful with her clear voice in my ears and gorgeous face delighting my vision.

"I am afraid I was blessed with an ear for music," I said when she asked me to sing a verse, "but cursed with a voice that causes children to weep and milk to curdle."

She laughed. "In that case, I will beg your pardon and recall my request. Shall we head into the rose garden, Richard? The air beneath these trees is very close, do you not think?"

On our way across to the new rose garden, Cecilia took my arm and leaned on me a little. It was a pleasant feeling. I wondered if I plucked one of the roses and presented it to the lady whether King Edward would have my head plucked from my shoulders.

"Why are you unmarried, Richard?" she asked.

"An interesting question, my lady," I said, temporising so I could gather my thoughts. "I have concentrated on waging war rather than on love."

"Love?" she said, as if she was shocked. "But what has love to do with marriage, sir?"

I glanced down and saw that she had a twinkle in her eye.

"You did not marry for love, my lady?" I asked.

She sighed. "Dear me, Richard. I had no choice in my husband. I thought that I would be blessed with children and that I could love them, at least. But God decided otherwise."

I swallowed. "I pray that you are so blessed in your next marriage, my lady."

She grasped my arm and looked me in the eye. "If I ever marry again it shall be for love. Children are a blessing but my heart wants only the companionship of an honourable man."

"An honourable man," I repeated, my mouth dry. Was that what I was? Was it something I could ever be? "Well, my lady, I sincerely hope that—"

Before I could continue, a great crowd came bustling from the royal apartments. For half a moment, I thought we were under attack but then I realised it was a member of the royal family, surrounded by an enormous number of ladies, servants and guards. The party was rushing across the courtyard and through the gardens.

Cecilia and I at once moved aside to allow the swishing wave of garish frocks and nattering nobles past us.

"Sir Richard!" Princess Joan called to me from the centre of the pack, shouting over the enormous noise.

The chattering died down as the chaotic procession slowed to a stop right before us.

Princess Joan was fourteen years old and about to embark on the journey that would take her away from England, possibly forever, to a foreign kingdom. It was the duty of such ladies to undertake such things but surely there was never a one of them who did not find it a hard task. Still, one day soon she could expect to become the wife of the heir to that foreign throne and bear him sons. Her husband would one day be king and she would be the queen and her sons would be kings after them.

And she would be travelling in style. All the talk for weeks had been the size of Joan's trousseau which was said to entirely fill one of the four ships that would take her and her retinue south to Iberia. The princess would be travelling in as much comfort as was possible in those days and she would be well protected. I had even spoken to a few of the two hundred veteran archers escorting her, for I knew them from Brittany and from Calais. They were hard men, as hard as they come, forged in the fire of battle where they had seen the weaker of them, their brothers and cousins and friends, struck down by blade or sickness, so that only the strongest survived. Being chosen to protect King Edward's precious daughter brought them more pride than their hearts could bear and more than one of them had tears in his eyes when he spoke of his new duty.

I bowed low. "I am honoured that you remember me, my lady."

"How could I forget you, sir," she said, smiling and pushing her way through the ranks of formidable matrons. Joan turned to the Lady Cecilia. "When I was but a girl, Sir Richard instructed me in methods by which to improve my riding. He was so effective that I beat Isabella in a race across country." She laughed. "The King was most displeased with me for that and he banned both of us from riding for a year. Of course, he never enforced it. I was so very sorry to hear that you bore the brunt of his displeasure when it was entirely at my insistence that you addressed me on the matter at all."

"Not at all, my lady," I said, unable to keep a straight face. "Your father merely sent me to Brittany for years with an army consisting of two dozen men. But I do not mind that now I hear how you finally bested your sister." I winked at her and she giggled until her matronly companion growled a warning.

"I am leaving for Castile," Joan blurted out to Cecilia.

"So I hear, my lady," Cecilia said. "You must be very happy."

Her smile grew tighter but Joan was clearly excited as much as she was worried about leaving her family, forever, to set up in a foreign court. Such a thing requires courage from a woman and she faced her future with fortitude. "I am happy. I cannot wait to embark upon the journey. They say that Castile is a beautiful land."

"It is, my lady," I said.

"Oh, you have not been there? Truly?"

"Not for some time. Yet I remember it well and my memories are fond ones. They are a fine people."

Cecilia lowered her voice and looked up at me through her eyelashes. "I am sure it is the fine ladies that you recall so well, Richard."

Joan gasped, thrilled at Cecilia's teasing. "Is it true, Richard?" Then her face fell. "Are the ladies as beautiful as they say?"

I bowed. "They are indeed lovely, my lady, but there is not one amongst them who could hold a candle to you." Joan's face lit up as her outraged companions huffed and dragged her away from us. "God bless you in your marriage, my lady."

"And you in yours," she said as she went, grinning at Cecilia and attempting a wink. "Remember to keep your lower legs in contact with the horse at all times, Lady Cecilia."

"Good God," Cecilia said, shocked, as Joan disappeared into the hall. "She is as uncouth as you are. No wonder she is so taken with you. If only you were a Spanish prince, Richard, I think you would have had an infatuated English princess for a wife."

I tried not to laugh, for Cecilia seemed to be rather jealous but I had nothing but fatherly affection for the dear child.

Poor Joan, the little angel. I heard what happened much later from one of those archers. On her way to Castile, they put in at

Bordeaux and her grand party was warned by the mayor there was a terrible sickness in the town and he advised that they leave.

Instead, they stayed. They had no idea what was in store.

But the archers, who were supposed to be housed in the town, noticed what was happening around them. Doors swung free in the wind and the homes were deserted. There were hundreds of bodies being buried in unmarked pits and the stench of death and decay began to waft over them. A wary bunch, they begged the leaders of the party to put out to sea immediately but they were rebuffed and then ignored. The archers explained how the sick people of the town were covered with swollen sores that emitted the fetid smell of putrefaction. In response, the noble leaders said that they would be safe in the castle, away from the town and the archers were instructed to keep to the town and to stop bothering the nobles. It did no good, and archers and lords alike fell ill and began dropping dead.

The leader of the party tried to save the precious and terrified Joan by fleeing to an estate in the country which would be free, they hoped, from the miasmas covering the town. That leader never made it, dying on the way from the terrible and unknown disease. I cannot imagine dear little Joan's terror. I imagine how she prayed in those days. I picture her in her bedchamber in the country, praying and praying to be spared as those around her died one by one.

A few days later, and in unimaginable agony, sweet little Joan died all by herself.

There were a handful of survivors from her party and these men made their way back to England as quickly as they could, hoping to bring warning of the terrible pestilence travelling the land.

By the time the first of them reached us, the pestilence was already ravaging England.

∞ ∞ ∞

There had for some time been ever-growing certainty about that terrible illness affecting the cities down in Italy and even rumours that it was spreading northward. I had dismissed it all so easily when I first heard and I know for certain that I was not alone. Few of us paid it much heed.

Few of us, that is, until the rumours became certain reports that the pestilence had reached England, finally. Even then, I do not know of anyone who thought it would be anything like the way it turned out. Still, people had enough sense to take proper precautions in case it reached their town or village or manor. The most sensible ones focused on praying that they and their loved ones would be spared and the wealthier sort took pains to make donations or undertake charitable works in order to head off the Lord's wrath, as it were.

As soon as it became clear that it would be a true pestilence, a plague, I returned to my manors in Suffolk to make my people ready. Lady Cecilia did the same and we parted in quite a hurried fashion. As I turned, from my horse, to look down on her before I rode away, a profound sense of dread descended upon me and I felt certain that she would succumb to this unknown sickness that crept toward us. For a moment, I considered insisting that she come with me to my lands so that I could better protect her but good sense returned to counter my romantic notions. As a widow, she had full responsibility for her own lands and she would certainly have rejected my offer. Besides, how could I have protected her against something that I could not see and did not understand?

Still, I regularly recalled the sight of her standing in her elaborate robe and headdress in the courtyard at the Tower for a long time afterwards.

I was the lord of two estates in the county of Suffolk, which stood and still stands on the eastern coast of England, northeast of London between the counties of Essex and Norfolk. The county was a fine place, as far as lowland, southern England goes, with bounteous green fields and leafy woodlands and gently rolling hills. It was no Derbyshire, of course, but then what is? The people were good and honest and toiled as hard as any ever did. The two manors of Hawkedon and Hartest did not make me rich but the land was so productive that I could provide a core of fighting men and afford most of whatever I needed. Whenever more was required, I obtained it from the Order's coffers.

The most important man a lord of the manor could employ was his steward, for all else flowed from him. My steward ran both estates, though a sub-steward was present at Hartest, the smaller of the two and in effect made all daily decisions. Both places were old but neither was a castle and they were rather comfortable. Other lords would invest in stone walls and towers but I could see very little chance of a new French invasion or armed uprisings against the King and his lords and so I sought always to make improvements to the domestic quarters, the kitchens and storerooms, or the workshops. I even had two chapels built. In particular, I added a new wing to Hawkedon, my primary manor, with two floors, and stayed there almost exclusively in as much privacy as I could maintain. The smaller manor of Hartest was better for hunting and when I was there I spent as much time as I could riding in the woods. Hunting was a social activity as much as a practical one but I preferred to provide meat for my table following excursions with as few others as possible. Mortals engage in ceaseless prattling about the most inconsequential topics and I can only feign interest for so long.

There was little I could do to shut myself away for as long as I wished, for my tenants came to me with a great many manorial issues. One man had not properly delved his drainage ditches and caused other men's crops to get flooded from the terrible rains and he had to be punished and make amends. There were so many cases of cattle and pigs straying and damaging crops or property that I quickly lost count. I had a few instances of poaching to deal with. It was never something I cared about but I had to pretend outrage and issue relatively steep fines. It was expected and if a lord was too lenient then the villeins and freemen did not like it, not one bit, even as they grumbled about the fines. There were greater crimes, and those committed by my own people against those from neighbouring manors, that I had to hear about but which were outside of my jurisdiction and would need to be deferred to the sheriff's court later in the year.

Of course, the talk from everyone was focused on the dreaded pestilence.

Many wanted to hear how the plague had affected London and were almost disappointed when I assured them that it had not occurred there before I had left it.

"What can we do to prepare, my lord?" the stewards and senior servants asked me in Hawkedon Hall.

I had no idea but I pretended that I did. "The pestilence is caused by bad air and so we must clean, brush, and wash all rooms and paths."

This they did with enthusiasm and returned to me, asking if they were now safe.

"The pestilence is caused also by rising miasmas from bogs and although our wetlands grow every day with these rains, we must now all avoid these places."

They nodded, keen to do so, for everyone knew that such places caused sickness at the best of times.

"But, my lord," my steward said, "the pestilence is also spread by the bad airs emanating from unwashed persons and from the foul breath of careless folk."

"Yes indeed," I said, "and so we must each make the greatest of efforts to wash our linen and our bodies as much as we are able. We shall send to the market at Lavenham and Framlingham for as much soap as possible."

My steward sucked air in through his teeth. "Hard to get soap in Lavenham, my lord, in these times."

"We shall go to Norwich if we have to."

"Very good, my lord," he said, though he seemed unhappy. "What about foreigners, my lord? Bringing their pestilential airs with them?"

"Quite right. We shall forbid anyone from Norfolk or Essex from coming into the manors without exception."

"Especially Essex, my lord."

"As you say, good steward. Anyone from the south or from the coast shall be strictly turned away from the borders."

"And also, my lord," the steward continued, "we must post sentries on the wells, at all hours. And the stream, also, I should think. Sentries night and day, sir."

"Sentries? But why, man?"

"But ain't you heard, my lord, that the pestilence is begun most of all by the Jews, what come creeping out from their low places to poison the wells of good Christian folk in the night so that we all fall dead by dinner?"

I sighed, for the Jews had been expelled from England decades before. It was common knowledge that plenty of them had changed their names and hidden themselves amongst the population, pretending to be Christians but continuing their dark rites in secret. No one ever met one of these secret Jews but everyone knew they were there amongst the townsfolk.

"If that is the case," I said, "surely they would be intent on destroying London, or Bristol, or Oxford, or York. Not Hawkedon and Hartest."

He sniffed, looking over his shoulder before turning back to me. "Colchester's got them new foreigners, sir. Might be they creep up here in the night."

"The Flemish weavers? They are good Christians, not Jews."

"Still foreign, sir."

"Post your sentries, then. But for God's sake ensure they are not armed or they will like as not spear Mistress Heyward when she comes to collect water one morning."

It was a Monday when the first people fell ill in Hawkedon and we all knew what it was, though at first there was still a tragic hope that it was an ordinary affliction that would pass.

A mere three days after the illness came, the first of my people died in blistering agony.

The villeins and freemen stayed in their homes and I stayed in my manor. What could I do? I was powerless. It was tempting to administer my blood to some of the pestilent but I saw how that path might save a life, or not, but would likely lead to my own downfall. Men and women grew suspicious of everything as they watched in helplessness as their parents and their children died first. But the strong and healthy, in the prime of their lives, died also.

I begged for our priests to come and to pray and to visit each of my people, especially the afflicted, and this some of them did. One kindly old priest rode from home to home, dealing out blessing and rites for four days without rest before dying in the night of the fifth.

In desperation, I sent for the finest physicians in the county and to the neighbouring ones, promising that I would pay whatever cost was asked. Just one of my men returned successfully and the doddery old fellow with a fat, red face that he brought back with him claimed to be a physician of the highest learning, although I had never heard of him. I met him in the confines of my solar in my private wing at Hawkedon, and had him sit with me while I asked what experience he had.

"I come from Ely," he said, proudly. "Where I have successfully kept the pestilence at bay throughout this plague."

"Indeed?" I replied, impressed. "Ely is an island in the pestilential fens and yet it is free from the spreading mortality?"

"Well," he said, spreading his stubby-fingered hands, "I have treated a great number of the afflicted. Some have even survived."

"What is the method of treatment? It seems to me that the servants die in more ways than I can understand. Some die where they stand and some few lay abed for a week and then rise, weakened but alive. What can be done, sir?"

He nodded, sagely. "It is a confusing story indeed. It seems as though it may afflict the victim in one of three ways. Most commonly, they fall ill with a fever that hits them very hard indeed. A day or two later, they break out in the boils, clustered in the armpits and groin. Many of these I have seen and they may grow to the size of an apple in a single night. If the sufferer is able to speak he will complain of blinding headaches and violent chills while his body sweats freely and uncontrollably. Within five or six days from the first signs of sickness, they will be dead."

"God preserve us," I said. "This is how my people have been dying, yes."

He held up a finger. "That is merely the first of the three forms, as I stated. Another form is rather better and if God decrees that I become afflicted, this is the form I wish to receive."

"Ah!" I said. "So, this is the gentler form?"

He laughed so hard that his face turned purple. "Dear me, no. I speak of those who die with almost no warning. Surely you have heard of these, sir? A man will kiss his wife goodnight in fine health and be discovered dead in the morning. You may soon find yourself witnessing a man or woman or child suddenly fall to the ground and begin a terrible shaking, with limbs and features rigid and quivering most violently. When you go to their aid, you will discover that they are quite dead, perhaps with putrefied blood oozing from their various orifices. It strikes with such rapidity that the suffering is certainly over quickly. Thanks to God's mercy."

I gripped my hands together in front of me. "There was a third form of death, you said?"

"Yes indeed. One where you might say it falls between the other kinds. It is preceded by terrible coughing which brings up enormous amounts of blood before their end. These poor souls take just two or three days from their first bloody cough to their burial but those days will be filled with agony as they struggle for every breath. They will vomit up their stomach contents, and then whatever water, ale, or wine you can get into them and then quickly it is blood that they vomit, almost ceaselessly. Their fingers turn black and die, as do the toes. No doubt the rest of them would follow in like fashion, if their body was not emptied of blood. This is perhaps the worst form of the pestilence."

There was nothing I could say in response. My instinct was to pray to God but there was a profound sense that He was not listening to our prayers. Worse, it was hard to avoid the feeling that we were all being punished by Him. But what monstrous sins had those living in that time committed that the people I had known earlier had not?

A letter arrived at my home from Stephen in the hands of a

young messenger who shook as he stood before me.

"Are you suffering from the pestilence, son?"

The messenger looked horrified. "Oh, no, sir. Thanks be to God. Simply cold and weary from the hard riding and…" He hung his head. "My father and my sister died not three days past, sir. Yet I am hale and in fine health, praise God, sir."

I took a full step backwards. And then another.

"You are one of Stephen Gossett's servants, yes?"

"Indeed, sir. And a fine master he is, sir. None better in all Christendom, so we all say, sir, especially in these days. Fair as the day is—"

"Yes, yes, I'm sure," I muttered as I broke Stephen's seal. Then I froze as I read the words, before calling one of my own servants over. "Escort this young man to the kitchens, see him fed well, give him good ale and provisions for his journey back to London. Give him a good, fresh horse. The black rouncey." I stepped forward and placed a hand on the young fellow's shoulder. "Tell your master I am coming immediately. That is all."

As they left, I read the letter again.

Richard. Regretfully, Sir Thomas and Lady Eva are struck down by the pestilence. They yet live. Please come at once. Your faithful servant, Stephen Gossett.

10

PESTILENCE

I RODE TO LONDON with all haste, taking Walter and a handful of healthy servants. The roads had degenerated since I last travelled them, with the surfaces washed out and pitted so deeply with eroded pits they were like elongated ponds. Worse, the ways had not been cleared of all the wild growth from weeds and bushes and felled trees blocked the way. Most were natural deadfalls but one seemed felled with a purpose.

"Robbers done it, sir," Walt said, riding to me with his sword drawn after investigating the trunk.

"I doubt they will attack us, Walt," I replied, though I drew my own sword and watched the undergrowth closely for the next mile or two.

We saw few other travellers and those that we passed we kept a distance from and they kept away from us, almost all covering their mouths and noses as they did so.

Rushing, we made the distance in three days which was as swiftly as anyone could hope for. Even so, I was fighting to control my distress over every mile. I had already lost John and now I was at risk of losing my dearest companion and the woman I had loved for longer than any other. Eva was no longer my wife and what passion we had once experienced was by then a century past but the thought of losing her was almost more than I could bear.

When I arrived at the townhouse, I did not pause to change or even to wash but strode into the house, scattering servants while I cried out for Stephen. He came clattering down the main stairs, banging to a stop on the steps before reaching the bottom.

"Richard, thank God. They are this way."

I followed, taking the steps two at a time, up to the rooms on the uppermost floor. Though it was a bright day outside, it was dark in the bedchamber and it took a moment for my eyes to adjust to the lamplight. I had slept in those rooms before and recalled how the windows allowed a pleasant view over the Thames and the ships that filled it. Now, they were shuttered and covered with heavy, dark cloth.

Stephen ushered me fully inside the larger of the two rooms and closed the door behind me. "The doctors said not to allow the bad air into the chambers," he explained, speaking softly.

Servants moved away from the bed as I approached, pulling back the linen curtain. A single candle, fixed to one of the bedposts, gave enough light to see that Eva lay within, her hair loose, wet with sweat and plastered to the sheets. Her face was waxy and pale and translucent as marble. The stench was quite foul. The only sign that she lived was her breathing, which was shallow and rapid.

"Eva?" I said, quietly.

She stirred and groaned and then fell silent.

"Is it truly the pestilence?" I asked Stephen, reaching down to touch her brow. It was fiercely hot and slick with sweat.

"She has the signs," Stephen said, then rushed to explain. "So the doctors tell me."

I pulled back the sheets. "Avert your eyes, Stephen," I said.

An old woman appeared as if from nowhere at my side, grabbing at my arm with her sharp little fingers. "How dare you, sir. You must not. It is unseemly, sir."

"She is my wife," I said to the servant, which gave her pause. I did not add that she had left me eighty years before but nevertheless she had been my wife for forty years before that and I knew her body almost as well as I knew my own.

"It is true," Stephen said, over his shoulder. His definition of truth was always a loose one.

"Even so," the old servant said, firmly.

"You are quite right, good woman," I said. "Would you be good enough to help me bare her shoulder?"

She peeled back the sheets and I lifted Eva's arm.

"Here, sir," the servant said, and handed me a lamp.

Holding it close, I saw the enormous black pustule half-filling her armpit.

"Dear God," I muttered. "There are more?" I asked. "Her nether regions?"

The old woman coughed to indicate that she did not think it

seemly to discuss it but she then whispered. "Yes, sir."

"How long?" I asked Stephen as I covered Eva again. "How long has she been like this?"

"Come with me," he said and led me across into the second chamber. Hugh, the squire, knelt at the side of Thomas' bed in prayer.

He got to his feet in that stiff-legged way that a man does when he has been at prayer for many hours.

"Sir Richard. Thank you for coming, sir. I know that Sir Thomas would be greatly pleased that you have come."

"How is he?"

Hugh took a deep breath. "The physicians say it is the strangest case they have seen. Thomas and the Lady Eva both, sir. How they are afflicted by the pestilence and yet cling to life, neither dying nor recovering, as some are said to do." Hugh glanced at Stephen then back to me. "Of course, we cannot tell the physicians about the Gift. Surely it is the blood that preserves them so, my lord?"

I nodded, patting him on the shoulder as I crossed to the bed.

Thomas looked like a dead man. His aged face had sunken further, and he was thin as a skeleton.

"Others I have seen suffering from this affliction," I said, "were crying out and raving from their pain."

"They have done so, many times," Hugh said. "After the blood."

"You have given them blood," I said, seeking confirmation, "and it does not cure them."

"For a time," Stephen said, softly. "It rouses them enough to accept a little broth, perhaps some morsels of bread soaked in milk or ale. The black blisters recede and they are often able to converse. And then their anguish begins anew. Eventually, they fall into this state of deathlessness until we rouse them again."

"Perhaps more blood would help? Increase the number and size of the draughts."

Stephen shook his head, sadly. "At first, I filled them both with so much that they vomited it back up. I also gave them blood once they woke, and again twice every hour, but still they fall back into this. I attempted giving them blood the instant they collapse, thus bringing them back to health over and over in quick succession. But there was no increase in effectiveness. Always, they return to this. And now, half my servants have fallen to the pestilence and more have fled this house and the city. I tell the survivors that bleeding them daily is what is keeping them free of the plague but every soul in the city grows suspicious."

"Suspicious of you?"

He waved away my concern. "Suspicious of everyone, of everything. Fear reigns, now. Ancient superstitions half-forgotten are being spoken once more. But my servants trust me and those that remain will continue to be loyal. I ensure I take very good care of them, with the best food I can find, hot fires to keep them warm and dry, even physicians for their families, if the bastard piss prophets can be enticed to attend anyone any more. No, my servants will be here to supply us with blood until this plague passes and our friends recover from their affliction."

"When the plague passes, they will also recover?"

"So the physicians said."

Hugh dared to speak up. "Some say it will never pass. We are dying one after the other until all will have perished and so this is surely the end of the world."

Increasingly, I feared that very thing. It certainly seemed far worse than I could have imagined, had I not ridden across some of the country and seen the horrors of London. Still, it is a leader's duty to provide strength and hope and so I searched for something comforting to say.

"It is a hard time, yes. As hard as any I have seen. Yet order remains in the streets, does it not? The dead do not lay in their beds but are buried by their loved ones and their neighbours. This is a pestilence, no more."

"What have we done to deserve it, sir?" Hugh asked.

"A great deal of evil," I said.

"And yet children have done no evil and they die also. Even more so."

"Some are saying," Stephen replied, "that God slays the children to punish the parents. And that the inexplicably random nature of the death is itself punishment for the wickedness of humanity as a whole."

"But if God is just, why would He do that?" Hugh asked, close to despair.

I wished to snap at him to ask a bloody priest but I held my tongue.

Stephen had an answer, as always. "One of the physicians told me the pestilential miasmas are due to a particular alignment of the heavens, and that God has no hand in this at all. That it is as natural as a storm."

"Of course it is God," I said. "He did it before, did he not? When he sent the Great Flood of Noah to cleanse the Earth."

Stephen bowed. "Of course."

Hugh was not satisfied. "But why—"

"Enough," I said. "Let us rouse them so I can cure them with my own blood. They have suffered enough, whether God wills it or not."

I decided that Thomas would be first. If anything went badly wrong, it would be he that bore the brunt rather than Eva. And I knew that he would not want it any other way.

Using the instrument, I bled myself into a cup.

"Should I..?" Stephen began, reaching out to take it.

I ignored him and sat on the edge of the bed. "Thomas?" I called. "Thomas, it is Richard."

He groaned and muttered.

"Come on, now, old man," I said brusquely as I lifted his head up. The hair at the back of his head was sodden with sweat and a strong, foul stench gusted up to my nose. My stomach churned.

I poured some into his mouth and he stirred himself, slurping at it in a most disgusting fashion. The effects began almost at once and he reached up to grasp my hand and tip the rest of the cup into his mouth while he gulped it down.

Thomas opened his eyes and gasped, then clutched at his stomach while he thrashed his head side to side. After a few moments, he sighed and sank back.

He looked at me.

"Richard."

"Thomas, thank God. You have returned to us."

"Yes, yes," he said. "What took you so long?"

"How do you feel?" I asked.

He considered it for a moment and sat up. I moved back as he pulled back the covers and got to his feet, standing in his sweat-soaked shirt. "I feel well," he said, speaking slowly and wiping his lips. "This was your blood, Richard?"

"You can tell the difference?"

"I have been drinking mortal's blood every day, or near enough. It is difficult to recall clearly. But yes, I believe this does feel different." Hope dawned on his aged features. "By God, I feel hearty indeed."

"Praise God," I said, turning to Stephen. "Now, let us see to Eva."

I was gratified when it went much the same as with Thomas. When Eva awoke and confirmed that she felt fully well, I gave her time to wash and be dressed and waited downstairs in the hall, drinking wine. Stephen's servants managed to find enough fresh produce in London to make for us a rather impressive impromptu feast to celebrate and first Thomas and then Eva joined us while the dishes were served.

Our first course was an array of boiled meats in sauces, of which my favourite was an excellent beef pottage in wine with herbs and spices. After that, we had meats in jelly with roast kid, and a dish of roast heron and one of woodcock which I devoured almost entirely by myself. The third course brought us dozens of small, delicate sparrows and swallows with bowls of fruit compotes, cooked with huge amounts of sugar. After that, when I declared I could eat no more, they brought out a half dozen cheeses which I tucked into with heroic vigour and good cheer.

"Bring us *hypocras*," I called to the servants, which was a spiced red wine that the produced with such alacrity that they must certainly have anticipated my order.

Stephen laughed. "Of course it was ready, Richard. Do you not think that I know you well enough, after all this time together?"

"Let us drink to your good health, my dear friends," I said to Thomas and Eva, raising my cup, and we did so drink.

"And to friends departed," Hugh said, raising his cup. We drank to John, who all of us missed.

"I must say, I am quite relieved to be rid of that terrible affliction," Thomas said. "I never felt anything like it in all my days."

Eva nodded. "And I never wish to again," she said. "It feels like..." she trailed off, staring into nothing.

"Well," I said, "it is all over now and all I can say is that I apologise for not being here sooner."

"You came as soon as you were summoned," Stephen said. "What more can a man do, Richard?"

Summoned. It irked me that he would use such a term when I was his superior in every way but I was in such a high mood that I let it pass. I often wonder what might have come to pass had I destroyed Stephen in his early days, instead of letting such moments pass and pass.

In no time, we were well on the way to pleasant intoxication.

"This was a fine meal, Stephen," Thomas said, "considering the circumstances."

"What do you mean?" Stephen replied, growing rambunctious with the wine in his belly. "This would be a fine meal in any circumstances."

Thomas shrugged. "For an English merchant, perhaps that is so. Speaking as a Frenchman of noble breeding, however, all I will say is that I look forward to when this pestilence passes and we can get some decent food in this hall."

As gibes go, it was rather close to the bone but Stephen laughed it off and so we all felt able to join in with the laughter.

Thomas was still chuckling when he popped some bread into his mouth and began coughing. I jumped up, thinking he was choking on his food, and thumped him on his back.

He coughed up a handful of bright, frothy blood.

We all stared at his hand, shining in the lamplight.

Thomas whispered the short prayer.

"God, no."

I turned to Eva. I will never forget the look of dread in her eyes.

His face contorted in pain, Thomas clutched at his guts and vomited onto the table before collapsing in a shaking fit.

Stephen called for his people and the servants came running.

"Eva," I said, kneeling by her. "It may not return for you."

"No," she said, "it has come again. I can feel it. Your blood, Richard. It did not work."

We tried everything that any of us could think of. I gave them more blood, of course. We gave them mortal blood soon after mine, or before, or both before and after. Stephen had the idea of concentrating my blood by heating it gently for some time. That seemed, if anything, to lessen its potency.

Nothing worked.

"We shall find a cure," I said, looking down on Eva, in her bed as the sickness descended upon her once again. "I shall not rest until I do."

"I know, Richard," she replied, patting my arm before turning away from me. I got up and trudged down to the hall.

Sitting with Stephen later with my head in my hands, I felt truly defeated. More than I ever had before. The pestilence was an enemy that I could not fight.

"There must be something," I said, for the thousandth time. "Must be some way to strengthen my blood."

Stephen shrugged. "What flows through your veins is already the most powerful substance on Earth. Yours and your brother's. And as much as I should like to empty him of his, he is not even in Christendom."

"It would take years to follow him to Cathay, Stephen, if that is what you are suggesting."

"I suggest nothing of the sort, sir," he replied, as if he was affronted. "Even if William was here, there is nothing to indicate that his power is any greater than yours. Is there?"

As tired as I was, I knew that Stephen was pushing me for information. He always was. It was his nature.

In fact, I had long suspected that my brother William was

stronger than me. Whether it was a factor of the blood in our veins or something else, I did not know but I felt it nonetheless. Perhaps Stephen sensed it too, in some way, and was seeking confirmation.

"We are equals, my brother and I, but if he were here I would string him from the beam there and drain every drop on the chance alone that it could help Eva. And Thomas." I thought for a moment, and idly spoke the next thought that popped into my head. "It is a shame that he killed our father so long ago, or else I could fetch him from Derbyshire and see if he is any stronger than his sons. Alas, William poisoned him when—"

I stopped speaking when I recalled something I had not thought of in quite some time.

If you do return to Christendom, you should seek our grandfather. The Ancient One. The old Lord de Ferrers was not our father's true father. Our true grandfather lives, and he is thousands of years old, Richard. Thousands! The things he has seen. The power that he has. You would learn a lot from him, brother, if you would but go to him. Our grandfather is in Swabia. In a forest, living in a cave. The locals live in terror of him.

"If power is what we need, there is one who may be stronger than I."

"Your brother?"

I scowled. "No, Stephen. Back in Baghdad, in that charnel house of a gateway, I made a deal with William. He told me of the immortals he had made in France and I agreed to not pursue him until he returned to Christendom."

Stephen nodded. He knew all this.

"William also told me something else. He told me that he had discovered our true ancestry. That my natural father was not descended from the de Ferrers family line but had been fathered by an immortal himself. A man who is thousands of years old."

Stephen sat bolt upright. "But you cannot make children, Richard. Neither you nor William."

"Our grandfather did. As did our father. That is why I think he may have more power in his blood than I do. The strength to create life. Perhaps it has strength enough to cure this cursed pestilence."

"Just a moment, please," Stephen said, shaking his head and closing his eyes. "Are you saying that your grandfather yet lives?"

I sat back and spread my hands. "I am relating William's words. As far as I know, he does not lie. To me, at least. But he may be mistaken or confused. He claimed to have visited him."

"Where?"

"Swabia."

"A fair distance from here, Richard. Where in Swabia?"

"In a forest. He lives in a cave."

Stephen stared. "That is it? How can we find him?"

"I would go to Swabia and search, I suppose. Ask around."

"How big is Swabia?"

I shrugged. "Big enough."

"It must surely be the size of Wales and just as mountainous."

"Even more so. And thickly wooded."

Stephen rubbed his eyes. "We must certainly seek this man out but I do not see how it will help us with Thomas and Eva. How long will it take us to travel to Swabia?"

"I can move quickly when I need to."

"Even so, how will we find one cave in a forest the size of Wales?"

"My brother found him. I will find him."

Stephen stood up. "You speak as though you have already decided."

"Do I?" I asked. "I suppose I have. Do you have a better idea?"

He waved his hands in the air as if he hoped to scoop one up out of the ether. "There must be one."

"Perhaps there is but until it occurs to us, I shall do this. Alone."

"Alone?" Stephen was appalled. "Take Hugh with you, at the very least."

Hugh was a good squire and a fair fighter but my instinct was that he was not up to such a challenge. "I shall take almost nothing but food and travel quickly."

"Take Black Walter with you, at least."

"Walt?" I said. "He is mortal. And ignorant. Close to useless."

"He saved your life once, did he not? You underestimate him, Richard."

"I doubt that is possible but you are correct, I shall need someone to take turns on watch and I suppose he is marginally more useful than a goose." I stood. "I will make preparations immediately. I will take Black Walter with me but no other servants. We will move swiftly that way. You and Hugh will stay here and keep our companions alive."

He looked stunned so I strode over and grasped him by the shoulders.

"Keep them alive, Stephen."

His eyes were wide. "I will."

I was going to cross a Europe deep in the grip of the worst plague it had ever known, in the faint hope of finding a hermit who apparently claimed to be thousands of years old as well as my grandfather. And I was going based on the word of my brother, who I had sworn to kill.

I must have been mad.

1 1

LAND OF THE DEAD

THE PORTS WERE CLOSED. No ships in or out across all southern England. I knew that it would be foolhardy to travel to the south coast and try to force passage across the English Channel from there, even though that would have been the quickest crossing. Instead, I headed north and east, up into that flat, marshy land called East Anglia. Although it was a fertile land, good for wheat, sheep and cattle, it was wet at the best of times and it had been raining steadily for weeks. When we travelled through it was as though the North Sea had risen up from the east to claim the land for itself. Roads were washed out. Rivers burst their banks and spread out to turn fields into lakes, ruining all crops not on the higher land. And that was few and far between. The landscape was often as flat as a table top.

"How will they eat?" Walt asked as we passed yet another field turned to bog. A man stood on a spit of land running to a cluster of houses, staring at the disaster. "How will they survive winter?"

"They will not."

There were fowl in the reedy ponds and wading birds on the mud flats. Deer in the woodlands. But unless there were enough survivors of the pestilence to hunt for them through the winter, the people would not fare well.

When we reached the coast, it took days of following it from town to town to find someone willing and able to cross to the continent. Even in that remote place, Walt proved useful. Well did he know the taverns in every town, and every hosteller and bar-maid, and these directed us to those who might have helped.

A few fishermen claimed to be able to make the journey but their boats were in appalling condition. Most simply refused to approach us, let alone converse. I considered stealing a boat and leaving a bag of coin but I could never have sailed it and Walt barely had wits enough to navigate his way up a gangplank.

It was a merchant who volunteered his ship, sailing master and small crew in exchange for an appalling amount of money. Due to the closure of so many ports, trade was so diminished as to be non-existent but still he was canny enough to know a desperate man when he saw one. We sold him our horses, as there was no possibility of taking them aboard the tub. Anticipating such a thing, we had not brought our best horses. Still, the awful price I got for them made me more irritated at the merchant than I had any right to be.

"Good idea, this, my lord," the merchant said as we agreed our terms, blustering in the loud voice merchants use when attempting to make a sale. "Get away from the pestilence to where it is safe."

"Do you take me for a fool? It is far worse everywhere south of England, as you well know."

His face turned white and he lowered his voice. "Then why do you wish to go there, sir?"

"I hear Ghent has an excellent brothel house just off the market square."

He went away, mumbling something about petty lordlings and Walter sidled up to me.

"That place ain't all it's cracked up to be, sir. Especially nowadays, I'd wager."

"Be quiet, Walt."

The crossing was remarkably unpleasant. It rained either all day or all night and sometimes both and the boat was seaworthy enough but it had a strange and at times quite alarming propensity to roll like a barrel.

Black Walt was completely unaffected by the motion, which was irritating in the extreme. We crept down the coast, taking advantage of the wind when it blew where we wanted and waiting it out when it did not. We sat in one cove for three days somewhere off the coast of Essex with the sky low and grey and the land lower and greyer. Local men on the land cried out that we were not to land under any circumstances. They made sure that we saw the huge longbows in their hands.

Blustering wind whistled and rushed through the mass of rigging like the wailing of a thousand widows. The boats rolled and pitched in the waves with relentless regularity, up and down, rolling one way and back the other. On every horizon, nothing but a haze like powdered bone. No man who was not a sailor knew whether we were being blown out to sea, on to the shore, or were making no headway at all. Such is the sea. Some moments out of a thousand, when all is well and the sun shines and the wind is stiff and steady and the ship ploughs through the waves toward home, it is of the purest joy. At all other times, it is deep misery that must be endured.

Eventually, we crossed the waters and were out of sight of land for a disturbingly long time and I was sure we would end up in Denmark, despite the sailing master's assurances. And yet he put us down on the coast of Flanders, just as he had said he would.

"Got to row you off onto the beach from here," he said as his ship bobbed at anchor off the coast. "We'll do it as the tide turns."

"If this is anywhere other than Flanders," I promised him, "when I return to England I shall castrate you and throw you into the sea so the fish can feast on your ruined nether parts."

He swallowed, hard. "This is bloody Flanders, my lord. I know these waters. Southwest is a fishing village called Eastend, and beyond that is France. Up the coast, northeast, the mud flats and shoals go on for miles. There is a harbour just up the way at a village they call Bruges-on-sea. You might find horses to purchase there, elsewise it's a walk into Bruges proper for you."

Walt shrugged. "Seems to know his business, sir."

"We shall see," I said, giving the master the full force of my death-stare.

The cold winter sea churned beneath the prow like the frothing mouth of a blown horse. Icy wind sliced through my clothes and chilled me to the bone.

We splashed ashore in the half-light of a grey dawn, wearing our padded armour coats and struggling to keep our over-sized packs from getting completely soaked.

"Going to be right hard buying decent horses for anything other than a king's ransom," Walt said as we trudged along the track to the nearest village. "But I reckon we can like as not help ourselves to a brace of them from some little lord's stables hereabouts."

"We are not thieves, Walt," I chided. "And the Flemings are our allies."

Walt scratched at his chin. "Seems like they're allies with King Edward in fighting the French but me and you are just a pair of foreigners traipsing through their lands uninvited."

"Nevertheless."

He shrugged and hitched his packs higher on his shoulders.

We were turned away from the village of Eastend by men with spears and crossbows who did not believe, or did not care, that we were English.

"Let us try Bruges," I said to Walt. He raised his eyebrows but said nothing.

The path to Bruges was almost empty and we met few travellers. The town was one of the biggest and busiest markets on the Continent, teeming with wealthy merchants and stuffed with skilled craftsmen, drawing locals from the lands all around and traders from everywhere in the world, when times were good. And yet it seemed as though we were almost alone as we approached the outskirts and suburbs. Even Walt was disturbed.

"Seems like things ain't going to go well for us in there, sir," he said, nodding at the walls and roofs in the distance.

"Nothing ventured, nothing gained," I replied.

A short while later, we passed by a father and his son sitting on their cart by the side of the road.

"Way's closed," the man said, turning to spit. Where one of his eyes used to be was a weeping sore that he dabbed at with a filthy rag.

"Do you mean to say that the town is not admitting travellers?" I asked him.

It seemed, as he squinted at me, that his French was not very good. "Way's closed," he repeated.

Walt plucked at my elbow. "Best make our way to a manor off in the country, what say you, sir?"

I shook Walt off. "They likely did not admit him on account of the appalling pustules in his eye, fearing him to be a plague carrier."

Walt wrinkled his nose. "What if the townsfolk detain us?"

"We shall not allow that to happen," I replied, tapping my sword. "Come on, you coward."

The men on the gate were suspicious but once they saw we were healthy and had coin to spend, they welcomed us like we were old friends, directing us to the places where we might purchase what we needed.

"Is the brothel house still open?" Walt asked but I shoved him in through the gate and apologised to the porters.

"Of course it will not be open, Walter. Besides, we have no time for that sort of thing, man. And you will certainly catch the plague in such a place. And catch it in your nether regions, like as not, causing your pestilential member to drop off by the middle of next week."

He nevertheless disappeared from our inn during the night, returning bleary-eyed but happy before sunrise and dozed in the saddle the next day.

Our four horses were good enough for the task and I felt hopeful as we set off because finding good mounts for the journey had been playing on my mind since leaving London. The rain threatened throughout the morning, fell lightly in the afternoon and ceased before sunset.

It was quiet on the road.

South of Bruges, in peaceful years gone by, that same road in late-summer was thronged with merchants and messengers, villeins and freemen, churchmen and beggars and endless servants. The road would be filled from edge to edge with carts piled with produce, riders with lords, children with chickens.

But not that day.

We came across a small group of poor folk wrapped in cloaks and hoods who retreated far into a field as we passed them and watched us for a good long while with dark looks until we were away around the next bend.

Walt turned in his saddle before settling down again. "I reckon we'll be finding trouble before long, sir."

The houses on the side of the road were silent and cold. Whether they had been abandoned or were filled with the dead, entombed unburied in their bedchambers, I could not say for we had no intention of entering any of them.

"What tongue do the folks around these parts speak?" Walt asked as we made camp for the night in a scrubby copse of coppiced ash and hazel a few miles from a village.

I covered my eyes and stifled a groan and cursed myself for not bringing Hugh along instead of Walt.

"You have been to this country before, Walt," I said. "Their tongue is Flemish. Most folk in the towns have French and the learned know Latin, just as it is everywhere. How did you converse with the pestilential harlot during your sordid excursion last night?"

"Oh, you don't have to speak to them, sir. You give them the coins and point at what you want."

"I am sure you do. It surprises me that the establishment is allowed to function at all, considering the keenness with which the men guard the doors to the town."

He shrugged. "Only a couple of old dears in there now, seeing to the locals. Fellow before me was keen as mustard on account of his wife died a few days ago and now he can get his end away again. Ain't take him too long, I tell you that much, he was in and out and looking happy as a pig in shit before I had time to sit down and take a sip of beer."

"Is that so?" I said, getting up to move further away from him. "I believe I shall prepare my own meal this evening, Walter."

Many a man of the knightly classes would despair at the notion of a meal consisting of a hunk of bread, a mouthful of cheese and a few slices of sausage, even if they were on campaign, and yet to me it has always been the simplest fare which brings the most nourishment to body and soul.

I had thought him asleep but Walt's weary voice drifted out of the darkness on the other side of the embers. "Sir?" he began, "is it true that you don't know the way? Only, our lad Hugh reckoned you don't know the way to this land called Swabia but I said Sir Richard wouldn't set out on such a quest without knowing where he was headed and no mistake."

"I do know the way," I replied. "It is to the south. We shall find our way the same way we do everywhere we go, Walt. By asking the way from one place to the next until we arrive."

The extended silence led me to hope he had fallen asleep but then he spoke. "How far south is Swabia, then?" I was about to hazard a guess but he continued speaking. "Long way, ain't it, sir. Long way to go to find a man who you say has a cure for the pestilence when it might be a lot of threshing for no nuts, if you catch my meaning, sir."

I caught his meaning well enough. Black Walter was unnerved by our venture. He was frightened by the creeping death all around, even if he was too simple-minded to know it in himself. And I was leading him further into unknown lands that were peopled with folk he did not know when all man's natural inclination when threatened with disease is to withdraw into a safe place. Into the arms of family and one's own home.

"All will be well, Walter," I assured him. "Rest easy, now, for all will be well."

In fact, it would not be well. Not at all. Especially for Black Walter.

∞ ∞ ∞

From Bruges, we made for Ghent, which was an even larger town. In fact, it was one of the largest and richest towns I had ever seen, rivalling Paris and was even larger, perhaps, than London. Unlike London, however, it was an almost pleasant place, as far as cities go. While London was just as mercenary and grasping at its heart, it was a magnet primarily for the poor, useless, desperate, degenerate, and the sinful, where Ghent was committed wholly to commerce and the people within were hard working and respectable.

Though there is no getting away from the fact that commerce is a soulless and empty pursuit, it is impossible to deny the benefits that it brought the people of Ghent. Merchants and their wives wore the finest clothes in colourful, embroidered cloth and the homes they built were tall and elegantly apportioned, some rising as if straight from the waters of the river. Their churches were impressive and the cathedral truly glorious. An enormous bell tower, still unfinished with empty scaffolding up two sides, soared above every other structure other than the cathedral's tower and the tower of the Church of Saint Nicholas. Within the city, a man could find the answer to all his needs, if he had enough silver. My needs were to obtain as great a quantity of salted and dried meats as could be carried.

"You may not enter," the porter said from the other side of the bridge.

"We carry no pestilence," I replied in French. "Our coin is good. I wish to spend a great deal of it."

The conversation was shouted across the short span of the

bridge because the porter's guards had ordered us to stop on the far side. Not that I would have forced the issue but two of the men held crossbows which they loaded and held ready and that demonstrated quite well that they meant what they said.

"None may enter," he replied.

"Do you have the pestilence?" I called out.

"No!" the porter snapped. "And we shall keep it this way. Be off with you, you French dogs."

Walt snorted. "Charming folk, the Flemish, ain't they."

I sighed. "They are merely protecting themselves." Raising my voice, I held a purse, heavy with coins, aloft. "This is for the men who allow us entry."

Three of the guards turned to the porter with hopeful expressions on their faces but the man cursed me and assured us that no man would enter, not for all the silver in England.

"What did he say about England?" Walt asked, putting his hand to his sword.

"Never mind that, Walter. We shall try the town of Brussels, further to the east. It has high walls but the men are not so full of their own importance as these bastards. We shall be there tomorrow before nightfall if we make good time."

The land all around Ghent was marshy but usually firm enough for them to raise so many sheep that the landscape seemed to be made from wool. Yet the rains had turned those grassy fields to ponds and the sheep were long gone. After another night sleeping like outlaws in the trees, we continued on the road to Brussels. It rose above the marshy land and so the going was far easier and we made it soon after midday.

Brussels was open and they welcomed us, for visitors had been fewer than they had ever known it.

"Pah!" a red-faced old innkeeper said. "That pestilence will never come to Brussels. We are good folk here, good folk, I say." He lowered his voice and glanced over his shoulder. "Other than my wife. She will certainly be afflicted. But, such is life." He shrugged.

His wife showed us to our bedchamber and she was a strongly built, rather handsome young woman who seemed perfectly decent to me.

"What on earth do you suppose that fellow meant about his wife?" I asked Walt over our beer and food later that evening.

"She be a harlot, sir," Walt said, hunched low over his pie and speaking with his mouth full, spraying flecks of pastry and gravy over the table.

I looked at the woman as she carried mugs of beer to a group of inebriated guildsmen on the other side of the ale room. "She seems to be a perfectly ordinary ale-wife."

Walt shook his head, still without looking up at me. "Pinched my arse, sir."

"She did what?"

"Earlier, sir, when you were looking at the bed. She pinched my arse and give me a saucy wink, she did."

"Why on earth would she pinch your arse and not mine?"

He considered it for a while before pointing at me with his knife. "You're too good for her, sir. A knight such as yourself is. You're pretending you're just an ordinary squire of middling means but it's clear as day from your bearing and manner that you're a man with noble blood and a practised harlot don't want to be getting involved with the upper crust or it'll be more than fines she'll be paying in court."

After regarding me warily for a moment, he continued to attack the meat within his pie.

"Are you mocking me, Walter?"

He looked up, aghast, radiating innocence. "Me, sir? Never, sir. Wouldn't even occur to me, sir."

I nodded slowly and he let out a breath before guzzling his beer and studiously picking the chunks of liver from every corner of the pastry crust.

It occurred to me that Stephen may have been right about Walter. I had perhaps been underestimating the depth of the cunning in my companion for many years. Never having spent so much time alone in his company before, I had always assumed his occasionally perceptive observations on the world were mere chance but I felt like I had just had a glimpse of his true self. His mask had slipped and the man beneath was illuminated.

Walt burped, cuffed his mouth and picked at something deep within his nose. I could not decide if he was truly so uncouth or if he was playing it up in the hope of throwing me off.

"What do you think of me, Walt?" I asked him.

He froze, one finger up his nostril. "Sir?" he replied, pulling it out.

"Do you wish me to repeat myself?"

"Just don't understand what you want from me, sir."

"You do not hold out much hope for our success in this venture, do you?"

He shrugged. "Seems like you always win when it comes to a fight, sir."

"Ah. But it seems like I always lose when it comes to everything else?"

"Don't rightly know about that, sir. But we been looking for the knight of the black banner for a long old time. Two years, is it? And we can't find him nowhere. Now, with this new fellow, you reckon you'll go to some distant land you ain't ever even been to before and find a man you ain't never met and who you don't even know the name of. Don't seem possible, is all."

I nodded. "I would agree with you but for the fact that the knight of the black banner knows we are looking for him and he is hiding. He is most probably travelling around from place to place. Or he was one of the knights of France who has put away his black banner and his black armour and is posing as an ordinary lord, in plain sight. Whereas the man we are searching for lives in a cave, and so can be found in one place. Hiding, perhaps, yet known to the folk of the surrounding area as a wolf man. As something ancient and terrible. All we need do is find stories of this wolf man in the towns and villages and search the local woods for traces of such a creature until we find him. It should be rather simple. Not easy, perhaps, but simple."

Walt scratched his face. "I suppose I don't really need to understand it, do I, sir."

A wise fool, indeed. "No, Walter."

He nodded, downed the rest of his beer, glanced around at the innkeeper for a moment and lowered his voice. "Right then, sir. That cuckold seems busy. I got to meet the alewife in the cellar about now so I will most likely see you on the morrow."

After Brussels, we headed south and passed through a landscape that I would come to know over four centuries later through battles at Quatre Bras and Waterloo. All I knew then was that it was Wallonia and that the villages and hamlets were terrified of outsiders. They hid from us or threatened us from a distance to keep away and we were glad to do so.

Our way south was hindered by the Ardennes, a land of dense forest and awkward hills, much fought over by Charlemagne. Assuming it might be hard going, I still decided to cut through the region rather than going around it by heading directly east but we found the road into a valley blocked by felled trunks. It was manned by a group of villeins who were wet and mud-stained but were armed with spears and bows and a few put on their helms as I approached on my horse. Walt was behind me to my left with the two pack horses.

"Good day, good fellows," I said. "We wish to pass through this land on our journey to the south."

"French, are you?" the lead man asked from behind their barricade. He gripped his spear so hard that his fingers were white.

Whether they considered themselves to be friends or enemies of the French, I could not guess, as in that area it could have been either.

"How much is it to pass?" I asked.

"Answer the question, Frenchman!" another fellow called from the rear.

I grinned. "Why, we are Englishmen and friends to all the folk of these parts."

"English!" they cried, and levelled their weapons at us and all began talking at once. Some to each other, most shouting insults and curses at us. I had no idea what the English had done to them but it mattered not.

"Please," I said, holding up my empty hands. "By God, will you listen? We mean no harm."

Walt rode forward from behind me. "Come on, sir," he shouted. "Let's be off from—"

I watched a crossbowman aim at Walt and I drew my sword. The bow clanked and the bolt shot straight and flew true. Without thinking, I swung my sword and knocked the bolt aside with a terrible clang that jarred my arm to my shoulder. Our horses, untrained in the ways of war, decided that they would much rather be elsewhere and we retreated, dragging our other horses after us until we were well clear of the men and their barricade.

"By God, sir," Walt said, "you knocked the bolt right out of the air."

"By God, so I did," I replied, laughing.

"We should go back there and slaughter the lot of them," Walt said, his face clouding over. "They would have murdered me, sir. Murdered me!"

"They were simply protecting their families from the pestilence. Even that fellow who sent a shot at you may not have meant to do so. You know what the levies are like. No nerves at all."

"Even so. It is the principle of the thing. The insult of it can't go unpunished, sir."

I must admit, I was tempted, and Walt could see it on my face. With a start, I realised that he was attempting to manipulate me by putting it in terms he thought I would respond to. Do my men truly see me as prickly as all that, I wondered.

"It is not worth the lost time," I said, finally. "We shall go back to the crossroads."

He said nothing but I sensed he had lost a little of the regard he held me in. For some reason, that bothered me.

∞ ∞ ∞

"Paris is filled with the dead," the priest said. "Fifty thousand, at least. Some say one hundred thousand. Rouen, too, is destroyed. Amiens has filled its graveyards, dug new ones, and filled those, too. The dead lie now in their beds, corrupted. Everywhere in France, it is the same."

We met him on the road and, unlike most other travellers we had seen, he was keen for our company. His name was Simon and he was heading home to Strasbourg from his parish in Normandy, where he swore that every one of his parishioners had died. The man had lost his horse at some point and was walking in shoes that were almost entirely worn away and his feet were in a terrible, disgusting state.

"Flanders yet fares well," I said. "They closed their towns."

Simon shook his head. "Sensible folk, the Flemish. Bunch of bastards. They do not have the pestilence at all? That is good."

Walt spoke up. "It's there alright. Cattle wandering without herdsmen in the fields. Barns and wine-cellars standing wide open. House after house empty and few people to be found anywhere. Fields lying uncultivated. It's there, sir."

"Ah. As it is all across France." He shook his head. "What did Man do to deserve such punishment? Are we not punished enough with our daily travails?"

"Some are saying this is the end of all things, brother," I said. "What do you say to that?"

"It may well be so," he replied, sighing and looking up at the darkness. "For how can those that live now go on in a world such as this? Perhaps when we are all dead, we shall all then rise and see Heaven made upon the Earth." He put his head in his hands and sobbed.

Walt leaned forward and held out a skin. "Some wine to ease your suffering, sir?"

Simon jerked up and snatched it from him. "Praise God," he said.

We each of us drank and in the morning we found that Simon had stolen one of our horses and some of our food and wine.

"I shall murder him," Walt said, shaking where he stood. "I'll bloody tear his throat out."

"Not before I do," I said.

But he had sold us a duck. He was most certainly not on the road to Strasbourg and we never found him before we doubled back and went on our original way again.

"All is well," I said. "We have one spare mount and coin enough to yet to buy another."

In truth, I cursed myself for trusting any soul and resolved not to let any man near us again. Walt was furious with himself and with me and he was mercifully silent for days on end.

We came to a small town named Saarbrucken where we found the people dying in great numbers of the sickness and so we did not enter for long. Bodies were being born in great numbers to the churches. Few spoke to us at all, save to warn us off but they did so without any malice. The dead were everywhere and the living were broken. Curates and parish clerks could barely keep up and they looked as though they were dead on their feet.

Passing on as quickly as we were able, we came to a well-fortified city called Stuttgart, where the buildings were grand and clean but the people were miserable and fearful.

A hooded monk, old and drawn, hobbled over to us with his hands folded into his belly.

"This is our punishment. All must repent. Confess. And repent."

"Yes, yes," I said, trying to ignore him.

"Do you know of the tale of a wild man of Swabia? A man like a wolf. Some call him the Ancient One."

The monk lurched away from me, muttering a prayer before seeming to lose his thoughts. "A ball of fire was seen above Vienna! Pestilential flame. The bishop exorcised it from the skies, praise God, and it fell to the ground. Praise God. A pillar of flame rises above Paris, from the depths of the city into the Heavens. Fire!" He stood as upright as he seemed able and raised his hands as he spoke.

"Stand back from him, sir," Walter said, drawing me away. "He has the plague."

I noticed then that the man's hands were black and rotten. Someone nearby shouted for the guards. As he was dragged away, his hood fell down and a woman screamed at the ruin of his face.

"He was a leper," I said to Walt. "Not a plague carrier."

Walt shrugged. "Same thing, ain't it?"

Heading further into the town, I kept an eye out for any man who might be likely to help me. A well-travelled man would be best, respectable in ordinary times but in dire need of silver and gold.

"Have you seen her?" a little girl with a pink face asked me in the marketplace. She was well dressed and the servant who was supposed to be taking care of the girl was instead arguing with a wine merchant about his prices. The child was perhaps ten years old and had spoken in good French, no doubt having heard me conversing with Walter.

"Have I seen who?" I asked the little girl.

She lowered her voice. "The *Pest Jungfrau.*"

"The Plague Maiden?" I said. "I never heard of her before. Who is she?"

The pale little girl was as delicate as a winter flower. Her big grey eyes filled her face. "A ghost. She flies across the land as a blue flame, spreading the plague. She flies from the mouths of the dying to look for her next hale body to fill with death. My mother died. My father will die, also. I think that I shall die soon."

"Take heart, dear girl. You may yet—"

The servant woman whipped about, seized the child's arm and dragged her away while giving me an evil glare.

"Poor child," I said to Walt. "How potent is their fantasy.

People are so impressionable, they can die of imagination itself."

"*Have* you seen it, sir? The Plague Maiden?"

"For God's sake, Walt."

Stuttgart had taken the view that the pestilence was a punishment from God and that their only salvation could come from being free from sin. The town fathers had acted to shore up moral standards by forcing unmarried cohabiting couples to either marry or separate. Swearing, playing dice and working on the Sabbath became crimes punishable by the harshest fines and penalties. No bells were to be rung at funerals, no mourning clothes were to be worn and there were to be no more gatherings at the houses of the dead to honour the departed souls. New graveyards were dug and all the plague dead were taken there rather than to their family plots.

Men came to close the market even while we were negotiating our purchases and they turfed us out.

"It has been noted that deaths are more numerous about the marketplaces," one of the kindlier officials explained in English. "And so we close the marketplaces. God be with you."

"Please!" I said. "We are travelling south, seeking tales of a wolf man. Some call him the Ancient One."

"By God," the man said. "You are madmen."

"Perhaps but have you heard of such a man?"

He shook his head, looking around to check that his fellows were not listening, and lowered his voice before speaking. "There is a wolf man in the *Schwarzwald*. Or many of them, perhaps. The tales are told to children to stop them going into the forest. It does not work."

"In the *Schwarzwald*? The Black Forest? We have heard much talk of this place. Can you direct us to it?"

He scoffed. "It begins here," he replied, pointing to the southwestern gate.

"Begins?" I said. "Where does it end?" I had a feeling I would not like the answer.

"I do not know. A hundred miles? Two weeks on horseback? The hills are large and many. The forest is dense and ancient. I must go now."

"Thank you for your—"

He grabbed my shoulder. "Do not go into the *Schwarzwald*." Before I could answer, he turned and strode away.

"What now, sir?" Walt asked.

"We go into the Black Forest."

1 2

THE BLACK FOREST

AN ANCIENT FALLEN FIR TREE allowed us the space to look out across the wooded mountain ranges to the south. The track we had taken up the hill wound its way down the other side and disappeared amongst the deep green needles of the pines below us. On the other side of the narrow valley rose hill after hill, growing fainter until they were lost in a white mist and merged with the sky. Smoke drifted above the dense canopy here and there. Somewhere, perhaps miles distant, a single axe blade smacked steadily into a trunk, the sound echoing between the hills. I could make out a handful of shapes that might be houses.

"God help us," Walt said. "We have no hope. None."

"Nonsense, man. We must keep on to the next village. And then the next. Someone will know of the Ancient One."

He mumbled under his breath as I led my horse on down the

track but I heard him clearly enough. "I'll be the bloody ancient one at this rate."

After Stuttgart, we had asked in the marketplace of a very fine little town named Calw about the man that we sought and had been led by a leather worker to an old woodsman who sat drinking in a beer hall. Only after buying him a half-dozen mugs of ale did his tongue loosen. The leather worker, whose name was Conrad, explained to me in French what the old man was saying.

"He says this Ancient One, the man who is sometimes a wolf, lives deep in the forest. That all woodsmen know to leave his lands alone and to fell no trees there."

"Ask him where, man. Where?"

"He says it would be very bad for you to go to this place."

"Surely, that is my business. Tell him I wish to know. I will pay him for the knowledge. I shall pay you, also, if you get the truth out of him."

"He says he swore to his father never to reveal this secret. He cannot do it for any money. He wishes us to leave now."

Walt cleared his throat and leaned into my ear. "Could always beat it out of him, sir?"

I shook my head. We would need a translator willing to participate in a crime and if we were caught we would be strung up by the local lord and his bailiffs.

"If he knows of the Ancient One, others will also know. We will continue."

Conrad agreed to act as our translator and guide, for a sizable sum, and so we went south and a little to the west, into the dark beneath the trees. Three days, we had picked our way into the northern Black Forest, before reaching that high ridge and looking out at the seemingly impenetrable mass of deep green.

Our guide, Conrad, had lost his parents and sister to the pestilence and his father's business was almost entirely without custom. He claimed he was unafraid of the forest and that the people were perfectly reasonable folk. When it came to the stories of the Wolf Man, he said he had heard them from other children growing up but his parents had forbidden him to speak of such nonsense. It was all a little close to heathenry for good Christian people. But no one knew any details. Only the hunters, the charcoal makers, the woodsmen and swineherds knew the details and most of them would never speak of such things openly and never to outsiders.

"All I need is one man who knows," I replied. "One man who knows on which mountain to search. Which valley to scour."

On the fourth day, we came to Hausach, a small village nestled on the flat bottom of a steep-sided valley.

It seemed as though everyone was dead.

The graveyard was lined with freshly-filled graves and a long trench had been dug as if ready to accept a host of bodies. Yet it was empty, and the sides had begun to crumble into the waterlogged hole.

"We should not enter this place," Conrad said, in between muttered prayers.

"He ain't wrong, sir," Walt said, speaking softly. "Horses are nervy."

"Nonsense," I said. "We have walked through pestilential lands before and remain free from the sickness. Come, now."

But nothing could convince our guide to continue on and Conrad took his payment and fled back to Calw as fast as his pony would carry him.

Walt climbed back into his saddle. "Well, I suppose we don't need one who speaks the local tongue if everyone is dead."

The next village was far smaller and seemed as though it had been abandoned for over a year.

"We need to find local people, Walter. They must be out there in the hills and under the trees but how can we find them?"

"Never many people in the woods in the best of days, is there, sir. If you want people, you find a town. To find a town, you follow the widest tracks."

"That will take us away from the deep woods," I argued. "And I know my grandfather is here. Somewhere. I can feel him."

Walt frowned and looked at me strangely before shrugging. "Going forward sometimes means going backward. You said that to me years ago."

"I very much doubt it. But we must find local people so let us go on."

On the empty road to Freiburg, a rainstorm began late in the afternoon that was heavy enough to make travelling further almost impossible and we walked our horses into the trees to look for a dense copse or ideally a rocky cliff to shelter against until it passed. A track led to a very fine stopping place consisting of a short defile that was narrow enough for a few tree trunks to have been thrown across them to create a crude roof.

We slowed as we approached because someone was already there.

Loosening my cloak, I checked that my weapons were free to be drawn quickly and let my horse trail far behind me to make space. Walter began to draw his sword but I waved him back. Walking into a travellers' camp with a drawn sword is as sure a way as any to start a fight.

"Good evening," I called out in French, raising my voice over the cacophony of the ongoing deluge. "We are simple travellers, seeking shelter."

Between the ten- or twelve-foot high rock outcrops on either side and beneath the roof was no more than a small family and a smoky little fire sputtering in the rain. A man stood with his son and behind them was the wife and a young girl. They were all soaked through and fearful.

"God be with you, good fellow. May we share your fire?" I asked as I approached, smiling. "We shall build it higher. We have food that we will share with you. We do not have the pestilence, as I am sure you can see. Lower your hood, Walt, show them your face."

The wife hissed something but the man looked us over and nodded. Presumably my wealth was obvious enough to allay his initial fears. The son glared with open hostility but was dutiful enough to follow the lead of his father as they took their seats on the logs around the fire.

"My name is Richard and my servant is Walter. Where do you come from, sir?" I asked as we settled ourselves.

The wife glared at the husband and he hesitated but he knew that to not answer at all would be extremely rude.

"Basel."

"Ah," I said. "You are heading north?"

Again, he hesitated before answering. "East." His French was heavily accented.

Walt busied himself splitting logs to one side and I left him to it.

"Is it bad in Basel?" I asked. He said nothing. "Of course, it is bad everywhere. Is the pestilence lesser in the East? We are heading southward but I do not know what our final destination will be as I am searching for a man, for a story of a man. Perhaps you have heard of a wildman who lives in the woods hereabouts? Some call him the Ancient One, or the Wolf Man. Have any other travellers mentioned such a man?"

The husband was confused and his wife scowled at his side. The son's eyes were wide with anger which was clearly aimed at me. He saw me as a threat to the safety of his family, which I most certainly was.

"We have heard nothing like that," the woman said, in rather good French, though there was something about it that made me look closer at her, and all of them.

The light was poor, her clothes were heavy and her hair was entirely covered. And she was drenched but she had a particular look to her. Pretty, in fact, and younger than her demeanour had suggested but her complexion was dark. It was a look that the husband had also, and of course the children were the same.

"What was your profession in Basel, sir?" I asked.

Both the wife and the son looked frightened and glanced at the husband, who clenched his jaw for a moment before looking down at his hands. His wife tutted and turned away. The son glared at his father with contempt, which he then turned on me.

"Are you Jews?" I asked but I already knew the answer. Walt stopped chopping wood and stared at them.

"We are travellers, heading east," the husband said, not meeting my eye.

"You are travelling alone? Just the four of you? How do you mean to protect yourself against those who would do you harm?"

The boy jumped to his feet, eyes filled with emotion. The father pulled him down while his mother scolded him. The little girl continued to bury her face in her mother's flank.

It was perhaps an unfair question to ask because clearly they had no protection and little hope of getting wherever it was they were going. Even in the best of times it would have been unlikely that a man such as he would have been able to long protect his woman on the wilder stretches of road. And at that time, when it appeared to be the end of the world and the civilising effects of the law was falling to pieces about us, they had no hope at all.

"Why do you not hire guards?" I asked him.

He scoffed and rolled his eyes, which was a strange response.

"Not all Jews are wealthy," the woman said, glancing at her husband. I took this to be a barbed comment aimed at her husband's failings but he nodded vigorously.

"We be very poor people, sir, and have nothing to offer anyone."

Now he had raised my suspicions, for no Jew took pride in his poverty, as a good Christian might.

"Not all wealth comes in the form of coin and gold, sir," I said, looking at his pretty young wife.

He looked horrified but she sat up straighter and held my gaze. The boy again stirred himself as if he was about to leap to his mother's defence but she muttered some foreign words to him and he sullenly stayed where he was.

"Perhaps we could pay you, then," the wife said, straightening the sides of her headdress and smoothing her clothing over her body. Even through the thick woollen layers, her womanly shape was quite apparent.

Despite myself, my ardour was raised. Without conscious thought, I entertained the idea of taking the woman to some sheltered spot close by to lay with her. It would have to be done against a tree or over some fallen trunk. She was offering herself in return for ongoing protection on the road, or even out of the hope that I would not murder her family that very night and take her anyway, before killing her, too. Rather rapidly, my ardour cooled.

The husband was looking down, while the woman looked at me steadily. She shook, ever so slightly. The strength of a woman, in what she is willing to suffer to protect her family, is the most powerfully-felt force in the world. Yet it is worthless without the physical and moral strength of a man to protect her. And her man was a weakling.

"I cannot travel with you eastwards," I said, "as my task takes me elsewhere. If we had been headed in the same direction, I would have protected you without any form of payment." The woman sagged, then, looking down. She took a deep breath. "But I would urge you to spend whatever coin you have to hire proper guards to escort you."

"We did," the wife said, glaring at me again. "They robbed us on the third day. They took all of our money, our jewellery. They even took my husband's and my son's weapons. Could you not escort us, good sir? Some of the way at least?"

"I can do no more than wish that God goes with you."

They nodded, sadly.

Walt approached and began to build up the fire.

"Was it you?" he asked them. "Was it you what poisoned the wells?"

"Walter," I chided him. "We are guests at their fire, are we not?"

He was surprised. "But they be Jews, sir. I mean no harm by asking but ain't it a fair question? I just want to know, is all."

"We poison nothing," the man said. "Never. Nothing."

I nodded. "It would not be the likes of these good folk, Walt. It would have been the elders and the priests of their tribe who did the poisoning. Besides, the learned physicians are certain that the pestilence is due to miasmas released from within the Earth, due to an alignment of the planets."

"Our elders poisoned nothing," the man said, sullenly. "We are innocent."

Walt scoffed. "The Jews might be many things but they ain't innocent, sir. We let you live in our towns, let you grow rich off our backs. You people are like fleas infesting our clothes, feasting on our blood. And this is how you repay us?"

Him and his boy stirred again but I knew they would do nothing. They were weaklings and soon they would be taken on the road and they would be murdered, for one reason or another.

"Leave them be, Walt," I said. "You are right that their people are never to be trusted by good Christian folk but here before us is nothing but a poor family who need our charity."

"Charity is for Christians, sir," Walt said, with such certainty that I hesitated to correct him. Possibly he was right, for I was never much of a theologian. "What was your profession, sir? Were you a money lender?"

"I am a goldsmith," he said, with pride.

"There you are, then, Sir Richard," Walt said, immensely pleased with himself. "A bloody goldsmith. What more do you want, eh? I never understood none of it my whole life. What do you want to live in our towns for anyway, goldsmith? Living protected by our walls, protected by our soldiers, eating our bread what we grew with our own hands. And what do we get for it?" He held up a hand and counted off on his fingers. "You steal our babies for your blood magic, you poison our fountains and wells and kill us off for no reason, you creep about at night changing into animals, you pretend to be one of us when it suits you while at the same time you demand special treatment because you ain't Christians, and... and..." he flailed around, desperate to find a fifth outrage so he could close his thumb also. "And usury. I cannot fathom why we allow them in our kingdoms at all, Sir Richard, can you? Of all the people of the world, the least trustworthy of all are—"

"All right, Walt," I said, "that's quite enough of your philosophising for one night, I think." I turned to the woman. "I do apologise for my servant. You will please excuse his shamelessness and general uncouthness. His intellectual deficiencies come not only from the lowness of his birth but I fear he is also halfway to being a Welshman."

The rain eased off and then stopped halfway through the night. Walt and I took turns to sleep because even though the man was weak, his son or the wife had enough heart to run us through and steal our horses if we let our guard down. Jews were devious, it was common knowledge, and I still wondered if the man could be trusted. They, too, watched us warily through to morning.

As we packed our belongings and prepared the horses in the halflight beneath the saturated, heavy forest, I watched askance as they loaded their sawbacked old pony.

"You said your guards stole everything from you," I said. It was quite clear that they had secreted something of value on their persons that the guards did not find, which they then used to purchase the packhorse and other supplies. If they had remaining valuables then I meant to impress on them that they needed to invest in protection, in spite of their previous failure in that regard. "How much do you have left?"

"Nothing," the man said, bitterly. "Be on your way, now."

"You cheeky bastard," Walt said, placing his hand on his sword hilt. "You be speaking to a great lord and you will show him the proper respect or I'll knock you into next week. You and your shit-brained boy. Hear that, lad? You want a thrashing and all, I take it?"

Stepping between them, I spoke to my soldier servant. "Peace, Walter."

He muttered under his breath but calmed himself and carried

on doing his duty.

"Go on, then," I said to the family, indicating the track back to the road. The man pushed his wife and the girl ahead of him and I was pleased to see his fear that I would do him harm. The boy led the horse by me and I stepped in his way. He was about thirteen and had his mother's good looks though he had the weak build and narrow chest of his people. His bitterness and anger and fear were understandable, considering what was happening in the world.

"Your father cannot protect your mother and sister," I said to him and I handed over one of my swords.

The lad was shocked but he snatched it quickly enough and hurried by me. He did not thank me.

"Why in the name of God did you do that, Sir Richard?" Walt asked, incredulous.

"It was a useless old sword," I said.

"I liked that sword," Walt said.

Blamed as they were for the plague, Jews were soon being massacred from Toulon to Barcelona and from Flanders to Basel and Strasbourg. Many were burned in their homes by the terrified townsfolk who believed that they were protecting themselves and their families while also taking revenge for the Christian deaths already caused. Others were executed by their towns or hacked down by angry mobs.

The Church pronounced that Jews were innocent of spreading the plague and the nobility of Europe issued edicts condemning the violence and sought to protect the victims.

In some places, such as Mainz, the Jews took the initiative and murdered the townsfolk first, resulting in massive reprisals from the populace. In more generous places, the Jews were given the chance to renounce their faith and become Christians, which many did. Those that did not were then righteously slaughtered. Tensions were so high that in other towns the Jews barricaded themselves in their own homes before killing themselves and their families rather than to allow the townsfolk the satisfaction of committing the acts themselves. Some even burned their homes down around themselves to deny the Christians the plunder of their worldly goods.

In time, the massacres lost momentum and ceased. Perhaps the townsfolk finally noticed that the Jewish people also died from the pestilence in great numbers. And it is the nature of mass hysteria that its manic energies cannot be maintained for long.

All of this began the eastward movement of Europe's Jewry to Poland and Russia. I do not know why the Poles gave refuge to the Jews. Walt had questioned why they wanted to live in Christian towns at all but it was clear to me. The Saracens had conquered the Holy Land and being subjugated by the Mohammedans was far worse than living amongst us, good and tolerant Christian folk. Still, they did not truly belong anywhere in Europe and they never would do, because it was not their land. They would always be regarded as strangers amongst us.

As I rode away that morning, I reflected that their plight as a people in some small way reflected my own. I was a man who did not belong but who had nowhere else to go. I existed within my society while forever being outside of it. In order to avoid persecution, I was forced to sometimes pretend to be something that I was not. Perhaps that was why I felt such sympathy for them, despite their dourness and possible hand in causing or spreading the pestilence.

It is likely that the family we met were murdered by robbers before they had gotten very much further along the road to the East. In the dark depths of that plague, strangers of any kind meant danger for desperate locals and had little value beyond what could be taken from them.

Shortly after our encounter with those poor people, Walter and I fell to calamity and sudden violence.

∞ ∞ ∞

It was an ordinary enough village, from a distance. A small number of painted timber houses, some rather large, clustered about a fine stone church. The river was clear and fresh and swift flowing before widening and slowing as it passed by the village.

"Graves, sir," Walt said, nodding to them as if I had not seen it. As if I had not already smelt the death.

"Let us pray that some yet live," I said.

It seemed at first that the place had fallen entirely but there was woodsmoke in the air and a large goat stood tethered to a post in a garden, chewing and watching us pass with its evil eyes. In the village square before the church, I felt other eyes on me. Human eyes, I was certain of it.

"Good day," I called out, in as friendly a shout as possible, hoping one of the survivors spoke French. "We are simple travellers looking to purchase supplies. Can you help us, please?"

A scraping sound brought me around to face the church as a priest emerged in his robe, wiping his mouth on a cloth. When I raised my hand in greeting, he smiled and came out from the church door, holding his cloth to his mouth.

"You are welcome," he said from behind his cloth. "Welcome indeed, sirs, to Wolfach. You come from France? In the name of God, I pray that you have news of how the plague fares there?"

"France, yes," I replied. "My name is Richard and this is my servant."

The priest was looking at me very strangely and I thought that he had detected the form of Norman French I spoke and perhaps even suspected that I was an Englishmen. His own version of French was quite different from mine, rather idiosyncratic in truth, with strange turns of phrase and I had to listen carefully to catch his meanings.

"Ah, pray forgive my manners. It has been the most trying time I have ever known and my mind is not what it was. My name is Peter. You must be hungry and tired from the road. Come, come. We shall find you something."

I dismounted and made for the church.

"No," Peter said. "Not there. We shall go to the inn. My brother is the innkeeper and he will have what we need."

The priest was a well-made fellow and no mistake. Almost of a height with me and broad in the shoulder. Still, not all men who are built for war are suited to it and he seemed to have the manner of a village priest, though he did look fair harrowed by the deaths. The doors to most of the houses were closed and marked with a cross.

"Have many survived, sir?" I asked. Our horses hooves echoed from the plastered walls of the houses.

"Some yet live and breathe, praise God," Peter said. "Enough to keep us alive, as long as no more perish. The dead are with the gods and the village will go on. And that is what matters." He raised his voice as we approached the inn. "Christman! We have visitors."

Before we reached the door, a huge man emerged. He had the look of his brother but taller, broader, with a skull like a granite boulder and arms like tree trunks. He wore a leather apron spattered with blood. When he spoke to his brother in their guttural tongue, his voice was as deep as the lowing of a bullock. After giving us a hostile glare, he ducked back inside.

"So many have died," Peter said. "We who are left must take on the work of the dead. The slaughterman and his sons died months ago. Here, let us sit on the benches out front so we do not have to smell the stench within. I have had my fill of death."

Walt tied the horses and began brushing them down rather than join me and the priest at the bench outside the inn. I knew then that Walt felt it too.

Something was wrong.

"Your brother is a giant, I see," I said to Peter as we sat. I made sure to face the doorway so the innkeeper could not come up behind me. "Are all men in these parts so well made, sir?"

He tilted his head. "Not all. Our father is a large man and all men grow from their father's seed. You yourself come from good stock."

I nodded. "Your father lives?"

Peter looked up at the sky. "Our father lives in another place and we do not know if he lives or if he has died. But I think that he lives." He looked at me suddenly. "To where do you go?"

"We are looking for the town named Freiburg. It is south of here, is that correct?"

"Southwest, beyond this valley toward the Rhine. Three days on good horses, if you are not running. What business do you have there? Are you expected by anyone?"

I sat back and allowed my right hand to fall into my lap so that it was close to my dagger. "Our business is that we are looking for a man." From the corner of my eye, I saw Walt turn to me and shake his head ever so slightly. I knew he trusted this man not a bit and neither did I but he was the first local we had found for days and even if he meant trouble, I thought we could fight our way out. Even the largest mortal, like his brother, was little when compared to my immortal strength.

"A man, you say?" Peter replied, speaking with forced lightness. "What man is that?"

"In truth, I do not know if he is a man at all. For they call him the Ancient One and also the Wolf Man."

The priest froze and stayed perfectly still. It seemed as though the very air around us stopped moving and a silence descended over the village. "Where did you hear those names? Why do you seek him?"

"I would be delighted to tell you. If you know where I might find him. What did you say the name of this village is, sir?"

He chewed on his bottom lip before replying. "Wolfach."

"Wolfach, I see. And is that name related to the tales of the—
"

I was cut short by a cry of warning from Walt.

"Watch out, sir!"

The giant brother, Christman, came charging around the corner of the inn behind me, moving with such speed that I barely had time to register the sight of him. His face, contorted with rage into a savage grin, filled my vision as I jumped up, knocking the bench down behind me and swinging the heavy pine table into the great charging mass.

It crashed into him but he knocked it aside without slowing and threw his weight onto me, wrapping his monstrous great arms about me and dragging me to the floor.

His grip was inhuman.

He held me from behind, so that his back was upon the ground and my heels drummed against the floor. Both of my arms trapped against my body, I struggled and heaved against him. The air was crushed from my chest and I fought for a breath. He may as well have been made from stone. Never, in all my life, had I felt such strength. Not even William's immortals had been so possessed with might. I used the back of my head to hammer at him but met only the flesh of his chest and shoulder.

From the corner of my eye I saw Peter rush to Walt and knock him down with a single blow.

Christman the giant squeezed hard, panting his bloody breath into my ear. I fought to strike him, any part of him, with my feet. Tried to roll him over so I might stand and throw him. I could find no purchase.

216

I was dying. Suffocating. My vision growing dark at the edges.

Walt leapt up, ran quickly to the nearest saddle and grabbed for a weapon. It was not there. I had gifted it to the boy on the road.

Peter stepped up behind him and stabbed a dagger into his back, over and over. Stabbing him in the chest and belly as he fell beneath the hooves of the terrified horses. Stabbed him a dozen times.

The giant grunted and squeezed harder, popping ribs and dislocating one of my shoulders.

I could not take a breath.

The world turned black.

13

THE ANCIENT ONE

THE PAIN told me that I was not dead.

Not yet.

I came back to myself slowly. Somehow, I sensed that I had been out cold for some time. Men on either side of me, holding me up between them, dragged me forward deeper into the blackness of a tunnel. The bare rock on either side and the rough floor beneath suggested I was in a cave.

My hands were bound. I was naked and shivering. The pain in my crushed chest and disjointed shoulder burned as they jostled me, handling me roughly as if I was a bag of meat.

My captors were Peter the false priest and Christman the giant who had crushed my body. I wondered if one of them was the Ancient One I was searching for.

Or if they taking me to him.

Either way, I felt a deep horror of how I had been bested and overpowered by those men. I was at their mercy.

There was no question of overpowering them. And yet I would not allow them to do whatever they were intending to do to me. I imagined that they were going to slaughter me. It seemed as though they were bringing me into some foul pagan grotto where I would be sacrificed.

It was the only explanation. The oppressive chill of the place seeped into my bones and the mass of the hard stone above bore down on me from all around. My bare feet dragged on the cold, damp gravel floor. Close echoes of their footsteps sounded in my ears.

I resolved to break free the moment they reached whatever destination they had in mind.

Perhaps they intended to chant their way through some depraved pagan ritual before slitting my throat but in case they proceeded without ceremony I would have to take the first hint of an opportunity.

Even if fighting were hopeless, even if it ultimately led to my death, I would not allow myself to die on my knees.

Light.

Up ahead, the walls reflected the yellow of candlelight and the hurried steps of my captors slowed. The smell of woodsmoke filled the cave and I imagined that they had some pagan fire up ahead that they would use to burn me alive.

I forced myself to relax, lest they sense I was about to break free and tear their heathen hearts from their chests.

We rounded a final corner whereupon they halted, threw me

forward with considerable force so that I landed on my front with my bound arms outstretched before me. The impact jarred me to the bone.

Before I could even catch my breath, I heard Peter and Christman retreating rapidly back the way we had come. None had spoken a word.

When I rolled over, I was struck by an image of domesticity.

A young woman leaning over a blackened pot that was suspended over a small hearth fire. She paid me no mind at all as she stirred the contents and the smell of food wafted from the pot. She wore a simple dress and her hair was covered.

Ordinary domestic furniture completed the space, with a table and two stools, a long bench for the preparation of food and the storage of earthenware. It was merely the fact that the walls of this home were rough-hewn, natural stone that demonstrated I was still within the cave.

I was thoroughly confused.

"What is this?" I asked in French, my voice loud.

The woman glanced at me with no expression on her face. I was startled to see that she was quite lovely. After resting her eyes on me, she glanced over her shoulder and then moved to the bench, turning her back to me.

A figure stirred in the long shadow of a bed set back into a dark alcove on the far side of the cave. I began shifting back, ready to spring to my feet and fight my way free.

"No."

The voice of the shadow was a rumble.

It was him.

The Ancient One.

His form was mere shadow and did not move. He spoke no more and yet I was overwhelmed by a terrible oppressive menace emanating from him.

"I have been looking for you," I said. "I doubted you were real."

He said nothing.

"Do you understand French?" I asked the figure. "I sought you out. I came here to find you. I have questions that I would ask of you."

The shadow stirred and rose. And rose. The man was massive. Tall, broad of shoulder, with a mass of brown hair on his head and a dense beard over a massive jaw. His eyes were deeply wrinkled beneath a jutting brow line and cheekbones. The way he moved was unnerving. He had the fluidity and stillness of a cat stalking a rodent.

"My name is Richard," I said. "My brother William spoke to me of you."

He grunted something and the young woman stepped away behind him without a word, her head lowered. When he moved around the fire toward me, I saw his full stature. He wore no more than a shirt, belted at his waist, and his legs and feet were bare.

His body radiated immense physical power. There was not an ounce of fat on him. The muscles of his legs were ridged and striated. His forearms were likewise crossed with bulging veins and deep ridges, as well as dark patterns on the skin in the form of dots and short lines arranged in clusters.

The Ancient One crouched, his feet crunching the surface of

sand on the compacted dirt floor. The face before mine appeared at first to be that of a robust man aged about forty years old and although his vigour was that of a younger man while his skin also had weathered lines about the eyes, like those of an aged shipmaster.

Those eyes were wide and his terrible gaze was difficult to withstand but I stared back.

My doubts that he was something other than an immortal, like me and my brother, evaporated.

But was he truly our grandfather, as William had claimed? Perhaps he did look like us, in some ways. Sheared and dressed properly, he could have passed for a noble in any court in Christendom.

He snorted and stood, rising above me and looking down.

"You are weak."

His voice was deep and effortlessly powerful. It took me a moment to decipher the words, as they were so heavily accented but he did speak French, of a sort. Every time he spoke, he would use some words in a form of Latin that I could barely comprehend, some words of Greek and other words in languages I did not know and often the order of the words in the sentences were unconventional. It took me time to restructure his sentences into something meaningful but the more he spoke the more I understood him.

"No. I am not weak," I said. "Your men surprised me. I could have freed myself. I hoped that they would bring me to you. I was looking for you."

"Weakness fills you. Pours from you."

He turned his back on me and returned to the bed.

The woman crossed to him and sat on his thigh while he snaked an arm around her waist. He stared at me while she stared through the fire blankly, in the manner of men who have seen too much of war.

I got to one knee, watching him closely for a reaction. When there was none, I stood fully upright before them in my nakedness.

As far as I was concerned, I was the strongest man in the world, other than that monster innkeeper called Christman, the Ancient One before me and, perhaps, William.

My body was powerful and yet my chest and shoulder ached from being crushed and dislocated. Still, I would not allow him to dismiss me so easily.

"Try my strength, then," I said, thrusting up my jaw and looking down my nose. My hands were bound but I was determined to show that I did not fear him. That I could best him.

In truth, he unnerved me.

My whole reason for seeking him out was in the hope that his blood at least would be stronger than mine but I did not expect him to be so imposing and disturbing in demeanour. Few men had ever frightened me. I did not mean to challenge him so in his home but his condemnation had wounded my pride.

He chose not to take me up on my offer. Instead, he looked me up and down, his lip curled and eyebrows raised. His eyes lingered on the mass of bruising on my chest and shoulder.

"Drink."

He spoke and shoved the woman away from him.

With a blank face she pulled up one of her sleeves, revealing a mass of crisscrossing white and pink scar tissue from her wrist to the inside of her elbow.

There was no hesitation before she sliced into her flesh and drained her blood into a wooden cup. This, she handed to me without a word or expression. With my wrists bound together, I lifted it to my lips and drank. It was warm and delicious.

Perhaps there was a hint of disgust in her eyes when she took the cup back from me, or perhaps I imagined it.

She turned away and then busied herself with serving the food at a table in the corner opposite to that of the bed.

Her blood worked on me quickly. My ribs cracked back into place with a sound like the snapping of a bundle of sticks. I rolled my shoulder around and it popped back into place. In mere moments my breathing was returned to normal, the pain was gone and I was at full strength once more.

The Ancient One approached, moving fluidly like a wolf on the hunt, and pulled a short knife from his belt.

I tensed, dreading that he was about to plunge it into my heart or across my throat. Perhaps it would be my only chance to overpower him, I thought, and if I had him at my mercy I could force him to answer my questions.

He came forward and I raised my hands, ready to grapple with him.

Instead, he gently took my hands and cut through the bonds at my wrist with a few expert strokes.

All the while he looked at me. He was taller than I was and

his hands were bigger than mine. I was conscious of my nakedness but I was determined to show no shame and no fear, neither.

When the woman had served the food, she brought me a linen shirt that I pulled on gratefully. She provided no belt and so it hung loose over me but it was better than nothing and I took the stool at the table across from the man who may have been my grandfather.

She brought a bowl of water for me to wash my hands, provided linen to dry them and then served the meal. The mutton and cabbage stew was surprisingly savoury, full of salt and sugar and other spices and I spooned it in just as soon as he began to eat. The hard oatcake served alongside was swiftly softened in the broth and helped to fill my belly.

When all was served, the woman busied herself cleaning the bench, took a pail and walked away into the darkness of the tunnel.

"I came from England," I said, not knowing where else to start. "There is a pestilence. A plague. A great mortality. Across the whole land. The worst the world has ever known."

He scoffed at that and I thought I saw the hint of a smile beneath his beard. "No."

"I assure you, it is quite terrible. Every other man, woman, child. Dead."

He nodded. "Many times, this has happened. When I first conquered this land, the men die before my sword cuts them down."

"When you conquered this land? Do you mean the village? When was that?"

He sat back and picked at his teeth while he looked at me. "Why come to me?"

"My people are dying. My companions. You see, William my brother and I made them immortal with our own blood, many years ago. Two of my companions have fallen ill with this pestilence but drinking human blood does not cure them, as it does for anything else that has ever ailed them. Rather, it cures them for only a few hours but it is not long before they fall ill again."

His face unreadable, he watched me as I spoke and I did not know if he understood anything that I was saying.

"Before my brother William went away to the East, he told me about you. That is to say, he told me that you were powerful. More powerful than I could imagine, he said. Whether he spoke the truth, I do not know, and yet I came to ask if your blood can heal my people."

It was far from the fine speech of introduction that I had rehearsed during the journey to find him but he was so strange that I did not know how to speak to him.

The Ancient One held my gaze. "William told me he made many such men by emptying them of some blood and giving them his to drink. I know what manner of servants you make with this act. Your blood will heal these men."

"And yet it does not. I gave them as much as I could spare and it was not enough."

For a long moment it seemed that he doubted me and then he looked disgusted. "You are weak."

I gripped the edges of the thick table. "I am strong."

"Strength would heal. Heal all ills. If your blood does not heal? This means there is no strength."

"No strength in me?"

He nodded, and gestured with the fingertips of one hand at my heart. "In your blood."

"How can that be? Surely there is some remedy that you know of? Some method of extracting the necessary potency from your blood that I could employ to heal my people?"

He frowned, not following me at all. I tried again.

"Would you give me your blood?" I asked.

"You ask your host for a gift?" he said, mocking me.

It was not merely difficult to understand his words but his meaning was confusing.

"I could give you something in return," I ventured. "I would pay any price."

"Any?"

"Well," I said, thinking of his knife, "almost any."

He snorted and shook his head. Though I struggled to comprehend him, it was clear that I was a profound disappointment to him. Or, at least, that he thought very little of me. Although preening courtiers often looked down on me, it had been such a long time since any man that I respected had displayed such open contempt for my character.

"I apologise, sir." I said, sensing finally that I had rushed headlong into a social transgression by asking for something immediately. Where I had merely hoped to explain why I was searching for him so that he would understand I meant him no harm, in truth I had acted with enormous impropriety. "I would like to speak of myself to you and also to seek your wisdom. I have many questions. Do you know about me? Do you know who I am? My name is Richard."

He inclined his head and touched his fingertips to his chest. "Priskos."

It was a strange name, to my ears at least, and sounded Greek. Whether it was his original given name, or one he had taken for himself, or a title of some sort, I did not know.

"Thank you for welcoming me into your home, Priskos, and for sharing your table with me. Forgive me if I am mistaken but my brother William told me that you were our grandfather. I do not know how such a thing could be possible. My natural father was Robert de Ferrers, an earl of England. A man of Norman birth who traced his ancestors back to before the conquest of England. How could you be his father?"

The woman came back with her pail, heaved it up onto the bench and busied herself cleaning up the meal.

Priskos barely glanced at her, preferring to regard me closely. "Sleep, now," he said after a while, and pointed to the blankets that the woman had laid against one bare stone wall. I would have to sleep on the floor, like a dog or a child.

What could I say? There was so much more to be said. I still did not even know if he could truly help me and time was wasting. Every night I spent away was another night that Eva spent in torment. Assuming she yet lived.

And the men who had ambushed me had murdered Walter.

It was entirely my fault. I should never have trusted that damned priest but he had outwitted me. I should have suspected that he was an immortal. One of William's, at least. And I should never have underestimated the huge innkeeper. My complacency had led to Walter's death and so, even with everything else, I had to find justice for Walter.

How could I get it? Other than taking revenge on the men who had captured me and dragged me hither to the Ancient One.

I was loathe to capitulate so easily to his demands and yet I was a guest and I wanted something from him. Either I had to comply with his commands or defeat him by force.

Even if I could overpower him without his men coming to his aid, I suspected after speaking to him that torturing the knowledge out of him would prove ineffective.

And there was something deeply unnerving about the man. He radiated violence like a wild animal. Like he truly was a wolf wearing the skin of a man.

"Very well," I said. "We can continue our discussion in the morning."

Priskos barely responded, as if it was of no interest to him at all. He grunted something at the woman and retired to his bed while she finished tidying away, extinguished all the candles and went to join him in his bed.

The bare rock floor beneath the blankets was more comfortable than I had expected due to the layer of sand and I quickly fell asleep. I awoke at some point in the night to the sound of vigorous yet brief rutting from across the cave. It was cold.

I wrapped myself tighter, rolled over and thought of Cecilia until I drifted off again. I recalled the way her eyes narrowed and her lips twitched in response to some jest I had made, and how her bosom swelled beneath her dress. *If I ever marry again it shall be for love. Children are a blessing but my heart wants only the companionship of an honourable man.* I resolved once again that I would ask her brother for her hand as soon as I returned. Assuming that she survived the pestilence, of course.

For all I knew, lying in that dark cave so far from home, the whole world could be on its way to annihilation.

As I drifted back to sleep, I wondered if I would even survive my meeting with Priskos, whether I challenged him or not.

∞ ∞ ∞

The cave was empty when I woke in the morning. A lamp was burning on the table but a slither of daylight lanced across the rear wall of the cave from some unseen crevice amongst the folds of the rock roof high above.

Tentatively, I felt my way to the exit and emerged, blinking, into green and orange sunlight. The woodland came right up to the opening and the understorey layer had presumably been allowed to remain dense as a form of concealment.

In no more than my linen shirt and with bare feet, I pushed through off the side of the track to void my bowels. As I was kicking the leaf litter over it, the young woman came crashing through the undergrowth with a bundle of firewood slung over her shoulder, her fair hair unbound, flowing as she bounded past. She wrinkled her nose but otherwise paid me no heed. It dawned on me that I had taken a shit on what amounted to her doorstep and I hurried after her.

"Good morning, good woman," I said. "May I carry that for you?"

She glanced over her shoulder but kept going until she reached a chopping block in small clearing and then dumped it all on the carpet of brown and yellow leaves littering the floor.

Dappled sunlight fell across her hair as she bent to the bundle.

"Allow me, madame," I insisted, dropping to one knee as I untied the bundle and eyed the axe stuck into the block. "Is your husband abroad this morning?"

She pursed her lips in a most fetching manner, then tucked a stray strand of hair behind her ear. It seemed that she understood no French and I did not even bother attempting English. I doubted a commoner such as her would understand much Latin.

Commoner though she must certainly have been to live such a life, she was as pretty as a princess. Although, I had seen plenty of princesses in my time and few enough could hold a candle to that girl waving a bee away from her face that morning in the Black Forest. Perhaps I was love-sick for Cecilia but that girl was strong, womanly, and made a dutiful wife even in a ridiculous dark cave in the woods and I was struck by the outrageousness of it all.

Where was her family, I thought. What on Earth was this Priskos doing with her?

I took up the axe and she stepped back as I swung, splitting the log in one blow.

"We were not properly introduced, madame. My name is Richard."

She bit her lip and looked down, clasping her hands.

"Would you tell me your name, my dear? Where are you from? May I ask how you came to live here?"

The woman looked around. A cold wind gusted through the canopy with a sound like the breaking of waves. After a moment, she opened her mouth to speak to me but then clamped it closed, threw her head down and hunched her shoulders.

Priskos strode toward us from out of the undergrowth. He did not hurry and his face was emotionless so his intentions were unclear but the woman's demeanour caused me concern. I gripped the axe, ready to defend myself.

Instead, he drew to a stop in front of her, placed a finger on her chin and tipped her head up. Her jaw was set and her eyes had returned to that blank stare I had seen on her before, as if she was looking through him. Without a word from either of them, she turned and walked by me, going off into the woods.

Without looking at me, Priskos held out one hand and I knew what he wanted. I handed over the axe, which he took and held by his side.

"You must leave," he said.

I could not allow that. There was no possibility of me leaving empty handed after all I had been through to reach him.

"I will leave when you have told me what I need to know."

Priskos stepped closer to me. His features were even clearer in the daylight and I peered with fascination at his eyes and his nose. Did he look like me? I thought I could see William in his features. The nose was the same. Those eyes were impossibly cold and clear. Perhaps it was my imagination but his eyes seemed to look into me. I felt like a child before him.

"Go home," he said.

"I need your help, sir," I replied. "Priskos, please. You know why I came. Can you help me to find a cure for the pestilence for my people?" I glanced at the bushes that the young woman had walked beyond. "One of them is a woman. My wife."

It was not quite true, of course. We had been married once and though my feelings for her were quite profound, we had not lived together nor laid together as man and wife for a hundred years.

He lifted the axe. I tensed, ready to leap forward to grapple with him. Instead, he rested the haft on his shoulder and tilted his head.

"Your blood cures all."

I stifled a frustrated sigh. We were going in circles. "I have no wish to quarrel with you but I assure you that it does not, sir."

He frowned. "Then, you are weak."

Again, he had said it. He spoke with such certainty that it was like a judgement from a king, or from God Himself.

Even as a child, few had ever called me weak. If anyone but Priskos had accused me of such a thing, I would have laughed in his face, and then crushed him.

But the conviction of his repeated accusation wounded me deeply.

"I am strong," I said, sounding like an impudent child even to myself. In response, he sneered. That made my blood boil. "Try my strength, then," I snapped, and stepped up to him. "Try it, sir. Try me."

For a moment, he appeared shocked and I was certain that he was going to explode with violence.

He laughed in my face and clamped a massive hand on my shoulder. "You should not be. I did not wish to make you. Your father did not know what you are. Your brother did not know. You are ignorant. But this not of your making." He thumped me on the arm with a friendly blow as powerful as a kick from a horse. "Come."

With a casual flick of his wrist, he buried the axe in the chopping block so quickly that I barely saw it. The head of the axe was buried almost to the hafting.

I followed Priskos back into his cave, where he indicated I should sit at his table once again. He served me with strong beer and sat in front of me.

"Your father? He is my son. I did not intend to make him." He turned to look at the entrance to his curiously domestic cave. "A man needs woman. Many years, I have been here, in this place. I take woman, she serves me until she grows old and weak. Then I take new woman."

He drank a gulp from his beer and wiped his lips and beard.

Many questions sprang to mind and I chose one. "What happens to the old woman?"

"I honour her."

"How do you honour her?"

"I drink her. I bury her."

My stomach churned, even though I had suspected it would be something like that.

"But why not let them go, sir? When they have fulfilled their usefulness to you? Surely they can do you no harm? Would it not be more honourable to let them live?"

He pressed his lips together as he regarded me. I was beginning to perceive that when he looked at me in such a manner, he was thinking one thing about me.

Weak.

"Blood gives strength. An old woman's blood is weak but this honours them. This is their final duty to their lord. Their offering. Their sacrifice."

I wanted to ask about the woman he had in his power now but I was already, in my heart, intending to rescue her from him and I did not wish to alert him to my concern for her.

"You said my father was your son," I said instead. "But who was my grandmother?"

He took a deep breath and a slight smile appeared beneath his beard. "Cunning woman. She bested me." He laughed, like a growl. "First in thousand years."

I wondered how old he was. "How did she best you?"

"I choose to not spill seed into woman. I choose not to make sons." He shrugged. "In this, some of times, I fail. I fill a woman. When her belly grows, I drink her. Take new woman."

"If your woman gets with child, you kill her?" It was monstrous. He was a beast. A demon. "Why? Why not allow them to bear children?"

He shook his head. "I make bad sons."

"Bad how?"

He licked his lips and pressed them together before answering. "Some are weak in mind, like Christman. Some are quick and

236

wise but fall to ambition, as did Caesar. Some try to kill me, their father, as Peter one day will. I see it in him. Some sons conquer world, like Alexander."

I was beginning to suspect that this man was himself quite mad. Perhaps he was my ancestor but how could I trust anything he said?

"Your sons conquered the world?" I asked.

Clearly, he detected the disbelief in my voice as he responded with a rueful smile. "So much is forgotten. You know it not."

"Indeed, please tell me. Help me to understand." When he yet hesitated, I continued. "You told it to William, sir. Why will you not tell it to me?"

"Your brother is like me. Your brother is man like his ancestors. Like my great sons."

I was insulted. "And what am I?"

He looked closely at me. "A Christian." He grimaced and turned to spit on his own floor.

"I am, sir. And proudly so. What else could I be? And William is a Christian also. For a time, he believed himself to be Christ reborn. Or an angel, perhaps. And then he claimed to be some incarnation of Adam, the first man, and he sought to recreate Eden upon the Earth. Did he claim to be something else when he came to you? I fear, sir, that he has no shame. He will speak whatever the listener wishes to hear, if it means he gets what he wants in return."

Priskos held himself very still. "No man deceives me. In here," Priskos thumped his chest, "William is conqueror. A man to remake world."

"I thought you said you killed sons like that."

He sighed. "They all fall to ruin if I do not. Once, I took kingdom to make it strong. I made mighty son. Philip was his name. His son was stronger, in some ways, but also he was mad. He conquered much and did much war but he could not conquer his own heart. His name was Alexander. William is like this. He burns with fire that destroys everything it touches and then it will destroy him, also. I had to put an end to his life to save his people."

I almost laughed in his face. Surely, I thought, this was proof of his madness. He believed that Alexander of Macedon was his grandson and although it sent a thrill through me to imagine that I was of the same blood as the most famed conqueror in all the world, I was sure of its impossibility. At least, it was highly implausible. How could this man who lived in a cold cave with a single woman to serve him have once been a mighty king?

"If you believed that William is like Alexander of Macedon, why did you let him leave here instead of killing him? What do you want from your sons and their sons?"

"It is every man's duty to conquer all before him. To make his name and his deeds live on in minds of his people and in blood of his sons. But sons of my sons make none of their own. Line shrivels to nothing and this drives great men mad. Alexander could make no sons, and so he brought his wife to his companion. But this is no good. Without sons, no man is complete. They destroy themselves. They grow angered at me. William will do this. It is his nature to do so. If he becomes an Alexander, I will put an end to him, also."

"And what about me?" I asked. "Do you mean to put an end to me?"

He regarded me. "You are not Alexander. You are not Caesar, nor are you Hattusili, Atreus, or Cleomenes. No."

Although I did not know some of the names he mentioned, I knew of course that I was being gravely insulted. I struggled to contain my anger. "What am I, then?"

"A man like Peter. One born to serve."

Whether he was attempting to anger me or it was merely incidental I did not know but it was having that effect on me.

Born to serve.

Was it true, I wondered? Was that all I was? A dutiful knight, when I could have been so much more?

"I am a knight," I said. "I serve a lord. I serve a king. But this is the order of things. Not servitude but duty, sir."

"I know what is a knight. One who serves. A servant is a slave. Slaves have traded honour for life."

I scoffed. "What about Peter, then? He serves you and so you do not kill him? Why did you allow him to be born at all?"

Priskos held my gaze. "A lord needs men to serve him. Who better than sons?"

"Is that why you allowed my father to live when he was born?"

The Ancient One shrugged. "A mistake."

So easy for him to rip my heart open. He had called me weak, called me a natural servant, and said my father's existence—and therefore my own—was a mistake.

Already, I was beginning to hate the Ancient One.

With great effort, I remained seated by gripping the edges of

239

the table. "How then did I come to be born? Who was the cunning woman who bested you?"

He furrowed his brow and looked through me into his past.

"I took woman I should not have taken. The daughter of lord. Yet I saw her, travelling through woodland far to north. I do not take daughters of great men. Trouble follows, always. I take strongest common women, as their fathers are afraid and if they come with their spears and torches, I slaughter them. Yet, lords have many swords and their men cause endless mischief."

His eyes wrinkled as he continued.

"But this girl. I saw her. I had to have her." He made a gesture to show how helpless he had been and then snatched at the air. "I take her. She fights me, for years she fights but I break her. Then, she loves me." His grin turned into a laugh. "She tricks me. Years, she tricks me, loves me in her words and deeds but holds hate in her heart." He nodded to himself. "Strong, strong woman. She seduced me with food, with water. All poisoned. That night, I spill my seed in her, for she has taken my heart and I have lost my mind in her. A woman's power. Belladonna, hemlock, you know these? I wake, fighting to breathe. She slits my throat." He used a finger to trace a line from ear to ear, and then he jabbed his thumb into his chest. "She pierces my heart. She flees."

He shook his head, sighing but he had a smile on his face.

"How could you survive such injuries?"

"She do good work on me. But I am strong. I come back. She flee north and west, returned to her people. They put her with lord for husband. Her belly must have already been big. Some weak men stand such things, if it brings him wealth and name of another greater than him. She flees across water, to the land of Britain."

"You let her go?"

"Perhaps I should have killed her. Killed child. But she fought. She won her life. My people would have sung songs of her."

"And that child was my father, Robert? So he was not the son of the old Lord de Ferrers?" I laughed in disbelief. I knew of course that a great many are deceived about the identity of their true fathers. After all, it had happened to me. And yet my father had also been a bastard, unknown to him. I wished that the old sod had known it before William had killed him. "Robert de Ferrers was not an Alexander either."

Priskos nodded. "No. So be it."

"But why? Why are you the way you are? Why is it like this? Why can I live on as I am, ageless and powerful, yet I cannot become a father? Why does our blood have such power that when a mortal drinks it, they gain our strength? Why?"

Priskos pointed up. The darkness of the jagged rock ceiling was like an infinite void. "Gods make it so."

I hung my head in my hands. "That is it? You do not know why you have this power?"

He frowned and jabbed a thumb into his chest. "I know. It is Sky Father who was my father. I am half god." He pointed a finger at me. "You have Sky Father in your veins."

I shook my head and scoffed. "The Sky Father? Is that it? I had hoped you would have true knowledge about our origins rather than some pagan nonsense about—"

I did not even see him move.

It was no more than a blur and a noise and then pain. He threw the table aside with such force that it smashed upon the wall with an almighty crash. His hands were around my throat and he hoisted me aloft as they squeezed into my neck under my jaw.

The strength in his fingers was inhuman and I could do nothing to resist them. I kicked out and struck at his arms but it was like fighting with an oak. Blood rushed in my ears and my vision darkened.

He tossed me to the floor like a rag and I clutched at the dry dirt as if to hang on to the Earth itself. Soon, my breath came back to me and I looked up at him.

"You worship the god of the wrong people," Priskos said. He pointed at me. "Your gods are the gods of sky, of thunder and lightning. Your gods are Sun and Moon and gods of lake and river. Your dead god is desert god, for desert people. God of death and of weakness. God of word, not deed. You must cast him off."

I sat up, rubbing my neck. I should have been angry but the fact that I had insulted him first gave me pause.

Also, I was quite terrified of his power. His strength was so far beyond my own that I was stunned.

Climbing to my feet, I looked him in the eye.

"You have it wrong," I said, warily. It was a risk to challenge him but I could not allow his insults against God to go uncontested. "Jesus is for all of us. For all of mankind. His message is for each of us as individual men and women, so that we may be saved and reborn."

We stood glaring at each other. Priskos kept his eyes on mine but turned to spit on the floor.

"You are fool amongst fools. But you do not know. Their victory is almost complete. Their madness conquered the strength of Rome when their strength of arms was too weak. They made great empire rot from the inside. They drove apart families with their lies. Jesus Christ was not one of us." He slapped his chest. "His words were never meant for you, for any of us. And yet you have them in your heart all same, corrupting you, making you weak. You must throw off dead god."

It was like the Devil was speaking to me, tempting me away from the light of Jesus Christ.

"I am a faithful servant of God and His son Jesus Christ," I said. "And I shall not waver in my devotion."

I thought he would be angry and braced myself for another assault. Instead, he seemed saddened. I felt I had disappointed him once more.

The woman came in, then and began to clear out the hearth. She took no notice of us or the smashed table.

"Did you ever make immortals by feeding them your blood? Did any of your sons or their sons? If mortals are drained of blood and then they drink from us, they become like us."

"This I have done."

"And what happened to them? You must have many sons and grandsons. And they must have made many immortals. Where are they all?"

"They fall."

"They are all dead?" I asked. "What about the men who brought me here? They are your sons, are they not?"

He scratched at his beard. "You must go home."

"I wish to," I replied. "Once you tell me how to save my people."

"Your ears are bad. Your blood saves them."

"But it does not!"

"Then your blood is weak."

I took a deep breath before replying. "Can my blood be made strong?"

He hesitated. "You drink blood of your enemies, yes?"

I nodded. "To heal wounds. To restore myself after battle."

"Seek more enemies. Strong men. Destroy them. Drink them."

"And that will make me stronger?" I asked, imagining finding and killing men, not because I was wounded and they were my enemies but because I wanted strength for myself. "But I cannot slaughter innocent men."

He scowled at that. "Then do not."

"Drinking the blood of strong men makes me stronger? More than the blood of weak men?"

He frowned. "But of course."

"What makes a man strong?"

"You do not know?"

"The strength of his arm or the strength of his will? Or do you mean a powerful, wealthy man?"

Priskos tilted his head. "These are all the same thing."

"Once, perhaps," I replied. "Not always today."

He nodded. "This world is mad. The weakness of your dead god infests the hearts of men. Weakness is worshipped. Failure is worshipped. Meekness celebrated. A world of weak men." His levelled his finger at my face. "This is your world."

"My world is a great one. We have built things that your barbarian people, whoever they were, could not comprehend. Have you seen the Cathedral of Notre-Dame in Paris? Or the one in Chartres? Once, I won a battle in the shadow of the Cathedral of Lincoln, an edifice more magnificent than any other. The spire reaches halfway to Heaven. It is a monument to the glory of God."

Priskos scoffed. "A monument to madness."

"How can you say such things? These achievements are greater than any other. What did your world create that was half so glorious and everlasting?"

"We created you. All of you. You come from us. We worshipped the gods and we gloried in the feats of men. Our monuments were the songs that were sung of them."

"Songs? Your songs are forgotten. Our castles and cathedrals will stand for ever."

His mouth twitched at the corners. "They will crumble to dust. Our songs are sung still. Names changed, tales twisted. And sung still."

I wished I had not come. It was all so abstruse and what little I did comprehend was hard to take.

"Yes, yes, very well," I said. "So I must kill and drink strong men to strengthen my blood. Their blood is best."

Priskos spread his hands and sat back a little. "Best? Well, the best blood is not of men."

I sighed, rubbing my eyes. "What?"

He smiled. "Best blood of all is blood of child."

I kept my eyes on him but it was clear he did not speak in jest. "A child's blood is stronger than a man's? How can that be so?"

"Child's blood hold's all force of life. What child may become is in blood. Drink this blood, take whole life. A babe's blood is best. From mother's belly, from breast. Or blood of girl who soon becomes woman."

"By God," I said. "By God, I shall never do such evil."

He snorted. "No. I know this."

I knew what he meant when he said it. *Weak.*

"William drank the blood of my brother's children," I said, suddenly recalling it. "My half-brother who was the son of my mother. William killed him, and his wife, and he tore apart—" I broke off, unable to speak of the horror.

Priskos regarded me coldly. "William understand this. William will take what needs to be taken. He will travel path to greatness. To everlasting fame. To glory."

"If doing evil is the price for your idea of greatness, I shall never pay it."

"Then you fail."

I nodded slowly, growing angry. "Because I am weak."

His smile grew into a grin, showing big yellow teeth. "It is law. Weak die. Strong live."

I shook my head. "As a knight, it is my duty to defend the weak from the strong."

"Yes, yes," he said, nodding. "This good, yes. This how we make our people safe. Our own people. Outsiders we destroy. This why to protect your people, you must become strong. Stay strong. Always."

"Very well," I said. "I understand."

Priskos seemed doubtful about my understanding but he did not pursue it any further.

"Enough, now. You will learn this, or you will die."

As I watched the woman, whose name I still did not know, bustling about the cave that was her prison, I resolved two things.

First, I decided that I would escape.

And I swore that I would rescue that woman and save her from her confinement at the hands of the monster who was my grandfather.

A true knight would save a maiden from the dragon. Arthur's knights, Sir Gawain and Sir Percival, would have risked all to rescue a lady from imprisonment. Lancelot's son, virtuous Galahad, would never have hesitated to do what was required.

One hundred and eighty years old, I was, and still a bloody fool.

1 4

RESCUING THE
MAIDEN

IN THE DARK OF THE NIGHT, I lay awake listening to the
steady breathing of the man who could kill me at will and trying
to get up the nerve to make my escape.

After eating a fair meal with me in something close to silence
at midday, Priskos had disappeared outside for hours.

I wondered then what he did to occupy his days. What
purpose he had taken for himself. Did he spend his hours praying
to his strange gods? Was he practising his skill at arms?
Contemplating the great mysteries? Whatever it was, it seemed to
be an empty life and a lonely one.

In his absence, I considered fleeing but did not know if I
would run right into him in the woods outside. The woman

would not speak to me and made an effort to be wherever I was not. Priskos returned before dark without a word and gestured that I should sleep on the floor again before he and the woman turned in.

I thought it likely that he would allow me to leave, should I ask it of him. But he had admitted to murdering his own sons and grandsons before and even more he had suggested that he felt it was some sort of duty to do so. He claimed that he had allowed William to leave but was that true or had William outwitted Priskos, as our grandmother had once done? And even if he had allowed William to leave, clearly he thought much less of me than he did my brother.

I was keenly aware that I was at his mercy, so fleeing in the night was a risk as it would certainly violate basic rules of hospitality to do so. Yet staying in the hope of being released may have been no safer and as taking action is almost always better than not doing so, I was certain that I would flee into the woodland. I believed that I could get miles away before sunrise, steal a horse and be away for good.

But the thought of leaving that woman there alone with him weighed heavily upon me. How could I in good conscience leave her in such a condition when I knew she was there against her will, facing certain death when he grew bored with her or when her belly swelled with a child?

And yet taking her with me would be an appalling risk. She would slow my progress so much that I doubted we could get away.

I knew what a chivalrous knight would do. But my noble act

for that woman may well end up condemning my dear Eva and my closest friend Thomas to an agonising death. Back and forth, my mind went, playing through all the possibilities. Perhaps I could restrain Priskos in his bed? But if I failed then that would certainly seal my fate. I had considered poisoning his meal, as my grandmother had done but even if I could have found the correct plants, I had no idea how to prepare them so that their presence would go undetected in his beer. I knew that my best chance would be to dash his brains out with a rock while he slept, and then to perhaps burn his body so that he could not recover. But even though the man was clearly evil, I was not prepared to murder him in his bed.

Just as I was erring on the side of cowardice, she stirred in her bed and then climbed from it. I could see from the light of the single candle that she pulled a shawl around her shoulders and stepped by me on her way out of the cave.

I took it as a sign from God to do the honourable thing. It seemed as though He wanted me to save her, that He was testing my faith and my honour, and I resolved to do as the Lord commanded.

Priskos continued to snore, his breathing regular and steady. I carefully slipped from my blanket and crept after her. As I saw the light grey outline of the world beyond, I heard her passing water near the mouth of the cave. She was startled when I appeared and I held my hands out to show I meant no harm.

Still, she held herself very still.

"I am leaving, now," I said, pointing at myself and then out into the dark woodland. "Will you come with me?"

Without hesitation, she grasped one of my hands and dragged me out into the world.

Dear God, I thought, give our feet wings and guide our way through the darkness.

We rushed headlong into the abyssal black shadow, our bare feet pounding the forest floor hard and fast and not caring that we cut our feet on the stones and twigs and thorns on the path. She seemed to somehow know where to go and so I allowed her to lead me for the time being, hoping as I did merely to get as far from the cave as possible before he began his pursuit, assuming he did do so. Would he wake once he sensed the warmth beside him turn cold? Or would he snore away in oblivion until the dawn?

Branches whipped my face and I stumbled on a rock, rolling my ankle and hobbling for a few steps until I recovered. She fell, later, and I helped her up to find her drenched in sweat and shaking from the cold and the exertion. How much further could she flee at such a pace? Her breathing was heavy and she fought for air. The unchivalrous thought that I should leave her was motivated by fear and I shook it off.

"Come," I said, softly, "we must continue on. As long as we can."

How much she understood, I still did not know, but she caught my meaning well enough. Soon, I was the one dragging her along as her pace slowed further and further. At last, it was unavoidable that I scoop her up into my arms so that I could keep moving with rapid, short steps. She buried her head in my neck but also I felt that she looked over my shoulder, behind me, watching for the pursuit that would surely come.

It was not long before my own breathing grew laboured and loud. While it felt as though I had run for uncounted hours, the sun was beginning to brighten the sky above the trees to the west. The shadows grew deeper even as the greys and purples of the pre-dawn edged the trunks and boulders all around.

"Is there a village?" I asked. "Near here? Horses? Where?"

For the first time in a while, she lifted her head and looked around with alarm. "Die klamm!" she said, pointing ahead. "The gorge!"

I had brought us to the edge of a shallow ravine. I could not see the bottom as it was too dark, though I could not hear a river below. Even if it was dry, I doubted climbing down into it would be the best decision.

"Which way?" I asked.

She pointed north and I hurried that way, being sure to keep the gorge on my right and to watch my forward step as best I could so that I did not stumble headlong into a side channel or some other fissure.

The sky grew lighter and my heart thumped in my chest like a drum. Although I did not wish to stop for long, I had to catch my breath for a moment and stretch my back while I put her down.

"Is there a village?" I asked, panting, "This way?"

"This way," she said, echoing me. The daylight was growing with every moment and I saw the fear and the determination on her face.

"Very well. Are you ready, my dear?"

"Osanna," she said, touching her fingers to her chest.

"A lovely name. Where is your own village? Is it far? Do they have horses for riding there?"

Before she could answer, something rushed from the darkness and struck me from behind.

I fell, hard. As I rolled and jumped to my feet I was smacked in the side of the head and my vision exploded. I drifted in and out of wakefulness as I was savaged and beaten bloody. It was so sudden that I felt little pain, just the sense of being thrashed. I had been trampled by horses more than once in my life and it was far worse even than that. Ribs snapped. It hurt to breathe. I lashed out and caught my attacker on his head and in response my forearm was grasped in a grip of iron and then my bones were snapped like twigs just above my wrist. I was screaming in anger and fear. My head hit a rock, or perhaps my skull was cracked with the back of an axe but I felt and heard the bones of my head breaking.

When I returned to consciousness, Priskos stood over me. I could barely move from the agony of my ruined body. It was light enough to see by but my vision was badly blurred. When I attempted to curse him, all I could manage was a strange moan. My jaw was broken.

He reached down and picked me up by the neck and held me in front of him. My arms did not appear to work and I was as helpless as a baby.

Without a word, he did something to my face, pushing his fingers against my cheeks. Only later, as I recalled the events, was it that I realised that he had pushed my left eyeball back inside my shattered eye socket.

Hoisting me up further, he twisted and threw me into the ravine.

∞ ∞ ∞

A noise woke me. Some steady sound at the edge of my consciousness pulling me back into wakefulness. Perhaps it was the smell of blood that roused me.

Though the ravine was in deep shadow, it was full daylight high above.

I was face down in soft leaf litter. I knew I was dying. Pain held me rigid but I forced myself to lift my head and look around.

The sound was the wheezing breath coming from the woman lying near me.

Her throat had been cut or punctured and her chest was covered with blood. Her eyes were open and her mouth moved.

I groaned and her eyes flicked toward me.

Behind her eyes, I saw terrible agony and hatred for me, who had failed her so completely.

With great effort, I dragged myself through the leaf litter toward her an inch at a time. The smell of cold, damp fungus in the leaf litter filled my smashed nose.

Osanna might have died at any moment and yet she clung to life, even though she surely knew she had no hope.

She lay motionless on her back. Not even her fingers twitched. It was such a fall from the edge of the ravine above that it was likely she had broken her back in the fall, if Priskos had not snapped it himself before throwing her down. Her legs were twisted and perhaps her pelvis was broken.

Pulling myself up to her, I believed I knew why he had done this to her. He had even cut her throat for me.

He meant for me to drink from her.

If I did nothing, she would certainly die and then I would die also.

That did little to make me feel better but my choice was really quite simple. Did I want to live or did I want to die?

I shifted myself, inch by inch, up to her throat and clamped my mouth over her wound. She was already cold to the touch and her blood sticky and thick about the wound but when I sucked, the hot blood flowed into my mouth.

It was not very long before her breathing stopped and her heart ceased beating. My belly was full enough and I turned over. Already, I felt the blood working in me and still I lost consciousness.

"Sir Richard," a voice said. It had been saying it repeatedly but I had been unable to respond. A hand slapped my face lightly.

I was cold and I shivered. It was late in the day and I had lain in shadow for hours in no more than a bloody undershirt.

"Walter?" I said, my voice a harsh croak.

Walt was alive? How could it be?

"Thank the Lord," Walt said. "Thought you was a goner, sir."

"Help me up," I muttered.

He had already carried me away from Osanna's body and he had mercifully laid a cloak over her face and chest.

"I saw you die," I said to Walt.

"And die I did, sir. Then those fellows, Peter and his giant brother Christman, poured a great cup of hot blood down my throat and then I was dead no longer. Peter told me some fanciful tales, so he did, and then later he told me my master needed me. Told me to take you home. Brought me nearby, gave me back our horses and even packs with supplies and pointed me to you. The horses are up there, sir, if you can try to stand?"

Priskos was up there somewhere, likely already back in his cave. After all he had done, I wished nothing more than to find him and kill him. Then again, he was stronger than I could have imagined. Attempting to take revenge on him would have certainly led to my death. And he had allowed me to live when he could so easily have killed me. Through that act, I sensed that he had gifted me life. I would be foolish to throw it away.

I got to my feet.

"Let us be gone from this damned black place."

It was a long way back.

To strengthen my blood, I had to find men, kill them, and drink their blood.

According to Priskos, if I killed enough of them, I would be able to save the lives of Eva and Thomas with the power of the blood in my veins.

1 5

BECOMING THE
DRAGON

I WANTED TO BE GONE from that evil land, with its close hills and black shadows beneath unnaturally upright trees.

On and on it went.

It seemed to me that we were followed and watched, from the darkness of twisted roots and moss-covered rocks beside the winding tracks. I pushed us onward, allowing little rest.

Every other step, I saw the dying face of Osanna, staring at me in condemnation of my failure.

Walter had died for me but he had been reborn as an immortal. I owed him a frank and full explanation of what that meant.

"What fanciful tales did Peter tell you?" I asked. "Why did

they bring you back from the point of death? They must have done so immediately."

Walt shrugged. "Peter said you might need a strong servant, if his father ever decided to let you go."

"What if he did not let me go?"

"Funny, sir. That's what I asked the fellow. Peter said if that happened, they would just have to kill me along with you."

"He explained that you needed to drink human blood from now on?"

Walt scratched his chin. "He said a lot of stuff what sounded like drivel. Lot of talk about living forever and whatnot. Wasn't following the fellow all that close, truth be told, sir. I never put much stock in the tripe that priests babble on about. I kept asking that giant what it was all about, on account that innkeepers tend to be the salt of the earth, but I reckon that big lad was simple. Proper simple. Never said nothing."

"What about when they let you go? When they gave you these horses?"

"He said you had gone and betrayed his father and you deserved death but you had to be saved. He was right angered about it. Bitter fellow, that Peter. Still, told me to do my duty and get you out."

It took a few days to explain it all to Walt, going over some of my life story a number of times before we left the *Schwarzwald* proper.

He took it rather well.

I did not, however, trust Walt with the knowledge that the blood of infants and young women was the most potent of all. He was not an evil man, far from it, but commoners have always lacked the restraint that comes more naturally to the better-born.

"So, he said you had been too *good*, sir?" Walt said, furrowing his brow. "You been too chivalrous and honourable and the like and so the blood what is in your veins lacks the strength to heal them? That what he said, then, is it, sir?"

We had ridden far to the north and the Rhine valley was down to the west. I was searching for a route down from the hills so we could head back to the lands of civilised Frenchmen who I could murder.

"Not in so many words. But yes."

"Bit of a surprise, that, though. Seeing how you killed about three score men before my own eyes since I first met you, sir."

"Perhaps I should have drunk their blood before I killed them."

"Can't see that sort of thing going down well with old King Edward, sir."

"No."

"But what if he was wrong, sir? The ancient gentleman. Perhaps it is not that your blood is weaker than his but this plague is worse than anything he has seen before in all his long years?"

"It oft surprises me how your profound ignorance does not hinder your ability to reason."

He picked something from his nose. "Yes, sir."

"I cannot know whether it will work. Yet there is nothing else but to try."

"You mean we have to kill some strong fellows and drink their blood, sir?" He curled his lip into a disgusted snarl as he spoke.

He was not one to shy away from a little murder when necessary but the thought of drinking a man's blood was anathema even to a man like Walt.

"Do you recall that I fought in Spain and the Holy Land with Eva as my squire?"

"How could I forget that part, sir?" He shook his head.

"For a time, because she needed blood every two or three days, as you now do, we would find wrongdoers in the camps or amongst our enemies and slay them so that she might drink from them."

"Dead men are revenged by their friends. You just got to do so. Dangerous work for you and the lady, sir."

"Perhaps. They were wild days, and men died everywhere from one thing or another."

"Wilder than these?"

"You know war as well as any mortal. You know how it is with companies moving from place to place, with disease in the camps, men deserting or fighting to death over some woman. If one is careful to take the worst, it can be done."

"Sounds like Brittany."

I grunted. "It does, that."

The germ of an idea began to grow. I had fought and killed from one side of the world to the other, leading men, following lords. Priskos had thought me weak for doing my duty but I had led warbands and caused havoc for almost two centuries. It was what I was best at. It was what I should have been doing all along, no matter what else my duty required of me.

"So, you and the Lady Eva was married, sir?" Walt shook his

head. "You know how to pick them and that be the truth. The Lady Eva has a right majestic pair on her."

"Do try to hold your tongue until we pass through this forest. I should hate to have to cut it out."

"Won't it just grow back, sir?"

"Good God, I hope not."

North of Strasbourg, in a wild, wooded place, we were set upon by robbers.

It looked like a dangerous place and I was already on edge. The sky was close and the shadows pressed in from beneath the trees and rocks.

"Any chance you relate that story now, sir?" Walt asked. "The one where you captured Mortimer in Nottingham, when King Edward was young? I should like to hear it, sir."

"Hush, Walter. Watch the flanks."

He sighed, because I often chided him with such warnings in dangerous places and usually nothing happened.

A shout pierced the air. Harsh and guttural, echoing along the trackway. We drew our weapons just as a score of desperate men descended on us from both sides of the road, all suddenly screaming their battle cries.

We cut them down to a man. Walt fought like the Devil himself, racing from the dead to the living to run the next one through with a mad joy on his face. I followed the last of them through the trees, spearing one in the spine and jumping from my horse to follow the last two on foot where I killed them with my sword.

Both pitiful creatures wept and begged. They were so thin and filthy. I killed them without a word and drank from them both.

Their blood filled me with strength. I was used to drinking it when wounded or exhausted and much of the power of the blood went into restoring me. But, drinking those men when I was uninjured and fresh, I felt how the full potency of the blood seeped into my bones.

I had a purpose. I would kill and drink, kill and drink, the strength from my next victim building upon that of my last so that I would grow to match the strength of the immortals Peter and Christman, who were apparently my uncles.

I would grow to be a match for my brother William whenever he returned.

If I drank enough powerful men, perhaps I could one day return to Priskos and beat the filthy bastard to death and throw his shrivelled carcass into a ravine.

Those scrawny, desperate robbers on the road had been a start but I would have to find warriors and lords, if I was to become what I needed to become.

Returning to the site of the villeins' ambush, I found a wild-eyed Black Walter standing over the whimpering forms of the wounded survivors.

They would not survive for much longer.

"You must drink their blood, Walt."

"God forgive me," he said, but in the end, he did not require much coaxing. Walt was a born survivor. Willing to pay the price for life, whatever it was.

I showed him how it was best and easiest to drink from the neck or wrist of a body where the heart still fluttered with vestiges of life and he sank his teeth into the wounds and gulped it down. Even when he heaved and vomited it back up, he drank once more.

All the men died and we left them to rot on the side of the road. Whether they had any families left alive nearby to bury them, I neither knew nor cared.

"Cold blood does not work?" he asked me later, when the bodies were miles behind us.

I recalled submerging myself into a vat of congealing blood beneath the hills of Palestine, so many years before.

"It works to heal you and will maintain your health. But it is not so potent as blood from a living man. And it congeals in your mouth and belly and it is quite foul."

"Living blood it is, then." He was quiet for some time. "What if those men had not come along? I would make ill?"

"You would grow weaker, the sunlight would burn and blister your skin even more than when you are satiated. And your pallor would take an ever greener tint."

"Green?"

"There was an immortal monk that I kept prisoner once. He would turn the colour of mould and rotting pears. As I recall, Eva would take on the hue of a mint leaf."

"Never been a man admired for my features. And I can keep my skin shrouded so as to not blister in sunlight."

"You would also lose your mind. Although, in your case it would prove difficult to tell."

"We always knew something was queer with you, sir."

"Who is we?"

"All of us. The lads. The men and the archers both. You and Old Tom and John and Hugh. Something off. Something to do with blood magic."

I scoffed. "How could you possibly know that?"

"The company servants would get bled regular, right? The young lads. Yet their blood would get taken off. We thought it was blood magic. What else could it have been? You was burning the blood, praying to Satan for your strength and your youth. All the lads thought so. Well, not so much that anyone would have done a thing about it. But that was what was said."

And I had thought us so clever. So subtle and cunning. But I should have known how a company of men can talk and talk so that a bunch of fools can together arrive at wisdom.

"Damn your eyes, the lot of you."

"Yes, sir. But what do we do for blood if we find no more desperate men?"

"If there are no men to kill and your time for blood is come, you may drink of mine. And my blood will keep you hale and steady. But we are now heading into pestilential France, where all men are desperate and two lone Englishmen will be welcomed not."

And I was more right about that than I expected.

∞ ∞ ∞

As we rode across the county, the weather grew wetter and wilder almost every day. I hunched in my saddle and plodded onward with nought but the thoughts in my head and the rain drumming against my hood or my hat. Always on my mind, of course, was the dead girl, whose life I had cut short through my witless romantic notions.

And often I pondered the condemnation that Priskos expressed over my worshipping of Jesus. He had called cathedrals monuments to folly. As if worshipping God was folly.

Your dead god is desert god, for desert people. God of death and of weakness. God of word, not deed. You must cast him off.

How could such blasphemy be truth? Of course, he was older than Jesus and from a pagan land somewhere to the east. And Alexander had been a pagan, as had Caesar, and yet they were sung of in ballads as heroes that upheld a kind of chivalric ideal. If they could be chivalrous without worshipping God, was it possible for me, also? I did not know what to make of it, only that I found it horrifying and intriguing in equal measure.

South of the fortified city of Luxembourg, we came to the outskirts of town where a large and bizarre group filled the road in a long procession ahead of us. They wore robes and sombre clothes with red crosses on their fronts and backs and almost all were men but there were some women at the rear. All wore hoods or caps, also with a red cross on, and they marched in silence with their eyes on the ground.

"Monks?" Walt ventured.

They moved in a long procession, like a chain, walking two by two. Two or even three hundred of them. At the front, down by the town, the leaders of the procession held aloft banners of purple velvet. As the first of them reached the town, the church

267

bell began to sound and it kept on with its ringing, over and over, as if it would never cease.

We followed the strange procession right into the market square, where they filed into a large circle and the townsfolk came out and surrounded them.

In the centre, many men stripped themselves to the waist so that they wore nothing more than a linen skirt down to the ankles. Their outer garments were laid reverentially in a big pile to one side of the open space within their circle, and I watched in confusion as pestilential townsfolk were dragged and carried to the mound of clothing where they took turns laying upon it while others prayed over them.

The robed worshippers began to march around and around the circle in a procession. In the centre, a powerful old man with a big beard held his hands aloft and chanted something.

All of a sudden, he cried out a command and all the marching people threw themselves to the ground, most violently, face down with their arms outstretched as if crucified to the floor.

The leader stalked among them and thrashed them on their bare backs with a switch, one at a time. Not all received such a punishment but a good number of them did. When he was done, he ordered them to their feet and each of them produced a heavy scourge from a bag on their belts. It was a short wooden rod with two or three leather thongs dangling from it and each thong was tipped with metal studs. With another command from the big bearded fellow, they each began to beat their backs and breasts in time.

The leader and three of his attendants walked amongst the

madmen, urging them to have strength and to pray harder.

On the far side of the square, the folk parted and a sobbing mother stepped forward into the magic circle carrying a bundle which she placed in the centre and wailed. A flap of cloth fell back and I saw that it was a dead child, not more than a year old, already turned black with putrefaction. Prayers were said over the poor thing and its mother but no matter how she wailed and how they prayed, the baby did not return to life and the mother was dragged away.

All the while, the mad worshippers continued to whip themselves bloody. And then they began to chant a prayer in time to their thrashing of themselves.

"What in the name of God is happening here?" I asked a tall man who stood far to the rear.

His eyes were shining, rimmed with tears, as he turned to me. "They mortify their flesh. Praise God!"

"Who are these men? Where do they come from?"

"The Brotherhood of the Flagellants," one man said.

"They come to us from the East," said another.

"From Bavaria."

"Hungary," said a woman. "So I heard."

"They said with their own mouths they was come from Nuremberg, Martha. Why don't you ever listen?"

I interrupted their argument. "What do they hope to accomplish through such acts?"

No one wished to speak the words until one young fellow turned and answered with a sob. "To end the plague!"

Their pace accelerated and the Flagellants threw themselves to the floor again and got to their feet to continue to the thrashing.

"What nonsense," I said, far too loudly, for a dozen or more townsfolk turned and gave me the evil eye. Some even cursed me.

"We should go, sir," Walt said, for he had a nose for trouble. Perhaps I should have listened but the orgy of self-mutilation fascinated me to such an extent that I could not draw my eyes from them. The fronts and backs of both the men and the women were beginning to spit more and more and the smell of blood was in the air as it was sprayed and spattered toward the crowd on all sides. Women were as enthusiastic as any of the men, their bared breasts bouncing and bloody as they whipped their flails around their flanks onto their fronts.

The big man in the centre, along with his three burly attendants, called out orders and lead the chanting prayer.

"Why do the leaders not mortify their own flesh?" I asked the folk about me.

Sensing criticism, they scoffed and scorned to answer.

"He is the Master," a lad who spoken before told me.

The Master shouted a command and the Flagellants threw themselves to the ground once more and fell silent but for their panting and wincing while the leaders strode amongst them, whipping a few of them.

"Should this Master not suffer his own punishments?" I said, speaking far louder than I intended. My voice filled the quiet square and the Master whipped his head around to me.

His eyes locked on mine.

Walt whispered. "We should go, sir."

"You!" the Master shouted, raising a finger to point at me.

A great rustling sounded as every face in the town square turned to mine.

"What great sinner is this?" he roared. "What great sinner is this that dares to interrupt our sacred rites?"

Walt began to turn his horse. "Time to retreat, sir?"

"I think so," I said and attempted to turn my horse about through the crowd.

"Yes!" the Master cried. "Yes, see how the sinner flees before our righteousness. Flee, you murderers and robbers. None you shall find but endless woe. The wrath of God on you shall fall."

I turned back to him.

"Richard. Sir," Walt muttered, looking at the outraged faces all around us. "My lord. We must—"

I sat upright and called across the square. "And who are you? Who are you to make such pronouncements? You who command these mad fools to beat themselves bloody while you yourself stand unharmed?"

A collective intake of breath echoed around the square and the faces turned back to him.

The Master's face above his beard turned the colour of boiled beetroot. Without a word, and keeping his gaze fixed upon mine, he untied the rope about his robes and shrugged off the clothes from his torso. The flesh of his muscular upper body and fat belly were white as chalk.

White, that is, other than the mass of red welts, pink scar tissue and weeping, pussy wounds that covered his back, chest and shoulders.

The crowd turned back to me as the Master, triumphant,

raised a hand to me once more.

"You shall know what it is to suffer for your sins. Bring him here!"

All at once, the townsfolk all around me surged forward, their faces grim and wild with righteousness. Hands grabbed my horse's bridle and tail and, already nervous, he began to panic. I fought him as the hands reached for my ankles.

"Unhand me!" I roared.

Walt was swearing at the men and women that grabbed at him. The crowd began to shout their encouragement and their rage built into a roar that filled the square.

I leaned over and punched the face of the man who had my right leg but three more grabbed hold of my forearm and began to heave me down from my saddle. I held on with my knees and yanked a dagger from my belt with my off hand and stabbed it down, striking flesh. They released me, shouting in anger that I had drawn blood.

More surged forward.

I realised that I was about to be ripped to pieces by a mob of mad, French peasants.

A rage filled me. A rage unlike any I had known. A rage that caused me to shake and growl like a bear.

My mind filled with visions of Priskos. His words. His assault on me. That violation.

I pictured my friend John being slaughtered by the black knight. I recalled the assassin that came so close to killing me in the Southwark stews.

Felt the agony of the bolt that had struck me in the face.

Saw Osanna's dying eyes fixing on mine.

Back in England, Eva and Thomas died in agony, over and over again, and only I could save them.

There was no decision. It was all instinct and blind rage.

I drew my sword and, screaming a wordless battle cry, I slashed down at the mob. My blade cut into the flesh of the faces of the nearest men. Blood sprayed up to splash across the crowd. My horse tried to flee but there was no way out. A young man leapt up behind me and I thrust my dagger around my flank and into his, sending him to his death. My blades stabbed down, left and right, killing and maiming men and women who still came at me.

Walt fought them also, with sword and dagger, so that the screams of the dying merged with the shouts of the madmen all around.

When one fell, two more took his place. It was as though there was no end to them. No satiating their lust for blood.

And there was likewise no bounds for mine.

It was a slaughter. They died and they died and I killed them with joy.

Without warning, it seemed, their hatred turned to panic.

Dozens were dead, scores were blinded or maimed, and instead of pushing forward the ones closest to us began to fight to get away. Pushing against the crowds behind to escape the terror that was my sword. My horse wheeled and rushed into whatever spaces formed, causing more panic. And their panic spread. Like soldiers breaking on the field, or a herd of animals sensing a predator in their midst, the townsfolk finally understood, on some primal level, that they were facing something that could not

273

be faced. They were fighting something that could not be beaten. Like a living plague, I charged from the dead to the living, bringing agonies and swift death.

The crowds parted before me and streamed away through the side streets, pushing the aged and the children before them and trampling those that fell.

My horse was wheeling and breathing in terror, so I climbed down and pushed him away. Walt stayed mounted, controlling his horse, while he chased away the rest of the madmen nearest to him.

The Flagellants alone had not fled, and I stalked toward them, wiping blood from my eyes and licking it from my hands.

A dozen of them rushed me with their flails and walking sticks. I smashed their skulls with my sword and threw them aside as I approached the Master, who stood his ground and prayed. His three attendants chanted some mad prayer and came at me with willow switches in one hand and wooden crucifixes in the other. I stabbed the first in his guts, cut the right hand off the next and the third dropped to his knees, weeping and praying to God with his head bowed like an invitation. With one swing, I cut off his head and kicked over his body.

The Master shook and tears streamed down his face into his beard.

I dropped my sword and seized him by the shoulders.

"Who am I?" I said, my voice low like a growl. It did not sound like my own. "Who am I? I am a sinner. I am a murderer. I am the wrath of God."

I sank my teeth into his neck and ripped out a chunk of flesh that I spat onto the ground. He screamed as I sucked the blood from his neck.

Walt grabbed me by the shoulder.

"People will see, lord."

"Let them see."

"These folk will talk."

"Let them talk!" I snarled. "Let them all talk. Let all France talk and let them tremble at the word of our coming. Soon, I will kill my way across France and they will fear me."

I drank more from the dying man until his heart stopped and I threw him down and raised my voice.

"Englishmen will drink the blood of the French." I shouted it so my voice echoed hard from the houses walling off the square. "Spread the word. The English will drink the blood of the French until we find the knight of the black banner. Spread the word. You fear the pestilence? *I* am the pestilence. I am Richard of Hawkedon and I will murder every soul in France until I find the knight of the black banner. We are the English and we will bring death to France!"

Walt recovered our horses and together we rode slowly out of town with eyes peeping from shuttered windows and half-open doors all around us.

We left scores dead and a market square drenched in blood.

It was a start. But I needed more.

1 6

STRENGTH

"DO YOU FEEL STRONGER, SIR?" Walt asked.

We had made it to the border of Normandy, coming at it from the south, and would soon be within striking distance to the coast. Then it would be a matter of finding a ship that would sail us home. I wondered whether Eva and Thomas yet lived.

Our camp was once more made amongst the trees away from the road. The weather had turned with the seasons and everything was wet. It reeked of mushrooms and brown leaves stuck to everything. My shoes were rotted almost away and the fires never dried us completely.

"Stronger?" I considered it. "Somewhat, perhaps."

Northern France had been ravaged by the plague such that it seemed at times that everyone was dead. Entire villages were empty. Others had no children or old folk. Everywhere was misery.

Walt sighed. "We need to kill more people, then."

I shook my head. "Killing these poor, starving villeins will not make me stronger. Not by much, at least."

Priskos had told me that the best blood came from unborn babies, and children, and from pregnant mothers, and from young maidens just into womanhood.

And also from great warriors.

Try as I might, I could not imagine killing babies, women and girls. Not even to save the lives of my companions.

I had tried.

In one hamlet, a starving girl of fourteen or so was alone in taking care of her very young brother and another little girl. Looking down at them after they came to beg for food, I considered cutting their throats.

"I will lay with you for some bread, lord," she said without looking at me, her skinny arms wrapped about her.

We rode on after I gave her all the food in my pack. Walt shook his head at my idiocy but I saw him quietly hand the boy an entire cheese. I was pleased to note that I yet retained some sense of morality. Did that mean I would never be strong enough to beat William?

"Could we not take some people and drink from them at will? As you do with your servants, sir."

"That is one way, indeed. It seems that is the way of many immortals that I have killed. It helps them to maintain the illusion of normality for the mortal world, just as it does for our order."

"So, am I now a part of the Order of the White Dagger, sir?"

"Good God, I suppose I shall have to swear you into it." In truth, I did not wish to sully the quality of our order with the likes of Black Walter, so that was all I said.

"You reckon we should take some slaves from the locals, then?"

"Priskos claims that one's power grows by drinking the blood of one who dies as you drink. They release their essence into you at the point of death."

Walt frowned. "That true, sir? It's better when they die?"

"I believe I have noticed a difference."

"Do you think that's what your brother William has been doing these centuries past, and that when he returns from the East he will be stronger than you?"

"Shut up, Walt."

There was nothing for it but to seek out strong men. And to kill them.

We found an ancient tower a few miles from Normandy outside a place called Senonches. The village was dead. It was surrounded for miles by dense oak woodland, all turned to gold and brown and decay.

The tower, though, was guarded by men.

It had been built probably centuries before and was no doubt even older than I was. The mortar between the stones needed repairing and grass and weeds grew from the cracks. A wooden palisade surrounded it, far newer but still rotting.

We reached it at dusk.

Smoke rose from within the walls and the sound of men's laughter drifted across the cleared ground to the trees where Walt and I crouched. Our horses tethered in a clearing half a mile behind us, we were dressed for war.

"How many, you reckon?" Walt asked.

"It does not matter."

I stood and walked across the soggy ground, pulling a cheap helm down over my head. Walt followed quickly. I considered going to the gates of the palisade but I knew I could not convince the men within to open the door so I aimed directly for the nearest corner of the stone tower. The ground was soft underfoot and I sank down into an ancient ditch up to my knees and fought my way out, emerging in a fouler mood.

Climbing the ancient walls was simple enough but not easy. Not in a wonky helm, and a gambeson with a sword dangling at my hip. I scraped the steel against the stones as I climbed, and I could hear Walt doing the same. If I could have taken both hands from the wall I would have ripped the useless helm off and thrown it down but I was committed.

As I rolled over the battlements, I knocked a stone from the wall onto the wooden boards of the roof, making a great bang. I helped Walt over and heard a noise behind me.

The hatchway onto the roof was opened by a man who stared, open-mouthed, as I ran at him across the roof. He pulled the hatch shut but I yanked it open before he could bar it and I jumped through into the chamber below.

The fall was greater than I expected it to be and I landed heavily, falling onto my face. I rolled and jumped up as the first man and another came at me. They were proper men-at-arms but they were not armoured and I wasted no time in stabbing the first in his chest. Walt slipped down the ladder and sank his dagger into the neck of the second.

Removing our helms, we each drank from the man we had killed until he was dead.

Walt stared at me with joy in his eyes as his man fell at his feet.

I nodded to him and we ran down to the chamber below.

To my surprise, it was a bedchamber, dominated by a great four-post piece with a sagging canopy. An old man lay abed with his sheets drawn up to his chin.

The door burst open and Walt killed the man as he came through. Three or four men behind, coming up the stairwell, turned and fled at the sight of it. Walt followed and I knew that he would have no trouble, for he had been a savage fighter even before being gifted with the strength of the immortals.

"Invaders," the ancient lord in his bed muttered. "Murderers."

"Who are you, old man?" I asked, crossing to him.

He raised his chin, exposing a wrinkled neck and unshaved white whiskers sprouting from his chin. "I am the lord of this place. Sir Pierre of Senoches. This is my tower. You shall leave, or die."

"Killed many men, have you? In your younger days, I mean."

He quivered. "Every death I brought was in honourable war. Your vengeance means nothing."

"Vengeance?" I replied. "You misunderstand, sir. I am not here for justice. You have not wronged me in any way. I am pleased that you were a strong knight. I honour you."

I slit his throat and drank his blood. It tasted old and wrong, for he was riddled with the diseases of the aged, but I hoped that some of the power he had in his youth had gone into me.

In the bailey below, I found Walt drinking from a dying man while two others huddled against the base of a section of the damp palisade, staring at us in horror and fury.

"Fight for your lives, you cowards," I said to them. "Where are your weapons? Fight and die with honour or die in the mud like worms."

They were mere men-at-arms, retainers in the employ of an impoverished lord whose tenants were all dead or gone. And yet they fought like heroes, thrusting with their spears and wrestling us with daggers in hand as they fell to our strength. We drank heartily from them and I felt my power grow.

At the coast, four days later, a company of eight men stopped us as we went from village to village to find a boat capable of crossing the channel so late in the year. I knew at once that the men who surrounded us were veterans of the recent wars. They were grim and wild-eyed. Most were scarred, missing fingers or an eye. Thin, desperate and iron-hard men.

It felt good to kill them, to cut them open and taste their strength. I could almost taste the evil acts that they had committed to survive the years of war and plague.

On the wide banks of the Seine where it becomes the sea, we found our way home. A trader and his family dragged their boat back into the water in exchange for a heavy bag of silver and for our horses. The crossing was unpleasant in the extreme and I thought for certain we would be dashed against the cliffs of

Dieppe or sunk in the churning dark waters. But the winds, strong as they were, turned mostly in our favour so that we made the crossing in five wild days.

We went overland to London with all the haste we could manage and arrived in the middle of November, having been away for little more than three months. With my heart in my mouth I rode into the courtyard, threw myself from my horse and hammered on the door of the house, shouting for Stephen.

Eva and Thomas were alive.

Opening my veins for them, they drank.

Each drank so much of me that I fell to my knees and then myself collapsed and was only revived through hot spiced wine and three cups of servant's blood.

Praise God, they were cured.

After two days with no relapse into sickness, dearest Eva wept with relief and embraced me closely.

When I was certain they were truly well, I told them what had happened. What I had done.

And Thomas was furious.

17

RECRUITMENT

"YOU DID WHAT?" Thomas asked me, his eyes shining.

"It was the only way."

Two days after my return, sure as we could be that they would not fall back into sickness, we ate in the hall.

After dismissing the servants, I had relayed the events of our journey to the south. Walt sat in silence and kept shovelling food into his face. We had both grown thinner but I had appetite solely for wine.

Elbows on the table, Thomas lowered his face into his hands.

"You murdered good men to save our lives?" he asked, without looking up. "I would rather have died."

Hugh, sitting beside him, patted Thomas on the back.

Stephen drummed his fingers on the table. "Hardly murders, were they, Thomas? It sounds to me as though Richard and

Walter defended themselves when attacked, as any man would have done."

"And the knight in the tower?" Thomas asked, lifting his face. He seemed tired. Drawn. Months of illness had taken their toll, perhaps not to his immortal body but certainly to his soul and to his heart. "That knight and his men were no threat to you."

"Enemies," I said, waving my cup and spilling wine over the side. "Enemies of England who would have fought us one way or another, one day."

"There is a truce," Thomas said. "You know they did not deserve their deaths."

His ingratitude was beginning to grate on me and I stared at him, feeling the anger burn in my chest.

"Well," Eva said, placing a hand on my forearm. "It is done now. The strength Richard gained through these actions has cured us and now we can go on, Thomas."

"Yes, yes," he said, bowing his head. "I am not ungrateful. It is simply that... for so long you have ensured we act entirely within the terms of the truces arranged between the kings. We do nothing that might risk them. And now..."

"I understand. As you benefit from my actions, you feel as though you had a hand in them. Do not trouble yourself with guilt. If there is sin here, it is mine."

He was unhappy and wished to say more but he was tired in his heart and he merely nodded.

I was irritated by his weakness.

Yes, I had sinned by killing when I had not needed to and I would have to atone. My sins had brought Thomas back from a terrible living death, and Eva too. They had wakened from an endless nightmare only thanks to my acting more like my brother and Priskos instead of by the code of chivalry.

A part of me had expected Thomas to fall to his knees and express everlasting gratitude for his deliverance. Part of me wanted him to do so.

"What I struggle to comprehend," Stephen began, "is that there are clearly many more immortals in the world than we knew of."

I nodded. "Yes, there are three more. Priskos, Peter the false priest, and the giant Christman."

Stephen opened his arms. "Are you certain? It is astonishing to think of this blood. The blood from you, Richard, that you have given to us." He rolled up his sleeves and examined the veins of his wrists, touching the skin reverently. "This blood that is in us, comes from so great a pedigree. It is the blood that flowed in the veins of Alexander. In the veins of Caesar. Think of what this blood has accomplished." He looked at us, eyes shining joy and not a little hint of madness. "This turns so much of history on its head, does it not? How many men like us have been turning the wheels of history down the centuries? How many famed ancients have been of this blood? It could be hundreds. Thousands."

"Only if this old man was speaking the truth," Eva pointed out. "He may be as mad as William."

I nodded. "Priskos may have been lying but I do not believe so. Mad, perhaps. But not a liar. And his strength." I closed my eyes and suppressed a shudder. "I cannot convey to you the power in him."

Hugh had his fingers across his mouth. "Surely, Richard, he cannot be that much stronger than you."

I scoffed at his ignorance. "Consider the chasm that exists between each of you and a mortal man." I looked around at each of them to see them nod as they recalled it. "That was what I felt when I struggled against the giant Christman. Perhaps that would also be the distance in strength between myself and Peter, the other son of Priskos. But the father himself." I grasped the edge of the table as I pictured him holding me aloft. "His fingers were iron. His arms unbending as an ancient oak. One might as well attempt to fight a mountain."

"Like a god," Stephen muttered.

"What was that?" Thomas said.

Stephen sat upright. "The pagans believed in gods that walked amongst mortals. They had stories of Hercules and Mars and Jupiter. Gods who acted like men, who could defeat monsters and cut down men like wheat."

Thomas snorted. "Pagan nonsense."

"Of course," Stephen said, waving his hand.

"He criticised God," I said, almost blurting it out. "He said that Jesus Christ was a god of death. The god of a desert people who was never meant for us."

"Disgraceful," Thomas said. "Surely, Richard, you put no stock in such blasphemy."

"Of course not," I lied. "And yet, Alexander displayed knightly virtue in his conquest of the East, and in his conduct with his enemies, and with women. And Alexander was a pagan."

Thomas scowled. "He had no choice but to be a pagan. We

have no such excuse. The truth and the light has since been revealed to us. To all mankind. For the sake of our souls, we must worship God and His son Jesus Christ. You see what becomes of a man who has not welcomed Jesus into his heart. This Priskos is a brute. A savage. And it is because he rejects God. Only through God can man rise up to take his place above the creatures of the earth, else we are condemned to forever act like beasts. All pagans were like this before Christ and all pagans are like this in the world today."

"You are right, of course," I said. Though I still had my doubts.

"Are we going to kill them?" Eva asked, looking at me. "Priskos and his sons."

I finished my cup and filled it again. Placing the jug carefully back on the table top, I picked up my wine and took a great gulp.

"The Order of the White Dagger exists to find and to destroy the immortals that William has made and to kill my brother for the evil that he has wrought in the world." I took another drink. "Priskos has done evil. Perhaps even greater evil than William. But he and his sons are sitting in a quiet corner of the world, doing harm only to the villages and people in the vicinity. One day, it may be necessary to cleanse them from the Earth also. Until that day, we may ignore them."

Stephen held up a finger, tilting his head. "Could Priskos or the sons be the progenitors of the black banner knight and his men?"

"He knew nothing about all that. He knew that William was granting the Gift to others and he even suggested he might have to kill William, if he caused too much trouble."

They all sat up at that.

"So," Stephen said, a small smile on his face, "why not let Priskos kill William?"

"He might not act for five hundred years, Stephen. Only once William unmakes the world, which we must not allow. And it is our duty. Would you allow another to fulfil your duties merely because they offered?"

He did not answer, which spoke loudly on what he thought of duty.

"What of the pestilence?" Eva asked. "How does it go across the sea?"

I shook my head, unable to describe it.

"Bad," Walt said, his mouth full of boiled pork. "Exceeding bad, Lady Eva."

"Here, also," she said.

Stephen sighed. "So many have died and yet the numbers of new deaths diminish. It seems that this is not the end of days after all."

"Plagues lessen in winter," I pointed out, "only to return in spring."

Thomas and Hugh nodded. We had seen it in many campaigns.

"The people are stunned," Hugh said. "It seems that the living are thankful beyond measure for their own lives, even while there is not a soul alive who is not terribly bereaved. It is beyond comprehension. There is nothing to be made from it. It is beyond reason, is it not? And so, as I say, the people everywhere seem dazed." He shook his head in wonder and placed a hand over his eyes, for he was a gentle soul, in truth.

"That may be so," Stephen said to me. "Order has not broken down in England. We still receive reports from the few yet travelling. Those that survive go on. In some places, half of the folk perished, so we are told. In others, merely a third, or fewer. And yet some villages seem to have been entirely lost. Our king and queen and the princes live. Most of the great men of the realm have so far survived. The soldiers, too, have fared better than others. It seems, from what we can tell, that the poorest, the oldest and youngest have died where the rich and the strong have lived."

"Good," I said, nodding and banging the table with my fingers. "Very good. As it should be. England goes on. When they are ready, King Edward and the Prince can go on with their war."

Hugh frowned. "Their war, sir? Is it not our war, also?"

"Not any more, Hugh."

"What about us?" Thomas said. "What shall we do if we are not fighting for Edward?"

I drank off my wine. "We shall winter here. Grow strong and healthy and wait for the weather to change."

"And then?" Eva said.

"We shall revive my old company of archers and men-at-arms and lead them into France. Not for Edward. Not to fight Philip. We will find the knight of the black banner and this time nothing shall stop us. If we must, we will burn all France to the ground."

∞ ∞ ∞

Eva came to me a few days later as I rested in my chamber. Rain pattered on the tiles above and on the walls outside but the chamber was warmed by the fire in my hearth and from the fire in the chamber below. One of the greatest creations ever developed in my long life is most certainly the chimney stack.

"Am I intruding?" Eva asked at the door.

"You could never intrude on me, Eva."

She smiled and shook her head. "What if you were privately entertaining the comely Lady Cecilia?"

I hesitated, surprised to hear her mention the name, before I recovered. "Well then I would most certainly endeavour to privately entertain you both, simultaneously, to the best of my abilities."

She scoffed, presumably at my abilities, and took the seat I held for her. "Do you mean to marry her?"

I sighed as I sat opposite. The green glass in the windows let in light and kept out the damp weather. Best of all, I could not see out across the cesspool that was London.

"Why would you ask me that?"

"I know you escorted her back from Flanders. You visited her at the Tower. She has written you four letters in these past three months."

A laugh escaped my lips. "You have been keeping note of my romantic liaisons?"

"I keep note of everything." She peered at me. "Of everyone."

"I had no idea you already maintained so many agents."

"When will you give me an answer?"

"Is it your business to receive one?"

She frowned. "My business? I care for you, Richard. I would see you happy."

I sighed. "I see." The rain gusted against the window. "Would you like a drink?" I poured us some wine but my hand shook, spilling the blood-dark liquid onto the table. "How can I marry the woman, Eva? She would get no sons from me. No daughters neither. She would age and wither while I went on. How can any of us condemn a mortal into such a life?"

"Have you told her that you cannot marry her?"

I wiped my finger in the dark wine spilled on the table. "I have discouraged her. Reminded her that I am good only for war and not for marriage. She knows I am beneath her, surely."

Eva shook her head at my stupidity. "You may as well attempt to fend off a bear with a honeyed chicken."

"What do you mean?"

She scoffed. "Tell her you will not marry her and then cease all contact. That is the kindest thing. Or..."

"Or what?"

"Would it be the worst life for her? You would not be such a bad husband. She is old. She bore no children in her first marriage. Her brother is wealthy but her name is not that great. Sir Humphrey Ingham is known to be a prickly bore and many a lord has already been put off by him, whereas you would never be intimidated by him. Cecilia is no doubt aware of that."

"She is not old," I said. "Anyway, I leave for France in the spring and I will not return until the task is complete. One way or the other."

"What if she is unmarried when you return?"

"She will not be."

"You do not have to allow your oath to drive you from happiness, Richard. You might have twenty or thirty years of contentment with Cecilia. Do not throw it away because you believe that you know what she wants better than she herself does."

"But I am a monster. I cannot allow her to enter into such a life without knowledge of all the facts."

"In what way are you a monster?"

"Come, now. You have seen the things I have done."

"I have done the things you have done. I do not consider myself a monster. And I do not consider you one, either."

"You might have done the odd monstrous act, Eva. But I come from a monster. Directly. It is in my blood."

She pursed her lips, frowning. "Perhaps the sins of the fathers will be visited on the sons for those who hate God, as Priskos claimed to do. But you are a good Christian."

I scoffed. "Never that."

"You were not. Not when I met you. But you have changed over the years. You have gown devout in your faith."

"Nonsense."

"It is Thomas," Eva said. "Did you know that? His love of God, his loyalty and respect for the Church. After decades together, his piety has rubbed off on you."

"God forbid."

She shook her head. "Admit it, Richard. You strive to be a good Christian, do you not?"

I sighed. "If I do, that may be that is why I have failed to find the black knight. I have been overly dutiful. Overly courteous to the kings and lords I have served. Perhaps I should be the one who is served by kings and lords. Let me be the monster and I will find the black knight and be feared also."

"Do you think Cecilia would like that?" Eva asked. "For you to be monstrous? Or would she rather marry to the man you are in your heart. A good and decent knight."

"She shall have neither." I drank my wine and poured another. "Perhaps I will write to let her know I will be gone for a long time. She will be free to forget me and perhaps it will not break her heart."

She laughed a little. "I doubt her heart is so fragile. I suspect she has a half-dozen other suitors dangling by threads."

"But you said—"

"Visit her, you coward. Do not write. But also do not tell her that you are taking your company to Brittany. Word would very likely get back to the King that you are jeopardising his treaties."

"I may be a fool when it comes to the ways of women," I said, "but I am not a drooling simpleton."

Eva nodded slowly as she considered my words, then shrugged. "Why are you willing to risk starting the war again? To risk falling out of favour with the King, likely forever?"

"For the rest of his mortal life, do you mean? Perhaps I have of late been overly concerned with the King's purposes, rather than those of the Order."

"And yet having the King's ear has helped us, has it not?" Eva asked. "You have said so repeatedly for fifty years. Social position unlocks doors that even wealth cannot."

"That is what I have told myself," I replied, "and whenever any of you had doubts, that was my response. Now, I wonder if I was not avoiding my true duty by waging war against the Scots and the Welsh and all the rest. It was simpler to do so rather than to carry out my true duty."

"For so long it seemed reasonable to believe that there were no more immortals left. Other than William. And our Order had to strive to maintain and develop our resources in the meantime."

"You mean to say that it was difficult to find them and so we gave up. No, no. That is not it. I should say that I gave up. Ceased trying. If I wished it, I could recruit hundreds of men and cut a swathe through France and we could torture our way to the truth. Someone would know. This is what I should have done decades ago, in the time of the first Edward, instead of amusing myself by killing barbarian Scots."

"You would bring the King's fury down on us."

I nodded. "So be it. One day, his son will be the King, and his son after him. While we will endure. What is the King, any king, compared to us?"

"A man powerful enough to wield the might of an entire kingdom."

That was true. "We have power, also. One of us is equal to hundred mortal men."

"Two or three, perhaps."

"A dozen. A score."

"Even if that were the case, it would mean we could defeat how many soldiers sent against us? Perhaps five hundred at the most? How many soldiers can a king raise?"

"I shall create more members of our Order."

"I see. How many? Who will they be?"

Her precise questions irritated me, as they always had done. I recalled how much I hated her damned practicality. "I do not know. Whatever is needed."

"How many, Richard?"

"A hundred, if need be."

She scoffed. "A hundred?"

"Damn you, woman, I shall make a thousand immortals and burn France to the ground."

"Very well," she said, "and who will these men be? Men you can trust, you have always said. Men who you could be certain will never turn on you, never betray us."

"Yes, yes," I said, waving my hand at her. "Why must your arguments always be so bloody well-reasoned?"

She smiled, and for a moment it was like we were man and wife again. But then we both recalled our separation and our smiles dropped.

"How fare you, Eva?" I asked.

Eva took a long, slow breath. She closed her eyes for a long moment and opened them again.

"I wanted to die. It was as though I descended into Hell, and climbed back out again, day after day."

"It cannot imagine the torment. Yet you endured."

"I did."

I reached across the table and held her hand. "In time, the memory shall fade."

She pulled her hand away. "You are changed," she said.

"I am?"

"You descended into Hell, also. You did it for us. You faced the demon of the abyss but it has hardened your heart. You fell. You died. You came back with these notions that you are monstrous, that you will burn and destroy. Death changed you."

I shrugged. "I have died before."

"You pass it off lightly but whatever you went through in that cave, with that man, has taken its toll on you. Can I even call him a man? The way you spoke of him. His power is terrible, is it not?"

"It is."

"You fear it."

I hesitated. "Yes."

"You have always had anger, Richard. You cloak it in jest, or courtliness, or chivalrousness. Even then, many can sense the danger in you. It makes men, even knights and lords, fear you. Fear what you might do. And yet when I look at you now I see that the anger has grown. It swells in your breast, it moves your limbs. It is closer to the surface and even I fear what might be should it burst forth."

I drank my wine. "I would never harm you."

"What did the Ancient One infest you with, Richard? Our Order exists to destroy men like him and yet you dismiss any notion of doing so."

"I created the Order to kill William and the ones he created. Priskos is something else."

"Something worse. At the least he is a killer of women and there is nothing honourable about that."

I gripped my cup so tightly that my wine spilled. Osanna would have lived a few more years if not for my idiot meddling. "Leave it, woman."

She licked her lips and swallowed. "Is it not worth discussing again? Unlike the black knight, unlike William, we know where these ones reside. Perhaps we should recruit an army, travel to Swabia and destroy him and his spawn."

"He deserves death." Even as I said it, I was not certain it was true. Was there much difference between his monstrous actions and my own? Perhaps he did deserve death and I did, too. "Even with an army, I am not sure we would be enough to stop him."

"Surely, that cannot be."

"Stephen said Priskos seemed like a pagan god walking the earth. He spoke truer than I cared to admit. Could a thousand knights stop him? I swear that I do not know."

"I have never known you not to seek revenge on every enemy. If you wanted to do it, you would find a way."

"I may need centuries to grow strong enough. And first, I must find and destroy the black knight. Then William. When that is done, I shall visit Priskos once more."

Eva peered at me closely. "What about the others? His sons, Peter and Christman? Perhaps you feel a certain kinship with them?"

She was right but I denied it, even to myself. "The only kinship that I feel is with you. And Thomas, and Hugh. And Stephen."

She smiled. "That is well."

"So, all else will have to wait. The black knight must fall. I shall recruit my old company," I said, "and take them to France.

Some of them, I am sure, would make reliable members of the Order."

"More commoners like Walt?" she asked. "You have always resisted it. You have not yet made Walt swear the Order's oath, have you?"

"These are desperate times. I will bring Walt into the Order and I shall make more of us. A select few, I think. Some of them fight better than knights I have known."

"How will you turn some of your company and not others? Surely, you will have to grant them all the Gift at the same time or none at all? You know what commoners are like. They have no restraint. How will you manage it?"

I laughed. "Will you stop thrusting your damned questions at me, my lady? Sometimes, a man must act and concern himself with the detail later."

She tilted her head and regarded me with a look. With her eyes alone, she expressed a thought as clear as if she had spoken it. "What do you mean, sometimes?"

I laughed again, because despite everything, I knew I was going to war again. A war on my terms.

And, whether I was a knight or a monster, there was nothing I loved more than that.

∞ ∞ ∞

Rob Hawthorn had been one of the wilder ones in his youth, when he fought for me in Brittany. Fighting and drinking like a madman, and he had been even worse with women. But he was a natural leader in spite of his carousing in the towns, for when we were fighting there was no steadier soul in the company.

Once when I led my men into an ambush near Rostrenen in Brittany I saw him standing alone, isolated from the rest of us, with two mounted men charging at him. I called out that he should run, or at least throw himself down. While I bellowed for the other archers to shoot, Rob put an arrow into one man's neck, and then calmly pulled another arrow from his bag, nocked it and shot the second man's horse in the nose, throwing the rider. Rob strolled up and cut the Frenchman's throat. When he turned around to us, he was grinning from ear to ear. It's fair to say that the rest of the men loved him for his steadiness and bravado and his legend amongst them grew until he commanded all of my archers.

It had been hardly a blink of my eye and there I was approaching his rather fine house where small children played in the yard, terrorising the chickens.

"Praise God, Sir Richard," Rob said, "I got your message, sir. I am greatly honoured by your presence." Touchingly, he was wearing what I sure was his very best clothing, as did his wife Agnes and his children.

Rob looked incredibly uncomfortable and stiff. His wife was a pretty young girl who watched all of her children like a hawk, without seeming to pay them any mind at all. She appeared nervous, as it was unusual for a lord to attend a commoner.

It would have made sense for me to invite Rob to the manor, or else simply instruct him by messenger. Agnes must have wondered what business I could possibly have in store for her husband.

"You honour me," I said, warmly, "by inviting me into your home. Please forgive me for bringing Walter, here, Rob. I am afraid, madame, that Walt's table manners are quite appalling. I will understand perfectly if you decided to relegate him to the servants table and in fact that may be for the best."

Walt hung his head in shame. "My lord Richard speaks the truth, madame. I ain't fit for proper company."

Rob laughed as he approached Walt and clapped him on the shoulder. "Black Walter, it is a wonder that you are still alive."

Walt glanced at me. "You don't know the half of it, Rob."

Rob had done well for himself. He had saved enough of the money he had earned during his years fighting to set himself up well in a three-bay house with a good-sized hall. The outside was covered in smooth plaster, freshly painted. Inside the dark hall, the central fire burned well with little smoke, and the mouth-watering smells of food filled the air. Rob gave me the best seat at the head of his table and he sat on my right while Agnes sat on my left and Walt sat opposite. The children sat at their own table nearby and Rob's servants busied themselves with the food, directed by Agnes. It was a well-ordered home. The plastered walls inside were even painted a bright white, and the rushes on the floor were mixed with copious amounts of lavender and other fresh herbs. The table was well laid with bowls, ceramic jugs and even silver serving spoons.

The food was good, hearty stuff and well-prepared. They must have spent a considerable sum on the fish and the meat and spices, perhaps in honour of my dining with them. We spoke of men we had known who had died, during the wars and during the Pestilence. The deaths of so many local landowners had been a benefit to men like Rob who had been able to buy up parcels for very little and his future was looking rather bright.

"God spared many of our family," Rob said, indicating his wife. "My wife's brother and his children excepted, of course." Agnes lowered her head in grief.

"There has never been anything like it in all the world," I said, though I thought of Priskos as I said it and recalled how he claimed to have seen even greater mortalities during his long life. "Though it is passed, now, and we may at last continue with our lives."

Rob seemed to catch a deeper meaning in my words and looked at me keenly.

Rob's eldest son approached toward the end of the meal. "Excuse me, sir," he said as he sidled up to me.

"Dick, leave the lord alone," Rob said.

"It is well," I said, smiling. "You are a well-made lad. How may I be of service, Master Dick?"

"Father says often that he saved your life in the wars against the French and swears he speaks true but my mate Will down Scatborough way reckons that ain't nought but a bunch of gooseberries."

"Richard Hawthorn!" Agnes snapped. "You mind your tongue, young man and beg the pardon of Sir Richard this very instant. Pray, forgive us, my lord, and know that he shall be thoroughly whipped for his impudence."

I tried and failed to keep a straight face. "Forgive me, madame. You must do as you see fit but do not thrash the lad on my account. Rob, may your boy join us at table?"

Rob had his own hand across his mouth as he nodded his assent and shifted aside on the bench, catching a look of some sort from his wife as the young master sat next to me.

"Dick, you should know that it is indeed the truth that your good father did save my life in the war and not merely once but many a time." I spoke a lie but it was not dishonest in spirit, for had I been mortal then Rob's loyal actions would have indeed saved me. "Once, a French knight's lance caught me just so, on my flank, and forced apart my armour where the buckles had loosened during battle. The lance sliced deep into the flesh of my belly and I do not mind admitting to you, young master, that the wound laid me low. Blood soaked me, belly and loins, and I would surely have perished that day, had your father not carried me, armour and all, upon his shoulder, away from the danger. He found me wine, clean water, and later he even persuaded a surgeon to come to heal me."

Young Dick's face was a mask of enraptured attention.

"You will have seen your father shoot, so you will well know what a fine archer he is. But you may not know that he has the strength of five men, and the courage of a lion. Do you know that I fought with the greatest Earls of England and even with Prince Edward of Woodstock and yet, I swear, lad, that there is no man I would rather have fighting at my side than Robert Hawthorn."

The boy slowly turned away from me, eyes bulging, to look up at his father.

After the meal, Rob offered to show me the new orchard he had planted and at once I agreed. The moment we were out of earshot of his house, he turned to me.

"Where?" he asked. "When?"

"Dartmouth," I replied. "Four weeks, if you can make it."

"I will be there. Who joins us?"

"So many of our company fell to the pestilence. Yet I hope we will have Hal, Ralf Thorns, Reg, Osmund, and Fair Simon, at the least. Also, Diggory and Fred Blackthorpe, if they are still at their farm. Gerald Crowfield is said to have returned, finally. Adam Lamarsh, if he is not in gaol. I would hope also to get Roger, Osbert, Watkyn, Jake, and Stan. I have sent a messenger to each but would you consider speaking to them?"

"I'll get them there, sir."

"Hear me, Robert," I said. "This raid is not sanctioned by the King. In truth, if the King were to know, he would likely forbid it."

"This is a personal quest, sir?"

"I never stopped hunting the man with the black banner, who killed our men that day near Crecy. Yet, I grew complacent. I did not try enough. No longer. I will tear France to pieces to look for him and then I will take revenge."

Rob's face grew tight. Unclenching his jaw, he nodded. "Deryk Crookley was my cousin, sir. And I fought with Paul since we were lads. The whole company loved them like brothers, Sir John, too, and were heartsore indeed when they got killed. All of us who remain will join you. Do not doubt that, sir."

His easy commitment worried me. I wished to make him

understand what he was agreeing to.

"We will be alone, Rob. We will be cut off from supplies and if we wish to retreat, we shall have to fight our way through. But we shall be a small enough band to evade pursuit while we live off the land and we will move rapidly. I do not know how long we will be there. How long it will be before we return home."

Rob looked back at his house. It was a good home. A home that all men wanted. A dutiful wife, a strong son, pretty daughters. I felt a keen stab of jealousy for the kind of life that I wanted more than any other. Though I knew it could never be, I thought for a moment that I would even live as a common man if I could have such a family. Without a home, without sons, I would never feel truly whole, no matter how many centuries I lived or how much glory I won in battle.

Rob sighed and chewed his lip. "Agnes will not understand."

I nodded. She would be right to be confused and hurt by him leaving. She would feel betrayed and rejected. Agnes would feel abandoned. By God, she would be abandoned. Rob was a man who had everything he needed to be happy and fulfilled. He had an heir to carry his name and continue the family, he had daughters to bring him joy, and his young wife could no doubt bear him more. He had over forty contiguous acres and more elsewhere in the hundred he had bought up. Already a man of good standing, and chief tithingman, he could easily become the bailiff of the hundred in time and his son would grow up to take full advantage of his father's wealth and status. Who knew how far young Dick would rise with such a start and with his father to guide him? His daughters might make excellent marriages, to merchants or lawyers or even the poorer sort of esquires.

It was certainly everything a man needed to be happy and fulfilled.

Except, of course, it was not.

A man also needed war. If you had fought in battle, and if you enjoyed it, then it was something you could never throw off. Even though war would bring you discomfort, pain, terror, and misery, it would also take you to a state of being that was far beyond anything that could be found in peace. Men like Rob knew, even if he may never have been able to put it into words, that war brought a man closer to God. It also brought you further into the world so that colours were more vivid and edges were sharper, before, during and after a battle. It brought you closer to the men you fought beside, the men you marched and rode with through burning sun and freezing rain, the men you shared your last piece of stale bread with, the men who picked you up when you were broken and roared your name when you won glory. It brought you closer to your brothers in arms than you were even to your wife and your children, or your father and the brothers you were raised with. Once you tasted that life, you could never be complete without it.

Even though it might leave his family without a husband and father, Rob Hawthorn could not resist going to war. He *had* to.

And he was right. His wife would never understand.

Although I knew that the best thing to do would be to cut off Lady Cecilia from all contact, I could not help but call on her before I left. Being cruel to be kind, I should have sent a terse letter but I could not bear the idea of her thinking badly of me and so I kept her dangling by a thread.

It was astonishing that she had rejected so many suitors as she was not growing any younger and she had to marry soon else her value would decline so far that she might spend the rest of her days as a widow before entering a convent. And that, I thought, would truly be a terrible waste.

Though I had only ever treated her rather badly, Cecilia seemed overjoyed to see me and rushed across the hall to me when I entered. She looked wonderful and if anything was even lovelier than I remembered. Truly, I marvelled as she approached, she was of elegant deportment and very pleasing and amiable in bearing. She displayed well the manners of the court and was so dignified in behaviour that she was more than worthy of reverence.

She held my hands and looked up at me expectantly, as if she hoped I would ask for her hand in marriage there and then.

"I must go away," I admitted. "For a long time."

"I see," she said, dropping my hands.

Of course, the poor woman was expecting I had come to ask her, simply to be disappointed once more. At least, I thought, it would be the last disappointment she would get from me, for surely she would accept one of her other proposals while I was gone. Especially if the King publicly denounced me once he heard where I had gone and what I was doing.

She escorted me to a fine chair in her hall and I sat while the servants brought food and wine before withdrawing to a respectful distance. I reflected that the lovely place I was in could have been mine. The servants could have served me and Cecilia every day and I could have shared her chamber every night. It would become my place and hers and our marriage would be a place for our hearts.

But it would forever be empty, of children and of hope for the future.

"Because I do not know for how long I will be away," I said, "I thought it best that I come. To speak to you."

"How kind," she said, pressing her lips together. "And where is it that you go, sir?"

"I am afraid I cannot say."

"Oh?" She was angry. "So it appears that you have said all that you came to say, sir, and you may now take your leave."

"My lady, you must understand that I do not tell you in order to protect you."

She laughed, bitterly. "You protect yourself, Richard. Do not pretend otherwise with me. I am not some two-penny prostitute who will nod and smile at your lies."

I paused, astonished at her vulgarity. Clearly, I had wounded her grievously.

"It is to France that I must go," I admitted, "but I cannot say more than that. Truly."

"France?" She gasped. "Has the war taken some new course I am not aware of?"

"No, no. Nothing of that sort."

"Then why do you go, sir? Is it merely to be free of me?"

"Cecilia, please. How can you say such a thing? It would not be fair to you for us to be married, we have spoken of this."

"You have spoken of it but it did not make sense then and it makes less sense now. You are running off to some woman in Normandy, I know it. Do not deny it."

"Where did you get this notion? I have no woman, my lady. None but you."

She scoffed at my words. "But you do not have me, do you, Richard."

"I wish that I could. But we cannot be married."

She came to me and knelt before me. "Not in law perhaps. But who shall give a lover any law? Love is a greater law than any written by mortal man. We could pretend to be married," she said, speaking softly. "Just for one night."

She looked up at me with those huge, dark eyes and long black lashes. Her pink lips were slightly parted and her breathing fast and shallow.

I wish I could say that I did the honourable thing.

But I am not as chivalrous as all that.

Her wanton passion and her remarkable ability in the bedchamber was startling to partake in. Tearing off her clothes with the help of her red-headed servant, she stood before me in joy and pride in her own nakedness. It was all I could do to keep up with her. She used her mouth over every inch of my skin and demanded the same from me. I was only too pleased to oblige. In fact, I obliged her all of the night and half of the next day. Thus in this heaven I took my delight and smothered her with kisses upon kisses until gradually I came to know the purest bliss.

While she rested in between bouts of passion, she had her maidservants bring us wine and fruit and she never once troubled to cover herself. We spoke of small things and laughed, though she also attempted to tease more from me regarding how long I would be absent, though she protested she was but making idle conversation.

"You were so very terse with me when first we met, My Lady," I said as she reclined in my arms. "I would never have known how sweet your lips could be."

She raised herself on one elbow and turned to peer at me, right close. "Men may shield their bodies with brigandines and mail but women must use cunning."

"Ah, so you were merely acting the hard-hearted creature when in truth you wanted me from the moment you laid eyes on me?"

She slapped her hand on my chest over my heart and poked me there with her sharp nail. "I had heard how you were a raging barbarian, sir. A vicious monster who delighted in murder and the ravaging of women. I had to show you with the cold steel of my words that I was not a lady to be trifled with or to be taken advantage of."

"And yet your cold steel warmed when you felt my mighty arms about you."

"Ha!" she scoffed and pinched my skin. "It was not your mighty arms but your kindness, sir, your gentleness that showed me what sort of man you truly were. A chivalrous man. A knight in your heart."

She kissed me on the spot where she had twisted and poked

at me.

"Come here, then," I said, pulling her to me. But she pushed me off and reached away from me to find refreshment from the bedside. After wine and fruit, she aroused my passions from me once more with her breasts, her hair, mouth and hands.

Although I was in Heaven itself, by midday I had to take my leave or I risked missing my own boat. When I raised the issue, she commanded me to leave without saying farewell and pushed me from her chamber before I could say more than a few words. The lady was wiping her eyes as she heaved her door shut with a slam.

A porter at her front door gave me an eyeful of judgement as I left the house but I heroically resisted knocking his teeth out and slamming his head into the wooden frame.

"Good day, sir," he muttered, bowing his head.

Outside, the sky pressed down like a sheet of melted lead. I dragged myself into my saddle, as weary and heartsick as a king that just lost his kingdom.

"You alright, sir?" Walt asked me on the road to the coast. "You look a little worse for wear."

"Shut up, Walt."

My company awaited us.

I had the immortal warriors Thomas, Hugh and Walt. I had twenty-one veteran archers commanded by Rob Hawthorn. With nine men-at-arms, their squires and the servants, I had fifty-two men.

Fifty-two men with which to invade France and find the knight of the black banner.

This time, I thought, *I will not fail. No matter the cost.*
But I had more to lose than I knew.

18

BRITTANY

MY COMPANY CROSSED FROM DOVER to Calais. My men brought their armour and weapons, we brought food and wine and equipment. I even brought across our best horses, which cost a fortune and quite ruined them for days afterward. It took five ships to get us all across and to avoid suspicion each left on a different day so that we appeared to be no more than the ordinary traffic to our little piece of England on the French coast.

It was still ours.

Earlier, in July 1348, the first truce ended and King Philip sent his greatest knight, Sir Geoffrey de Charny, against us. The Burgundian knight who had borne the Oriflamme in the army that fell back from Calais in 1347 was one of the commanders of an army sent to cut off Calais from our allies in Flanders. They were hampered by the terrible summer rains that had so threatened to spoil Edward's endless tourneys in England.

De Charny built a fort outside Calais and cut that road through the marshes to Gravelines that I had spent months keeping open the year before. But the appearance of the pestilence had cut short his campaign before he could follow up on his initial moves. Instead, the French moved to attack the cities of Flanders and so cut off our vital allies not just from Calais but from the entire war and that was where they had focused ever since.

My men claimed it was not for strategic reasons but because they were afraid of us and demoralised with their endless failures whenever the French went up against us.

Either way, Calais remained in English hands and so we crossed to there.

The town was a hive of activity and regular shipments brought a steady supply of timber, building stone and lime so that construction and repair could continue apace. What is more, bows and arrows were stocked in great abundance, as were spears and lances. Carts and wagons were unloaded in pieces, and oxen were driven down narrow gangplanks with much bellowing and cursing. A significant fraction of it all was organised by Stephen and the merchants who operated on his behalf. He was making a great deal of profit from the venture, while also fulfilling the King's strategic objectives.

And smuggling an entire company over in amongst it all.

I claimed to all who questioned me that we were on royal business and presented papers forged by Stephen and Eva as proof. The letters and their forged seals worked and we were soon through the gates heading south into France.

As the French forces were concentrated in the great estates around Paris and the armies were in Flanders to the east, we instead went west into Normandy.

My goal initially was to head for Brittany where I and many of my men knew the land, the towns and the people. Also, English allies held almost the entire coastal area and so there were many places we could be welcomed. And it was a place that we could always fall back to, should we need to do so.

Indeed, one of the King's Lieutenants in Brittany was Sir Thomas Dagworth, a man who we had fought with and who I hoped could be relied upon to provide me shelter and support. Of course, should he decide otherwise then I would most likely be driven from the duchy altogether. I hoped that would not be the case. In my favour was the fact that Dagworth had only about five hundred men in total and so my force of veterans would surely be most welcome, even if I insisted that I would remain independent of his command.

And I would most certainly insist so.

We made excellent time travelling across country and almost all local forces who came out to us simply stood and watched us go by. We set no fires and raided no homes. Well, few enough. I assured my men that there would be plenty of time for that. We made it in under three weeks and were in a very presentable condition when we came to Dagworth's castle.

Dagworth was originally from a village called Bradwell in the northern part of the county of Essex in England, which was not far from my manors in Suffolk and where many of the men in my company were from. I hoped the fact that they hailed from the same region of England would encourage him to welcome us as comrades.

Thankfully, he was surprised but pleased that we had joined him. He had fewer than three hundred men at arms and two hundred archers which was hardly enough to control the surrounding area, let alone impose his will on the entire Duchy of Brittany, which was larger than the entire country of Wales and had a population of hundreds of thousands.

Dagworth welcomed me to his table, along with Walt, and fed us very well indeed. The rest of my men crowded amongst the garrison down in the hall and grew increasingly raucous as the beer flowed.

"You are doing well, I see," I said after the fourth course of meats and sitting back to drink my wine.

Some of his men grinned and said that was very true but Dagworth grimaced.

"I do as well as I can. The damned routiers take and take from the country so that many of the common folk suffer even more from the soldiers than they did from the pestilence."

"Surely not. How bad has it become?"

Dagworth pressed his lips together, glancing at his men. Some shrugged, others grinned, and Dagworth nodded.

"Most of the inland castles were taken by the various captains that we have out of necessity employed. Many of them, unfortunately, are led by and made up of German, Dutch and Flemish mercenaries. I do not mind admitting to you, Richard, that I have very little control over them. Even more so than when you were here last, they increasingly act like little kings, lording it over the common folk of the towns they occupy and the lands about them. They are all ransoming the districts that they control. In return for payments to the mercenary captains, the inhabitants are not too badly assaulted by the companies occupying their area and, if they are lucky, they are defended from the other captains in neighbouring districts and from the wandering bands that go from place to place."

"It at least sounds to be more formalised than when I was last here. Before Crecy."

Dagworth sighed. "Indeed. They are dug in like ticks. Each garrison captain has marked out his own ransomed district and informs those in surrounding districts. Where they fall into disagreement about the borders, it is the inhabitants that suffer but it has settled somewhat into stability."

Walt grunted. "Sounds like a good deal to me, sir. Our king ain't paying for the garrisons but we have loyal men keeping the castles for us all the same."

Dagworth nodded. "Except they are no longer kept for us so much as kept out of the hands of the French. And should King Philip or one of the Dukes decide to roust them out one by one, what could they do to resist? And as I do not pay them, I have no control over them. And the common folk suffer. Dear God, how they suffer. I wonder if there will be any remaining to rule over once the war is won."

Once the war is won.

The words, so often spoken, hung heavy over us all like a curse. When the captains and lords spoke them, it was with hope and expectation that Edward would someday be the King of France and her dominions and his loyal men would all be great lords, living in peace and abundance. When the common soldiers spoke the same words, it was said flippantly as if they knew that the good times of plunder and murder would never end.

Once the war is won, when Hell freezes over.

"With your permission, Sir Thomas, I should like to take a tour of these towns. Inspect their defences. Speak to the commanders of the companies."

Dagworth sat back, chewing on the roast leg of a heron. "If it were anyone else, Richard, I would laugh in his face. As it is you, I believe you might just be able to do it. But tell me, sir, why would you do this for me? Anyone of these rogues could turn on you."

"I seek a man. A particular knight who I saw at Crecy. A knight with a plain black banner, fighting for the French. No one knows who he is, where he is from or where he has gone, but I mean to find him and put an end to him."

"All this?" Dagworth said, gesturing out of the window at my company. "All this effort. This expense. For one man?"

"A knight, his squires and any who associate with him, yes indeed, sir. It is a matter of honour."

He nodded, slowly. "I will write you a letter, though I doubt it will open as many doors as you might hope."

I shrugged. "Any door I need open I shall break into pieces."

"He complains about the *routiers*," Walt said as we rode west, further into Brittany, "and yet he's robbing his own lands three ways from Sunday and all, ain't he?"

I had to agree with Walt that the people of Dagworth's lands seemed broken and destitute. Bridges were not being maintained and roads were washed out all over. The thatch on houses was rotten and sagging, as if they lacked the will or the wealth to repair their own homes. Fields were fallow and meadows grew wild with no livestock to eat it.

"The English," Thomas pronounced grandly, "are excellent at making themselves rich from others' misfortune."

Rob laughed at him. "It's us that's making the misfortune, too, Tom."

That brought a cheer from the others and Thomas and Hugh scowled at them. Neither was a Breton and yet they must have sympathised with the people of the duchy even more than I did.

Our destination was the fortress of Becherel in the northwest of the duchy, a castle under the command of Hugh Calveley and his band of *routiers*.

His men refused me entry.

"I come under the authority of Sir Thomas Dagworth," I called up to the wall. At my side was Walt, Thomas, Hugh and Rob. The rest of the company held far back but within sight so that the men in the castle would know I was not attempting a ruse but also that I was not to be trifled with.

A few moments later came the shouted reply, along with a round of mocking laughter. "You can shove Dagworth's authority up your arse."

"When I get inside your walls," I said, "I am going to strike that man so hard he shall wake up in the infirmary pissing blood. Tell your master that Richard of Hawkedon is here."

The laughter faded into nothing and half an hour later the great doors were opened and Sir Hugh Calveley waved me in himself.

"Richard!" he cried. "What a delightful surprise."

"Sir Hugh," I replied. "Bring me that man."

His face coloured. "What man would that be?"

"You know what man."

"It was a jest, Richard. They did not know who you were. Thought you were one of Knolles' men come to bother us again."

"Bring me the man."

"Richard, I cannot—"

"A commoner cannot treat a knight with such disrespect and avoid punishment, can he, Hugh?"

"Why go to such trouble over a bloody archer?"

"Trouble? There will only be trouble if you deny me."

He nodded to one of his men who went away into the base of the tower and a few moments later a big man with a ratty face came stumbling out. He had the massive shoulders of an archer and was a veteran of perhaps forty-five.

"What do you say to Sir Richard, Esmond?"

Esmond looked down. "Beg your pardon, my lord."

I walked slowly toward him and he began edging away until the man-at-arms behind shoved him on the back. "Are you ready to receive a blow that will rupture your bowels?" I placed my hand on his shoulder and lowered my head. "Are you, man?"

He shook and nodded.

With a stomp of my foot, I thrust my fist toward his belly, shouting in his face. I stopped the blow before it connected but he fell back, crying out and tripping over his feet. He fell into a heap.

The courtyard erupted into laughter and Esmond was helped up, dusted off and led away while the others mocked him.

"Come on," Sir Hugh said, "let's get you fed and find out what the bloody Hell you are doing in my lands."

His table was not so well stocked as Dagworth's but he had an astonishing amount of fish, from the river and from the sea, as well as wading birds and fowl.

"All the fisherman in Dinard died," Sir Hugh said. "But more fisherman came." He pointed his dagger at me and waved the point around. "The lords all around complain that their peasants have died from the pestilence or say that we murdered them or starved them. But, mark me, Richard, mark me. There are always more peasants." He opened his arms. "And they come. They come from wherever the bloody Hell they come from. Like flies on a cow turd."

"Are you calling your lands a cow turd, Hugh?" I asked.

He scowled. "Why have you come, Richard? What do you mean to do with those men you have out there? You will never take this castle, you know that, surely? We outnumber you ten to one."

"More like three to one, Hugh, and those odds would not be enough to save you if that was my intention."

He scoffed but did not argue. "Why, then?"

"I seek a man. A knight who fought by Philip at Crecy. A knight with an all black banner."

Hugh shook his head. "And this knight is here?"

"He may be. What do you know of him?"

"Nothing. No knight I know of has a black banner. Who would have a black blazon, sir?"

"The heralds did not know him. None knows him. And yet he exists. He was there. Someone in France must know him."

"Then why not seek him in France?"

"Someone is helping him. Keeping him hidden. Or else he is a known knight who fought incognito to protect his identity. Who would do such a thing? What if it was a man who should have been fighting for England. Perhaps he was a Fleming? Or a Breton? Perhaps, God forbid, an Englishman."

Sir Hugh scowled. "I was not at Crecy."

I leaned forward. "Precisely, Hugh. Precisely."

His jaw dropped. Then he laughed, wiping a hand across his brow. "Come now, sir. Come. You cannot suspect I would fight against the King? Why would I do such a thing?"

I pursed my lips. "Who knows how the mind of a traitor works? But no, of course it could not be you, Calveley. You are as loyal as a..." I trailed off, leaving the unspoken word dog to fill the gap. "As loyal as any dutiful knight in the kingdom. All I ask is that you keep an eye out for word of the black banner. I will pay handsomely for any true word that leads me to him."

"Handsomely?" he said, looking me up and down. "Is that so?"

I sighed and took out a purse which I emptied into one hand. A cascade of sapphires, rubies and emeralds filled my palm.

Hugh's eyes grew.

"While you and the other captains have been gathering men and castles these last few years, I have been gathering gems, gold and silver."

It was somewhat true but most of the gems I had taken from the grave of a Mongol lord a hundred years earlier on the other side of the world.

"I shall send word," Hugh said, licking his lips and nodding. "All my men will ask wherever we go."

I poured the gems carefully back into the purse. "I want only true word, now. There shall be no payment for false words and threads that lead to nothing."

"If he is here, we shall have him for you."

With one English captain in my pocket, I went looking for more.

∞ ∞ ∞

We crossed back and forth across Brittany, sometimes raiding the lands of those *routiers* who denied us entry or tried to chase us off.

My men were good and I led them well.

Still, some men fell to wounds or sickness. Fair Simon took a scratch on the forearm in a scrap with some of Robert Knolles' men at a place called Gravelle down near the Loire. When he fell, he tumbled head first into a patch of boggy ground which was never good but the lads cleaned him up, cleaned and dressed the wound and we went on our way. He tried to hide it for a day but his sweating gave him away and when they pulled his arm from beneath his coat the stench was overwhelming.

"Am I going to die, lord?" he asked me.

"Yes. Say your prayers, lad. We will all be here with you when you go."

"Oh," he said, looking down. "That's good, then."

We lost Ralf Thorns in an ambush near Vannes when I stupidly split my forces in an attempt to surround an enemy who was not there. We all make mistakes but it was old Ralf who paid the price.

Adam Lamarsh came down with the flux and he emptied himself inside out between dawn and dusk one day on the banks of the Vilaine.

One by one, we lost archers and men-at-arms. One of the servants fled, looking to make for the coast. I ordered them to bring him back so I could talk some sense into the man but they brought him back dead. They protested that it was an accident and I accepted them at their word but I knew they had punished his disloyalty with death.

As the leaves turned to gold and yellow and brown in that first year, we tallied up nine dead.

Thomas was worried. "We are not yet beyond Brittany and yet we have lost so many. We must take on more men."

"Plenty of *routiers* about, sir," Walt said. "God knows, they would follow you."

"Men I do not know. Do not trust. I will take none on. We yet have enough to see off any trouble that comes our way."

"What about, you know, sir," Walt said, lowering his voice. "Giving some of the lads the old Gift, then?"

I scoffed. "Whenever the thought crosses my mind, I take one look at you and it puts the matter to rest."

He pursed his lips and nodded slowly. "Fair enough, sir. Fair enough."

In the second year, we lost thirteen more. Never a good number and it meant we were down from over fifty men to just thirty. With so few, there was less we could attempt and so less we could achieve.

"Would you not consider it now, sir?" Hugh asked me after we buried another archer beneath an old oak in northern Poitou. He lowered his voice as the other men trudged away from the grave. "Giving the common men the Gift?"

It was raining lightly. Our men were weary and wounded and needed somewhere to rest through the winter. We had to take a fortress and use that to wait out the bad weather but my men were hardly capable of defending themselves, let alone launching a ferocious attack on a walled town or tower.

"I thought you agreed with Thomas?"

Hugh nodded. "We should bring some men from the other companies into ours, yes. You say you would not trust them but we would watch each new man like a hawk. But also, sir, I think it would be a great boon to us if you would consider turning a few more men-at-arms, at least. There are so few left."

"Most of our archers fight as well with a sword or mace as any man-at-arms," I said. But my company suddenly appeared small and the men round-shouldered and tired. They could not keep up with the immortals. Still, they were savages at heart and once they were given the gift, I suspected I would have to fight to control them and some I would have to kill anyway.

"Find me a knight who has no family or future and I will consider him. Not these ruffians, Hugh."

My resolve lasted as long as it took for most of my remaining men to be slaughtered.

19

IMMORTAL COMPANY

WE ASSAULTED A SMALL FORTIFIED town under the command of a tough old French knight named Charles of Coussey who had three times as many men as I did and all of them veterans.

But I wanted Charles. I needed to take him. Rumours had circulated for months that he was murdering local girls but that was far from an uncommon occurrence for *routiers*. Only when word came from Sir Hugh Calveley that this Charles of Coussey was stealing young women from villages, marrying them and then murdering them before taking another, was I struck by the similarities to the vile Priskos.

"It could be him," I said to Thomas. "The black banner knight himself."

"Or one of his men," Thomas replied.

"We must take him."

It was late October in 1351 and I intended to take the town and fortress at Tiffauges, discover whether Sir Charles was the man we sought and then, either way, use the town for the winter.

I had but thirty men remaining and just twenty-four of them were fighters. Tiffauges was a small town but the fortress was far beyond our strength if we attempted any sort of frontal assault. The archers favoured drawing the enemy out and ambushing them but they had seventy men and would not send all out at once, leaving us with the rest within the walls being on high alert.

Walt wanted us to launch an attack on the walls during the dark of the night. He thought we could kill enough men in their beds before they could form against us. But they would be spread in houses throughout the little town, along with the poor townsfolk who suffered under the routier occupation.

"It would be chaos," I said to Walt.

He nodded, blank-faced, not seeing a problem.

After many days exploring the land all about, I came to a decision.

"The town is too well defended for us to take it. It is too large for us, anyway. We shall find somewhere else to overwinter. All we need is to take Sir Charles. If he is the knight we seek, we shall take revenge for John and our brothers. If not, we shall ransom him back to his men, if they will pay for him."

Thomas coughed. "What about justice for the women he has killed?"

"We are not here for them," I snapped.

He was a wily old knight, that was certain, and he was happy enough where he was, all tucked up safe in the town's keep, on the little hill looking down on the few houses and the church below. But his men had to come out to look for food and take tribute from the starving villages all around.

These men we took.

We took their horses, their food and their wine. We took their lives and their blood.

From Charles of Coussey's perspective, he had sent out a handful of men who did not return. Such things were common enough. Men desert for better lords all the time. So Coussey sent more riders in their stead but this time he sent fully half his force. Almost forty riders.

"This is madness," Thomas said as we watched their approach from the ridge in the woods two miles from town. "We cannot defeat so many."

"You and I could take that many all by ourselves," I said, turning from him.

But they were expecting an ambush in the woods. Of course they were. And they broke into three groups, the first riding along the road while the others came behind, separated by over a hundred yards.

"Should we call it off, sir?" Rob asked me. His men were concealed on both sides of the road, ready with their arrows.

"No," I said, though my heart raced at the thought of what was about to happen. "Bring down as many of the first group as you can then withdraw up the hill. We shall make a stand and take them as they come for us. They will give up before long and ride home to tell Sir Charles about us."

My complacency was going to cost my men dearly.

Our arrows flitted into the first group of riders. All eleven of them were hit with an arrow to either horse or man. But the survivors raced straight for us with cries of red murder in their throats and the other two groups came galloping to their companions' aid.

I did what I could to forestall them, as did Thomas, Hugh and Walt. But our enemies were so spread out between the trees that we could not reach and slay enough of them before the riders overtook us and ran down my fleeing archers. Stout and brave fellows that they were, they fought the mounted men with their bows, their swords, and even their bare hands. But many fell and no matter how many enemies I killed, they refused to flee from us. I killed man after man but I also saw my own men lying dead or crying out in agony and I wondered if I would have any men left to salvage from the utter disaster.

And then I saw him.

Up the hill, on a white horse, with his sword blade raised and visor up, roaring in fury and in victory.

It was Sir Charles de Coussey himself urging his men on from horseback in very fine armour and the most magnificent clothing. He was a big, burly fellow, gesturing theatrically. His fitted surcoat was a vivid yellow with a black cross emblazoned on it.

That was why the enemy were fighting with such uncommon ferocity. That was why my men were being slaughtered.

Their lord was amongst them.

He had been leading the third group of riders and had charged through the trees up the hill to the ridge to cut off my men and kill them all. Charles de Coussey was filled also with a ferocious energy and vigour and made an inspiring sight.

I was moving before I considered the bodyguard around him. I ran as though my armour was nothing, closing the distance in mere seconds and pushing through his men without attacking them.

A growl of rage grew in my throat and I speared my blade through the neck of de Coussey's horse and sawed it out, spilling the hot blood from the terrified beast. I yanked de Coussey from the saddle and stamped my foot on his face through the open visor. His nose crunched and I pushed my weight on him so that he could not rise.

His men came at me all at once and I fought them off for a few moments before Thomas, Hugh and Walt caught up with me and killed the bodyguards. The remaining enemies fled back through the wood toward the town and I let them go. Charles de Coussey was suffocating on his own blood but we got him upright and he coughed it out well enough while he was trussed up tight.

"Send to the servants beyond the ridge and have them bring up the horses," I said to Walt. "Thomas, Hugh. Let us find any man of us who yet lives."

"It is Rob, sir!" Hugh called a few moments later from just along the hill.

I went crashing through the undergrowth and found him on his back, coughing up blood all over Hugh. A broken lance point had taken him in the gut, front to back.

"We shall remove it," I said. "Hold him steady, Hugh."

Rob grimaced as he spoke. "No point. I'm done for."

"Yes," I replied, hurrying to remove the armour from my left arm. "You will die. But if you wish it, you can be reborn stronger than before."

He was confused and dying and did not understand, especially when we slid the lance from his guts, being careful to hold the wound tight so we did not rip him apart. In his confusion and agony, he followed our directions and drank down the blood that I gave him.

I poured it in and he drank and was turned.

So many more were close to death. I had a choice to make. Grant the gift of immortality to the dying remnants of my company or resign myself to failure. Recruiting new men who would be willing to follow me as the others had would be close to impossible and, even if I could, it would set me back months or years.

There was no time to hesitate.

I offered life to my strong men-at-arms Hal, Reginald, Osmund, and Watkyn, and the archer Randulf. They all took the chance, though they knew it to be blood magic and they barely comprehended what they were agreeing to. Ultimately, though, it was as stark and simple a choice as the one I faced in whether to offer it. Few men, when offered life over death, ask to first see the terms.

We were safe enough in the darkness of those woods but it was a tense night, crouched in the undergrowth and tending to my poor soldiers as they lay in the leaf litter. It took a long time to turn so many but they all lived to see the dawn, other than poor Reg, who died writhing in agony after drinking my blood. For some men, the Gift simply does not take.

When the surviving archers understood what had happened to their brothers, they each wanted to join them in immortality. With those men, healthy as they were, I took the time to explain that they would be slaves to blood and that their chance for ordinary life would be over.

They wanted it anyway though I could see they were not considering the consequences. And because I needed them, I cursed them also by granting them the Gift of immortality. So the archers Osbert, Jake, Lambert, and Stan were soon welcomed into the brotherhood of the blood.

The six remaining servants I would not change because my men needed their blood to drink and, in fact, I required more of them just so I would have enough for the bloodletting needed to keep my men thriving.

I had lost fourteen men in the failed ambush, including some of my best. Men who had followed me for years. Men like Nicholas Gedding, who would sing ditties to his bow to make his mates laugh. And Roger Russet the sturdy man-at-arms who never said much but always did what he said he would do. Gerald Crowfield, another one who had been a stocky labourer when I found him but who had turned into a damned savage soldier after a few months in the crucible that was Brittany. And Fred and Digger Blackthorpe, brothers who had died protecting each other.

It was a disaster that would have been the end of most routier leaders. What soldiers would follow a lord so incompetent? But my company was not dead. I had lost so much but I had gained eight more immortals. Three men-at-arms and five archers.

These along with Walt, Thomas, and Hugh, made for a force equal in effective strength to a mortal one of perhaps three or four times its size. There were few companies in France capable of withstanding a dozen veteran immortals.

After the disastrous ambush, we had dragged Sir Charles de Coussey with us and although much of the time I had his head covered by a sack, I had not bothered to hide all of the bloodletting from him as I turned my men.

When, three days later and many miles away, I leaned him against an ash tree by a swollen river and removed his hood, he stared at me in horror. His eyes wide and wary and jittery.

"Yes," I said, smiling. "I am Satan himself. But I hear you are quite the murderer yourself, Charles." I wagged my finger at him.

He ground his teeth and glared but said nothing. Sweat ran down his face and his eyes seemed unfocused.

"Hungry are you, Charles?" I asked. "Thirsty? What a terrible host I am, not giving you water for so long. Dear me, and your nose is such a bloody mess it is a wonder you did not suffocate, sir. Here, watch me drink this wine." I slurped at it and smacked my lips. "Would you care for some?"

He nodded.

"What was that, Charles?"

"Yes." His voice was thick with his broken nose. "If you please."

"What a polite fellow you are." I had another sip. "Tell me, Charles. Are you the man I am looking for?"

He seemed to be somewhere between horrified and confused, which was understandable.

"What do you want?" he managed, blinking as the sweat ran into his eyes.

He did not look well at all and I nodded to Walt who crossed and gave Sir Charles a drink of water. He gulped it down, gasping. Thirst is a terrible thing and he was suffering mightily from it.

"All I want, Sir Charles, is to ask you some questions and then I shall ransom you back to your men. What do you think about that?"

He pursed his lips. "I know who you seek."

I raised my eyebrows. "Oh?"

"Everyone knows. You are Richard of Hawkedon and you seek a black armoured knight. You are offering a reward for him. I will tell you all I know in exchange for the wealth."

I laughed. "Your reward shall be that you will live. If your answers are true. If I think you are lying, I will gut you from hip to hip and leave you tied to that tree so you can watch the wild dogs eat your entrails. Now, what do you know?"

"The knight with the black banner. I saw him."

I shook my head. "I doubt that."

"It is the truth, sir. I saw him three years past, in Orleans, meeting with Jean de Clermont. He wore blackened armour, with a surcoat of a black field. His man held aloft a black banner also."

"Who was he? The black knight?"

"I know not. I swear it."

"Oh, you swear it? It must be true, then. Why were they meeting? Jean de Clermont is the lord of Chantilly and of Beaumont."

"De Clermont has been made a Marshal of France and he

governs Poitou, the Saintonge, Angoumois, Périgord and Limousin for the new King John."

I whistled. "And the black knight was there? In armour? For the ceremony? What did he look like?"

"It was from afar, across the field. I did not see his face but they seemed to be on good terms, sir. On good terms. Jean de Clermont laughed at something the knight said. Other lords around me noted the knight and asked each other who he was but none there recognised him."

"What else can you tell me?"

De Coussey shifted in discomfort and looked like he was going to be sick. "Nothing. I beg your pardon but there is no more."

I watched him for a while. Thomas raised his eyebrows. Walt shrugged.

"I think I will kill you anyway," I said.

"Sir!" Thomas said. I went away with him a few paces. "Richard, you cannot kill him. You took him as your prisoner. He has given his word he would not flee. We have treated him very poorly already and we must not slay him."

"He is a murderer, Thomas. Even worse than I am. He kills women."

"It is nothing to do with him, Richard, nor his actions. To kill him would demean us. It would demean you. A chivalrous knight saves his own soul."

Walt was at my elbow. "Begging pardon, sirs. But the lads was all heart set on ransoming the bastard. Running low on coins, a bit."

"Very well, let us offer him back to his men. If they will have him."

His men did have him, though it was for a pittance as they swore they had not a penny more in the entire town. But Charles de Coussey seemed sick and dying when we handed him over outside his town and I did not expect him to live much longer so I did not feel too bad about it.

"What now?" Thomas asked.

"Now we must capture a Marshal of France, the governor of Poitou, the Saintonge, Angoumois, Périgord and Limousin. Jean de Clermont. For he has met the black knight, face to face."

Hugh looked to Thomas rather than me. "But does such a man not have a sizeable force?"

"Hundreds, perhaps," I said, lightly.

"Thousands," Thomas said. "Thousands of mounted men from the Loire to the Dordogne."

Walt looked around. "There's only a dozen of us, sir."

"A dozen immortals," I said.

"Even so, Richard, I do not think that we can make war with a Marshal of France."

"We shall not make war on him. We will burn his lands from the coast to the marshes. We will burn his forests and his vineyards. Destroy his villages and his mills."

"He will never come out himself."

"We will make him come. And then we will take him."

It was easier said than done.

∞ ∞ ∞

I had my men make new banners and paint the design on what few shields we possessed.

"A field of red, with yellow flames beneath rising up to touch the white dagger in the centre of it all. We shall be the White Dagger Company. And we come from Hell. Let us let the people know."

Some were disquieted but most grinned like madmen at the thought of the fear it would instil in our enemies.

There was so much land to cover. We went from place to place, flying my banner, and causing what destruction we could. We took from the people and made ourselves rich, though we had to spend everything we took just to stay alive.

Local lords sent their men after us and some we killed and drank from, others we ran from. Because there was always the next village or valley to attack.

When things grew too difficult we travelled across to the next county or to the farthest reaches we could. Other times we went to ground or fell back into the chaos of Brittany.

The immortals were thrilled with their new strength and stamina. They wanted to slaughter every soul in France and make themselves kings. I needed the help of the steadier men to keep them in check and had to dominate a few with my own hand. I could depend utterly on Thomas, of course, and on Hugh who was ever the dutiful young squire even as he entered his sixties.

Getting the attention of such a great lord as Jean de Clermont was close to impossible. Especially as he was almost always in Paris. One year he spent in England and another year he spent near Calais, leading negotiations with the English. I was undecided on whether to chase him there or to continue on the path of destruction.

"The men do not wish to leave," I said to Thomas one winter. "They are revelling in their power, here in the Périgord."

I had taken an old fortress for my men and although it was cold and damp in places we sat by the crackling hearth fire and filled our bellies with warm, spiced wine.

Thomas watched the fire as he spoke. "You know you could order them to follow you. And they would. It is you who does not wish to leave."

"What are you saying?"

He looked at me. "You love this burning and looting."

"And you know its purpose."

Thomas rubbed his eyes. "You love it for its own sake."

"All I want is to find the black knight."

He sighed and looked to Heaven for a moment. "You are lost in it. You must find your way back to virtue."

I laughed. "You are mad, sir. You hang on to notions of chivalry. Do you not think that we are past that now?"

He stared at me, the fire flickering on the side of his face. He looked old. "I know you think you have gone beyond proper standards but we must hold on to our honour. It is not a line that one crosses but an ideal that one must always seek. We do this by following the code of honour that dictates our actions no matter how often we fall short."

"When I say that we are past chivalry, it is not only us that I speak of. You and I. Not us alone. How can you not see that the world has changed around us, Thomas? Where are the true knights, now? Who decides the battles? Brutes like Walt and archers like Rob. Mercenaries from Italy and massed levies from towns. The great lords seek earthly power. None care about crusades in the Holy Land. I tell you, there are no true knights left, Thomas. If there ever were any. It seemed as though, in my youth, that knights strove to achieve greatness for the glory of God and for their king. Now, they seek only to further their family name and consolidate power and wealth. It is all so base. Why should we alone hold ourselves to such ideals when no other does? By so doing we merely hobble ourselves while the monsters of the world have free reign."

"Perhaps all you say is true. But what other men do does not have to dictate your own actions. You can yet be virtuous. You can be chivalrous in war."

I shook my head as he spoke. "No, no. It is too late for all that, brother. There can be no chivalry in this war. It would not lead to victory and our oath to the Order of the White Dagger comes before all else."

"Then go to Calais! Find Clermont in the negotiations, charge in amongst the diplomats and cardinals and cut off his head. If you wanted to do it and cared nought for the consequences, none could stop you."

I looked away into the fire and Thomas scoffed.

"Precisely, sir," he said. "You are not so far gone as all that. You are a knight still in your heart and would not carry out such an act and call it victory."

I laughed, without humour. "Which is it, Thomas? You

criticise me from both ends. Do I love pillage too much to be a knight or am I too virtuous to achieve victory? Make up your mind, sir."

"It is you that must make up your mind, sir. Will you have victory through honour? Or victory no matter the cost?" He bowed his head. "I will, of course, do as you command."

He left me alone to ponder it. Once, when I was a boy, I wanted only to be a knight. And then I wanted to fulfil the chivalric virtues through my actions. But over time, perhaps even before I had ever met Thomas, I had forgotten how to be courteous. I had grown arrogant and vain. And even then, I had not gone far enough to achieve the victories that I could have had if I had thrown off virtue entirely.

Virtue was all very well but perhaps it was more than I could afford when what I needed above all was victory.

King Edward had wanted victory and so he had thrown off knightly ideals on the battlefield. Using masses of archers instead of knights had led him to victory over the virtuous, chivalrous French.

Priskos my grandfather had conquered lands in ancient times before there were such notions as chivalry and Christian decency. He said that William would achieve greatness because he had thrown off the shackles of those very things.

Thomas was a knight from the days when it had still meant something. And so was I but I was also more than Thomas could ever be. I had the blood of heroes and conquerors in my veins. The blood of monsters and tyrants. Kings who had known victories that lived in legend.

"I will have victory, then," I said, speaking to the fire.

∞ ∞ ∞

Four years, we burned those lands. Four, long, bloody years. We killed hundreds of men sent against us and still Jean de Clermont never came to deal with us directly. He was always with King John in Paris, or so we thought.

My men were a concern. They enjoyed the blood drinking and the slaughter of the men who tried to stop us, whether they were levies or mounted professionals. Rob and Walt managed to keep them in check but I fretted at times about what I had unleashed. Oft times in the night I would consider getting up and slaughtering them all rather than have them go on.

But I did not.

I needed them.

And I could not see much difference between them and me. If anything, I was worse because I had made them, I led them and I knew that it was not the honourable path in a way that they, as ignorant commoners, could not comprehend.

We wrought so much death and chaos that even the English in Gascony sent word that we were to be stopped. It was an order from Prince Edward himself, ruling over the many lords and factions of Gascony like he was already a king. There would be no safe haven in the south for us and I doubted whether I would have any lands in Suffolk to return to, if I ever succeeded in my quest.

By itself, it was not so much of a loss. But it meant that I would certainly never marry dear Cecilia, or any other lovely English woman for that matter. Not for a long time. I avoided seeking word of her but I got messages from Stephen and Eva every now and then, many months out of date but always Eva mentioned pointedly that Cecilia remained unmarried. I felt sorry for her. It happened with some women, who were more useful as a potential wife than an actual one and so were dangled until they grew too old and joined a convent.

It was such a terrible waste. Still, knowing as I did the lustful wantonness of the woman I expected she was enjoying the delights of the bedchamber while she yet could.

In 1355, we became trapped in the vast marshland in northern Poitou by a massive group of knights and spearmen. We had been surrounded and expertly pushed back into the boggy landscape close to the coast.

Jean de Clermont had not come himself but he had finally sent someone close to him named Rudolph de Rohan, a powerful lord who commanded de Clermont's troops and ruled over vast lands for his master the Marshal of France.

After so many years of practice, my men were as good as any could be at setting and springing ambushes. Those that had not the discipline for such work had long since been killed due to their own folly and so all that remained under me were cunning, strong-willed fellows. Despite being so heavily outnumbered, we remained confident that we would prevail. Indeed, we delighted at causing the enemy companies to dance to our tune.

The marshland was deceptive to men who had no direct experience of its fickle ways. There were dead men and dead horses down in the shallow waters, and hundreds of sheep and cows, too. Green grass would stretch for hundreds of yards in all directions but there might be just a single track through it capable of carrying a man and his mount.

We drew them in deeper and deeper until we ambushed our hunter Rudolph de Rohan. Two score of them charged my exposed archers only to ride headfirst into a sucking bog. As they abandoned their horses and struggled away on foot, our arrows killed them all.

Another dozen followed us into the darkness of a wood at sundown where my men charged their flank and speared them to death. When their friends came to retrieve the bodies, we killed them, too. From these men we took the best horses, the best weapons and armour, and we were soon the most well-equipped bandits in Christendom.

Rohan's men grew so dispirited that many began deserting their lord. Along with the casualties we inflicted, he had just forty-five soldiers when we finally surrounded and trapped his company.

Sheets of rain fell and soaked us thoroughly, washing the blood into the rivers and bog all around.

Though they fought to free themselves, we killed his men and made him watch while we drank the blood from his loyal captains and followers.

Lord de Rohan fought like the devil but we brought him down last of all and my men held him and revelled in his anguish. The lord was angry and he almost wept in despair as he witnessed us murdering and drinking his best men. He knew that his campaign against us had led to total and complete failure.

"So it is true," Rohan cried, disgusted and furious. "You are monsters. You are evil."

"Yes," I said. "And we mean to have your master, Clermont. You will lead us to him."

Rohan regained his composure. "No, no."

"I do not wish to *kill* him, Rohan," I said. "Merely to ask him questions about the black knight."

He blinked. "Who?"

I smiled and held my arms out. "You know who. The knight who wears black and bears a black banner. Your master Clermont has met with him, so I am told. I would so dearly love to meet him, also."

Rohan looked between me and Thomas and the others. "You are *friends* of the black knight?"

I was confused. "If he were my friend, I would know where he is."

Rohan frowned, looking around before staring at the ground at my feet. "I know of the black knight. He is evil. Like you. He drinks the blood of men. Like you."

"What did you say?"

Rohan took a deep breath before answering. "The black knight. He drinks the blood of his enemies. But you know that, do you not? You are all the same. All of you? Even you, sir?"

He had not seen me drink blood but I ignored his probing question.

"You know of him. So what is his name?" I said.

Rohan shook his head. "No one knows."

"De Clermont knows."

Rohan shrugged as best he could with my men holding him. "Perhaps. He is in Paris."

"Why is he in Paris?" I said. "Is he helping King John to assemble the army of France?"

Rohan hesitated and I knew it was true. "You will never reach him."

"I will kill the black banner knight and all of his men, no matter how far they are from me today, nor how well protected."

Rohan laughed bitterly but I did not understand why until later.

"Have you seen the black knight with your own eyes?" I asked.

"From afar."

I looked at Thomas. "Why is it always from afar?"

"He was meeting with the Dauphin." Rohan sneered. "I was not allowed near, of course."

Thomas and I exchange a puzzled look. "He was meeting with the prince? When was this? What year did you see him? Do you mean the new King John of France?"

He shook his head. "The prince who is the son of John. The young Charles, the Dauphin of Viennois, who will be John's successor."

"But he is just a boy."

"He is seventeen or eighteen years old," Rohan said. "And already a bright man. That is, so they say."

"I hear," Thomas said, "that the boy prince is a weakling. Pale, sickly, and strangely proportioned."

De Rohan paused but then nodded. "He is that, also."

"Who is the black knight, Rohan?" I asked. "What is his name?"

"I swear on all that is holy, I know not."

I stared at Rohan, unsure whether to torture him or not.

"We should let him go," Thomas said. "It would be the chivalrous thing to do."

"What is that to me?" I replied. "I think I shall cut him to pieces and scatter him in the bogs."

"Please," Rohan said. "Please, no. I have great wealth. Ransom me and you will be rich. All of you will be made rich, if you ransom me."

"We do not need your money," I said and saw how many of my men shot me hostile looks. "But I shall let you go. Find your master Clermont in Paris and tell him that I am coming for him. Tell him that nothing will stop me."

He scoffed but said that he would relay my message.

"And Rohan?" I said before we sent him off. "If I ever see you again, I shall kill you."

He laughed as he rode away.

We broke out of our encirclement and headed east for a time to get away from the mass of men sent to catch us. But we ran into more troops, and more. It seemed as though all of France was up in arms.

"Something significant is happening," I said to my men. "Something we have not seen for years. It is true. It can no longer be denied. France is going to war."

"Where?" Hugh asked. "Calais again?

"They are gathering south of Paris. Garrisons are being

strengthened in the south and west. There can be only one place. They mean to invade Gascony and to drive out the English once and for all."

"What do we do?" Thomas asked. "If Clermont and the black banner knight are with King John and with the Dauphin, they will be surrounded by an army. How do we get through that?"

"I must get myself captured by the English," I said. "Immediately."

20

THE PRINCE'S

CAMPAIGN

IN EARLY DECEMBER 1355 the Prince of Wales called the leaders of his army to the fortress of la Reole overlooking the Garonne. It was Englishmen almost to a man but a handful of the best of the Gascons were also invited. Men who had fought with us for years and had neglected their own lands and lives to fight almost constantly for English interests. Proper soldiers, like the Captal de Buch, Auger de Montaut the Lord of Mussidan and Elie de Pommiers.

Although, most of the other Gascons were tucked up nice and warm in their homes and cuddled up to their wives or a soft servant girl, the bastards.

It was exceedingly cold when I walked up to the gates of the town of la Reole in my best clothes and spoke to the sergeants on the gate.

"My name is Richard of Hawkedon and the Prince has ordered me captured. And that is well because I would very much like to speak with him about an important matter." They gaped at me, their faces pale and lips blue from the cold. "It is a matter of considerable urgency, my good fellows."

The men looked at each other. "You what, sir?"

"I am the captain of the White Dagger Company. You may have heard of us?"

They held me in a small, cold room in the fortress of la Reole for three days without contact with any of my men or servants. Although I was fed and given wine, they did not provide me with a servant of any sort and it was quite clear that I was being treated as a prisoner, whatever my legal status might have been. Not that anyone would have cared to consider the law as far as I was concerned. In Gascony, the Prince of Wales' will was all the law any man would know.

I was brought into his presence eventually and they did me the courtesy of removing my chains and allowing me to wash. Still, my best tunic was filthy and threadbare and I am sure I looked quite the ruffian to the Prince when he looked up at me from the table at the top of the hall.

Their recent meal had been cleared away, though the smell of it yet filled the air and the tablecloth remained in place while the wine still flowed freely.

At the Prince's side were the Earls of Salisbury, Oxford and my own lord Robert Ufford the Earl of Suffolk, all scowling and casting disapproving looks. The Gascon lord Jean de Grailly, known as the Captal de Buch, stood with the other prominent Gascons still loyal to the English. Sir John Chandos stood to one side trying to keep the smile off his face.

With horror, I saw that Sir Humphrey Ingham, my dear Cecilia's brother was also in attendance. His glare radiated something between disgust and rage.

I smiled at him before turning back to the Prince.

"Your Grace," I said brightly as I was acknowledged, "my lords! What a pleasure it is to see you all here and all so hale and hearty at that. It has been far too long since I have seen you all."

A couple of them shook their heads while others turned to the Prince.

He scratched at his cheek while he regarded me. The young Edward truly did look well and I was pleased to see how he had continued to grow into a well-made man with all the stature and presence of any of his illustrious ancestors. If anything, he was taller even than his father. It was not hard to see the Lionheart in him, and of course he was every inch the Longshanks.

"What am I going to do with you, Richard?" he asked, sighing.

And, I noted, he was every bit as arrogant and condescending as those very same forefathers.

"Do with me, Your Grace?" I asked, pretending to be as innocent and guileless as a newborn lamb. "Why, I would expect that you might use me and my men in your imminent attacks into Languedoc."

They began to splutter in outrage until the Prince waved them into silence.

"What makes you think I mean to move now?" he asked,

speaking mildly.

Because I have been doing this since before your great-grandfather was squeezed from the royal nethers, boy. I thought the words but did not speak them, though the temptation was great.

"Forgive me, Your Grace. I have been everywhere in France over the last few years and I have heard and seen a great deal. For instance, I have heard how the leading men of France are urging King John to strike back at their enemies in Normandy and Picardy and also down here in Gascony. It is no secret that the nobles feel dishonoured that the French Crown has been pushed back on all fronts and the lords wanted their king to throw back King Edward from Picardy and also smash you here in Gascony. And although King John continues to hesitate to commit himself, they insist that he take decisive action. As we speak, they are now raising an enormous sum through taxes which they will use to raise the King's army."

"What does all that have to with anything?" Salisbury asked, scowling.

A handsome man with a big nose, he was just a year or two older than the Prince but through his military competence had risen to become one of the most trusted English commanders. I had fought with his father, the old earl, when this Salisbury was just a boy but the man before me was one of the new generation that was far from impressed by my earlier exploits. I had stood near to the King as he knighted the eighteen-year-old Salisbury along with the Prince and a few others after we landed in France before Crecy. But I was swiftly realising that meant nothing to the new men.

"It is in the air, sir," I replied.

Their faces turned to a sea of frowns.

"What in God's name are you blathering about?" Sir Humphrey Ingham spluttered.

I lifted my arms. "War, my lord." I looked at each of them in turn. "I can smell it. I can taste it. It is all around us. It fills the air from Paris to the Périgord and every man, woman and child there knows that the war proper will be rising up just as soon as the French can muster their huge numbers of men from all the regions of the country. Even now, they are coming in, mounted and on foot. In dozens and hundreds." I smiled at them. "And of course, here you all are, my lords. The finest fighting men in all England, all gathered here in this one place. Why? Are you here to celebrate Christmas together?"

I got a few smiles from that but the Prince fixed me with a dark look.

"Richard, speak plainly, will you." My lord the Earl of Suffolk spoke up. "Are the French prepared to defend an assault from Gascony?"

"No, my lord," I said. "They are preparing to invade Gascony."

"Nonsense," Salisbury said, turning to the Prince. "We would have heard about this."

"My men have taken many messengers in the last few weeks, most heading south from Paris, and we questioned them quite vigorously. The French know, sirs, that Lancaster has summoned men to muster at Southampton after winter, with horse and equipment, ready to attack Brittany in the spring, as soon as the weather turns. They know also, that a second fleet is intending to sail from Plymouth to here, bringing supplies and more men to reinforce you."

"Good God," Suffolk said, raising his voice above the growing muttering. "Their agents have improved."

"If it is true," Ingham growled.

"And yet," I said, quickly before their attention wandered. "And yet, they do not suspect you plan to strike against *them* before spring."

"Who says we plan such a thing?" Salisbury asked.

I shrugged. "If you are not, then you damned well should be. The towns are well stocked and under-garrisoned. It will be spring or even summer before France's grand army can be brought to bear on you. If you divide your forces into three or four, each army will be large enough to raid at will. Even to take possession of many places, if you are willing to garrison them. If your armies remain close enough that, if threatened by a royal army of the French, you can withdraw and form together at one of a number of prearranged places."

They looked at me without speaking and I knew that I had either spoken their own plan to them or else I had outlined a better one. Either way, they seemed quietly impressed.

"He is yours, by law, Robert," the Prince said to the Earl of Suffolk. "What would you have us do with him?"

Suffolk bowed. "He may be my man by law," he said, glancing at me, "but we all know that he was only ever your father's man, Your Grace. Whatever crimes he may or may not have committed these last few years, I believe that the King has looked the other way in greater crimes, over the decades since he gained the

Crown."

"Decades, yes," the Prince said, turning to look at me with narrowed eyes. "How is it that you continue to avoid the ravages of time, sir? Since I was a child, there has been talk where you are concerned of dark things indeed, though I shall not speak them."

"I shall," said Salisbury, looking down his fat nose at me. "I shall damned well speak them, if you will pardon me, Your Grace. It is witchcraft that is spoken of, when men speak Sir Richard's name. Witchcraft, blood magic, sorcery and demon-worship."

For a moment I considered remarking that it was cuckoldry that was spoken of when men spoke Salisbury's name, on account that his first wife had secretly married another before she married him. But I reflected that it was probably best not to mention it.

"I made no pact with the Devil," I said.

"You will wait to be asked a question before speaking again," the Prince said, growing angry.

The meeting was getting away from me once again. What could I do but bow and stay silent?

"My father always told me that I could rely on you, Sir Richard," the Prince said. "No matter how strange you are. No matter how violent your tendencies and how absurdly old-fashioned your manner of speech and style of clothing are, I could always rely on you to get the necessary work done when it comes to matters of war."

"He is a wise man, Your Grace."

"Perhaps he is," the Prince said, "or perhaps he *was*. Unfortunately for you, he is not here to protect you this time." He turned to his sergeants and gestured at me. "Take this man and lock him up until we are well gone from this place."

I forced myself into stillness as three armed soldiers moved to surround me. To resist might mean my death but even if it did not, it would be the end of me in the eyes of the lords of England.

Suffolk cleared his throat and I was pleased to see that he had remembered he was my lord. "What about his men, Your Grace?" he said.

"His men?"

"A score or so of them," Sir Humphrey Ingham said. "Brutes, the lot of them. The murderers and thieves who have slaughtered their way back and forth across this land for years. They must be taken, too, Your Grace."

"Must they, indeed?" the Prince said.

"They have slaughtered their way through the King's enemies, sir," Suffolk countered.

"And so have blackened the King's name," Sir Humphrey replied, sharply. "Their deeds reflect badly upon the English amongst our allies here in Gascony and in France and they should suffer the consequences."

The Prince raised his chin. "What would they be, Sir Humphrey?"

"That is not for me to say, Your Grace. But if it were, I would hang the lot of them, strike off their heads and stick them on pikes above the walls of Bordeaux."

"A waste, Your Grace," Suffolk said, "of their considerable talents and experience. We could use men such as they. Even a score of them."

"I am sure you are right, Suffolk, but I am yet inclined to hang them."

I held my tongue but glared at my lord.

Suffolk bowed. "Many of them are from my lands, Your Grace. Let me take them on. If they put a foot wrong, they shall hang."

"Fine, fine. If you can find Hawkedon's men, you may use them." The Prince gestured at me. "But I will have none of your mischief making, Sir Richard. You have caused enough havoc on your own. Take him away."

I could have fought my way free, perhaps. But to do so would have involved killing Englishmen and perhaps even a great lord or two. And then I would have truly been an outlaw. Any Englishman who saw me could have killed me and indeed they would have sent a large number of soldiers to hunt me down. It was trouble I wished to avoid.

So instead I bowed to the Prince and wished the lords well before I was escorted away from the hall by the sergeants. Suffolk caught my eye and winked, which was encouraging but I also saw Sir Humphrey's dark looks. He knew, I am sure, that his sister loved me and so Humphrey rejoiced at seeing me disgraced.

Far from the hall, the sergeants courteously asked me to step inside a small room above the armoury on the outside of the eastern wall and then slammed the door behind me.

I have been in worse prisons than the chamber they locked me inside. There was a straw mattress and I even had a slit window with which to look out at the men leaving over the next few days. While I waited, I fretted about my men. Thomas would lead them well, of that I had no doubt, but he was not like them. He did not understand how they thought and if they were pressed hard then I wondered if they would follow his commands.

Would they continue to respect the bloodletting schedule I had established? Or would they demand ever more from the servants? If they followed my orders then Walt and Rob would support Thomas and together they would control the others and all would be well.

Surely, they would be quick enough and wily enough to evade any men sent after them. Even though I had faith in them and their abilities, still I watched from the window and listened at all hours, fearing to witness them being dragged into the fortress to face justice.

On the third day, the Prince left. It was with rather more fanfare and general fuss than most nobles might but it was concluded efficiently and when the last of his long train of servants and soldiers had peeled away, I knew it was time for me to leave.

When the old man opened my door later that day with a big cup of wine and a loaf of bread, I stood to receive him. He was as wrinkled as a decrepit shoe and lame, dragging one foot from an old injury but he had a way about him that suggested he had once been a fighting man.

"Step back, sir," he said, as he had said before. "Stand to the window, sir, if you please." He pulled the door all the way open and stepped inside. "Go on, sir, if you want your wine, sir."

This time, however, I did not follow his instructions.

"I am afraid, sir," I said "that I shall be leaving now."

He looked alarmed and a darkness descended across his face.

I had caught a glimpse of the man he used to be.

"We got guards. *Guards.* Soldiers on the walls, porters on the gates. You ain't getting out, sir. Now, what say you just move to the window and I'll not tell the steward nothing?"

"Do you enjoy your work, man?" I asked him.

"Can't fight no more," he said, shrugging. "Ain't got no family. Better here than dead in a ditch, sir."

"I am curious," I said, sliding slowly forward while keeping a reasonable tone, "about whether you can still ride well?"

"Ride?" he asked, confused.

I slid forward while smiling and holding my arms out.

"I could use a man like you. A trustworthy older man who has seen his share of action. You could help steady my wilder ones."

He frowned. "But I'm the assistant to the head steward of—"

All of a sudden, he noticed how close I was and he sucked down a huge gulp of air, ready to cry out for help.

My fist connected just under his ear as he turned. I intended to silence him but he collapsed like a sack of mud and his skull bounced hard on the stone floor. I considered tearing his neck open and drinking him dry. But that would have been most unchivalrous. And I thought I could probably do without his aged blood.

Taking the keys on his belt, I locked him in the room and crept carefully to the stairwell. I could have fought my way out, charging from guard to guard, knocking each on his arse. But sometimes, a man simply has to brass it out. I straightened up, brushed myself off and strode down the stairs like I was about official business.

It was clear that the Prince had not been committed to keeping me locked up for long. Perhaps Suffolk, before he left, had advised the garrison to stay away from me. Whatever the reason, I was not accosted. I nodded to servants and called out good day to the soldiers I saw. A few frowned, possibly unsure of who I was, but I simply waved and smiled and nodded my way to the stables. I ordered a boy to prepare a horse and he jumped to it quite smartly. Mounted, I rode out through both gates and crossed the bridge out into the country with the farewells of the bemused porters in my ears.

I rode to find my company. I hoped that they had not turned into wild beasts without me.

We had a grand English raid to join.

∞ ∞ ∞

When I found my company at our agreed meeting place two days later, they were in a state of high agitation.

We stood in a wooded hollow at the edge of a boggy field in the flood plain of the Garonne. It was very cold and they were irritable and hungry from waiting so long for me.

"Suffolk's men have been searching the valley for us," Walt said, glancing at Thomas. "Some of our lads want to kill the soldiers, sir. Have a bit of a drink of them, like."

Hugh edged closer and lowered his voice. "The brutes would not listen to reason, Sir Richard."

Thomas held his chin up. "I explained that you would prefer

them not to."

I clapped him on the arm. "I am sure that you had to explain it at length. Well done, sir."

He nodded.

"My lord the Earl of Suffolk," I told them all, raising my voice, "has been given leave by the Prince to take us under his command."

They grumbled and cursed but I held my hand up before continuing.

"The Prince's armies are to undertake a series of raids, all along the border. There will be plunder like you would not believe. We will follow Suffolk's contingent and keep our heads down. I will take no orders, not from the Earl of Suffolk, and not even from the Prince himself. Not unless they are orders that suit me and suit our search."

This they cheered and I could see how their faces flushed with the prospect of blood and riches.

"But mark me well, you men." I waited until their faces dropped and they fell silent. "Mark me that my orders to you shall be obeyed. Every one, without delay or question. The English and the Gascons are off limits. We shall have plunder and, in time, we shall have a battle. But what we need above all is to bring the black knight to us. Wherever we meet him, be it in siege or in skirmish or in open battle, we shall find him and take revenge. That is why we are here. That is the only reason we are here. If any of you forget that, I shall have no more use for you. Do you understand me?"

They swore that they did and I took them at their word.

We joined the great raid.

There were over two thousand English soldiers, all told, and a few hundred Gascons. These men were divided between the various leaders and the leaders assigned planned routes for the march. Salisbury made for Sainte-Foy on the Dordogne River. Prince Edward made his headquarters at Libourne along with Chandos and Ingham. The Earl of Suffolk was directed to Saint-Emilion and my company followed.

From places of strength, each commander sent raiding companies outward as they advanced, to widen the frontiers of the destruction and to pull more lands into what was effectively English dominion. The poor French on the Gascon border had never known an assault like it.

Our columns pushed eastward into the Agenais. Warwick invaded the Lot Valley and took fortified monasteries and important bridges. A force led by Chandos and Ingham marched right up the Garonne and captured forts and castles all along the valley. The largest contingent was led by Suffolk, Oxford and Salisbury. Charging along the fertile and wealthy Dordogne we stormed fortresses in the barony of Turenne, taking Souillac and Beaulieu and many more.

It was ideal land for those who could fight like *routiers* and after the main forces moved on, that land became infested with bandits for almost two years.

Through it all, my company kept apart from the mortal men, making camp away from the others and keeping to ourselves. And when it was time to fight, we did as we wished, taking a village or a fortress whether another group had claimed it first or not.

364

The soldiers under Suffolk learned to keep away from us.

For a time, our detachment made as if we were going to assault the great town of Poitiers but then we swung south away from it, rode like the devil and assaulted the walls of Perigueux during the dark of the night. While we held the town, the French reinforced the castle and held it, so that both sides warred unceasingly and the townsfolk, caught in between, suffered greatly from the arrows, fire, and fury.

All of the great French lords of the border regions, whose duty it was to protect their people from the aggression of the English and Gascons, did nothing. The cowards cried that they could not act against us until King John's mighty army, yet assembling at Paris, arrived in the southwest.

What weakness they displayed. What a betrayal of their obligations. It would have been far better for their people and the lords' immortal souls if they had fought and died.

"What is the point of a lord saving his own life," Thomas asked me, "if he does not do his duty?"

Our assaults had taken eleven towns and seventeen castles in just a few weeks. It was nothing, perhaps, compared to the vastness of all France but still the local lords saw who was strong and who was weak. The Prince sent a stream of messages and bribes to the lords of the bordering regions until by spring a number of them transferred their allegiance from John King of France to Edward Lord of Gascony and future King of England. These lords brought almost fifty more towns and castles under English authority.

Prince Edward's successes in turn encouraged King Edward

back in London to prepare his own invasion force so that he could assault from the north while the Prince of Wales attacked from the south. The Duke of Lancaster prepared for an invasion of Brittany.

The freezing weather finally passed and, in April, a detachment including my company raided deep in Quercy and laid siege to the fortified village of Fons and its royal garrison, and to the massive fortress of Cardaillac.

I recalled the name and realised it had once belonged to a knight named Bertrand I had travelled with from Constantinople to Karakorum. Sir Bertrand had been turned by William into an immortal and I had killed him in the entrance hall to a house in Baghdad. A sordid, low death for a mean bastard of a knight. And then the descendants of his cousins ruled Cardaillac, high on its cliff, until we came and assaulted it without warning. The locals put up a spirited defence but their spirit was not enough and we killed them almost to a man, ransoming the few survivors off to their families.

Local order collapsed following the raids and the country all about fell to banditry. The land there was so rich with crops and vineyards, it was as close to an Eden as one can get outside of England. Robbing the country blind and burning what could not be taken was as disgusting as it was delightful. Captain after captain peeled off from our main army and began taking places of their own while our companies raided deeper and deeper.

The locals despaired. Our soldiers were become depraved through decades of war and they, surrounded by abundance and safety until then, were like innocent lambs to the slaughter.

366

The southern parts of Poitou fell entirely into English and Gascon hands and the cities that remained free, like Poitiers itself and the ancient castle of Lusignan, turned inward to shore up their own defence and abandoned the other cities to their fate. And so, with France in great disunity, we picked them off one by one.

My own company even rode through the dilapidated walls of Poitiers and seized goods and men, including the Mayor of Poitiers himself who we stole away and then ransomed. It was so daring that we deserved everlasting fame for the act but the land was in such chaos, such an orgy of theft and destruction, that it was lost amongst a thousand other stories.

Still, we knew through it all that the French would come eventually. That there would be a reckoning for all the destruction. That fact led it all an even greater sense of urgency and madness.

All the while, in the north, the French army grew.

King John had summoned all those lords holding noble fiefs to join the army with a retinue and equipment appropriate to their status. The same was commanded from the towns who had to supply equipped infantry and crossbowmen.

Lancaster gathered an army of two-and-a-half thousand in Normandy from the garrisons of Brittany. It was a terribly small army but they were all veterans, all were mounted and two-thirds of them were our savage, brilliant archers. Moving swiftly, they plundered great riches in Normandy, took thousands of fine horses, and caused havoc before withdrawing for safety. King John offered battle and Lancaster declined, for his job had been to draw the French to him and in this, he had succeeded.

While in the southwest, our main army moved north toward the Loire. The Prince unfurled his great banner, quartered in red and blue with the arms of England of France.

And we began to burn.

We assaulted and looted abbeys. We crept across the county of La Marche like a plague, sacking town after town in the lands owned by the great Bourbon family. Soon, we crossed the River Creuse at Argenton and again the crossing was uncontested by the French.

"Where are they?" men asked each other.

"Do not ask," others said. "Make yourself rich while you can."

All the men knew that the French could easily outnumber our small army by two or three or more times and not even our veteran soldiers thought we could stand against that so deep into French territory. We were in the heart of France and could not run for the sea like we had always had before in Normandy and Brittany.

The army destroyed the town of Issoudun so thoroughly that much of it remained uninhabited for years after we were done with it. The small garrison sat in the keep and watched us from the walls. We did not bother them and they left us to it.

"They are cowards," Hugh said, with uncharacteristic venom. "They should come out and fight."

"They would die," Rob said, gesturing at the men on the walls. "And for what? For this little town?"

"Even so," Hugh said. "It would be the honourable thing to do."

"They are not knights, Hugh," Thomas said, softly.

"Even if they were," Walt said. "It'd be a stupid bloody knight who charges into this lot. That be a glorious death, Hugh? To be hacked apart by the sons of tanners and labourers?"

What could Hugh say? His sense of honour was offended every day by the sight of so many Englishmen destroying his beloved country. It was hard on both Hugh and Thomas but the older man had the strength of character to find some level of personal accommodation with the world as it was.

The French had received a fleet of galleys from Aragon and so King Edward found himself suddenly unable to cross to France and join up with the Prince. Instead, Lancaster was ordered to take his two thousand veterans south from Normandy to meet us in September.

Joining the two armies together was critical and yet it seemed to many of us to be impossible.

"Do you truly believe," Thomas asked me, "that Lancaster can lead so many men across two hundred miles of hostile country and make a rendezvous without being trapped and destroyed?"

"Only time will tell," I said, though I doubted it also.

We were watched and followed, day and night, by French scouts. The mounted men were always watching from every horizon, relaying our movements and actions back to the French.

"Want us to kill them, sir?" Walt asked.

"Good God, no.

"They'll tell old King John where we be at."

I pinched my eyes and cursed the stupidity of the common man.

"We want them to see us, Walt. We want them to see how few we are, how spread out we are, how much loot we are weighted down with. We want the French to come. We need the King to bring the Dauphin and the other great lords so that the black knight comes with them."

"Right you are, sir." Walt lifted a hand and gave them a friendly wave.

They turned and galloped away in panic.

The local lords assembled their forces but still they kept away from us, preferring to hide on the other side of the Loire and wait for King John to bring enough proper soldiers from the rest of his lands to crush us.

And, finally, praise God, he was coming.

Our men reached the River Cher and put every building to the torch for a distance of twenty miles in all directions. The country burned.

Chandos and Ingham took a force to Aubigny where they clashed with a group of eighty French men-at-arms. The fighting was hard but the French were defeated, many captured and the rest driven off. Irritatingly, Humphrey Ingham won great plaudits from his skill and bravery in the sordid little scrap.

The Loire thereabouts was flat and boggy and the trees were of willow and alder on the higher patches of land among the endless reedbeds. After all the rain that summer the river was enormous. It was wide, deep and fast flowing and could not be forded.

We found that there was no way across.

The main body of our army came up behind the advance

companies and occupied the burning towns and country.

"Where are the bloody French?" I asked Thomas, for the hundredth time. "Can they not see what we are doing to the heart of France? How can any king allow this to happen to his country? To his people?"

"Perhaps we should ride north," Thomas said, "and ask them?"

I nodded. "A fine notion. But we need not ride north. There are Frenchmen hereabouts, are there not?" I sat up in my saddle and turned to find the man who was my shadow. "Walt? Take Rob and bring us back a few French scouts, will you?"

Walt looked exasperated. "I thought you said we was to ignore them, sir?"

"Just bring me a damned Frenchman."

Before sundown, my company dragged three men back to us. They had ropes about their necks and all three had been beaten roughly about the face.

"Where is your king?" I asked them.

"We will tell you nothing," one of them said, his face rigid with fury and contempt. "Nothing."

"Very well," I said.

I sliced my dagger across his throat, lifted him and drank the blood from his neck while the other two men cowered and sobbed in horror. Before his heart stopped, I tossed him to my soldiers, who grabbed him and supped from the wound, passing him around like a wine skin.

"Now, sirs? What can you tell me about the location and the intentions of King John?"

They died the same way as their fellow scout but before their blood fed my company they admitted that the French would confront our army on the road to Tours.

"How far does that be, sir?" Rob asked.

"Tours? It is merely sixty or seventy miles west."

"That mean there's going to be a battle this week, sir?"

"It depends on the courage of the French."

Thomas and Hugh took no part in such brutality and though they rarely gave voice to it, their behaviour spoke loudly enough. I did not like disappointing Thomas but I needed victory, not honourable failure.

Sixty French men-at-arms and a few hundred infantry guarded the crossing of the Sauldre at Romorantin. The Prince decided that he had to drive them away and so ordered the taking of the walled town and its ancient keep.

"Why get bogged down with this bloody lot?" Walt asked while we watched the army assembling for the assault. "We always leave big towns or garrisons what burrow in to keeps like tics. Waste time here and the French army will cut us off."

"With any luck," I said, brightly.

Thomas answered Walt's questions properly. "We cannot allow a force made up of hundreds of men at our rear as we advance on Tours. If the French do stop us on the road we will have those men in that town attacking us from behind."

Rob nodded. "Still a risk to stay in place for so long. What if they hold out in there? Look at the size of the bloody walls, Tom."

"It certainly appears to be a tough place but it is old and will fall, in time. Perhaps this will be where the French catch us. This

372

is what we want, is it not? Then we shall find the men we seek."

"He is right," I said. "We must have the heart of the black knight and then we shall rejoice, even if the cost is the destruction of our entire army and the death of every Englishman in France."

My men were appalled but I cared nothing for that. My enemy was so close now, I could almost taste him.

"While we're here," some of my men said, "perhaps we might get involved, Sir Richard? Lots of gold in that town. Women, too."

"And we would be of great help to our soldiers," Hugh said, eagerly.

"No," I snapped. "I need you all alive and well for the coming battle. I will not lose any of you in some pointless siege. Let the mortals spend their lives."

Thomas glanced at me and I was ready to tell him to take his chivalry and shove it up his arse but he simply turned away in silence.

In the end, it was a brutal assault on the little town. Our men stormed the walls and the garrison retreated into the citadel. Three long days of struggle, the Prince's army tried to winkle out those men inside. Our miners undermined the walls while our siege engineers threw up three moveable assault towers and the soldiers launched repeated attacks on the keep from every direction at once.

The men were exhausted but the Prince urged them all on. He swore that it had to be done swiftly or it would be the end of the army.

All the while I prayed to see the blue and yellow banner of the

King of France appear on the distant horizon. But no one came to save the town and the assaults continued until the keep was set on fire. It burned all through the night and in the morning the garrison surrendered.

We headed for Tours.

The delay had cost us. The French were coming, out of sight somewhere to the north, every man knew it now. But where would they catch us? I considered sending a message north to let King John know where we were but that would have been treasonous and besides, it was hardly necessary.

Every mile on the road to Tours, with the River Cher on our left, I expected scouts to report that the way was blocked.

And yet we reached Tours unopposed.

"Perhaps I should send word," I muttered to Thomas. "Clearly, King John is a coward or utterly incompetent. Perhaps if he knew how tired we are, he would take heart and come to meet us in the open field?"

"Anything you did or said would be mistrusted by the French," Thomas replied. "They would certainly think you had been sent by the Prince and suspect a trap. It may even drive them away from us."

"God damn his cowardice."

Lancaster was on the other side of the Loire with his two thousand men but he could not cross to us and we could not cross to him, for the French had broken every damned bridge across the great river from Tours to Blois. It was a serious setback. Our armies were suddenly more likely than ever to be destroyed one by one, despite being so close as the crow flies.

The Prince, bold as a lion, decided to take the city.

Tours was big. It was well defended by the river and by walls and towers enclosing the city and the castle. The citizens had dug ditches and raised ramparts and palisades. We wanted to burn them out but the endless rain did not allow it. Men experienced with assaulting towns were thrown at the walls but they fell back every time.

And then the French came.

Finally, the combined French army crossed the Loire just thirty miles upstream at Blois and came charging down at us. We were suddenly at great risk of being caught tween Tours and the enormous army of the King and so the Prince did the only sensible thing he could.

He ordered us to flee.

The army abandoned everything that we did not need and charged south, crossing two small tributaries and making ten miles before dark caught us.

In the morning, we found that the French had sent envoys.

They wanted peace.

"Bloody cowards," I said. "We cannot have that."

"But we do not need a battle," Thomas pointed out. "We wished for the French army to come within close proximity so we could seek the black knight."

"Yes, yes," I said, irritated. "But how do we now find him if there are twenty thousand enemies spread across miles of country? I need to see his black banner held aloft, Thomas."

"There's truly more of them than us?" Walt asked.

"Twice as many, at least," Rob replied. "So the scouts are

saying."

"That is what they always say," Hugh pointed out.

"I think this time it is true," I said.

"And every one of them a man-at-arms on fresh horses?" Walt frowned. "While we're saddle sore, injured, and wet to the bone? What are they afraid of?"

Rob and his archers laughed. "This," Rob said, stroking his bow stave.

Walt shook his head. "When will they bloody learn?"

"Learn what?" Rob said, offended. "How would you fight us?"

Walt shrugged. "Either do it or don't do it. But farting around it don't do nothing."

The envoys spoke at length to the Prince about truces and treaties. But the Prince replied that there would be no peace. The King of France was here with an army and if he wanted peace, he would have to fight for it.

It was a very fine sentiment, somewhat undermined by the fact that we immediately turned and ran south once more. King John had the local forces in addition to his own army of mounted men and also the young Dauphin had arrived with another thousand men-at-arms. The black knight had to be amongst them.

Our lords were desperate to join up with Lancaster's army in the west while King John attempted to get around us to the east and cut off our retreat. He was so close on our heels that his men reached our nightly stopping point just hours after we left it. And our brave Prince made a difficult decision.

He waited.

The Prince held his army at Chatellerault, in the hope that

Lancaster could reach us there and cross while we held the bridge.

French scouts watched us and ours watched them. The great French army was somewhere to the northeast and heralds gathered between our armies as the inevitability of battle grew.

"Surely," I said to Thomas. "Surely, this is it. I cannot stand it any longer."

"You know how it goes," Thomas said. "There has to be the will to fight from both armies. We are getting tired, now. If Lancaster does not come? We will try to run. And King John? Will he have the courage of his ancestors? His kingdom is not a happy one."

"There will be no avoiding it now," I muttered. "Surely."

Yet his words concerned me. What if the French pulled away again and my enemy disappeared once more? "But let us find him now, Thomas. Let us go to the French. Find the black banner amongst them. And slay him there."

"You have been patient for years," Thomas said. "You can wait a few days longer."

"What if he flees, Thomas?" I said, almost pleadingly. "We could charge into the enemy now. Right now, Thomas. We could do it."

Thomas, God love him, nodded slowly. "Perhaps. He will likely be with the Dauphin. Deep within the army. Imagine it. The press of men and horse. Even our strength could not throw down thousands of horses and men. Our company will certainly be stopped before we can reach him. No, no. It cannot be done. You must wait, Richard. Take heart. Have patience, sir. Take the time to pray."

I scoffed in his face. "I will go alone, then. One man on a horse is nothing to them. I will call myself a Frenchman. There will be so many of them, they will not know the truth of it until I am in striking distance."

"You would assassinate him, and kill his men also? Even if you could achieve such a thing, you would give yourself away in doing the deed and the French would tear you apart."

"Possibly."

"Certainly."

"Then so be it! If he never leaves the side of the Dauphin, how can I hope to kill him?"

Thomas stroked his chin. He needed to shave. "You shall have to wait for the battle."

I hung my head. "You said there may be no battle."

"Eventually, there will always be a battle."

Thinking of Priskos, I imagined what Alexander would do. What would Caesar do? Would they act? They had commanded armies and I had one company. Patience and steadiness were virtues but I could wait no longer.

"I must make an attempt," I said. "If they are too strong, I shall return. But I must see the banner, Thomas. I need to see it. If I can reach it, I will."

"Take Walt with you."

"He will give me away with his presence. Even a fool can see that Walt is an Englishman. Look at his features, Thomas. Despite his colouring, he is the most English thing you ever saw, is he not? Or Welsh, perhaps, I will allow. But I am stronger now than I have ever been and need no man's help. I shall do it alone."

"You need a good man to watch your back."

"Perhaps you should come with me?"

He thought about it. "Without me, the company will turn feral. Even Rob cannot control them now."

I left them in the dark of the first night. I took Walt with me. Leaving my men was a mistake.

In my wrath and my haste, I was throwing away the steady work I had done over the previous years to uncover as much as I had. Because I was so close, I could not temper my frustration but still I believed that I could not fail. Thinking of my immortal ancestors made me feel as invincible as Priskos, as vigorous as Caesar, and as mighty as Alexander.

Patience is a conquering virtue. And vanity is the deadliest sin.

2 1

DECEPTION

BY MORNING, I WAS CLOSE enough to smell them. The French were moving around us along the roads to the east. Moving in their thousands, spread out over many miles. I rode into them and simply asked.

"Where is the knight of the black banner? Have you seen the Dauphin's mystery knight? You, sir? Do you know of the knight of the black banner? Where is he, sir?"

I asked a dozen, a score, a hundred, as I rode back along their lines. Some men were angry, calling me a dog, a swine, or an Englishman. From most of these, I simply rode on, calling out cheerfully and with encouraging words, before asking my questions again.

"Who has seen the Dauphin's black knight? Where is he?"

"With the damned Dauphin, you fool!" one man shouted, to

much laughter.

"Where is the Dauphin?"

A series of shouts came back to me from knights, squires and pages.

"With the King."

"At home with your wife!"

"Up your arse!"

Their laughter filled the air as I rode on, trying to get deeper into the masses of riders coming the other way. We were cursed and damned for going in the wrong direction but I kept claiming that I had a message. Everywhere I looked it was more knights, lances and pennants, banners, and shining steel. The whole day passed in that way and by evening I was cursing myself for wasting my time.

"We'll go back home to the lads now, will we, sir?" Walt asked, speaking softly.

We watched as the enemy broke up into hundreds of tiny camps on whatever dry area of field, copse, or hedgerow they could find. Some lit fires but most did not bother. It was not cold.

"The King, the Dauphin, and our black knight will pass this way eventually. We will wait another day until–" I grabbed Walt. "Look, there. Is that not the blazon of Jean de Clermont?"

A rider cantered south beside the road in a coat emblazoned with the red and gold coat of arms that we knew so well. Behind him rode a squire and a young page.

"Is it?" Walt asked, with his nose in his pack. "Do you want some of this cheese before it goes bad?"

"Let us take him, Walt. Come on." I rode to intercept him

and called out a greeting while waving my hand. "Thanks be to God, sir. I have been looking for you all day."

His face expressed deep irritation. "For me? Who are you, sir?"

"For your lord, sir. I have a message that I must give to him."

He sighed dramatically and rolled his eyes. "Very well. Hand it over. Who is it from?"

I had no letter, of course, and made no move. "It is a message I must relay in person. Where is your lord tonight?"

He eyed me closely, looking me up and down. I was quite filthy and everything from my clothes to my horse's caparison was plain and mismatching. "Who did you say you served, sir?"

"Pierre of Senoches," I replied, plucking a random name from my memory. "My lord owes yours a considerable debt and he finally is able to pay it."

The knight frowned, as well he might, for the debt was a fiction.

"Here, see for yourself." I pulled out the purse I kept close to my body at all times. "Come closer, sir and see."

He was very wary indeed but his curiosity got the best of him and he watched as I tipped the garnets, emeralds and sapphires into my palm.

"My God," he muttered. "Where did your lord come into such a fortune?"

"He took it from the English. The fools are so laden with treasure stolen from our brothers across France that they cannot move for it. We routed a company of them and took this and much more from them. Much more. Perhaps you would assist us in bringing the sum of the debt back to your lord?"

"More?" he asked, astonished.

I pointed into the trees. "Just a small chest, sir, but we cannot carry it between us," I jerked a thumb at Walt. "And our wagon cannot travel this road as it is. If you and your two men there would consider sharing the coin between you, we could bring it to Lord de Clermont all together?"

His face lit up at the prospect for enriching himself and bringing his lord a great prize. "Certainly, sir. Certainly."

I narrowed my eyes and tipped the gems carefully back into their purse. "Only if you swear that your men are trustworthy. I shall have none of it pilfered and so come up short in the final accounting."

"They are trustworthy," he said, with greed in his eyes. "I swear it, by God and upon my honour."

I nodded slowly. "Very well. If you say it, sir, I shall believe it. Come, we are camped not far into the woodland there."

He followed us, still wary, but his fears suppressed in the hope of easy booty. Perhaps the knight and his squire were intending to kill us when we gave them the gold to carry. Perhaps they were even going to do their duty. Whatever their intentions, I never gave them the chance to act upon them. When we were alone and two dozen yards from the edge of the wood, I threw myself at the knight and dragged him down while Walt bundled the squire to the ground. The little page almost got away but Walt charged him and plucked him from his horse. We had to beat them around rather a lot to get them to be silent. The page pissed himself, poor lad, and I told him to be silent or he would be killed. He nodded, eyes as wide as saucers. The squire remained insensible for some time.

"I have questions for you, sir," I said to the knight, who sat leaning back against a tree trunk.

He spat blood out and it dangled from his chin and dripped onto his chest. In the distance, men laughed in the darkness. His eyes darted left and right before coming to rest on me again.

"No one will come for you. But answer my questions and you shall go free."

"You are English," he said, bitterly. "I knew it."

"I am looking for the knight with the black banner."

He glanced at me, suddenly fearful. "I know nothing."

"And I know that your master is friends with him. Tell me where they are."

He scoffed and I held up a dagger to his face.

"I have skinned men alive," I said, which was not true. "I have become very good at it."

He licked his fat lips. "You are the man who has been searching for him all day."

"You heard about that? Who told you?"

"My lord was told. Earlier today. In my presence."

"What did they say?"

"They said that the Englishman Richard of Ashbury was looking for..." he trailed off.

Ashbury, I thought. I had not gone by the name for decades. No man alive knew me by that name, other than my immortals.

And William's.

"Was the black knight there with him?" He looked away and I grabbed his jaw with my hand and squeezed, staring into him.

"Was he there?"

He nodded as best he could. I did not release him.

"Who is he? You saw him? You saw his face? Who is the man you saw? Who is the black knight?"

I pressed my dagger gently to the underside of his eyeball and held it there. His breathing became panting and tears welled in his eyes. He blinked and they flowed down over the point of my blade.

"Charny," he whispered, so softly it was like the hushing of a mother to a child.

"I did not hear you."

He gasped and blurted it out. "Geoffrey de Charny."

I sat back on my arse, staring. "I do not believe it."

"I swear it." He rubbed his face and touched his eye to check it was intact. "Sir Geoffrey de Charny. The black knight is Sir Geoffrey de Charny. It is a secret known only to some. To my lord and to the other great men. He uses the black banner to fight where he has been ordered not to by the King, and by the previous king. And so de Charny protects his honour."

I scoffed, almost disbelieving it still. "He protects his name, not his honour, you fool. Do you know what he is, son? What he *truly* is?"

The knight frowned. "He wishes to do what is right for the kingdom. For the Crown."

Oh?

"Not for the King?" I said. "But for the Crown? And what is right for the Crown but not for the King? Come on, out with it. No use holding back now. I truly will take your eye if you hesitate and take them both if you lie."

"To fight for the Dauphin," he blurted. "My lord Jean de Clermont and Geoffrey de Charny will help the Dauphin to do what the King cannot. We will push the English from France forever."

I shook my head. "He wants to put a puppet on the throne and so make a kingdom that my brother can take when he returns."

The knight frowned. "Your brother?"

Walt coughed. "Kill them now, sir? Have a little drink, like, before heading home to the lads?"

All three of the prisoners looked so weak and pathetic that I was disgusted by them. "We'll bind them. Gag them. Tie up their horses. Perhaps someone will find the fellows before they die of thirst."

Walt grumbled that it would be easier to do them in rather than muck about with ropes and whatnot. But after the revelation that Geoffrey de Charny was the black knight, I suddenly did not have the heart for murder. I had a vague sense that Thomas would have disapproved of it and I wanted to act chivalrously. And I thought that, so close to victory, I could afford to be magnanimous.

If I had known what was coming, what I had set in motion with my bull-headed blundering, I would have killed them all. Even the boy. It would have made no difference to the outcome but vengeance is a matter for the heart and the balls, not the head.

"Time to go home now, sir?" Walt asked when the men were trussed up tight. "Catch up with our lads?"

I looked around at the crow-black woodland. The sky above the trees was cloudy and there were no stars. Walt's immortal night vision was better than mine but I did not wish to go staggering about all the hours of darkness looking for our tiny company amongst ten thousand soldiers.

"In the morning. We know that Geoffrey de Charny is our enemy. And now he can hide no longer."

But hiding was not what that monster had in mind.

∞ ∞ ∞

The French were everywhere even before dawn, creeping through the trees collecting firewood, looking for somewhere to shit, or to take a woman. There were plenty being dragged along with the armies, willingly or otherwise.

We walked our horses through the darkness in the general direction of the English army. As the morning grew brighter I noticed that some of the trees were already beginning to change into their autumn colours, mottling like rust on an old blade. Spiderwebs hung with glistening dew across every path, some with black spiders waiting in the centre for the flies to wake and come blundering to their doom.

The French voices all around us thinned and soon we heard Englishmen shouting insults, in the way that friends do.

I discovered that the Prince was still at Chatellerault and so our army had not moved. Three days, he had waited, hoping to strengthen his army with the men who could give him the edge in the coming battle.

It was not to be.

Lancaster could not make the meeting place. His two thousand veteran soldiers were stopped at every turn by guarded crossings and fortresses filled with large garrisons. And King John in the meantime, sent his army well in front of us to the south.

It took us all morning to pick our way beneath the trees, across fields and through two villages. My company was still encamped in the little wood where I had left them. Acorns crunched beneath my horse's hooves as we rode up toward the group of my men, all standing and watching me approach.

"Thank God, sir," Rob said

"Where is Thomas?" I asked, aghast that he had abandoned our brutes to themselves. Although, they seemed to be behaving themselves. If anything, they were a bit pensive. "What is it, Rob?"

"Letter came, sir. First thing this morning." He held it out to me. "From a bloody Frenchman, sir."

I yanked it from his hand and read it aloud to Walt, my heart racing ever more as I did so.

"To my brother knight Sir Richard of Hawkedon. After many years of searching, by the grace of God, I have finally discovered the identity of the knight of the black banner. This man fought in disguise at the battle at Crecy and his men also stole a shield from me bearing my coat of arms. Although I am certain of the truth of it, I cannot divulge this to you in writing. If you still wish to find this man, I shall be at the chapel in Liniers at midday today." I looked at Walt. "It is from Sir Geoffrey de Charny."

Walt looked at the sun above us as I screwed up the letter in my fist.

"Thomas said he had to go meet him," Rob said, backing up from me a step. "Took Hugh with him. Told us to give you that if you came back. Only been gone a little while, sir."

"It is from Geoffrey de Charny," I repeated to Rob, who nodded, fearful of my boiling rage. The rest of the men drifted toward me. "Listen, all of you. This is a ruse. A bloody trap. This bastard de Charny is the black knight. Do you hear, men? Thomas and Hugh have gone to meet the black knight but they do not know it. Mount your horses. Weapons and helms. We will kill de Charny and all who ride with him, do you hear me?"

My heart was in my mouth as we rode south through the woodland. My horse was sweating and exhausted but I pushed him harder.

Thoughts revolved in my head as I cursed myself to the rhythm of my horse's movement.

I was a fool. A damned fool. I had been so close and I had ruined everything. I had shown myself to my enemy by barking the words *black banner knight* up and down the French army.

Of course it had gotten back to him. Someone saw me, perhaps one of his own immortal squires. Someone who knew my true name. And then Geoffrey de Charny had set a trap for me.

A trap I would have walked into if not for finding Lord de Clermont's man. Perhaps I would have suspected the truth but Thomas thought he recognised in de Charny a truly chivalrous knight. An honourable man who brought forth the righteousness and decency in those he fought with.

Please, Thomas. Please, do not trust him.

We charged into the tiny village of Limiers. It was hardly more than a hamlet, with a smattering of cottages and gardens about a small wooden chapel.

The ground was much chewed up by hooves but there were no horses outside the building.

The chapel door stood flung open. A black chasm leading into emptiness within.

"Maybe Tom and Hugh chased after them?" Walt ventured, pointing along the road through the village which disappeared beyond hedgerows and hills. "Can you hear them horses galloping?"

Rob ordered some of the men to pursue the riders and others to stay with me.

I ignored them all and rushed through the open door.

The taste of blood filled the air. It was a small, dark place, with a square window high up over the shrine to some unknown local saint.

Thomas' body lay on the floor in a pool of blood. It flowed still from the tattered flesh across his neck.

My friend's head lay against the far wall next to the altar, with sunlight falling full on his anguished face. I stepped closer and saw how his expression in death was fixed in surprise and outrage.

"Sir!" Walt called from behind me, drawing my attention to our other dear companion. "I'll see if I can find a priest."

Hugh lay against the side wall, eyes wide and flicking about while his mouth worked in silence. His throat trickling blood from a great gash across the front of his neck.

Both of his arms had been cut off between the hand and

elbow.

Hugh's eyes swam with tears and agony.

"Sir," he was trying to say. "Sir."

Blood issued from his lips and he coughed, spraying

I knelt in his blood and took his head in one hand. "Drink from me."

Shaking his head, he mouthed in despair. "No, no."

He held up the ruin of his arms before his eyes, staring at the space where his hands had been.

He preferred to die than live so disfigured.

I shook my head. "Forgive me, Hugh."

"De Charny," he said in a wet whisper, blood filling his mouth.

"I know," I said. "I know de Charny is the black knight. I swear to you I shall kill him. That's enough now, son."

"And... and..." He coughed, causing blood to spray up and the gash in his neck flapped open. I placed my hand over it, feeling the hot blood pump out beneath my palm to soak my hands in it.

"Rest easy now, good Hugh. Go to God, son. You have always done your duty. You fought well all your life. You lived with honour. Go to God. Go to God."

He closed his eyes. In a few moments, he was gone.

I looked up at the men of my company. Their faces reflected the misery and the anguish and the anger that boiled in my breast.

We buried them in the village

And I went to make a battle.

22

POITIERS

PRINCE EDWARD LED HIS ARMY south through the woodland with the intention of getting in front of the French army on the road to Poitiers as they crossed the Vienne. The forest was dense and dark and filled the land between two valleys.

It was a hard march. Forcing horses and wagons through dense woodland is difficult enough and doing it quickly was taxing in the extreme. Even so, the men managed to cover over twenty miles that day using the woodland tracks.

And the route kept our army hidden from the French scouts. They knew we were somewhere close by but they had no idea how close we were to them. In truth, neither did we, for our foremost groups stumbled upon the French rearguard quite suddenly and fought a sharp action. They were more surprised than our men, though, and seven-hundred French men-at-arms routed as the sun went down. Our army pulled back into the black shadows of the woodland.

It was safe within but we were between two rivers and there were no springs to be found in the wood from which to water the men and horses.

Before daybreak, we were already moving west, toward Poitiers, hoping to get away from the French army that we knew were nearby.

But the French were already drawn up in battle order on the plain before the city.

"By God, sir," Rob said as we observed them from the shelter of the woods. "Look at the bastards."

There were eighty-seven banners held aloft over the French army. Eighty-seven bannerets with their companies and God alone knew how many ordinary knights. Thousands of men-at-arms, plus infantry and crossbowmen.

"There will be no escape now," I said to Rob.

"Bloody hope so," said Walt.

"Won't the Prince try to flee anyway? We are outnumbered and outmatched."

"Our route to Gascony is blocked. We have nowhere else to go. And this is good battlefield territory."

It was good land to live on, too. Low hills covered with woods and green pasture. Miles and miles of abundant vineyards in every direction. A place made beautiful by the generations that had lived there since the days of the Romans. It would soon become a place for death.

The Prince conferred with his lords and led the army to a

hilltop just north of a village named Nouaille. The French were about a mile away, just beyond the brow of another hill. And our army established itself in battle order.

Warwick and Oxford commanded the vanguard on the left, his far wing where the ground fell away into marshland toward the river. Salisbury commanded the right and Edward took the centre. We had about two thousand archers, three thousand men-at-arms and a few Gascons.

This would be our battleground.

Behind us, the wood of Nouaille gave us somewhere to retreat into, if we were overrun. In front was a thick hawthorn hedge which ran right across the hillside. Here and there were copses and scrub and everywhere across the hills were rows and rows of vines. On our right flank, where there were no natural defences, the archers dug deep trenches and pits to protect themselves from a mounted charge.

It was a good place to fight.

But the English were afraid. Fear was in the air. At Crecy, we had been as confident as an army could be.

On that hillside outside Poitiers, there was a sense of impending doom.

Every man was hungry but even worse was the thirst. After the twenty mile march the day before and the hundreds of hard miles before that, legs and arses were like jelly and thighs raw.

All the men knew we were outnumbered, with at least two of them for every one of us. Many were shaken by the fact we had missed meeting up with Lancaster. Those two thousand men were on everyone's minds and some were even convinced they would come to our rescue in time, no matter how much it was explained that was impossible.

Also missed, desperately, were the thousands we had left behind to guard Gascony. All of them sitting warm and dry for months, eating all the food, drinking the wine and bedding the women, while we stood shivering and thirsty waiting to die on a French hillside.

The French sent their priests and envoys out into the fields between the two armies.

Prince Edward and the leading nobles rode a little way forward toward them and they came closer to meet him.

I jumped on my horse.

"Sir?" Walt said.

"Stay here."

I rode out after the Prince and the great lords, feeling the eyes of the army on me. I was disgraced, an outcast, practically a criminal.

Ever since I had escaped my half-hearted imprisonment in Gascony, I had kept well away from the lords of the army. My presence was barely tolerated within the mass of the general soldiery but still, I rode out alone behind the great lords and their retinues and lurked where they could not see me without turning. No one else came to stop me. I knew none would dare.

A French cardinal came forward toward the Prince on foot with his arms stretched out, tears in his eyes.

"Your Grace," he said, voice quivering. "I beg of you that you listen."

Edward sighed. "Say it quickly. This is no time for a sermon."

The cardinal stuttered into his speech. "Your Grace, I beg that you consider the appalling deaths of the good Christians that shall happen in this place if battle is joined. Your men, there, so many good and decent men, will surely be slaughtered. Your royal person, your loyal nobles beside you, and the common folk that follow you, are in the gravest peril where you stand. Please, my lord, let you not tempt God with pride and vainglory. I beg you, in the name of God and by the honour of Christ and the Blessed Virgin to grant a short truce so that negotiations may be held. I swear to you that my brothers and I shall do all in our power to assist you to come to some accommodation in this matter. If you will allow it, we should have a conference between the kings of England and France and so avoid the terrible slaughter that you must suffer."

I laughed and a few men turned around to look at me.

"What are you doing here?" Salisbury growled, pointing his ample nose in my direction.

"You cannot mean to treat with the French, Your Grace?" I called out.

Edward turned and gave me a death stare. I gave him one back and mine was far more practised.

"Get him away from here," Edward said to Oxford, who nodded. However, he wisely made no move toward me.

The cardinal and his men glared at me. "Your Grace, a truce would be—"

"Yes, yes," Edward said, waving his hand. "I suppose a short negotiation would be in order. We owe it to God, do we not?"

The cardinal beamed. "Praise God! We shall at once return to the King of France. There is a hill just there, between the hedge and the vines, where two groups may sit in peace."

Bowing and praising God and the Prince, they left and rode away over the hill.

I shook my head as they went. "We hold a fine position," I said loudly as the lords turned in to each other.

"You do not hold anything," Salisbury called. "You are not welcome here."

Oxford nodded. "You may take yourself away from the Prince's presence. Immediately."

"We can kill them all," I shouted. "We can murder the lot of them, Your Grace. Why delay?"

Warwick sneered. "Our men need rest, you fool. This way, our men can recover from the march."

Humphrey Ingham took up the haranguing. "Hold your tongue, Hawkedon, you blustering bastard. You claim to know so much about—"

"There is no water here, sire," I said to Edward, projecting my voice over theirs. "Our men will have to ride to and from the rivers for as long as we stay in this place. All the enemy has to do is guard the banks and wait for us to die of thirst or attack. We must invite an attack now, today."

The Prince pursed his lips and looked back at our army. The men stood, spattered in filth and all cloth darkened and heavy with rain not yet dried. They looked anxiously down at their lord and future king.

"It is done, now," he said, his tone surprisingly reasonable. He looked at his lords. "Let us see what they have to offer. In the meantime, send companies to collect as much water as we can and have them drink while they are there."

They glared at me but again made no move to drive me away. Each of them had experience and they were good soldiers. But they knew my reputation. Most had seen me fight. They had heard my advices over the years to the King and to his nobles and they knew that whether my words were listened to or not, I was usually right.

But despite all that, the negotiations out between the armies lasted all day and continued after sundown. For all his confident talk, it was clear that Edward wanted to avoid a battle.

He, too, was infested with the sense that we could not win.

I had to force the battle or else I could not kill Geoffrey de Charny. I needed them to come for us and whether de Charny fought in the open or under the black banner, I would cut my way toward him and tear his heart out.

But only if there was battle.

The proposal from the French was galling. They said Edward had to surrender all his conquests in France over the last three years and he had to pay tens of thousands of pounds for the damage caused by the great raids. In return, the Prince asked to be betrothed to a daughter of King John, and she would bring the entire county of Angouleme as dowry.

"Absurd," I said when I heard the details but Edward seemed to be open to it.

When it went back to the French, they changed their minds and after sundown their message came back to us.

"You have destroyed too much of France to be paid for by any sum. You are trapped in your position, your men are exhausted from their ceaseless destruction and you are out of supplies. You have no source of water and so you cannot stay where you are. But you cannot escape. Any agreement you make with us would have to be confirmed by your father the King and in the meantime you would throw away our terms and continue your onslaught upon our soil. You will have no agreement from us."

"Why did they go through all this?" Oxford said. "Merely to throw it all back in our faces?"

"They are delaying because it suits them, you bloody preening fools," I said, unable to contain my anger at their stupidity. "We can only lose by such delay while they only gain. We eat the last of our supplies while their numbers continue to grow beyond that damned hill."

Although they knew it was true, they despised me for my disrespect towards them and they pretended I was not there.

The men of our army sat all through the day and in the night each man lay down on the ground and slept.

Thousands of men laying across the hillside beneath the stars. Small fires flickered everywhere. A few fellows gathered around a candle or two, talking in low voices. Pages and other servants traipsed back and forth through the mass of men, some holding lamps aloft as they went.

"How can there not be a battle?" the men in my company asked me. "How can we be here and them over there and not come to blows?"

"Ain't you daft sods never seen two blustering drunks?" Walt answered them. "The two biggest mouths in the alehouse, shouting each other hoarse and cursing each other's mother and puffing up their chests, only to allow themselves to be pulled away by their mates? Seems like that's what this is here, if you ask me. Two biggest bastards in the room, each afraid of getting his block knocked off."

"How do you make such men come to blows?" I asked Walt.

He shrugged. "No one wants to see that, do they, sir. Just want to finish your ale and go home to a woman, that time of night."

Rob leaned forward. "Some craven old bastards wait for a man to turn away before thumping him on the crown."

I nodded, the germ of an idea taking root.

"Nah," said Walt. "You want to drive your knuckles into a man's kidneys, if you be hitting from the back. Liable to break your hand, cracking him on the dome in such a manner."

"Unlike you, Walt, I ain't got experience hitting a fellow in the back."

The men laughed.

"Come now, Robert," Walt countered, "from what I hear it told, you like most of all to pound a man solely from behind."

I walked away while they roared and argued with each other. Most of the soldiers on the dark hill were quiet and pensive but men prepare for battle in a thousand ways and it has always been the same.

Some laugh and joke, others tremble and others weep. Many, I know, think of home and family and what they might go back to if they live through the next day. And they dread to never see it again.

Myself, I had no home. Not really. And yet I thought of

Cecilia and the home that I might have had with her, for a time, if things had been different. If I had chosen differently. If there was any home at all, it was the house in London and if I had any family it was Eva and Stephen alone. Poor Thomas, and Hugh with him, were gone forever.

Both men, I had given a longer, ageless life than they would have had otherwise. But still they were dead because I had not done my duty protecting them from the danger I exposed them to.

I walked by an armourer who sat hammering dents from pieces of armour plate while another sharpened weapons nearby. Pages queued up for either one man or the other, their arms full of blades or helms.

I had lost John, and Thomas, and Hugh, to Geoffrey de Charny.

He had taken so much. His reputation as the greatest knight in Christendom irked me almost as much as anything else. The fame that he had cultivated had come from his prowess in battle and in tourneys and jousts. Prowess enhanced due to his immortal strength and speed. It was deceitful, dishonest and I wished I had done it.

The soldiers around me on that hillside joked and complained and said their private prayers.

My prayers would wait. Instead, I swore by God and Jesus and all His saints that I would have vengeance.

In the morning, a rider came to ask for a truce of one year. Prince Edward replied that he would agree to a truce extending from that day to next spring but no longer.

"They will give us no truce," I said, exasperated. "This is nought but to delay us further. We must force battle today or we will wither and die like vines in a drought."

"How can we force them to attack," Warwick said, "when they are seeking to delay."

I had been thinking about it. "The hotheads amongst the French lords will have been urging King John to attack us since yesterday, or even earlier. Especially the ones who were not at Crecy. They will see us as weak, needing only to be assaulted for us to crumble. They are surely being held back by cooler heads and the reticence of the King. All we need do is tip the balance."

"Yes, yes," Warwick said, scowling. "But *how*, man?"

"We turn our backs."

They stared at me.

"We withdraw." I smiled back at them. "At least, we should *appear* to be withdrawing. What can they see of us, from over the hill?"

They looked out across the rolling hills and hedges.

"Nothing," Oxford said.

"Their men see us," Salisbury said, nodding at the scores of riders atop the far hill a mile away. "And they will ride back, frantic, telling their masters all at once what they see. And they will surely act to catch us while we are in disorder."

Salisbury may have been a miserable bastard who disliked me intensely, but he was a damned fine soldier. He smiled and the others began nodding with him. Even Sir Humphrey Ingham, who seemed delighted by the proposition. Salisbury and Ingham turned expectantly to the Prince.

"Raise your men's banners aloft at the rear," Edward said to Warwick, "and have them advance them into the wood. Go with him, Humphrey."

They turned to make it happen, enjoying the prospect of tricking the French.

"Best tell the men, my lords," I said to them, loudly. "We would not want any of them thinking we were running away." I raised my voice. "Not when we are about to slaughter the French." A few of the common men near us raised their voices to cheer me and I grinned at them. "Pass the word, lads. The Prince is going to trick the French. But we are all staying right here. This hill is England, today, boys. Pass the word."

Salisbury nodded once at me and turned to make his way to the right flank.

I made my way to my company.

"Going to be a fight then, is it?" Walt said. He lowered his voice. "The lads are getting a bit thirsty, sir."

"I know. There will be a battle today if I have to ride out and charge the French alone. We shall be away from here tomorrow. They can drink then."

"If any of us live to see tomorrow," Walt said. "Sounds like there's a lot of French knights." He spat at his feet.

"We are in a very fine position. Do you see? Their numbers do not matter so much as they cannot get around our left due to the marshes and the hill. How will they get through those hedges, there?"

Walt frowned. Rob answered. "They'll have to come through the gaps where there's no hedge. They just have to. Proper hedges, them."

"And so they will have to come on in a narrow front there, and over there, and right here, before spreading out again to attack our front line."

Rob was grinning as he strung his bow. "They'll be all herded together. All nice and tight and packed in there. It'll be lovely work, lovely."

"It'll be a bloody slaughter, all right," Walt said, nodding. "And then they'll be through and they'll slaughter us in turn."

The priests came out and started to say Mass.

Many men-at-arms filed away up the hill with their lords.

Walt jerked his head at them. "Knights up there, sir. Knights dubbing their men, making them knights also. Great honour, that, if we win. Great honour for a loyal man to be so dubbed by his knightly lord." He looked at me expectantly.

"The day you are knighted, Walt, will be the day the notion has lost all its meaning."

He hung his head and walked away by himself.

Edward came forward on his magnificent horse and turned to his men. A hush fell on the army as we strained to hear his shouted words. He had a fine, loud voice and it carried well but the wind blew most of it away.

The Prince's men came around, shouting out the written orders as they went. "You shall keep strictest discipline in the lines! No man shall waste time securing prisoners! Do you hear? No prisoners to be taken."

Rob looked over his shoulder at Warwick's banners on our left as they waved rearward into the wood. "Supposing it *ain't* a trick, sir?"

"What's that, Rob?"

"Oh, nothing, sir."

"Spit it out, man."

"It proper looks like Warwick is retreating, don't it? Look at Ingham's banner, there. It's halfway to bloody Bordeaux. But still the enemy waits up there. And if the French don't attack now, then we might as well make it an actual retreat, right, sir? The rest of us can follow him?"

I had a sudden thought. Perhaps it was I who had been tricked by the Prince. Perhaps he had in fact ordered Warwick and Ingham to retreat and that was what he intended.

Aghast at the thought, I rode out through the rows of vines toward the French. "Fight me!" I shouted at the men on the far hill. "Come and fight, cowards. Any of you, come fight me. All of you, come to me and fight."

A mass of horsemen crept over the brow of the hill and began to cross the fields toward us. More and more appeared and streamed after the ones in front. I counted scores, then a hundred and when I saw it was perhaps five hundred men mounted on destriers with their lance points glinting and their pennants snapping in the wind, I turned and rode back toward the Prince.

"Here they come, Your Grace."

"Yes," Oxford said as I rode up, "thank you for you pointing it out."

"They are aiming for Warwick," I said, watching the Prince closely. He screwed up his face and turned to a man on a swift courser at his side. "Ride to Warwick! Tell him to hold his position against the assault."

"Look!" Chandos said, pointing with his sword. "Their men separate. Two columns."

I nodded, seeing the riders pick their way through the trees and bushes. "They mean to charge the archers on both flanks. Drive them away or kill them before the main assault."

"Oxford," the Prince snapped. "Lead the archers into the marsh around the left flank."

The Earl of Oxford blinked once and then charged his horse along the front lines toward the men. In the distance, the two columns of French cavalry formed as they drew closer to us, ready to smash into our formations.

They charged into the disarray on our left flank and penetrated the lines where Warwick's men had pulled back. They were fighting to hold the French from breaking through and sweeping in behind us. Out beyond them, on the farthest left flank, Oxford ordered the archers to slog out further into the marsh. The horses could not charge them there but they were able to shoot into the rear and flanks of the French horses. The horses died. Falling, throwing their riders, and panicking, the enemy horses took terrible damage from the storm of arrows and the attackers were driven off.

On our right, the enemy column came galloping up the hill toward our archers. The dense hawthorn hedge on that flank was broken only by a gap so narrow that no more than five riders abreast could make it through at once.

Our archers began shooting.

As the French squeezed through the gap, the arrows smashed

into them causing terrible damage. Still, their armour protected many of them and they came on through the hedge and opened out into a wider front and, horses blowing, they readied to charge.

Salisbury ordered his men forward to meet them and our men-at-arms, hundreds of them, stepped rapidly forward with their visors down and their polearms raised. The French charged into them and our men hacked at the riders and horses with their long-handled hammers and axes and the enemy thrust with their lances.

My lord the Earl of Suffolk had his blood up and he rode down to the archers shouting at them to advance on the right and shoot into the flanks while he and his men guarded them.

The French assault was overwhelmed. So many fell, and yet they fought on.

Until they fled.

The assault on our right collapsed and they rode away while our men cheered and hurled insults after them. A few archers kept up shooting at the backs of the men riding away, taking down a handful more horses, until they were ordered to stop. So many dead and wounded French lay on the hillside in front of us. Some of the archers walked out to them until the Marshals of the army roared at them to get back into their formations.

"Why can't they grab a bit of loot, sir?" Rob asked.

"The battle has barely begun."

"Killed hundreds of them," Walt said.

"And here come thousands more," I said.

For the first proper assault was coming toward us across the rolling hills. They came on in good order, on foot, in all their glory. The banner at the centre of them all was that of the Dauphin. He was just eighteen years old and leading the vanguard, as our own prince had done at Crecy aged just sixteen. But their prince, the Dauphin, was a weak little streak of piss and ours was a damned hero.

When their well-ordered lines came to the hedge, they had to break up and come through the gaps to get to us. Once again, our archers unleashed a storm of iron and steel on them. Many fell, some dead, more wounded, as they emerged from those gaps.

But still they came on.

Thousands of French men-at-arms assaulted our lines. They fought us for hours. And a hard fight it was.

When they could make no headway against us, they retreated back down the hill.

Our men wanted to chase them away but we knew we had resisted but a portion of their army and our keenest men were held back.

Only later did we discover that the Dauphin was then spirited away from the battle. Some said it was on the orders of the King of France but in truth it was the actions of Jean de Clermont and the other conspirators who wished to place the young and weak Dauphin on the throne. The Duke of Orleans followed the Dauphin from the field, as did the Count of Anjou and the Count of Poitiers. And they took the entirety of the second line of battle with them. Thousands of French soldiers under the command of those men marched right off the field and away into France, abandoning their king to his fate.

A shocking, treasonous betrayal.

It cost the French a third of their army but still they had their third battle, the rearguard, commanded by King John himself and it was large enough by itself to match our entire army.

They came forward to the roar of trumpets and drums, his men shouting and cheering as they came.

"This lot seem keen," Walt said.

They held the King's banner aloft and beside it was the unfurled Oriflamme. The sacred, inspiring, red banner of the King of France since the days of Charlemagne which declared that no quarter was to be given.

Beside that was the banner of Geoffrey de Charny.

"Our enemy is with the French King," I called to my men.

John Chandos heard me shouting but misunderstood my words. "By God, Richard. We do not wish to kill King John."

"Shut your idiot mouth, Chandos. There will be a cold day in Hell before I need your battlefield advice."

The trumpets sounded over and over and the men beneath them roared like the sea in a storm. Their armour shone in an array of blue, gold, red, and silver. A riot of colour across the front.

They were keen. And they had every right to be. That third battle was filled with the finest knights in France.

And they were fresh.

We had been fighting for hours and our men leaned on their weapons or sat on the churned ground. Men breathed heavily and drank whatever last dregs could be found and ate any morsels their men had hidden away. Fighting saps the energy from your limbs. A minute feels like an hour. Two hours can finish a man for days. And yet our toughest test was coming.

Before the French knights came their crossbowmen. Hundreds and hundreds, perhaps thousands. Unlike at Crecy, these men held their enormous shields aloft as they came forward and so protected themselves from the arrows of our men. Our archers unleashed their arrows but they hit only wood and steel. Our men's volleys slowed until they all but stopped.

"Out of arrows, sir," Rob said.

I ignored him, keeping my eyes fixed on de Charny's banner. Like the Oriflamme and the King's banner, it was at the rear of the advancing French lines. I would have to smash through hundreds of knights without being swarmed by their number. *Unless*, I thought, *unless I can come at them from the rear.*

"Send for our horses," I said to Walt. "Take our men to the rear." I left them and pushed further to the centre. "Your Grace!" I shouted, shoving my way through the masses of men toward him. "Sire. They are held here. Fixed here. Horsemen can get around to their rear."

The Prince ordered the Captal de Buch to take fifty men from the reserve and whatever mounted archers had arrows around the right flank into the rear.

I turned to go with him and the Prince shouted at me. "You will remain, Richard."

"Fifty men will do nothing," I said, scowling. "I am taking my company, mounted, to charge the Oriflamme."

"You will not!" he shouted.

"I am going to kill de Charny. If you have any sense in your fat head you will send every man you can with me."

I turned and pushed my way through the men as the lords of England shouted their disapproval.

"To me, men," I called to my company. "Mount your horses. De Charny is there, do you see his banner? He holds the Oriflamme. We will kill any man who stands in our way, whether he be French, Gascon, or English. Whether he be knight, lord, or king. For Thomas! For Hugh! For the White Dagger!"

My men roared and I led them along the rear of our lines, throwing clods of earth as we galloped, sending archers scurrying and cursing us. At our farthest flank I turned to the north and rode on beyond the French. My men, not the finest riders and not on the finest horses, caught up with me. "There!" I said, pointing to the distant banners. "We stop for no man. Unfurl the banner! Get it aloft."

My great war banner was raised. The white dagger on the red field with golden flame reaching up.

"Death!" I shouted. "Death!"

My men shouted with me and we rode along the rear of the French lines to the centre, where the King's bodyguard turned to meet us. They were on foot and as our charge faltered, they surged around us. My horse was struck and he stumbled.

"De Charny! The Lord of Hell is here," I shouted. "Hell has come for you!"

My horse was killed and I threw myself off, stumbling into the arms of my archers Watkyn and Osbert, who pushed me upright again.

We cut our way through the masses, my men fighting like lions. Like demons.

My sword was yanked from my grasp and I took a mace from another man before smiting him with it. It was hot beyond belief in my armour. The sounds of clashing arms and men's cries filled my head. I was struck with weapons and gauntleted hands grasped at my shoulders, my helm. Pole weapons were shoved, unseen, between my legs, as enemies tried to trip me. Falling even once could very well mean death.

They were so many and my men were swarmed by French bodies. It was chaos. I saw Hal Brampton, my sturdy man-at-arms, go down under a dozen men and their daggers worked their way through his armpits and groin. His visor was pulled open and they stabbed him in his eyes and face until his screams stopped.

Osmund was overrun by my side and before I could reach him, he was borne away by masses of enemies. I cried out for Walt but I had no idea where he was. One of my archers, Lambert, stumbled in front of me. He had lost his helm and had a torrent of blood gushing from his skull.

"Get to the rear," I shouted at him. "I will restore you later."

He nodded and took one step away before a heavy bladed glaive swung down from nowhere and hewed his head in two down to the neck.

I was shoved forward, blows ringing on my back and shoulders. Enemies were all around me and I did not know if any friends remained. Had my entire company been killed or lost? It seemed as though I would never reach the French King. Never reach de Charny and the Oriflamme. Never kill the black knight.

And the English mounted knights came. Finally, the Prince had sent them after all and they smashed into the rear of King

John's men, knocking down knights and squires and spearing them with their lances. The press of men was suffocating.

I surged forward, throwing enemy knights down before me. I hammered my mace into the King's standard bearer and he fell, along with the King's great banner.

"De Charny!"

He was there, with the pole of the Oriflamme in hand, striking down English knights like wheat. Finally, my enemy was before me.

His two men beside him were immortals also, their inhuman strength undeniable and irresistible.

I killed the first one, crashing my mace down on his shoulder until my weapon broke. I wrapped my arm around him while he hammered at my helm with his sword and I worked my dagger through the tattered mail beneath his armpit and through his ribs into his lung. I swirled it around, opening the wound and working my way toward his heart. His knees sagged and he fell against me. Reaching down, I tore off his helm, ready to stab him in the eyes.

It was Rudolph de Rohan. A lord who I had once held in my grasp before sending him back to his lord Clermont.

"You," I said, breathing heavily.

He had deceived me and I had let him go. I had never considered that he would have fought as a squire to a mere knight. But what did such things mean to immortals? I had been a fool again. I had wrought so much destruction and killed so many but I had still not killed enough.

Seeing me distracted, Rohan thrust up with his sword and it slid inside the armour of my right arm, cutting me deeply.

Enraged, I stabbed him in the head and bore him to the ground.

Blood poured from my arm, soaking my sword-hand.

A cry of warning alerted me to the incoming blow but I managed no more than to see it coming and lean away.

A poleaxe hit me flush on the breastplate. The inhuman force knocked me onto my back and I could not breathe, nor see.

It was not a blow from a mortal man.

De Charny was on me. I got my arms up as he swung his poleaxe again down onto my head. The haft on it had broken and he gripped it close to the head of it, striking hard against my helm, my gauntlets, and my breastplate. Such force and fury that I could not block the blows, nor grasp the weapon or the man. I rolled to the side to get up but his weight and strength bore me down and he struck me so that my world turned dark.

It was suddenly bright.

My visor was gone and de Charny kneeled over me with his arms raised, the massive steel polearm over his head. I reached my hands up. Pieces of steel from my gauntlets were hanging down from the ragged leather gloves.

He was dragged away.

I climbed to my knees in time to see Rob twist de Charny's helm off his head before holding him down with his archer's strength, magnified by his immortal power.

And Walt sawed Geoffrey de Charny's head from his shoulders with a broken sword, crying out in an animal roar at the barbaric brutality of it.

I staggered forward as Walt lifted de Charny's severed head. The eyes were open for a moment and it seemed as though they focused on me in rage and in horror, just for a moment, before the eyes rolled back and the lids closed.

"My dear fellows," I said, hearing the emotion and exhaustion in my voice as I spoke. "Walt. Rob." I could say no more, overcome with the knowledge that they had saved me. Both men seemed to be in as bad a condition as I was and yet they stood and grasped my arms and grinned with me.

The King of France fought on with his youngest son, a lad named Philip. Almost all of his bodyguards had fallen. The English could have killed the King easily but they shouted at him to surrender and yanked his weapons away from him. A great press of English and Gascon men-at-arms pushed in on him but King John would not submit. The crowd about him were furious.

My wounds were painful and I wanted to drink blood. But I could see that he was going to get ripped apart and that was no way to treat a king.

"Everybody back!" I shouted in English. "Get back from him you bloody filthy dogs!"

A few parted and I pushed into the front of the crowd.

"Why do you not surrender, my lord?" I shouted in French, my voice carrying above all others.

"I shall surrender only to a knight," he shouted back. "As will my son."

"I am a knight," I said. "I swear it to God."

The crowd around us quietened as they watched.

He hesitated and then pulled off one of his gauntlets and held it out to me. I stepped forward and bowed as I took it in my left hand. I must have looked quite a sight. My armour dented and hanging off me. Blood streaming from beneath what remained.

"You are my prisoner. You shall be safe. Have no fear."

"My son also," King John said, and pulled the young Prince to his side.

"He's mine!" someone shouted behind me and surged forward to grab the King from me.

Another voice from the other side shouted. "He's mine!"

Then they all began shoving forward and I pushed back their grasping hands. Walt appeared by my side, and Rob also, slapping at the greedy bastards as they tried to take my prize from me.

King John raised his voice, though it shook as he spoke. "I am a great enough lord to make you all rich!"

We pushed against them. "Get off him, you faithless dogs!"

And then the Earl of Warwick and his men, all mounted, pushed through the crowd.

"Stand back on pain of death!" Warwick's men shouted. "On pain of death, I say!" Their swords were drawn.

The crowd backed away.

"You, too, Hawkedon," Warwick said.

"The King has surrendered to me," I said. "He is my prisoner and in my care."

Warwick sneered. "I will be damned before I allow you into the presence of the Prince ever again. Step back."

I recalled how I had spoken to Prince Edward and the great lords of the realm. It was a breach that I could never repair. And I realised I did not want to do so. It was irrelevant. My enemy was dead.

"I pledged to protect you and I have. The Earl of Warwick is an honourable man who will keep you safe. You and your son."

I bowed and stepped back while Warwick and his men dismounted, bowed low before King John and took him away. The men-at-arms, deprived of the riches and the spectacle, turned back to find other prisoners and to loot the bodies of the fall all around us.

"Walt," I said, "Rob. Where are the others?"

Rob hung his head. "Dead, sir."

"Hal? Osmund? I saw Watkyn fighting at the end, surely he is not dead?"

"All of them," Walt said.

Rob looked me in the eye. "To a man."

"Good God Almighty," I said, looking at the sky. "We must bury them."

My men had been spent in breaking through the French centre. Without their immortal strength and veteran skill, the battle could yet have swung in the favour of the French. Each of my men had fought and killed a dozen, a score, of enemy knights. They had helped me to cut a swathe deep into the royal retinue, bringing me to our immortal enemy. They had paid for my revenge, and the Prince's great victory, with their lives.

We buried Hal, Osmund, Lambert, Watkyn, Osbert, Randulf, Jake, and Stan. I said my prayers over them and gave them my thanks. Also, I gave thanks to God and humbly requested that He take care of my men. So many, I had sent to Him, both friends and foes, over the long years.

All told, the Prince's army lost no more than fifty men-at-arms and a few hundred archers and spearmen. There were hundreds of wounded, though, and every man who stood was exhausted beyond measure.

Well after the battle, I heard about the French losses from the heralds. Two-and-a-half thousand men-at-arms were struck dead on the field. Their armour and wealth was well stripped by the end of the day and, without coats of arms to go by, the heralds had difficulty identifying the bodies.

As well as Geoffrey de Charny, his ally the lord Jean de Clermont was killed and scores of other great lords and nobles. We took three thousand prisoners, including fourteen counts, twenty-one barons, and fourteen hundred knights. Marshals of France, Archbishops, the leaders of the kingdom, all were in our hands. Each one would be ransomed for a fortune.

But that was not for us.

Just before sundown, I led Walt and Rob to the top of the hill by the wood. Our brothers had been killed. We were exhausted and hurt. They wanted blood so I gave them each some of mine. Enough for them to recover. My arm was hurt but I would live so I could wait.

"How many times is it that you have saved my life now, Walter?"

He smiled. "A few, sir."

"Why?" I asked him.

He was confused and opened his mouth to answer. I wondered if he would say it was because I had lifted him up from his poverty and given him wealth. Or if it was because he thought he needed me, now that he was an immortal.

In the end, he shrugged. "It is my duty, sir."

Rob nodded slowly as Walt spoke.

"You are an honourable man, Rob," I said to him. "Trustworthy, loyal, and honourable."

He bowed his head. "Thank you, sir."

I had taken two rather fine swords from the field, having lost my own. These swords, I placed before me.

"Kneel. Both of you."

They did so, glancing sidelong at each other.

"This is your oath. You will safeguard to your uttermost the weak, the widow, and the helpless. You will be without fear in the face of your enemies. You will be loyal by word and deed and serve your lord. Be humble and courteous everywhere, especially to women. Serve Jesus Christ and protect those who worship in His name. Be the terror and dead of all evil-doers and be just and brave in battle."

They so swore and I struck each of them across the face with the flat of my hand to dub them. Then I presented each man with a sword.

I dragged them to their feet and embraced them in turn.

Walt had tears streaming down his cheeks. Rob looked astonished.

"Let us go home, brothers."

2 3

THE GREAT STORM

"SO OUR ENEMIES ARE all dead," Stephen said. "It is over."

I thought of my brother, out there somewhere in the East. Destined to return. I thought of Priskos and his sons and wondered what it would mean for the future.

"For now, at least."

We made it home from Gascony to London by the summer of 1357. I was allowed to keep my land and my title but as I dare not show my face at court or call on any great lord, especially my own, the Earl of Suffolk, I was unsure what to do with it. It was beyond time for me to leave England but I delayed leaving.

We sat in the townhouse in London and ate well. Stephen, Eva, Walt, and Rob. The remaining members of the Order of the White Dagger.

Stephen nodded. "All this time it was Geoffrey de Charny and

I did not have the wit to see it."

"You did see it. We all did. Yet he managed to turn our suspicion away from him with that business with the stolen shield. It was a mistake."

"A costly mistake," Stephen said. "Our dear friends. Dead, because of my failing."

"Yours, yes. And Eva's. And mine."

"He is dead," Eva said. "Him and his men. Whatever business they were up to, to put the Dauphin on the throne, is finished."

"And yet the Dauphin is regent while his father is the prisoner of King Edward," Thomas said. "Is that not precisely what they wanted?"

Walt spoke up. "But there ain't none of them alive to whisper in his ear none, is there."

"No immortals," I said. "Plenty of lords."

Walt shrugged. "Sounds about right, to me."

"What I still do not understand," Stephen said. "Is why they sent that ruffian to kill you in Southwark."

I shrugged. "He is dead. They are all dead. What does it matter?"

None had an answer for that.

"When do you mean to go away again?" Stephen asked. "Where will you go this time? To crusade against the northern pagans?"

I waved a hand. "Perhaps. For now, we shall return to Suffolk," I said to Walter and Rob. "You can be with be with your family for years yet, Rob."

He nodded, keen as mustard to get back to his wife and

children.

"I will give you the manor at Hartest, Walt. You can be the lord there, now."

"Me, sir? I wouldn't know what to do with it."

"You will be all right. And you might even take a wife, now. Settle down for a few years."

"Don't want a wife, sir. The man who has no wife is no cuckold, and that's the truth."

"Not all women are deceitful, Walter. But, wife or no wife, you are a knight, now. No man may have position without duty. And so you will run it well and you will take care of your servants and tenants."

He held up his chin. "I will, sir. I surely will."

In the courtyard a few days later, Eva embraced me before I mounted my horse. She placed a hand against my cheek.

"I am so sorry about Thomas."

"Thank you."

She took her palm away from my face and took my hands in hers.

"You know that Lady Cecilia has married."

I took a deep breath. "I heard it on the way home. Some fat fool. Not a proper knight at all. Never been on campaign. Wealthy, though."

"I am certain she will be deeply unhappy."

I smiled. "I do not want that."

"She sounds like a lusty one. And lust is addicted to novelty. Perhaps you might have her anyway, when the fat fool is not looking."

"I do not want that, either," I said.

"Of course," Eva said, patting my hands. "Do you want me to kill him for you?"

I laughed and embraced her again before mounting my horse. "I think I have had enough killing for a while."

"Does that mean you do not consider yourself a monster after all?"

Before I rode away into the vile filth of London, I considered it.

"We shall see."

It seemed certain that I would not have to fight again for a long time. Perhaps decades.

But I was wrong.

∞ ∞ ∞

In late 1359, the King summoned me to Windsor Castle.

The war had gone remarkably well. After the Battle of Poitiers, Prince Edward had sent word of the victory back ahead of us.

"We take no pleasure in the slaughter of men," King Edward had said, which was a lie. "But we rejoice in God's bounty and we look forward to a just and early peace."

He seemed right to be so confident that, after yet another catastrophic defeat, the French would sue for peace on almost any terms. With all the leading men of the kingdom either dead or prisoners, their lands had fallen into chaos, anarchy, and rebellion.

After the battle, there was essentially no French army in the country and yet there were thousands of well-organised, highly experienced English armies in Brittany, Normandy, Calais, and Gascony. The French were surrounded and on their knees. In panic, they recruited townsmen to protect against the assault they were certain was coming for Paris.

But the English did not want Paris. Instead, our armies overran what little resistance remained near our strongholds.

The French commoners turned against the knights and nobles who had robbed them for years through endless taxation only to lose battle after battle or to run away in ignominy. And then they were informed, all across the land, that new taxes would be raised to pay for the enormous ransoms required to free their lords. What was more, the assaults of the English and Gascon free companies had increased now there was little threat of resistance.

The people had bent as far as they were able, and then they snapped.

Paris revolted. An eruption of violence took hold of the city as the merchants and common folk rose up against their lords and the Dauphin. They tried to force political changes through violence. The Dauphin attempted to negotiate and delay and said he would consider their demands.

He then ran away from Paris.

The capital city exploded in chaos again. Coinage collapsed. The mob sought to enforce their terms. They attacked royal buildings and set fire to noble's houses with burning arrows while they pillaged official's homes and rampaged through the streets.

Some lords cowered and prayed and pissed their

underclothes. Others abandoned law and honour and took up banditry and murder, like the *routiers* of Brittany.

All through this, King John, still a prisoner of the English, attempted to negotiate his release, negotiate with his lords, with the Dauphin. He was still the King but he was not present in his kingdom and so little could be concluded.

King Edward wanted John to give huge concessions in return for being set free and meant to hold him for as long as it took to extract this from the French.

The political mess was so chaotic that it hampered diplomacy and the talking dragged on for months and years.

Truces were allowed, conferences were held, peace terms were negotiated almost endlessly. Edward wanted the world and he felt he could demand it. He was willing and able to launch more massive attacks on France.

And that was when he summoned me back to him. It was done quietly, and I was shown into his private chambers with no announcement.

"Dear God," King Edward said. "How do you do it, sir?"

I knew he was referring to my everlasting youth. "It is my innocent heart, Your Grace."

He scoffed and almost laughed but then his face fell. "How old are you, Richard?"

The King of England was in his late forties and looking rather as if his best years were far behind him.

"To be honest, Edward, I have lost count. But I must be fifty, I suppose."

"I am surrounded by young men. Or men who appear

youthful." He shook his head. "You have the devil in you."

"Perhaps."

"My son says so."

"I would never disagree with the Prince, Your Grace."

He smiled. "I think you embarrassed him at Poitiers. I hear you shouted at him. Called him a fool in front of the army."

"Unforgivable actions."

"Spare me your false contrition. I do not need it."

"You called me here for something."

"I am going to war again." He did not sound pleased about the matter. "I will only get the victory God wishes if I take Paris."

"So it is true."

"I would have you with us."

Even though it was gratifying to hear it, I was surprised. "It is a great honour to offer my sword in service to you again, Your Grace. And yet, the lords of—"

"Are they the King of England, sir? Or am I?"

Inclining my head a little, I smiled. He had rarely been one for outbursts but the war had been hard on him, even if he had not been the one fighting it in person.

He cleared his throat. "You have always been able to achieve that which other knights would find difficult."

I knew that he meant I would do dishonourable things, if he asked me to. And I would achieve them and hold my tongue about it.

"Certainly, Your Grace. Whatever you require."

"If you do this and can manage to control yourself, you will be welcomed back in full honour."

That was not something I needed, or wanted. And I felt no desire to go to France again and do whatever it was that the King had in mind for me. Possibly, he wanted someone killed. Perhaps the Dauphin. Or perhaps even King John himself.

I sighed.

Edward scowled. "Are you ungrateful, sir? I offer you this chance at redemption and you can think only to huff and blow like an old maid? Damn you, then, Richard. And Damn Humphrey too. Leave me."

"Humphrey?" I said. "Sir Humphrey Ingham? What does he have to do with it?"

"He is the man who asked me to bring you back in."

"Why in God's name would he do that? He despises me."

"I always believed that Sir Humphrey Ingham regarded you highly. After all, he requested that you be the lucky one, of all the knights of the realm, to escort his lovely sister home after she was widowed the first time."

"Sir Humphrey asked for me personally? But why would he do that?"

"Practically begged me. I told him you were a rogue who could not be trusted with his sister but he insisted and as he had done well for me I granted his request. As I recall, now that I think of it, he put a word in with Suffolk and my son to ensure that you would be released from confinement when you were thrown into gaol before the Poitiers campaign."

"That is quite peculiar. The few occasions we have crossed paths in person, he gave every indication of despising me."

"Perhaps he does. Many do, Richard. But all men know that

when you set your will to a task you see it completed. He was thinking of his sister's safety and who better to protect her from robbers and pirates than the biggest robber and pirate of them all."

"Thank you, Your Grace."

"And now, I expect, he wants you for his sister again."

"Cecilia is in trouble?"

"Trouble?" The King waved a hand. "Her second husband has suffered a tragic accident while riding. The fall killed him dead. Oh, do not worry, the Lady is well. But, of course, she bore him no children, she is now really rather old, and she is considered to be somewhat unlucky. It is the convent for her, that is for certain. Unless..."

"Unless some great, desperate fool is willing to take her as his wife."

The King smiled. "So, I shall see you again once you join the army in France, sir?"

∞ ∞ ∞

I rode hard for Cecilia's home. When I arrived, it was as though she was waiting for me. Everything was ready. Food, wine. Her bedchamber.

Even though she was in the middle of her thirties, she was still quite lovely and had the energy and enthusiasm of a girl half her age.

We spoke little until we lay naked and tired on her sheets,

looking up at the underside of the canopy. One of her maids brought wine and then left, leaving us to catch our breath in the candlelight.

"I missed you," I said.

"Clearly, sir," she replied. We laughed.

"I am very sorry about the untimely death of your late husband."

"Yes. I am in mourning."

Growing serious, I turned my head to look at her. She was not smiling.

"I wish I had not left you all those years ago. I hope your marriage was not too difficult for you."

She sighed. "He tried to get a child on me. I could not stand it. He soon gave up. Much preferred hunting and drinking."

"An often fatal combination."

"And boys."

I turned to look at her again. "He was a sodomite?"

She laughed, bitterly. "I do not think he went so far as that. He just enjoyed touching them a little."

"Dear God. I do not know what to say."

She reached over to her wine beside the bed and drank a sip. I ran my fingers idly down her flank as she turned and stretched herself out.

"He was a child himself, in truth. He was terrified of me, and rightly so. Still, I withstood him as long as I needed to," she said. "And when I knew you had returned, and Humphrey gave me leave, I broke my dear husband's neck."

Astonished, I began to lean over onto my elbow to ask if she

430

was speaking truthfully.

She whipped around as fast as a striking snake.

I saw a glint of bright steel raised high.

Before I understood what was happening, she stabbed me through the chest, between collarbone and nipple, with a sword.

It ran right through me to the hilt, through the mattresses below and into the oak bed beneath. My blood welled up and flowed across my chest beneath the crosspiece.

The pain was incredible but it was nothing compared to the horror of what had happened.

I grabbed the sword and tried to pull it out. It was stuck fast.

She had missed my heart but only just and I could barely breathe. I coughed and sprayed blood over myself.

Cecilia was staring at me with wild victory in her blue eyes.

She laughed.

"I did it," she said to herself. "My God."

The betrayal was more than I could bear. Her laughter echoed in my empty soul. I grasped the sword hilt with both hands and, cutting my hands, heaved.

It slid slowly up through my body, slicing through flesh and bone and lacerating my organs as it followed the path. My body seemed to suck the blade into itself as if it did not want to come free.

As the sword came loose from the bed beneath me, Cecilia's laughter turned to a scream of horror.

"Eustace!" she shouted. "Eustace!"

Almost at once, the door to the chamber burst open and the damned steward marched in with sword in hand.

Cecilia, shamelessly naked, jabbed her finger me. "He frees himself!"

Eustace snapped at her to get back and stalked forward to finish me.

I gripped the blade and pulled it up and up, out of my sucking chest wound, hand under hand. The stocky steward rushed me and thrust with his sword where I lay. I rolled away across the bed just as I pulled the last of the steel from my body. Blood gushed out of me and filled my throat.

The steward rushed around the end of the bed, hooking a hand around the final post and aiming a cut at my face. I lurched back away from it and, holding the blade in both hands, blocked his next cut before falling back over a low table beside the bed and crashing into the wall. He stood back, watching me warily. It seemed as though he was afraid of me, even naked and bleeding. But I realised he was merely waiting for me die.

Angry, I stumbled forward with my sword in my hand.

Cecilia jumped on me and held on to my sword arm with her immortal strength.

"Now, you fool!" she yelled at Eustace.

He came forward, sword ready to strike.

Lifting her up, I threw Cecilia, naked, at Eustace. He lowered his blade and ducked and she hit his considerable mass with a thud and fell to the floor. I grabbed her by the hair and yanked her up and tossed her away against the wall.

Eustace rushed me like a bullock charging a half-open gate. I thrust my sword into his neck, sliding the blade down into his body, before ripping it out again as he fell past me onto the bloody floor.

The porter came rushing in and froze two steps into the doorway. His eyes wide and his mouth open. He stared at his dazed, naked, bloody mistress pulling herself to her feet.

"Help me," I said to him, or tried to, as the blood filled my throat and I coughed.

He had a sword in his hand. The porter's face changed from horror to fury, and, seeing I was so terribly wounded, rushed at me to finish me off.

Instead, I knocked his blade aside, grabbed him, slit his throat and drank his blood as his heels drummed on the floor. He was simply doing his duty but I wanted to live, and so he had to die.

My wound burned as it knitted together, the lancing pain like being run through again, but the pain went away and I was healed. The blood covering half my body was already beginning to dry.

"Why?" I said to Cecilia, pushing her to the floor again before she could regain her feet. "Why did you do this?"

She sneered, her beautiful face twisted in contempt.

"Why, Richard? *Why*? To protect ourselves."

"You and Eustace?" I pointed with my sword to his body.

She laughed a bitter laugh. "You think yourself so wise and yet you are a fool."

"Who, then? Geoffrey de Charny? You are his?"

She shook her head. "You know nothing at all."

"I know that my brother William made you. He made Geoffrey de Charny and his two squires. That brute Eustace there. So many of you under my nose. By God, you sent that big filthy bastard to kill me in the stews."

"No, Richard. Not I. We were not supposed to kill you. Only to discover the others that you had gifted immortal life. That arrogant merchant, Stephen Poole. Others, though, we suspected. The woman who travels to Bristol. Other soldiers. But my dear Humphrey could not contain his jealousy and he sent Jacob to kill you. I warned him that you would not fall so easily."

"Sir Humphrey? Of course, it had to be your brother."

She grinned. "My *brother*. Ha! I never met him until my lord William brought us together. In time, my Humphrey and I fell in love. We have often lived openly together as husband and wife. For many decades. And at other times we pose as siblings so that we both may marry into wealth or position." She laughed, suddenly, flicking her unbound hair. "I had you dangling, did I not? And yet you refused to marry me for so long. A shame. We could have lived together. Shared a bed together. For years." Rising up on her knees, she opened her arms wide, displaying her nakedness. "It could have been delightful, sharing each other all this time, dear Richard, if only you had not been so bull-headed about it." Her eyes were wide and sorrowful. Her skin, pale and perfect.

"Why?" I asked. "Why, why? Only to now murder me?"

"Oh," she said, tilting her head. "I am so sorry for that. But Humphrey said that you had to be stopped before you undid everything we have worked so hard for. And you also had to be punished for murdering Geoffrey. He was the best of us, so Humphrey liked to say. If you ask me, Geoffrey was the most tiresome bore this past hundred years. Always wittering on about honour and jousting and such. But I did not want to kill you,

Richard. I do have such affection for you."

"What were you planning?" I asked. "For what purpose did William make you? Why did he bring you all together?"

"Oh, they do not tell me such things. I am afraid I would not know."

"Do not play the silly maid with me, Cecilia. I know you well enough to know that you are not a simpleton."

She smiled and sat back, still kneeling. "You are so kind."

"You are trying to control the Crown of France, are you not? You were behind the plan to kill King John and take power through controlling the Dauphin? I have put a stop to all that."

She sighed. "Yes, you are so very clever, Richard."

"But your brother. That is, Sir Humphrey. What is he..." I trailed off. "Sir Humphrey is Prince Edward's man. Or pretending to be." I recalled how the Prince had changed over the years, turning from valiant golden prince into a darker, meaner spirit. Surely that was in part due to Ingham, whispering in his ear for a decade. "Is he going to kill King Edward?"

She laughed. "I may not have killed you. But I have delayed you. Humphrey has already sailed with the King and you will not have time to stop him. When the King falls, Prince Edward will rule. And through him, us. Other plans shall have to be made for France. King John remains a prisoner in England, does he not? Humphrey shall find a way, he always does. And soon, our lord will return at the head of a great army and the crowns of England and France will be his. And then we shall rule all Christendom for eternity."

I scoffed. "Once you have served his purposes, William will

discard you. He will rule alone and you shall have nothing."

"No!" she said, rising up onto her knees again, her bare chest thrust out before her. She jabbed a finger at me and spoke with such passion that she quivered. "He swore his undying love for me. For me! I shall be at his side, ruling as his queen. As the Empress of Christendom."

"You and William—" I began.

She leapt to her feet, snatched a dagger from Eustace's corpse and stabbed up at my groin with a scream of fury.

It gored the inside of my thigh even as I twisted away, jumped back, and brought my sword down on her neck.

She fell, her head almost entirely severed.

I dropped to my knees beside her and held her as she died. The blue of her eyes dimmed and her eyelids fluttered closed. Her hand lifted toward my cheek only to fall before she reached me.

Chasing out the servants from her home, I put her chamber to fire so as to burn the bodies. No doubt the servants would be raising the hue and cry to have me captured and tried for murder. Two of the deaths were matters of self-defence but I was certainly guilty of the murder of the porter and so the name and persona of Richard of Hawkedon would have to be abandoned.

I rode south to find Rob and Walt.

We had to find passage to France, join our army on campaign, and save King Edward's life before he was assassinated by the immortal Sir Humphrey Ingham.

By the time we caught up with the army, Edward's campaign was in full effect. He wanted to take Paris for England or at the least cause so much destruction and terror that the French would finally seek terms.

Hundreds of ships crossed back and forth across the Channel, taking vast quantities of supplies to the army and I had to pay a great sum to get one to find room for us. In Calais I paid a fortune for a few good horses and we hurried on. All the while I prayed Edward yet lived. The spring had been remarkably warm and dry but it was after Easter by the time we rode south in the wake of the devastation.

Riding those long miles, I tried not to think of Cecilia but I kept going over it all. Recalling all the little things over the years that should have alerted me. Her childlessness in itself was not enough but her continued youthful beauty as the years went by certainly should have been. I was simply infatuated with her. With who she pretended to be, that was. Perhaps it was only ever blind lust. I wondered if anything she had said and done had ever been true.

She had said I thought of myself as wise. But that had never been so. It was clear that she did not know me as well as she thought. And that made me feel better. I may have had a false idea of her but clearly she had one of me also.

I told myself that I had thrown off the betrayal. And yet I found that it was on my mind for a considerable time after the anger turned to melancholy.

Our army was unopposed and the English had burned villages

and towns all around Paris to the south. Places like Orly, Longjumeau, Montlhery. The great army marched up to the walls of Paris and cut it off from the south. Our garrisons across northern France cut it off from the north. Inside, food shortages and subsequent price rises caused the population to panic. Edward had forced displaced people from the surrounding villages, towns, and suburbs into Paris and all those within the walls knew that in their future lied starvation. Smoke from the burning homes and villages drifted across the city and flames could be seen coming ever closer as the English army marched back and forth outside the walls, turning the rich suburban homes into charred timbers and ash. All the while, English trumpets blew and the kettle drums sounded.

The Parisians were too afraid, or too wily, to leave the safety of the walls.

It did bring the French diplomats into urgent negotiations, but the obstinate fools delayed and delayed and our army suffered from the usual maladies. And so the King decided to reposition the army, moving west away from the city and then to the north.

That was where we found them.

By the town of Galardon, with the towers of Chartres Cathedral silhouetted against the swirling grey sky in the distance across a vast open plain. The weather had finally turned and dark clouds gathered overhead. Beneath, our enormous, filthy army spread in shadow across mile after mile of flat French countryside.

The land burned beyond and the men were miserable because everything had been picked clean a thousand times over and there was nothing left to steal.

"How we going to find him?" Walt asked as we stared at the trudging lines of horses and men and banners held aloft waving in the growing wind. "Find him, that is, without giving the game away."

I knew he was thinking of our search for the black knight and how our actions there led to Thomas and Hugh being killed.

"And when we do find him," Rob said, while I recalled it. "How do you mean to apprehend him without men stopping us?"

"We have no time for cleverness or subtleties," I said, drawing my sword and raising my voice above the wind. "I will ride up to Ingham and murder him. Then we shall flee and stay away from the English until all living are now dead."

Rob hung his head and said nothing.

Large blobs of rain began to fall, here and there, pinging loudly when they hit steel or drumming on the dry earth.

I raised my voice and called out. "Where is Sir Humphrey Ingham?"

A sergeant rode over to us, looking me up and down. I was dressed well enough but I had left my armour back in England. We all had.

"Can I help you, sir?"

"I seek a man. A knight named Sir Humphrey Ingham."

He looked at my naked sword and the fury on my face. "If he has angered you, sir, you must take your disagreement to the King."

I snarled. "I will cut off his damned traitorous head."

In the distance, thunder rumbled.

"A traitor? Sir Humphrey? Surely not, sir?"

I scoffed. "He is Brutus. He is Ganelon. He is Judas. The King himself is in danger. Where is Ingham?"

"But..." he stammered. "He is with the King, last I saw."

"Where, man?"

He raised his hand and pointed south. A cluster of banners whipped and twisted in the far distance and one of them looked like the King's own arms.

I spurred my horse and raced forward through the men with Walt and Rob riding as well as they could behind me. It would not do to get too far ahead of them, so I slowed.

The rain came down harder and harder until the heavens opened and the rain came down in sheets. Men all around us covered their heads with whatever they had and trudged on.

"There is the King!" I shouted to my men, pointing with my sword.

King Edward and his lords came on in a hurry, no doubt hoping to reach some sort of shelter miles beyond, or at least outrun the sudden storm.

The rain gusted into my face like a thousand tiny whips. The ground turned to mud and the rain ran across the surface like a river. My horse slowed to a walk, lifting his hooves up high and stepping through the morass.

"Get on, will you," I shouted at him, raking my spurs on him.

Lighting flashed overhead and almost at once thunder sounded, powerfully enough to be felt through the earth. The men all around me hunched and fought their way onward through the storm. There was no shelter to be had anywhere for miles around and so all they could do was go on.

The rain, already as heavy as any I had ever seen anywhere in the world, suddenly got heavier. My horse would not move, so I dismounted and he jumped away through the muck. Peering behind me, I saw Walt helping Rob to his feet. One or both of them had been thrown from their mounts.

"Come on," I said, fearing that I would lose the King's men, who were so close.

I lifted my knees high and fought through the liquifying mud. Soldiers were shouting at each other in fear.

As the rain eased off slightly, I caught sight of the King and his men, dismounted and fighting to hold on to their panicking horses. I thought I could see Ingham there by the King's side but it was so hard to see.

It suddenly turned cold. Bitterly cold, like the deepest winter had descended.

"What is this?" Walt shouted in my ear. His eyes were wild. Shivering violently, he and Rob clung to each other like drowning men.

I had no answer for what it was. Never in my long life had I known anything like it. Underfoot, the flowing water drained away but the mud began to freeze, even as we walked through it.

Men wailed all around, fighting their horses, fighting to hold on to supplies as the wind whipped up and blew away blankets, sheets, clothes.

The King's men clustered around him, I hoped protecting his royal person from the elements. Ingham was there amongst them. I could see him.

"Stop!" I shouted. "Edward! Beware!"

I thought, perhaps, that Ingham turned and looked in my direction. But my voice was carried away by the hurricane and the temperature dropped further, turning the ground to ice. Men were blown off their feet and some rolled along the ground.

Rob got his leg stuck and together with Walt we pulled him out before the ground turned as hard as iron.

"Hurry, now," I shouted in their ears and they nodded, drawing their swords.

As we pushed through the wind, the rain turned to hailstones. The smallest of which was the size of an acorn and most were the size of a fist.

Men fell in their scores as they were struck by the storm of hail. A cacophony rose above the roaring of the wind to become deafening as the deluge of stones struck helms and armour for miles around. Men cried out in pain and terror. Horses ran in wild panic or lay down on the ground in despair and agony.

Soldiers fell down dead or insensible from the impacts. The King's men, many covering him with their bodies, dropped under the assault. Felled by enormous lumps of ice or collapsing from the relentless driving impact from thousands of smaller ones, knights and lords crawled through the crunching ice underfoot into hollows.

Leaning against the driving wind, I struggled on, step by step. I passed two knights huddled against the belly of a dead horse that lay on its side, one leg jerking in the air.

Other men struggled on, bent double, headed across the plain as if there could be salvation elsewhere if only they could reach it.

Two of Edward's bodyguards held the King between them,

442

making off through the ice and wind. The others had fallen behind or were knocked insensible all about us.

Behind Edward, Sir Humphrey Ingham stalked forward.

He was making better headway than the King and his men, gaining on them with every step.

In his right hand, he held a long, thin dagger.

I roared a warning but my voice was whipped away as soon as it was spoken.

Pushing forward, fighting the wind, I forced one leg forward and another, lifting my knees up and down with my watery eyes on the ground.

I was so close.

When I looked up, Ingham was an arm's length behind the King. He reached out with his left hand to grasp Edward on the shoulder. His right was pulled back with the dagger in his hand.

"Ingham!" I shouted with everything I had.

He half turned in surprise and with that moment's hesitation, I lunged forward and stuck my blade into his leg. It hit his armour but it was enough to trip him. I stumbled forward and dropped down on him.

Ingham grasped the blade of my sword and ripped it from my grasp, throwing it behind him.

I locked my knees either side of Ingham and lifted his visor with one hand while I drew my dagger.

He stabbed me in the body, just beneath the ribs. God, it hurt. The dagger was long, and sharp as Satan.

With my free arm, I trapped his arm and blade inside my body, and I stabbed him in the face with my own blade.

The King was shouting something. His bodyguards came forward.

I stabbed Ingham again, over and over.

My men pulled me away.

Edward was there, pushing his two bodyguards away from him. The hail was easing off, turning to sleet. And the wind was no longer strong enough to blow a man to the ground.

"Richard!" the King shouted.

"Ingham, sire," I said, wincing. It hurt to speak. "He was going to kill you."

Edward looked at the body and then back at me.

He nodded once.

"I saw the blade," the King said, scowling and shaking his head in wonder. He broke off. "You are hurt."

"All is well, Your Grace," I said, clapping him on the shoulder. "All is well." Raising my voice, I waved over his bodyguards. "Get him somewhere safe, will you."

"Why?" the King said. "Why would Ingham do this?"

"He was paid by the Dauphin's men," I said, lying easily. I had rehearsed my accusations. "Paid to assassinate you. I discovered the plot and came to warn you."

"God love you, Richard," the King said as they tugged him back toward safety.

"Come on," I said to Rob and Walt, as the storm passed. "It is over."

24

THE DEATH OF THE KING

"THE ARMY WAS FINISHED after that," I said to Stephen, weeks later, in London. "And Edward's resolve to continue the war must have crumbled."

We sat in the hall together for what we knew would be the last time for a generation, at least.

"I cannot fathom it," Stephen said, shaking his head. "How can a storm be so powerful?"

"God can do as He pleases," I said. "And He decided to do what the French could not."

All told, we lost a thousand men to the storm and six thousand horses. There was never a storm like it in all my days, before or since. It was undoubtedly a sign from God that He wished Edward to end his war and so that was what Edward did.

The Treaty of Bretigny brought the war to an end. He agreed to drop his claim to the throne of France. And in return, the French recognised all that Edward and the English Crown had won in the war.

Edward III obtained, besides Guyenne and Gascony, Poitou, Saintonge and Aunis, Agenais, Périgord, Limousin, Quercy, Bigorre, the countship of Gaure, Angoumois, Rouergue, Montreuil-sur-Mer, Ponthieu, Calais, Sangatte, Ham and the countship of Guines.

What is more, these lands were to be held free and clear, without doing homage for them.

After twenty years of war against the mightiest kingdom in Christendom, King Edward III had established a truly mighty empire.

My own quest was also over.

It had taken far too long and I had almost destroyed us entirely. My decisions had led to the deaths of my brothers Thomas, John, and Hugh.

But we had uncovered the whole nest of snakes in the end. We had, perhaps, saved the lives of two kings and disrupted my brother's plans for the domination of two nations.

Decades before, William had given the Gift to a number of French and English knights and left them with instructions on how to prepare for his return. I had been looking for them for so long and now, it was over. It was time to leave England and hide elsewhere for a few decades.

Eva would stay in London for a few years to manage the trade and the information network, posing as Stephen's widow.

Stephen would move to Bristol and pretend to be Eva's steward, taking care of things there. We would maintain correspondence and all would watch and listen for signs of William's return.

I kissed Eva and embraced my brothers in the hall of the London house and went on my way.

England, on top of the world for a moment, did not fare well.

Prince Edward administered the lands of Gascony and all France, ruling like a king. But he became embroiled in the knotty and interminable web of shifting alliances between all the rulers in that part of the world, from Castile and Aragon to Poitiers and Bordeaux. He fought in dozens of battles where generally he won. And he wrestled in diplomacy with hundreds of lords where generally he failed.

And fate turned against our prince.

In 1367, when Edward was in his prime at thirty-seven years old, he was on campaign in the disgusting heat of a Spanish summer when his entire army fell to the bloody flux and other common maladies. The Prince was himself afflicted so terribly that he never fully recovered. His body went into a long and painful decline.

Some men whispered that it was divine punishment for his black dealings with this lord or that. Others thought he had been poisoned and it had rotted his body from the inside.

Over the coming years, he was stricken with dropsy so that his limbs and body would swell to enormous size. He could not even ride and had to be carried in a litter here and there. A shameful and emasculating fate.

One by one, his great friends and allies, like the capable soldier John Chandos, died.

In 1370, Edward's eldest boy, another Edward who was just five years old, died from a resurgence of the Black Death.

The pestilence would return every few years and take more from our people. Mostly children, and so each generation was aggrieved in their hearts beyond all recovery.

It was the death of his eldest son and heir, on top of his own endless physical agonies, that broke the Prince's will. There was another son, Richard, who would one day become King of England. But a man can only bear so much pain and, when he was back home in England for his boy's funeral, Edward's flux returned and drained him of his will.

Bloated, pale, and weak, our Golden Prince died in 1376 aged forty-five.

King Edward would make it just one more year before himself succumbing to age and the ravages of grief.

He was never the same after the storm. After the peace he had won. All his life, he had fought for victory and when he achieved it, he found himself broken by the effort.

His boundless energy and enthusiasm were gone. Used up in the fight. Perhaps it was the toll of decades of physical exhaustion and from being thumped about the head too many times in battle. God knows, that seemed to do for the wits of many a knight I have known.

After the peace, he passed much of the leadership of the realm onto his son and even though the Prince of Wales had struggled with international diplomacy in a way that the King never had, old Edward left him to it.

Queen Philippa, who had brought forth from her womb thirteen princes and princesses for England, died in Windsor in 1369 and the loss brought Edward very low indeed. He had loved her dearly.

His health failed him more and more and by the summer of 1377, he was never out of his bed. The King's mind had long been failing but his wits were by then almost gone. His days were numbered and he would soon depart for Heaven.

My own heart was breaking at the news coming from England of the King's demise. It was a risk, perhaps, but one I could not resist.

I went to see my king one last time.

∞ ∞ ∞

Stephen's wealth, connections, and well-placed agents bought the necessary access to the palace at Richmond and, after waiting all day, I was shown by one of Stephen's men into the King's bedchamber.

The smell was appalling and his servants all had cloths tied across their faces.

"Who is that lurking there?" the King said. His voice, once so powerful that in a single breath it could move the hearts of a thousand knights, had become the rasping whisper of a dying old man.

"It is Richard of Hawkedon, Your Grace," I said, coming

forward. "I thought you asleep."

"Asleep? No, no. I never sleep. Never get enough. Too much to do. Come here, man."

I went forward and bowed, before taking a knee beside him.

He frowned. "Is that you, Richard?"

"It is, Your Grace. I came to speak with you."

"Well? What is it you have to say?" his eyes flicked up around the room. "Where are we? Is this... Villeneuve?"

"This is Richmond, Edward. We have not been at Villeneuve for twenty years. Twenty-five, perhaps. That was where the lords of Calais surrendered their town to you. After we beat the French at Crecy."

"It seems like another life," Edward whispered. The corners of his mouth twitched and he lifted a skeletal hand toward my face before letting it fall back to the bed. "Another life for me. But perhaps not for you, Richard. How is it that you are unchanged from that day to this? They always told me you were not one of us and now I see how right they were. Or have I truly lost my mind after all? You are an impostor, perhaps. His son, or grandson, pretending to be my friend."

"They were right," I admitted. "And yet I am the same man who was at your side that night in Nottingham when you were newly our king."

"Do you recall it as I do, I wonder?"

He was testing me and his mind had degenerated so far that I am sure that he believed he was doing so with subtle cunning.

"I recall it clearly, Edward," I said. "You were all so young. The lords around you were loyal but they needed a little encouragement and the belief that they could help you destroy Mortimer. And I watched from the edges as you slowly grew to become the man I knew you could be. After you married Philippa, you changed. Marriage often does that to a man but the stakes were so much higher for you than for ordinary men."

"Oh," he muttered, clutching at his sheets. "Dear Philippa. Gentle, compassionate Philippa. She was stronger than iron, you know. She would have had Mortimer's throat slit in the night if it meant being done with him."

I smiled at the thought. "I admit, sire, that for some time I planned to murder Roger Mortimer myself. My friends convinced me that it would destabilise the kingdom and of course they were right. But I kept a close eye on Mortimer and his bodyguards. Your mind may be going, Edward, but no doubt you recall the humiliation of the Great Council in Nottingham where Mortimer called you untrustworthy and accused your men of plotting against him." My voice shook as I spoke and tears pricked my eyes. "You were the King and he spoke in such a way. The outrage could not stand and it was my friend Thomas who literally held me back from storming to Mortimer's chambers that very night and delivering to you his head."

Edward laughed at that. A laugh that ended in a cough. "Your friend had good sense. You talked me into taking action, finally."

"You did not require much persuasion, Edward."

He smiled. "No."

"On the morning of the fateful day, I told you of my plan and you merely nodded. I was proud of you. Later, I gathered twenty-two of your companions and brought them to the culvert outside, below the castle, which you unlocked for us with your own hand."

"Who were our companions that night, Richard?"

"Let me see. Montagu, Ufford, John Neville. John Moleyns was still there. The three Bohun brothers. Humps was perhaps twenty-one and Ned and William were not yet twenty."

"Steadfast fellows," Edward said. "Thank God for those men."

"Thank God for those tunnels beneath Nottingham and for your courage. Our companions were in a very high state but you were the embodiment of calm and your steadiness in turn calmed them. It was quiet and we saw few servants but those we swiftly subdued. The garrison commander was loyal to you and so we were not challenged until we entered your mother's apartments."

"My mother," he muttered, shaking his head. "Do you recall what she cried?"

"Your mother beseeched you most fervently. Fair son, she called, have pity on gentle Mortimer."

Edward nodded in confirmation, though clearly it pained him to recall it and so I continued.

"Mortimer was in a chamber adjacent to hers and when I threw open his door, his men cried murder and attacked me. Two of them, I killed, though there were others I merely wounded. Mortimer was quick to give himself up rather than fight. As much as I wanted to paint the walls with traitor's blood, I knew it would be better for you if I restrained myself."

Edward chuckled in his throat. "Two dead and half a dozen wounded is my Richard when he restrains himself," he said.

"I continued to restrain myself, if you recall. As the sun came up, we went out into the town and took all of Mortimer's supporters lodged there into our custody. And soon, Mortimer received the justice that he deserved. I rejoiced at the sight of him dangling at the end of that rope. It pleases me still."

"So long ago," he sighed, "and yet also no more than a blink of the eye." He squinted at me. "Do you never grow old, Richard?"

"Not so far."

"What are you, Richard?"

A dozen thoughts crossed my mind.

I am a blood-drinking immortal. I am the progeny of a mighty ancient conqueror whom someday I must kill. I am the bastard son of a bastard son. I am cousin to Alexander and to Caesar. I am a murderer. A failure. A fool.

"I am a knight, my lord. An English knight." I smiled. "A very old one."

He narrowed his eyes. "How old?"

"I have lived over two hundred years."

"Is this madness?" he asked, an edge of horror creeping into his voice. "Is it my madness?"

I took his hand. "Not this, my lord. Strange beyond reason and yet it is truth."

He sighed and closed his eyes, so that I thought he was asleep. But he opened them and spoke earnestly. "Will you look after my son? See he makes a good king, will you? I think perhaps he does not know how much he needs the love of the people and the loyalty of the lords. Help him to know, will you, Richard?"

He had forgotten his son was dead. It would be the King's grandson, Richard of Bordeaux, who would take the Crown. I did not have the heart to correct him.

"I will, Your Grace."

He smiled and lay back.

It was a lie in more ways than one. I could not stay in England to watch over the young king to be.

"I failed, did I not?" he asked.

In many ways, perhaps he had. But he had done more, been more, than most men who ever lived.

"Failed? How can you say such a thing? You defeated France, my lord. Again and again."

"God wanted me to stop," he muttered.

"That He did. But He also helped you capture the King of France."

"Oh yes." His tone was one of surprise and he chuckled to recall it and I saw the merest hint of the energetic young man I had first known. "But that was not God but you, Richard, if my memory does not fail me." He closed his eyes and his voice fell to a whisper. "You gave me France."

I bowed my head. "I have lived a long time. Served many kings. You were a king that England deserved. And it has been an honour to serve you, Edward."

Whether he heard me before he slept, I do not know, for I was escorted from the chamber.

Three days later, the King was dead.

∞ ∞ ∞

After leaving England, I went to Castile but there were too

many Englishmen there, fighting in free companies under veteran captains for this lord or that, and so I went to Italy.

I found the same there, only more so. Thousands of English soldiers in dozens of companies fighting for one city against another. Some companies rose and others fell. I was welcomed for my skill at arms in any of them but I had had enough of the base, mercenary nature of their endless squabbling. And so, I went further east for a while before eventually returning through the Italian wars to England.

Walt was beside me through all of it. He was proud to call himself Sir Walter of Hartest and he strove always to live with the honour of a knight. The fact that he failed more often than he succeeded could not be held against him, as all knights struggled so whether they were a peasant or a prince.

The code of chivalry was ever an ideal to reach for, and to sometimes fall short, rather than a standard to live by.

In truth, I could well have done without Walt's constant stream of unsought opinions but not without his steadfast companionship.

Rob Hawthorn spent as much time as he could with his family until the talk of his agelessness grew to endanger the legacy of his good name.

It broke Rob's heart to leave them but he had done his duty by making strong sons and daughters and had established a robust family line that would continue on down the centuries without him. His son, Dick, was a man grown by then and ready to inherit. Stephen helped Rob make a faked death by reporting the sinking of a ship that did not exist and so the son took over Rob's land

and became the head of his family. As is right and proper.

When Rob left England to join us in Italy, he left a kingdom in upheaval.

Richard II appeared at first to be another fine king in the making. When he was just a boy, he took a personal role in quelling the terrifying rebellion of the commoners of Essex and Kent. In 1381, the ungrateful masses of those Godforsaken counties stormed London, killing and robbing like crazed savages. Only the physical presence and the wise and goodly words of the young king served to calm them. After the fools were disbursed, they were rounded up and quite rightly sorted out once and for all. Sadly, this early success may have been Richard's finest hour.

He lost his crown to his cousin, Henry Bolingbroke, who was a truly great knight in his youth and a rather mediocre king. But he fathered Henry V who took the throne shortly before I returned to England.

Henry V was, perhaps, an even greater king than Edward III. I was proud to serve him, though I was careful this time to avoid becoming his friend and companion.

I resolved to live and to fight like a knight but I could support the King from afar. This I did through my personal strength of arms, and those of my knights Sir Robert and Sir Walter, and through funding King Henry's campaign with loans from the coffers of the White Dagger.

We fought France again, of course. And again, we thrashed them so completely that it shook the French to their souls.

During the Battle of Agincourt, our English steadfast archers fought like bloody heroes. They also, by order of the King, slaughtered a great mass of the captured French nobility, which much increased the numbers felled on the field.

It seemed as though England was poised to subjugate all of France, for the French Crown was promised to Henry's son and heir, who ruled as Henry VI.

But tragedy struck. The victorious Henry V was in his prime, the most celebrated man in Christendom and the most magnificent King of England who ever was, when he was destroyed by dysentery. Surely, the most ignominious way to meet one's end.

Henry VI was just a boy when he inherited and, without the hero king, England's nobles could not keep their hands around France's throat for long. And when he grew to manhood, Henry VI was both weak and mad.

Dear old England suffered.

All through our weakest times, I fretted for us, as I knew that my brother would one day return to Christendom, and I feared that it would be at the head of a great army seeking to conquer it.

As it turned out, I was quite right about both his return and the army he was leading.

But it was decades more before my brother made his traitorous move.

We kept a close eye on the Black Forest but my grandfather and his sons lived quietly, ruling through fear over the villages nestling in the valleys around them. All it cost those people was the sacrifice of a lovely young woman every few years to the monster that lived in the woods and they could pretend to the outside world that all was well. One day, I would pray, one day,

Lord, I will put Priskos and his sons to the sword. But I would have to grow far stronger, and I would have to defeat William first.

For the longest time, I believed that we had routed out William's nest of immortals. We could find no more. Not in France or England, or Italy or Spain. Every trail led nowhere.

And then, after years of searching, we finally uncovered another one of William's spawn in France. One we had missed. One that I had overlooked with my own eyes. A man lurking and biding his time in one guise or another for decades and centuries until his evil could be contained no longer.

When I finally found him, he had made himself into one of the great nobles of his time. A Marshal of France and a hero of the battles that threw the English out of his lands forever.

A man so depraved he fashioned a raving mad peasant child called Joan into a parody of a soldier and set her on a path that led to her appalling death, screaming and bound as the fire destroyed her flesh.

A monster with a heart so dark that he consumed children like capons, bathing in their blood even as they screamed their last.

A heretic who called upon the power Satan and all the demons of Hell in the towers and dungeons of his fortress home.

But that is a tale for another time.

AUTHOR'S NOTE

Richard's story continues in *Vampire Heretic the Immortal Knight Chronicles Book 5*

If you enjoyed *Vampire Knight* please leave a review online! Even a couple of lines saying what you liked about the story would be an enormous help and would make the series more visible to new readers.

You can find out more and get in touch with me at dandavisauthor.com

BOOKS BY DAN DAVIS

The GALACTIC ARENA Series
Science fiction

Inhuman Contact
Onca's Duty
Orb Station Zero
Earth Colony Sentinel

The IMMORTAL KNIGHT Chronicles
Historical Fiction - with Vampires

Vampire Crusader
Vampire Outlaw
Vampire Khan
Vampire Knight

GUNPOWDER & ALCHEMY
Flintlock Fantasy

White Wind Rising
Dark Water Breaking
Green Earth Shaking

For a complete and up-to-date list of Dan's available books,
visit: **http://dandavisauthor.com/books/**

Printed in Great Britain
by Amazon

57888584R00279